Commendations for *The Bike Cop*

"*The Bike Cop* combines the right amount of humor, politics and suspense for a fun detective tale with an irresistible lead!"—*Clarion Reviews*

"Digger has spent his life crisscrossing the line between the 'townies' and summer vacationers in the Port, making him a fine instrument for the author's riffs on both. A light, breezy and entertaining beach read." —*Kirkus Reviews*

"Bruner is a skillful writer who, drawing on his legal background and familiarity with life in a resort town, keeps the plot moving and holds readers' interest. Bruner has done an excellent job ... Entertaining ... *The Bike Cop* is a perfect beach read."—*Blue Ink Review*

"There is nothing like The Bike Cop series and a little time at Kennebunk Beach to make you feel better."—**Gary Tito, Pharmacist, The Colonial Pharmacy,** Kennebunkport, Maine

"The Bike Cop series has a positive message about our community in a thrilling plot line. Like our corned beef hash, the book has the perfect recipe for a best seller!"—**Bonnie Clement, HB Provisions, Kennebunk (Lower Village), Maine**

"What fun to step back in time and be reminded of the Port's good old days. Whether you're a local or a visitor, you are sure to enjoy the antics and local places involved by the Bike Cop and his new side-kick, Kristy Riggins."—**Tina Hewett-Gordon, General Manager, Nonantum Resort, Kennebunkport, Maine**

"Digger Davenport, the Bike Cop, is becoming a household word around here. What an exciting read about wild events in our community of 'Port Talbot.' It's impossible to put down ... like one of our whoopie pies ... legendary!"— **Christine Faiella, Owner with Jim Faiella of Bradbury Brothers Market, Cape Porpoise, Maine**

"What's better than coffee and a good book? When the coffee is from Coffee Roasters of the Kennebunks and the book is one of Bruner's legal thrillers in The Bike Cop series. So fun to read about our community years ago in 'Port Talbot.'"— **Sandra Duckett, Owner of Coffee Roasters of The Kennebunks, Kennebunk (Lower Village), Maine**

"Bruner's first book in The Bike Cop series, *The Greater Weight of Evidence*, has been a real success in our store. I have no doubt that the second, *Son Over The Yardarm*, will be equally strong in sales."—**Bill Gallant, Mail It Unlimited, Shopper's Village Kennebunk, Maine**

THE BIKE COP

in

Shadows of Dog Island Light

James H. K. Bruner

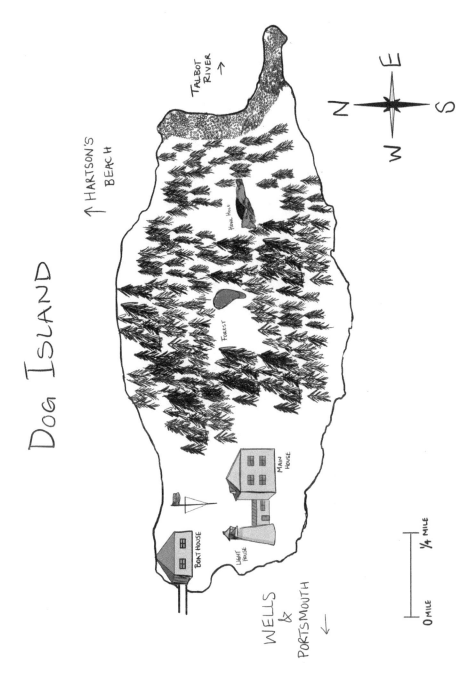

Dog Island

Talbot River →

↑ Hartson's Beach

Howl Hulk

Forest

Main House

Light House

Boat House

Wells & Portsmouth ←

N W S E

0 mile   ¼ mile

Softcover ISBN: 978-1-7330380-2-7
Ebook ISBN: 978-1-7330380-3-4

Library of Congress Control Number: 2020914062

Published by

The Proverbial Lawyer Publications
www.theproverbiallawyer.com

Produced by
Great Life Press
Rye NH 03870
www.greatlifepress.com

Contents

DEDICATION

No one has sacrificed more in the preparation of the Bike Cop trilogy than Gretchen, my wife of close to 40 years. We met in Kennebunkport, Maine, during a summer like any one of the ones featured in the Bike Cop series. She is to me as Kristy is to Digger. We keep writing our exciting script together by the grace of God.

I also dedicate this book to my friends on Parsons Beach. They have a terrific history and heritage that has nothing to do with this book's plot. But to the extent they have stood together as a huge extended family and not only weathered the storms of life but have succeeded, each on their own merits, they are an inspiration to this author and, indeed, our community.

CHAPTER 1
Savannah 1860

Jonathan Hartson walked with a determined step down to the quay on the river bordering one of the busiest cities in the South. In 1860, since Eli Whitney's cotton gin transformed the cotton market, Savannah, Georgia, had become a boomtown. Hartson paused to watch as bundles of his recently ginned cotton were loaded aboard boats of every size and type. He squinted. "Well, I'll be… It's the clipper, the *Great Republic!*" The four-masted bark had been built a few years earlier in southern Maine, a few miles from his home on Hartson's Beach in Port Talbot.

Hartson tapped the breast pocket of his morning coat, which made the chilly November breeze tolerable. Having felt the item in his pocket that was a key part of his mission, he turned to the south off River Street and passed City Hall and the customs house.

As he left the noise and bustle of the docks behind, a most unsettling sound of shrieking and wailing invaded his surroundings, echoing off the walls of the city buildings. While he knew where the wailing was coming from, he nonetheless spun around to experience the cacophony reverberating off the stately facades of the urban buildings. Voices and cries swirled about the air as if he were caught on a battlefield in the demonic realm.

His stomach lurched and he paused to mop a sudden sweat from his brow with a linen handkerchief. Before returning the monogrammed cotton cloth to his pocket, Jonathan stared down at it. Cotton. The tightly woven fibers in a crisscross pattern were marred slightly by the grime from his forehead. "Forgive me!" he uttered passionately. He stuffed the cloth into his perfectly creased pinstriped britches and pressed toward Johnson Square for what was being hailed as the grandest slave auction in all of the Americas.

The penchant that Savannah's city planners had for building homes and businesses around central squares and parks was an enviable example to the rest of the country, and Johnson Square was the epicenter of the design. Today the park was filled with scaffolding, stages, tents and covered wagons teeming with dark-skinned people chained in groups. The whites kept their distance and stayed near the covered bleachers provided for their viewing pleasure. Jonathan checked his breast pocket again reflexively as he approached the auction registration table. As he stood in line with a glum look on his face, a short, portly man with a shiny red face interrupted by hairy grey muttonchop sideburns slapped him on the back. "Jumpin' Jehoshaphat! A slave-buying Yankee! Hartson, it sure is good to see you here. Hope you brought some of your gold?" the man taunted, making a clear reference to the well-known Hartson fortune. Hartson looked around to see who had heard this bulbous blowhard call him a Yankee. All eyes burned toward him.

"Braxton, I simply cannot get over your southern hospitality... so gracious!" Jonathan replied in an elevated voice to remind the audience of their widely touted virtue. It had the desired effect of cooling and diverting the crowd's hot gaze. After all, Abraham Lincoln had just been elected president of the United States days earlier and even though Lincoln was not from the Abolitionist Party, the South was smarting because he was from a new antislavery group called the Republicans.

Braxton retorted, "Pierce Butler's loss is our gain. Had he waited any longer, the property wouldn't fetch any more than Job's turkey."

Jonathan smiled. "Pierce tried to make a go of it, but his cotton tonnage just kept falling."

Braxton interrupted, "His rib cleaned him out in the divorce. She hated our way of life anyway." Shrieks from a nearby tent pierced the conversation. A mother was being separated from a child.

"Uh, yes, right, Braxton. See you at the exchange Monday." Jonathan quickly pulled away with a bidding paddle in his hand, unable to communicate with the business associate due to the loudness of the wailing but more to Jonathan's own inability to think clearly given the inhumanity of what was taking place a short distance away.

Jonathan beelined for the tent where male slaves were waiting to be put on the auction block, which was a large stage situated in front of a set of bleachers for the bidders. Registered bidders could walk through the large tent where black males were ankle-chained in groups. Overseers with rifles also walked among the forlorn slaves. The members of the security detail uniformly wore wide-brimmed cowboy hats and had bullwhips neatly coiled at their hips as if they were just coming from a cattle roundup on the range.

Hartson asked an overseer, "Might I examine those over the age of twenty?"

"Over there!" was the gruff reply from a red-eyed cadaver reeking of stale booze. Each slave had a number painted on his right shoulder. Shoppers squeezed the forearms, shoulders and legs of the goods. The slaves stared expressionlessly straight ahead, focusing on a point in the distance, perhaps very far away. Some bidders, as they went down the line of the shackled, had no qualms about checking the dental configurations of black men twice their size, pulling at the lower jaw, pushing the specimen's head back and peering in his gaping mouth.

Jonathan Hartson allowed some space to develop between himself and the other gawkers. He deftly reached into his breast pocket and pulled out his shopping aid. It was a white card with an unsolved mathematics equation written on it. It had a three, then an "X," then a seven followed by an "equals" sign and a blank line for the answer. It was like an oversized flash card any child would use in school. Keeping his back to the overseers, Jonathan propped the card on his chest and fastened it there with a lapel pin worn for this purpose. He squarely faced each slave and sidestepped down the line, noticing that most slaves refused to look at him or the card. Precautions needed to be observed because speaking back and forth was prohibited.

Jonathan was nearing the end of the line. He had passed a tall dark-skinned slave and was in front of another when he heard "Twenty-one" whispered to his right. He sidestepped back and stood in front of the man, looking around to see where the overseers were. The coast was clear. He looked into the eyes of the tall man, a perfect specimen of the human form. The slave held Jonathan's gaze and whispered, "The product is twenty-one, mastuh," then returned his eyes to a distant point. With one hand, Jonathan squeezed the man's arm, with his other hand he flipped the card over, revealing another question in cursive writing. *"What is your surname?"* The slave glanced down quickly. He smiled faintly and whispered, "Lincoln." Jonathan returned the ironic smile, given the coincidence of this sharing a name with the man who had just become president. Hartson winked and stuffed the card back in his breast pocket, noting the number painted on Mr. Lincoln's shoulder. *Twenty-one.* Hartson did a double take at the number while Lincoln gave a slight smirk, staring off into the distance.

CHAPTER 2

A Victorian Christmas

The black horse and carriage, presently covered in a blanket of white snow, rolled sprightly up the tree-lined entrance road of the mansion on the river. The commanding four-story Federal-style edifice was known by all as Royal Orchard. Perhaps more impressive than the many fruit orchards surrounding the house was its view, which overlooked fields and pastures rolling down before the bold oceanfront known as Hartson's Beach. The large estate was the main home of the Hartson clan, a family with roots they traced back to England via the *Mayflower*.

Just as the carriage came to a stop, a tall dark figure jumped down and ran to open the other door of the carriage. "Stop it, Tombo! You're free," Jonathan Hartson said kindly.

Tombo Lincoln looked up and smiled. "Yes sir, indeed. So why is it that you tell me what I can do and what I can't? Am I not free to jump out of the carriage and do backflips to open your door?"

Jonathan rolled his eyes. "Of course, but if you want to make me happy, please back it off a bit. We're in Maine now, it will seem… unseemly."

Tombo, who was usually referred to as Tom rather than by his birth name from the Upper Niger Valley, retorted in an professorial fashion, "I understand, Mr. Hartson. Maine's positioning in the slave debate is very important ever since being admitted as part of the Missouri Compromise in 1820. I will tone it down, sir."

Jonathan shook Tombo's hand as he stepped down from the carriage. "Thank you, Professor Lincoln." Looking up at the driver, Jonathan asked,

"George, can you show Tom his quarters in the trainer's cottage, after you men bed down the mares, please?"

"Yes'm, Mr. Hartson. Welcome home," replied the driver in an overt dig at the southern dialect. Jonathan and Tombo glanced at each other, signaling perhaps more ostracization was to occur, even in the progressive state of Maine. Hartson let the slur pass without correction but thought it better not occur again or there'd be a swift reckoning. George Eaton had been the overseer at Royal Orchard for years and had raised his family alongside the Hartsons, albeit in a servile role.

Suddenly a flood of children came pouring out of the oversized Dutch door of Royal Orchard. "Uncle Jon-Jon! Merry Christmas!" Jonathan knelt to hug the throng of nieces and nephews, all children of his brother, Theodore Hartson. Theodore was four years older and had married upon graduating from Dartmouth College. Jonathan too, had graduated from Dartmouth and then moved to Savannah to run the family's cotton gins.

"You ninnies, what are you doing in bare feet?" Jonathan teased.

One of the more spirited boys went running into the snow-covered apple orchard in his bare feet and pajamas. "Look at me! Look at me! I don't care!"

Theodore, known as Ted, came down off the wraparound porch and gave his brother a hug. He nodded toward his son running in the orchard. "Let's see how long he lasts. Merry Christmas, brother. How was your trip?"

"Merry Christmas, Ted. It's good to be home. Say, didn't Father lay the rail from Portsmouth to Portland? It's brutally rough. It's given me lumbago, by golly!"

"Well, don't bring it up with the old man. He's not in a mood to hear anything about his railroad. The western line lost some men and their wives to an Indian attack in Nebraska. He wants to go to Washington and raise hell, but he can barely walk!"

"He may want to stay away from DC for a bit until we see what these rebels are made of," Jonathan warned as they both turned to enter the house. The little barefoot rapscallion streaked between them and headed straight for the fireplace to warm his frozen toes.

"He doesn't have to go to Washington. Royal Orchard has been designated an outpost by the United States Military Telegraph Service," boasted Ted.

"Jonathan Hamilton Hartson!" Agnes Hartson, the matriarch of the family, swept towards her son, her arms outstretched.

"Merry Christmas, Mother! You look lovely and the house is decorated so festively."

"Oh, Jon-Jon, I have been so worried about you down there."

"Now, Mother, all is well, I promise. I've certainly missed you, your wisdom, and your good cooking, though!" They embraced as the other family members lined up to greet their relative returned from the South.

Henry Hartson bustled into the welcoming committee, leading with his gold-handled cane, which stabbed hard against the oriental rug. The family backed away deferentially to allow the men to embrace. Jonathan hugged the wizened body of the industrialist known throughout Europe and the Americas. "Father, you look wonderful."

"Bull hockey boy, but thank you!" The old man, a full foot shorter than his son, steadied himself and reached both hands up to Jonathan's cheeks in order to get a good look at him. "I hope you voted for Lincoln and his new Republican party last month."

"Father, you know that wouldn't have been good for business!" Gasps could be heard from the entourage. The industrialist's eyes widened. "I am jesting, sir. Lincoln was not on the ballot in Georgia. The whole Republican party is *persona non grata*."

Ignoring the remark, the old man turned slowly to allow others to greet his son. "Now you know the importance of the Electoral College. If it were not for that newfangled factoring system, Lincoln wouldn't be inaugurated this March." The old man stabbed his cane on the floor with a heavy, rhythmic cadence as he headed for the study where his bourbon awaited.

Jonathan called after his father, "Will I see you at the inauguration?"

From the study Henry shot back, "Yes, dressed in my best... wearing my Dartmouth green tie, fully reposed... in a hearse!"

Agnes cried out, "Henry! That's not funny!" The other family members tried to conceal their mirth. Jonathan then greeted his sister Sarah and his sister-in-law Florence.

Jonathan marveled at the fourteen-foot Christmas tree with small candles balanced on its limbs. It was trimmed this year as always, with strings of cranberries and popcorn, while blown glass ornaments from the Old World displayed timeless images of the Celtic cross and Nativity scene. The center hall stairway with its sweeping banisters was lavishly wrapped with laurel leaf garlands, and spruce boughs sat upon the fireplace mantles. Adding to the beauty were evergreen sprays highlighted by the sconces on each wall. The arrangements filled the house with the unique smell of Christmas in New England and stirred up memories. "Balsam Fir," Jonathan mused as his mind wandered to fond childhood memories and the many things he missed while living in the South.

At the formal dinner that evening, the men agreed to convene in the morning to discuss their textile mills in Biddeford and Saco, the cotton operation in Savannah, and the shipping business that connected the two operations. Sarah would participate as the clerk to keep the corporate minutes. Henry made it clear he wished to remain silent on matters affecting the rail business and his investments in the American Land Company.

CHAPTER 3
TITANS OF INDUSTRY

The next morning in the dimly lit study, Jonathan, Theodore, and Sarah sat in burgundy leather captain's chairs arranged in an arc around Mr. Hartson's gleaming mahogany desk. The brightest spot in the room was the beauty that radiated from Sarah. Her large blue eyes were set in a perfectly shaped oval face distinguished by high cheekbones and thick, lush eyebrows. Her full mane of rich sandy-blonde hair fell over her broad shoulders and framed her creator's artwork perfectly. As befit the patriarch, Henry was propped up in a red velvet throne chair that accentuated his slight frame. Behind him was a Palladian window with red velvet curtains that matched the throne-like chair. The window framed a commanding view of the river and the ocean off in the distance.

Tombo brought in an armful of long logs for the large fireplace. "Excuse me, Mr. Eaton said you would need some wood in here." Tombo's presence caused everyone but Jonathan to turn and stare at the large black man as he handled the logs like they were kindling sticks. After stoking the fire, Tombo exited without a word.

Sarah spoke first. "Who in tarnation is that?"

Ted answered, "That, Sarah, is Jon-Jon's Man Friday."

Henry Hartson erupted; He is not a slave... dear God, no!"

Jonathan sprang toward the door. "Tom! Excuse me, could you come back? I'd like to introduce you." Tom returned and stood tall at the door. Sarah could not help but blush as she beheld the giant physique of the quiet, humble man. She focused on what she regarded as his perfect facial features: a broad smile with luminous white teeth, radiant eyes that were expressive and kindly, all set within a handsome face the color of black tourmaline. "Sarah, Theodore, Father, please meet Tom Lincoln, formerly of Savannah, Georgia, now of Port Talbot, Maine."

Ted stood and gave Tom a hearty handshake. "Welcome to Maine."

"Thank you, sir." Tom nodded. Sarah was dumbstruck. Tom nodded toward her and simply said, "Ma'am." He looked to Mr. Hartson. "Nice to meet you, Mr. Hartson." Henry simply nodded, a half-smile on his face.

"Tom's birth name is Tombo," said Jonathan. "He recently adopted his surname 'Lincoln.'" A broad smile came over Tom's face, which caused everyone else to smile as well. "Tom, my brother referred to you as my Man Friday. What does that mean to you?" Ted started to stammer and blush. Jonathan held up his hand toward his brother. "Shh, let him speak."

Tom stated plainly, "I am, indeed, Mr. Jonathan's Man Friday in that we share a mutual respect as depicted in the novel *Robinson Crusoe*. Daniel Defoe wrote the book in 1719. When Mr. Jonathan and I first met, I was a slave in shackles at an auction. I had been educated and introduced to Christianity by Mrs. Butler, the wife of my former owner. Mr. Jonathan purchased me in a fiery bidding war, and he has freed me. I prepared my papers of manumission for his signature and sent them to the court here in Maine. They certify my freedom..." Tom's lips began to tremble. "... from... slavery... thanks to Mr. Jonathan." A tear slid down his dark, handsome face, and he quickly brushed it away.

He continued, "I come from the Upper Niger Valley in West Africa and am part of the Mandinka tribe." Tom looked at Jonathan. "Shall I continue, sir?"

Sarah found her tongue. "Please do, Mr. Lincoln," she said in a soft, sultry voice.

"When I was a boy, my family was killed by a neighboring tribe, and they enslaved me for several months," said Tom. "They then sold me to white men for a jug of rum. In Georgia, I was offloaded at Butler Island south of Savannah. Mr. Pierce Butler became my master."

Henry Hartson interjected, "I knew a Major Butler from Philadelphia."

"Yes sir, that was the grandfather. Major Butler started the plantation on Butler Island. The grandson married a British subject named Fanny Kemble. Miss Fanny taught me everything I know. She was a Shakespearean actress in England, so I had to learn all the parts. She taught me mathematics, Latin, philosophy, card games, accounting, and how to sail. In fact, we learned that skill together by trial and error. She loved to sail to Savannah and to the Spanish port of Fernandina on Amelia Island in what is now Florida. The pirates and smugglers of Fernandina were able to get anything Miss Fanny desired."

Henry, making a great effort to stand, held out his hand. "Tom, welcome to Royal Orchard. It is an honor and a privilege to have such talent on our staff. I hope you find the arrangements to your liking and if not, I'd like to be the first to know if Jonathan, or Ted, here, is not around."

Tom took the handshake as his cue to bow and start backing out of the room. "Thank you, sir, at your service."

Jonathan closed the study door after Tom. Sarah was slowly shaking her head. "Unbelievable. He has a better education than mine from Mount Holyoke!"

Ted asked his brother, "How much?"

"Well. If it weren't for the SOB who kept bidding me up, Tom would have cost a lot less. As it happened, I paid nearly two thousand dollars. Double the typical price."

The senior Hartson waved his hand as if to dismiss the subject. "Worth every penny. Good job, Jonathan. Now, let's move on."

A loud metallic tapping noise suddenly filled the room. Sarah moved over to a round marble top table on which sat a contraption with knobs and a spool containing a ribbon of paper. The spool started to spin out the thin paper marked with dots and dashes. "Ted, hand me that codebook on Father's desk. This is from E. Cornell..."

"That's Ezra Cornell," explained Henry. "What's he want? He and Joe Henry set this up here a couple of months ago. Sarah has taken to it like a bird to flight."

Sarah haltingly interpreted the Morse code, frequently darting her eyes between the codebook and the ticker tape spewing from the strange machine.

"USMTS reports..." Sarah looked at Ted. "Write this down just in case. *"United States Military Telegraph Service reports... S...C... has seceded... from Union.... More states expected in days. Pres Buchanan states secession not legal but government cannot stop it. President-elect Lincoln briefed. Federal government and Military travel south of MD line restricted. Stop."* Sarah looked at Ted. "Did you get that? What did I say?"

Ted looked at his younger sister in wonderment. "How did you do that?"

She repeated urgently, "What did I say, Ted?"

Ted handed the written note to Sarah. "You said, 'Johnny, get your gun.'"

Henry Hartson pounded on his desk. "Buchanan is absolutely worthless! He applauded the Dred Scott decision, too. Despicable Democrats!" His two sons looked at each other and rolled their eyes.

Jonathan spoke up. "Father, Buchanan is a lame duck until March when Lincoln gets sworn in. Cut him some slack."

"Never!" bellowed the elder. "Read the Dred Scott decision! No, I'll read it for you!" Henry yanked open his desk drawer and put thin half-glasses on his red nose, then started waving a scrap of newspaper pulled from the same drawer. "Chief Judge Taney, Buchanan's fellow Democrat said, and I quote, '*They had, for more than a century before, been regarded as beings of an inferior order, and altogether unfit to associate with the white race either in social or political relations, and so far inferior that they had no rights which the white man was bound to respect, and that the negro might justly and lawfully be reduced to slavery for his benefit.*' Hmph!" Henry looked up from the paper with a flush rising in his cheeks. "Unconscionable! Then the idiot held the Missouri Compromise unconstitutional! Where does that put the great state of Maine, I ask you?"

"Right, Father, point well taken. Can we talk about our business in Georgia?" Jonathan urged gently. "I have to go back there lickety-split and protect our assets from the rebels and who knows… maybe from the Federalists too… if they come riding into town."

Henry sat on his perch, exhausted from his fevered speech. Ted sat down, too. Sarah tapped out a brief message signaling receipt of the message from the military service. She returned to her chair to take notes and carefully pleated the ticker tape message and placed it in a folder.

Jonathan approached the sideboard and poured a dram of bourbon into a snifter and brought it to his father. Henry simply said, "Bless you, my son." He swigged a generous portion and sat back in the chair, waiting for the tonic to take effect.

Ted looked at Sarah. "Do we have the balance sheets for the cotton gin activities here?"

"Only as of the first two quarters of 1860 when Jonathan came to Maine for his July Fourth vacation."

Jonathan sat in his chair and picked up a leather satchel from under it. Handing a sheaf of papers to his older brother, he said, "This brings us to the end of the current fiscal year. The cotton exchange is closed until January 10. You'll note the operations to Victoria Dock, London, are exceptional."

Ted asked, "What kind of assets are we sitting on right now in Georgia?" Sarah dipped the fountain pen in the inkwell and tapped gently, then poised herself to write.

"Let me see those papers, please." Jonathan reviewed several sheets. "Not taking into account the coinage from Spain and France because of the demonetization by law a few years ago, we are sitting on $6.8 million dollars' worth of gold coins and ingots in our vault on Bay Street in Savannah."

Henry seemed instantly revived. "Don't forget the gins themselves and my new schooner, *Vigilant*, built right here in town!"

Ted said, "Yes, Father, good point," but rolled his eyes slightly. The boys understood one another. The gold, and only the gold, needed to be moved to safe ground immediately to avoid expropriation by the South or the North.

Sarah piped in. "Maybe this is an idiotic question. Why are we not holding banknotes and paper currency? They're much easier to move."

"Not idiotic at all, Sal-Gal," Jonathan said affectionately. "We hold about $100,000 in paper in each city to…"

Henry barked, "We are old-fashioned, Sarah! I have trained these boys to convert all proceeds over $100,000 to gold or silver on a regular basis in case of a run on the banks or a depression in currency value."

Sarah risked another question. "But the sheer space the coinage takes up must be a consideration."

"This is true," Jonathan confirmed. "When Congress passed the Coinage Act of 1857, which demonetized our foreign coins, instead of trading in the foreign coins to the US Treasury at a pathetic rate, we started smelting the coins into silver and gold ingots or bricks. We imprinted the ingots with a crude rendition of the Hartson crest." Jonathan nodded toward the colorful depiction of three deer heads, each with a top-heavy set of antlers, in a framed painting hung over the fireplace. "We have about fourteen tons of precious metal down there."

The business meeting moved on to such topics as the removal of the assets in the South and the potential interruption of cotton delivery to Britain and Canada and their mills in Biddeford and Saco. Jonathan suggested procuring cotton from Morocco and Egypt to keep the local textile mills operational. They discussed plans for anticipating the military's material needs and opportunities if hostilities escalated. As usual, Sarah kept meticulous minutes of the meeting and even included the telegraph tape as evidence of the good business judgment being exercised, given the risks in the southern market.

CHAPTER 4

DOG ISLAND LIGHTHOUSE

After lunch Ted and Jonathan saddled their horses and moseyed down to the beach for a private conversation in the ocean air. "There's a perfect building site right there," Jonathan said, pointing to a bluff on a point of land at the end of the mile-long, crescent-shaped beach.

Ted looked at Jonathan. "Crescent Point! Would be a good name, wouldn't it?"

A gleam came into the younger brother's eyes. He yelled, "First one to the rocks of Crescent Point lays claim to it!" And they were off in an instant. Jonathan was higher up on the beach and his gelding started to bog down in sand that looked no different than the sand closer to the water but was significantly softer.

Ted, in the jockey tuck position, took the lead and yelled under his right armpit, "Sucker!" as he crouched forward with his face buried in the mane of the white horse in a full gallop.

Jonathan had to drop behind his brother and move toward the surf for his mount to get better purchase in the harder-packed sand and recalculated his route by veering toward the waterline at the inner side of the arc of the beach so he could make up lost time. He muttered to himself, "It's geometry, Teddy boy!" and coaxed the horse onward.

Ted looked to the left at his brother's route and the proximity of the rocks and started veering to the left, too. "Come on, boy! Let's get 'em!"

But it was too late. Jonathan's angle would allow him to reach the rocks first. By the time Ted got on the closest trajectory, he had fallen a full length behind his little brother. Jonathan, not looking back, yelled, "Who's the sucker now?"

Ted made up a half a length, but the rocks were upon them and they both backed off the reins. Ted conceded, "It's yours, little brother! Well done!"

Jonathan, panting as much as his horse, huffed, "Thank God, because you get Royal Orchard as the eldest!"

Ted shouted between breaths, "But I'll have to take the forest lands too… just to heat it!"

The brothers dismounted to give their steeds a rest and walked them up to the dirt road that ran parallel with the beach, stopping at the pond, which had a thin layer of ice on it. Ted's horse led the way to the edge of the pond and punched its hoof at the ice, broke through, and began drinking. "Your horse may be faster but mine is smarter," said Ted. Jonathan had to agree because he had to punch a hole in the ice for his own horse.

The brothers walked the horses back towards Royal Orchard. Jonathan stopped, looking out to sea. "What are we doing with that island out there? Do we still own it?"

Ted paused too and brought his horse around to better see the small mound three miles out in the ocean. A spire with a triangular symbol to caution sailors during the day was barely visible. Ted walked around to the right side of his horse and reached into the saddlebag to retrieve a brass spyglass.

"The Massachusetts Humane Society, with permission from Father, built a life-saving station out there but volunteers were hard to come by. You can see the house on the right side." Ted passed the spyglass to Jonathan. "Now funding is available from the US Life-Saving Service, which is, of course, run by the Revenue Department."

Jonathan coughed. "Of course. Get the smugglers first and the sailors in distress second." As Jonathan scanned the rolling hills and crashing surf of the island, he asked, "Are there still dogs out there?"

"Yes, I've heard that somehow the wolves or wolfhounds have been able to survive since the Indian encampment was out there. They eat rodents and fish and drink the brackish water from the pond out there. The mangy beasts are omnivores and eat grass, rose hips, snakes, insects… basically, anything that moves. They live in the grottoes on the high ground to the left." Jonathan scanned to the left. Ted continued, "You remember when the wind was right, and the sea was calm, we could hear the howling at night?"

"It was quite unsettling. It gave me nightmares. I could hear them all the way up at the big house," Jonathan agreed.

Ted pointed again. "There's a large grotto or cave out there on the left called Howl Hole, the opening of which faces this way. It acts like an amphitheater, directing those primal cries in this direction. In the 1680s, four shipwrecked people, including an Indian, survived in the cave until rescued by the Abenaki. I think the Abenaki set up encampments in the warmer months and brought their dogs out there. They must have left a litter or two behind, and the beasts have survived all these years. What is strange is that the breed is quite large and has the look of an Irish wolfhound. Their snouts are quite furry. Maybe the Vikings left them behind?"

With the telescope still raised, Jonathan asked, "Are they friendly?"

"No, they're basically wolves or wolf-dogs, and now Father wants to convene a hunting expedition to eradicate the herd. He wants to then rename it Liberty Island."

"Of course he does…but isn't he a little late? I think New York took the name already."

"The Revenue Department doesn't want the name changed because of the confusion to mariners relying on sailing charts," said Ted. "It would take an act of Congress… which Father is seriously contemplating. Just last week, the revenue people wrote a semi-threatening letter that they would take the island by eminent domain if we did not build a lighthouse out there. Steamer traffic, business and pleasure trips between Boston, Newburyport, Portsmouth, and Portland, is on the rise."

"What did Father say? If I couldn't guess."

"He crumpled the letter and called them a bunch of Marxists and vowed to fortify the island."

"Why don't we just let them take it?" Jonathan asked. "Eminent domain requires just and swift compensation by the government. It'd be nice to receive a check from the federal government for a change. Right?" he reasoned.

"Not a chance, Brother. That's too sensible. Father actually wants to keep Dog Island in case influenza sweeps through southern Maine again." Ted turned his horse to continue walking. Jonathan remained where he was, scanning the island with the spyglass.

After a few moments, Jonathan exclaimed. "I've got an idea!" Jonathan turned his own horse and caught up to his brother.

"Oh no, Jon-Jon... you got that devilish look again... it's the same look you had when you had me help muscle the railroad switch and sent the hog train into Preble Station in Portland! Not good, little brother."

"No, this is serious, Ted. I've got a plan for our problems in the South. You know how we were talking this morning about how moving the gold could get us in trouble with each southern state as well as the federal government...not to mention bandits?"

Ted looked around as if to be sure no one was listening on the desolate beach road. "Now I am seriously worried, but go on. What are you scheming?"

"Well, we build that lighthouse. We pull the brick ballast from the schooner and replace it with the gold ingots. Then we put the brick ballast in the cargo hold along with some fine Georgia pine and head for Dog Island to build the lighthouse. Best of all, we do it under the authority of the Revenue Department! Maybe they will even pay for it." Pointing dramatically to Dog Island, Jonathan continued, "We secure the gold in the lighthouse and the grottoes out there until the hostilities die down!"

Ted silently looked at the island with a faraway gaze. The wind picked up and Ted shivered visibly. He turned up his coat collar and looked at his brother. "Where do you get these ideas from? You're crazy, kid... but... I love it! Let's do it! Is it legal?"

Jonathan laughed. "I love your priorities. Only after confirming we should do it, do you ask if it's legal. That's perfect. Yes, it's legal." Jonathan continued with the confidence of a lawyer advising a client, which always annoyed his older brother. "Here is why: the gold itself is ours. As we ginned and sold cotton and shipped products, we paid the tariffs in full. And we have the paperwork to prove it. So, we are merely moving our property from point A to point B. Our reason for secrecy is that we can't be sure government agents on the state or federal level will believe us. They may take joy in impounding our profit to fight over it in court for a portion. Our consciences can be clear on this point."

Hardly taking a breath, Jonathan continued, "Further, we need to scurry about to avoid robbers and pirates. We do not know what instability this secession business will produce. Why wouldn't Georgia create a new tax and tap us for a war effort? Or here in Maine, you know Father's detractors already think he is profiting off slavery. They'll impound his accounts here as contraband of war!"

"War?" exclaimed Ted. "You seriously think the South is going to go to arms over slavery?"

Jonathan looked off in the distance, searching for words. "I believe it will be Lincoln who will not tolerate the secessions. The North needs the raw materials and extended growing seasons of the South to feed the bloated cities of the North. The South, in true southern fashion will say," Jonathan switched into a perfect southern accent. "*Go on now… leave us be. Let a sleepin' dawg lie. Let's part as friends. Let us pursue our view of life and economy based on slavery. Y'all up North set up the slave economy by making all the slave ships and receiving the profit in New Yawk. So, don't get all righteous now over it. You want to run your economy without slave labor, go do it! But live and let live. We gonna be takin 'er easy down heyah.*"

Ted was smiling as Jonathan did his redneck impression, but then Jonathan added coldly in his normal accent, "No Ted, Lincoln is going move on the South. Then those prideful, hot-headed southern dogs will fight to the death over it. I've heard their resolve in Savannah. It's coming. We have to sell now and sneak our gold out of there because war is imminent, I promise you. I didn't want to say anything in front of Sarah and Father, but we must act now. Frankly, I could be drafted if I don't get out of there quickly. You, being married, are probably safe up here in Maine from the draft. But Father's cotton profits from the South are not safe up here in Union banks. We need our own vault up here."

Ted stopped walking because they were getting near the barn and he noticed George Eaton and Tom were coming to get the horses. George appeared to be telling Tom to hurry up. Ted quickly focused on the issue at hand and assumed the mantle of older brother by urgently whispering, "Jonathan, we will pursue the lighthouse project. I'll get Father to agree and set it up with the revenue boys. Then I'll get the thing engineered and prepare the foundation out there and shore up the landing rails. You're in charge of the exit strategy in Savannah. We will speak in code on the telegraphs and posts if needed. Let's keep the project just between you and me. When we have secured the vault on Dog Island, we can bring Sarah and Father in on the secret. Got it?"

Jonathan reached his hand out and whispered before the hired hands were too close, "Got it, Brother. It's for their own good. It gives them deniability. I'll load the gold on *Vigilant* and sail for Port Talbot as soon as possible. I'll probably arrange for a decoy shipment of currency and valuables by prairie schooner or that security fellow, Allan Pinkerton."

Ted shook his younger brother's hand firmly and then pulled Jonathan to him in an embrace. "God help us."

CHAPTER 5

RE-ENSLAVEMENT BY CHOICE

Jonathan's Christmas visit to Maine came to a hasty close with news of more southern states seceding. The day after Christmas 1860, the Hartsons' telegraph on the table in Henry's study clicked to life with the news of Fort Pulaski at the mouth of Savannah's port being strategically occupied by order of the governor of Georgia. The ticker tape indicated that the federal forces left the fort they had built without incident. The news sent a ripple of concern throughout Royal Orchard. Everyone knew that Jonathan was returning to Savannah shortly.

Jonathan walked over to the Trainer's Cottage not far from the main house. Tom opened the door. "Come in, Mister Jonathan. Can I offer you some hot tea?"

"Yes, that'd be great, Tom. I need to talk to you about life here while I am away. Are we alone?"

"Yes, sir, we are." Tom poured tea into a pair of camp-style metal mugs.

Jonathan began, "While I am in Georgia, you will assist Mr. Ted in some special projects."

"Excuse me, sir, for interrupting, but I am returning to Georgia with you. I have thought about it and it is my free choice, if you will have me."

"Tom, it's too risky," said Jonathan. "You could be walking into a death trap. The prospects of being re-enslaved, or worse, are extremely high. You know it is illegal in Georgia to free a slave. They will not recognize those fancy manumission papers from the Maine court. In fact, having such documents on your person might be fatal. You have to stay in the North and there is plenty to do here."

"Sir, I know all that," Tom replied. "The person who is in greatest danger is you. You are a known Yankee. You will be immediately suspected of being a spy. The way I figure it, I am your best cover until we get out of there. I think if I am in the right clothing and carrying a sad countenance as most slaves do, I am safe. I am a valuable piece of property protected by the laws of Georgia, like a fine horse. All I must do is play slave, and you play mastah. In fact, the harsher you are to me, the better. You being a Yankee openly berating your slave will win the hearts of the southern gentry." Tom concluded his pitch by wrinkling his face at the ironic word "gentry."

Jonathan sipped his tea as he thought about Tom's proposal, then stood to look out the window as the snow fell and shrouded the large barn in the distance. Before Jonathan could say anything, Tom added in an animated voice, "Besides, Mastah, it's some cold here. I'll die if I stay!"

Jonathan spun around to see a wide grin on Tom's face and started laughing. "Well, if you do come back with me, your last name is Lee or Davis. It ain't 'Lincoln' once we get past Philly." Jonathan paused. "Are you sure you want to do this?"

"Yes, Mastah, I sure." Tom replied in the vernacular of his former southern peers. "I'z gots to get into character like Miss Butler taught me. I done figured, Boss, that you're gonna need a faithful servant to dos what youz gots to do down theyah in cotton country. I owe you my life. How's that for faithful? And to be honest, Mastah, I think there's not enough room for me and Mr. Eaton on this here plantation."

Jonathan asked sharply, "Has Eaton been a problem?"

"I think he'd fit right in with the rest of the gentry in Savannah," Tom replied.

"Well, he is a favorite of Father's and I can't see upsetting that apple cart…yet."

"Hey, Boss, I don't want to upset nothing, please, forget it. I just rather stick with you, come hell or high water, and I expect we will see a little bit of both."

"Okay, Tom, get your gear together. We catch the train in the morning. Dress civilized 'til we cross the Mason-Dixon line and then it's back to slavery for you."

"Yes'm, Boss! I can't wait. Sweet Jesus, here comes the sun, yessuh!"

* * *

Jonathan and Tom boarded the train south of Port Talbot in the town of Wells. They sat together in the coach, though blacks who did not accompany a white person had to sit in a different car. The farewell at Royal Orchard was accompanied by tears and wailing as if the two were being sent off to war – which, in effect, they were. Sarah had given both Tom and Jonathan a crash course in operating a telegraph. Henry Hartson had come around to the notion of yielding to the federal revenue department and constructing a lighthouse on Dog Island if the boys promised to pursue renaming it Liberty Island.

As the train drew closer to Philadelphia's Broad Street Station, Tom quietly pulled a burlap sack from Jonathan's carpetbag on the rack overhead. He slipped out while Jonathan slept, heading to the Negroes' car toward the back of the train. He ducked into the small washroom and changed his clothes, putting on an off-white, pullover linen shirt and a pair of cotton trousers cut off at the calves. He opened the window of the moving train and threw out his refined clothing. He hesitated before throwing away the leather shoes. "If I'z keep 'em, deyz gonna string me up fo' thiefin,'" He muttered as he opened the bathroom door and headed through the car of black people sitting on wooden benches. He checked inside his burlap sack to see an apple and a half loaf of crusty bread from the Royal Orchard kitchen. The crust had sat drying on the counter to be crushed into breadcrumbs for Mrs. Hartson's famous baked stuffed haddock.

As the train jerked to a stop in Philadelphia, Jonathan awoke, disoriented by the surroundings. The train station was flooded with black people walking in every direction, looking for relatives traveling freely or as escapees from the South. Jonathan remembered the mission and knew where Tom was, if he hadn't simply run away. After all, Tom did have his freedom card issued by the court.

The first-class car started to fill with high-society folks headed south. A gentleman sat down across from Jonathan. "Good evening, sir," the stranger said.

Jonathan did not want to talk to anybody about anything, so he nodded politely, gave a curt "Evening," and looked out the window.

"Where are you from?" asked the stranger.

Jonathan replied quickly, "Georgia. And you sir?"

"By Jove, Georgia, too! The little town of St. Mary's. And you?"

Dread coursed through Jonathan's being. "Savannah," he said as he stood up. The train started pulling away, and as planned, Jonathan was headed off to find Tom. "Excuse me, sir, I need to check my steerage." Jonathan walked back to the colored car. Only one kerosene lantern hung there, swinging to the sway of the train. Shadows danced on fixed dark faces. Jonathan squinted and muttered, "Poppycock, this is fruitless. I can't see a blessed thing."

To his right, he heard a whisper. "Mastah Hartson? It's Tombo, boss." Jonathan, looking to the right, still could not see a thing. Then Tom leaned into the light and smiled. "Tombo, you okay? Do you need anything?"

"I'z good, Mastah. I gots food and there's a drum of cool watah over theyah, sir."

"Okay, boy. I'll check on you in the morning," was Jonathan's gruff response. "We should be in the Carolinas by then. Big day tomorrow boy, you heyah?"

"Yes, Mastah. I be ready, Boss."

Jonathan pivoted stiffly without a parting salutation and headed back to his seat. As he re-entered the car, the gentleman from St. Mary's stood up and asked if Jonathan would join him for a libation and some food in the dining car. Jonathan relented and introduced himself. "Jon Hartson, Savannah."

"Nice to meet you, sir. Derek Olmstead, St. Mary's." They shook hands and Derek led the way to the dining car.

After ordering whiskeys and the pot roast, the gentlemen settled into a lively discourse. Jonathan explained his work milling cotton. Derek explained his trade as a commercial fisherman with several boats at the Port of Fernandina in Florida and his private docks on the St. Mary's river. He recounted the early days of Fernandina during the flux between Spanish and US rule. It became clear the fisherman was no apologist for the slave trade. He owned no slaves and paid his boatmen, both black and white, equal wages based on the haul.

Jonathan hinted at his shipping endeavors, focusing on how, in the uncertain times, it became necessary to employ different exit and entrance points from the southern coast. "What does your boat draw?" asked Derek.

"When fully laden, 12 feet, empty, 6 feet."

"Come visit me in Fernandina or at my private docks in St. Mary's,"

Derek invited. "As long as there are no moon tides, I can accommodate your depth. What I can not accommodate is a smuggler, however. I cannot be sure how things will be viewed in the coming weeks and months. One day cotton is king, the next it's contraband."

Jonathan was warming up to the man. "Oh no, I have come too far in life to engage in smuggling. I am not sure what is going to happen to my cotton trade. I am actually looking at diversifying by hauling southern pine to the shipbuilders up North if this infernal dispute doesn't interfere."

"Well, we have a lumber mill in St. Mary's less than a mile from my docks."

"How long a sail is it from Savannah?"

"A day sail… a good day," replied the fisherman.

"Well, I will certainly think about it. Do you have a card? I'm not sure it makes sense to go south to sail north, but you never know."

The next evening the train pulled into Savannah to the sounds of gunfire in the streets. The residents seemed to be celebrating news of the state's vote in favor of a secession convention in Milledgeville, Georgia. The traveling partners exchanged their goodbyes. Jonathan found Tom waiting by the tracks. Tom jumped to grab the carpetbags of his "master" as he descended the stairs of the train.

"Mastah Hartson, sir, shall we go, sir?"

"Yes" was the swift reply. "Follow me, boy!" Jonathan led the way to the carriages waiting outside the station. He bellowed at the cabbie, "Seven Bay Street!"

The Hartson townhome overlooked the Savannah River and was just west of the docks. Once inside the house, Jonathan reached out to shake Tom's hand. But Tom ignored the gesture and shuffled to the large windows looking out over on the street and river beyond. Tom bowed his head several times as if he were obeying commands and drew the drapes closed. He then went to the second floor and did the same. Only after he returned did he shake his master's hand. "So far so good, Mastah Hartson. May I take my leave, mastah? My bones are creaking and cracking."

"Of course, Tom. Tomorrow we start loading *Vigilant* and head back to the safety of Port Talbot and Royal Orchard.

CHAPTER 6

1980 ADEMPTION REDEMPTION

Rick Eaton, the great-great-great-grandson of George Eaton, the original overseer at Royal Orchard, tiptoed out the side door of his single-wide mobile home on a back road in Port Talbot. There was no front door. He was trying to avoid being interrogated by the ball and chain, as he called her. He could still hear her snoring through the trailer's tin walls. Rick slithered into the beat-up olive-green '68 Ford Mustang and only clicked the door partially shut. Now that he had read about the new Hartson archives in the newspapers, he was taking the first step, an early-morning mission, to correct a wrong perpetrated against his family by the Hartsons. Rick Eaton did not want to explain his scheme to anyone. He pulled out of the rural driveway as quietly as the car and crunching gravel beneath it allowed.

As he turned toward New Hampshire on his mission, Rick recalled the conversation with his father years ago regarding the Hartson settlement. "The lawyer called it ademption, Ricky," his father had tried to explain. "It's when a gift in a will or trust is spent or lost before the giver dies… it never becomes part of the estate. It ain't there."

"Pops, it's called it a rip-off, plain and simple. They used fancy legal mumbo jumbo to deny us what's our fair share of the Hartson estate."

"Now Ricky, just calm down. This was many years ago. We know that the intentions of Henry Hartson never worked out. Ted Jr. put a bequest in his will in 1925 that your grandfather would receive a 20% interest in the cotton textile mills in Biddeford. Ted Jr. was making amends for his father's failure to honor Henry Hartson's word to give a double portion to Great-great Grandpa George."

Rick's father continued, "When Ted Jr. passed away in the 1950s, his bequest to the Eatons was supposedly worthless. The cotton mill was supposedly belly-up. When it came time to issue the stock, the corporation had closed. No stock could be issued. My lawyer, Sanford Beach, said the Eaton bequest adeemed."

"That's fancy legal stuff, Dad, because the Hartsons have been selling the land where that factory was, even to this day!"

"Ricky, after our claim was thrown out by the judge, our lawyer said the case was over unless we could show company assets were hidden from the court," his father replied. "Then Grandpa died, and I didn't have the will to fight the Hartson machine any longer. Plus, I was still on the payroll and was trying to keep things gentlemanly. Ted the fourth was a real gentleman, too. He explained how all of the cotton manufacturing was moving south. He said his buyers could get the same product quicker and at half the price from a mill in Alabama or Georgia. No unions, cheaper labor, more advanced factories, and easier access to fuel for the coal-fired turbines. It shuttered the plant here. Then he offered us the land and the mobile home. I settled right quick with him, son. Mr. Beach advised me to do it, too."

Rick slammed the steering wheel as he remembered his father's capitulation to the millionaires. He recalled telling his father, "What if those southern mills are Hartson companies with different names? Do you know? The Hartsons are wealthy, and they're making a fool of you! Pops, stop being a pushover! You slaved your whole life at Royal Orchard. I slaved there too, until I couldn't take their smug and snobby orders. You have failed to get us our due, and now I'll have to get it. Thanks, Pops!"

* * *

Trying to keep a clear vision of the road to New Hampshire, Rick wiped the tears from his eyes as he recalled this conversation and how rough he was with his father. He wished he could take it back and apologize, but now his dad was gone forever, having died four years earlier. In honor of his father, Rick was as determined as ever to make the Hartsons pay. He believed the fight over the inheritance, while his dad still worked for the

Hartsons, had been too much for his dad to deal with. Thus, Rick blamed the Hartsons, not only for his family's poverty, but also for his father's untimely death.

Dressed in his Sunday best and a John Travolta-style *Saturday Night Fever* wig, Eaton sped through the White Mountains of New Hampshire towards Dartmouth College. His mission was to redeem his inheritance. He pulled into the empty circle in front of the college's Tuck School of Business and parked in the no-parking zone. He figured with it being the end of May, the school's spring session was over. He straightened his wig, walked up to the receptionist, and pulled a newspaper out of his backpack. The headline read: "Dartmouth Business School Home to Hartson Records."

"Excuse me, miss," he said. The coed looked up. "I'm a business student at St. Francis College in Biddeford, Maine, where the Hartson family owned the textile mills. I am doing a research project on the Lowell Method of textile production, which the Hartsons perfected. I'd like to review these business records if possible." He pointed to the headline.

"Of course! We are very proud of the new acquisition of records. It is so rich in business and family history from the turn of the century." the receptionist replied cheerfully. "We love helping students at neighboring schools. Do you have your student ID?"

Eaton fished through his wallet and pulled out a marred ID card. "It's all I have. It got scratched up when I locked myself out of the dorm room. I tried to use the card to open the door."

The receptionist, who was about the same age as Rick, giggled. "Oh, I hate when that happens. I know that trick. It can pop the door right open."

"Sometimes," Rick sighed.

She squinted at the name on the shredded ID. "Is it Wilhelm?"

"Yes, Wilhelm Harding, but everyone calls me Willy." Rick fluffed his Travolta hairdo for effect. The girl blushed and giggled again as she reached for a clipboard for the visitor sign-in. She filled in her part of the information and passed the board to "Willy" to sign. He signed in as Bill Hardin.

"If you need any copies, they're ten cents each. Documents in cellophane are not to be removed from their covering. I'll show you to the cabinets containing the Hartson archives, and you can view them at the table. Just let me know if you need copies."

After showing Rick the cabinets, the receptionist left the room. Rick casually looked around at the ceilings and walls for closed-circuit TV cameras. Nothing. He began rifling through the drawers, which were arranged chronologically. He homed in on George Eaton's years of service from 1830 to the mid-1880s, which also covered the period of the untimely deaths of the Hartson brothers, Jonathan and Theodore, due to the influenza outbreak.

In one area of the cabinet lay a leather folder with a flap and a rawhide tie string. Rick opened it and saw corporate minutes, resolutions, and letters with wax seals that had been opened. He then pulled out many folded strips of paper ribbon. The thin strips were marked with black dots and dashes. He shoved it all back into the folder and continued to rifle through and pull documents from other parts of the cabinet, stuffing them into the leather portfolio as he worked. He tied the fancy folder shut, stepped back from the files, pulled his shirttails out, sucked in his gut, and shoved the thick file down the front of his pants. He billowed his shirt in front of his stomach, grabbed his backpack, and walked toward the reception area.

"You're done already?" the girl asked.

"Oh, no, I just remembered that I'm in a no-parking zone and this is going to take a while. I shall return!"

"Oh, okay, but hold on a second. Can you step over here? We have to search all backpacks. Do you mind? I'm really sorry."

Rick put his elbows on the counter and leaned over, allowing his shirt to "tent" over his stomach. The girl looked in the backpack and pulled out the newspaper article. "This is all you brought?"

"Yeah, man, I'm in trouble on this project. It's my only lead so far!" They laughed together. Rick quickly pivoted and added, "I'll be right back." He hustled toward his car. A campus police car was parked behind the vehicle. Rick carried his backpack in front of his stomach and called out, "Sorry, officer, just had to pick something up."

The officer was in his own cruiser with the window down. "You must be from Maine."

"Yes, sir. How'd you know?" Rick played stupid.

"Only Mainiacs park in no-parking zones." The officer pulled away slowly with a self-righteous look on his face.

Rick waved politely with a forced smile and hissed quietly, "Live free or die, you pompous pork chop!" He slid the backpack under the car seat and headed back to his rural location on the bottom rung of society's ladder in Port Talbot.

CHAPTER 7

THE VALEDICTORIAN

Eaton's grey trailer with black shutters was not far from Hartson's Beach. The land on which the trailer sat had been part of a larger Hartson tract well inland from the beach itself. The trailer and the property were first occupied by Rick's father when the Hartsons "gifted" them to the Eatons. It was meant to settle the bequest snafu, which was intended to reward the Eatons for more than a century of faithful service. Rick had lived there all twenty-two years of his life. It was around the fourth grade that Rick began to feel the stigma of trailer living. "How's the land yacht?" or "how's life in the rock 'n' roll hall of shame?" were frequent questions from the bullies on the school bus.

Rick did his best to cope with this ridicule from peers and the dysfunction of parents whose major enterprise was distilling spirits in the backyard. Rick found relief by getting good grades and earning praise from his teachers. He quickly earned a reputation as a brainiac who preferred to be alone. The harassment waned as Rick learned to verbalize his own form of wit. He could out-debate his detractors and had a knack for inventing nicknames for bullies that would catch on among classmates and foment ridicule of the bullies, all at the hands of the other students. Rick dubbed it *boxing by proxy*.

In his speech four years ago as valedictorian of Talbot High, Rick delivered a manifesto extolling the virtue of vengeance as a motivator for achieving one's goals in life. The address had the sound and feel of a classic youthful rah-rah graduation pitch, but it was shrouded in twists of phrase that mostly masked the darkness of his thesis. Occasionally, during the delivery, parents would squirm in their seats and look at one another, whispering, "Did he say what I think he said?" A portion of Rick's speech included the following;

> *My fellow students, today we embark on a new venture… life after high school. For some, it is straight to the sea, or a land-based job, others to college and still others to trade school. It is my hope that you will develop talents to succeed like I have utilized in my tenure here. I am so very proud to be your valedictorian. I could not have done it without you."*

Rick paused, and a smattering of applause reverberated in the auditorium. Many knew he had been picked on and wondered why on earth he would now be thanking his tormentors.

> *The strategy for success that I use has precepts, rules, or methods which, if constructed properly, will drive you to victory. Much like a formula in chemistry or a theorem in math. I call it* lex talionis.*"*

Rick Eaton looked over toward his Latin teacher, who was very popular with the students. The professor was seated on the stage wearing a black graduation robe with the crimson hood of Harvard hanging down his back. Rick pointed to the teacher. *"Dr. Clough gets it. Lex tal- lee- own-us"* Rick pronounced the Latin term slowly and phonetically as he pointed toward Dr. Clough and led the audience in a round of applause for the teacher. Dr. Clough's smile and pleasant nodding started to wane as he mentally translated the odd Latin phrase. His face turned white and worried. *The law of retaliation.*

> *The concept is to build your drive by identifying the source of your pain and failures in life, name them, and then declare war on them! Rocky Balboa understands lex talionis. Rocky's beginnings as a debt collector for the mob was the perfect first job.* Lex talionis *was being put into motion.*

Rick lifted both arms like Rocky during his victory run up the stairs in Philadelphia and started to loudly hum the theme song. *"Na na nah… na na nah… Na na nah… na nah!"* Rick turned around with arms and fists up at the podium, and the students went wild with applause. The adults looked bewildered. Rick went on. *"Rocky's lex talionis resulted in Apollo*

Creed going down and going down hard!" Rick bellowed the word "hard" for effect. There was more applause from the students.

> *Today America celebrates landing Viking One on Mars, folks. Mars! Imagine that. The craft left Earth less than a year ago and landed today. Think about the drive, the determination, the guts! Know this: our space program is built on lex talionis! We identified the source of our pain and our failure...the Russians! With Kennedy's leadership, we vowed to beat them and beat them we did! Lex talionis! Say it with me!* Lex talionis!

The students roared the Latin phrase.

> Lex talionis *is all around us. Seize it. Harness it! Pummel your adverse forces with lex talionis!*
> *Look in the market. Beta tapes versus VHS tapes?* Lex talionis! *Bye-bye, Beta!*
> *Look in the environment! Ozone layer versus CFCs?* Lex talionis! *Bye-bye fluorocarbons!*
> *Life is short. Don't put up with those who oppose you.* Lex talionis!
> *Port Talbot Senior Class of 1976? Go get 'em!* Lex talionis!

As Rick returned to his seat, the students started chanting *lex talionis* repeatedly. After several nerve-wracking minutes for the adults who were opposed to a message centered on vengeance, the principal calmed the crowd and continued the ceremonies.

* * *

After graduation, Rick's free ride to St. Francis College as a pre-med student came to an early termination in the spring of his freshman year. The appeal of St. Francis' medical program was that it fast-tracked students to becoming a licensed doctor within three years following undergrad studies. So, it was particularly odd to hear of his sudden leave of absence. Most everyone thought it was because of the death of his father the preceding Christmas, during his first semester of college. Only the anatomy professor and some classmates knew the real reason for Rick's expulsion.

Human anatomy was Rick's favorite subject at the college because the anatomy labs were so robust. The college was so invested in its medical training that it maintained a morgue on-site so that students would have no shortage of cadavers. The entire room was maintained at a temperature just below 40 degrees and contained an open three-level hydraulic shelving system that allowed for easy withdrawal and study of each corpse.

Just before spring break, two events diametrically opposed to one another occurred: exams and Mardi Gras. Rick, fueled by some whiskey, got the ghoulish idea of throwing a Mardi Gras party for the dead. He pulled fifteen cadavers down from their temporary resting places and propped them up in various poses and costumes. Some were naked, wearing only beads and feathery masks. Others were partially dressed as members of a royal court, complete with a king, a queen, and jesters. Some had cigars wedged between their frozen gray fingers. Others sported red lipstick and held plastic champagne glasses. Eaton single-handedly arranged the motionless group into a semi-circular tableau facing the glass windows of the observatory auditorium. Rick made sure to open the curtains so that students would immediately see the diabolical "die-o-rama" when they entered the assembly hall for class.

* * *

Rick had worked through the night and sat in the back of the class with a small cassette recorder to pick up audio of the students' reactions as they entered the room for the first period of the school day. It took some a few moments to realize what they were looking at. Many gagged and ran out. Screams sounded down the hall, and soon students were prevented from entering the room, though they tried. Rick had decided he better run, but when he got up to exit, the door was locked. He jiggled the handle and when it was opened, he stood face-to-face with his anatomy professor. Rick's smile said it all.

Professor Woodring, suppressing outrage and alarm, asked with a deceptively calm smile, "Is this your idea of fun?"

Rick giggled. "It's probably the best party I have ever been to!"

The smell of stale alcohol assaulted the professor's nostrils. Woodring forcibly backed Rick into the observatory and shut the door behind them both so the students could not hear them. Woodring looked over Rick's shoulder at the grisly display and spied a bottle of Old Grand-Dad whiskey on a dissection table. "Is that your whiskey down there?"

Rick spun around. "Shoot, there it is. I've been looking for that." Sirens whined in the distance.

The professor, still feigning a smile, gripped Rick's shoulder and asked, "So was this Mardi Gras creation your idea, or did you have help?"

Rick, thrown off by Woodring's smile and calm tone, said, "Yup, it's all me. I was just having a little fun. Check out the girl on the right, she's a work of art... then I added the beads and mask."

The professor glanced at the naked cadaver seated upright, wearing only a feathered mask and the beads draped over her ample chest. That was all he could take. Woodring lunged at Rick, began throttling him by the neck, and yelled: "You sick..." Just then, campus police stormed the classroom and knocked them both to the ground. Screams and chaos enveloped the area as more students beheld the exhibition. Eventually, Rick was escorted out in handcuffs, never to return to the school.

His sudden expulsion, combined with the death of his father earlier that school year had pushed Rick over the edge. His father, who had worked at Royal Orchard his entire life, left his only son the single-wide trailer plus a modest sum of money. His father's death ignited Rick's desire for vengeance on the Hartsons for weaseling out of the promise of inheritance. The promise had explained the family's continuous loyal service to the Hartsons for all these generations. In Rick's mind, it was now time for *lex talionis*.

* * *

After being bounced from the pre-med program, Rick used the intervening three years to nurse his alcohol addiction with the money left to him by his father. He also used his time to research what had actually happened to the Hartson wealth and his own family's financial entitlement. Rick made forays down to Royal Orchard where he had once, for a short time, worked. The Hartsons were always gracious in receiving him, but kept him at arm's length. Rick sensed their aloofness and concluded they were in on the denial of his share of Hartson wealth. Rick had the anger and energy to seek the truth, plus he had figured he had time to kill. The newly created archives at Dartmouth gave Rick the break he needed in his search for revenge.

CHAPTER 8

The Queen B

After returning from Dartmouth and hiding the car in the garage next to the trailer, Rick sat in the dining area of his home and pored over the sheaf of documents he had brazenly stolen from the college archives. The front of the leather portfolio was embossed with the Hartson family crest. He stared, mesmerized, at the three deer heads, each with an unusually prominent rack of antlers. He sipped from the pint bottle of Old Grand-Dad whiskey. Rick was proud of being the great-great-great-grandson of George Eaton, the original overseer at Royal Orchard at Hartson's Beach. Rick thumbed through the yellowed papers and muttered to himself, "Liars, thieves, profiteers… rip-off artists…"

"What's that, Ricky?" asked the heavy-set girl who walked in from the narrow hallway. The mobile home rocked as she approached.

"Nothing! I wasn't talking to you," Rick snapped as he shut the portfolio.

"Wow, that's a cool folder!" she said, ignoring Rick's rudeness. She reached for the portfolio but Rick slapped her hand. "Don't touch, Brenda. This is none of your business! This is a family matter."

"Ain't I family, Ricky?" Brenda asked coyly. She rubbed her ample belly. "Ain't *we* family?" She nodded toward her baby bulge.

Rick spun the cap off the whiskey and took a long haul. "This is Eaton business, Brenda. I gotta concentrate."

"Oh, let me guess, three years since college boy got booted, and you're still trying to figure out how to shake down the Hartsons. You should use your smarts for something worthwhile. Isn't this home enough?"

"No, this tin can is not enough! The Eatons made it possible for the Hartsons to survive. They owe us big-time! This trailer is chump change! Back in the late 1800s, the Eatons almost died of influenza, trying to save the Hartsons' hides. They nursed the ingrates back to health. So they owe their very lives to my family! Both granddaddy and my dad told me we were to receive a double portion of inheritance from Ted Jr. You know what a double portion is, Brenda?" He didn't wait for an answer. "Yeah, me neither, but all I know is we were to receive a twenty-percent share in the Biddeford Mill, and that's a lot! Daddy said the Hartsons told the probate judge that the mill was worth nothing. Hartsons put it in bankruptcy right at the time the estate was being split up. They called it ademption. A fancy term for rip-off. What did Eatons get? Nothin'! Zilch! Nada! Except for this 'land yacht' and it's sinking fast."

Rick was raging. He barely took a breath. "My dad, God rest his soul, never gave up his belief that the mill had value. He did not believe their fortunes had dwindled. He was sure they were hiding the money just to deny the Eaton grant that was promised all the way back to Henry Hartson himself. Pops settled for the best he could... this old tin can. I promised him I would continue the search for justice. If I can show fraud in the documents or hiding the money of the estate, the distribution gets redone. Pop's lawyer said he needs proof, and he will do the rest. So, Brenda, I must concentrate on family business. You understand?"

Brenda patiently listened to Rick's all-too-familiar rant and reached for the leather portfolio again. "Where'd you get this?"

Rick pushed her hand away. "Don't touch, okay?" he barked.

That was it for Brenda. She bent over Rick, rubbing her belly, and whispered harshly, "Well, you better figure it out, Mr. Genius, cuz there's about to be another mouth to feed at Chez Eaton. And the for-sale signs down at Hartson's Beach don't look like a flim-flam to me. The clocks are ticking. And listen here, you loser, if you so as much as touch me the wrong way again, I'll have you back in jail in a heartbeat. Can you say domestic violence?... I knew you could."

Rick gritted his teeth, looked away, and swigged the whiskey again. He picked up the papers and his bottle and rushed out of the trailer. Brenda cackled like the Sea Hag in the Popeye cartoons. Rick could hear her husky laughter even out in the garage where Brenda made him go to smoke his cigarettes in anticipation of their bundle of joy. Rick was fuming, all right. After he lit up a cigarette, he threw a gnarly soup bone to his dog, who was also kept in the garage in a penned-in area away from big bad Brenda. Rick barked a foreign word at the dog, and the black-faced Belgian Malinois shepherd with the light tan body immediately sank to its haunches and began gnawing on the bone.

Rick's mind settled down as he inhaled deeply. He glanced sideways at his Mustang and reviewed the day's excitement in New Hampshire. He thought aloud, as he had always done as a child. "Thanks to Mr. Porkchop's activities today, my little pony, you're getting a fresh coat of paint. It's just what you need for the summer... Candy apple red? No, something innocuous... chestnut brown, my little pony? Yes, suh! That'll do it."

Rick looked overhead at the rafters and flicked on a flashlight, scheming for a hideaway above the double-bay garage. He continued to mutter to himself and the huge dog. "Samson, above you is a war room. You protect it. Right, Sam? *Lex talionis*, my friend. It's coming." He flicked on the shop lights, which flooded the garage, and lifted a stepladder into Samson's penned area and propped it against the wall. He grabbed the Hartson artifacts and climbed the ladder. Samson watched his master disappear overhead into the eaves and returned to his sinewy snack. As Rick focused on the documents in his hideaway, he too had a bone of sorts to chew on. Samson's gnawing and licking below could just as easily describe Rick's antics as he pored over the documents in his secret office.

CHAPTER 9

DIGGER OPENS SEASIDE

The very afternoon of Rick Eaton's Dartmouth caper in late May 1980, Digger Davenport returned to his summer home on Ocean Avenue in Port Talbot. The mansion, affectionately referred to by the summer folk as a "cottage," was perched high on an ocean bluff. The locals swore the house was the one featured in the gothic soap opera, *Dark Shadows,* and thus it gained that nickname. The mansion's real name was simply Seaside.

Digger was a tall young man with dark curly hair and piercing green eyes. He had just successfully completed his junior year of college in New York. He was ready for a break before starting his third summer season as the bicycle patrol officer for the town. He would have the oceanside manse to himself for a few weeks before his parents arrived from their winter home in Lake Placid, New York. As soon as he got in, he went to the front closet to fire up the hundred-amp Fisher tuner and Technics turntable. He thumbed through the mix of albums on the rack above the sound system. He passed the *Bert and I* records of his parents, skipped Herb Albert's *Whipped Cream and Other Delights*, and snatched up the Jethro Tull album *Aqualung*. Holding the edges of the vinyl record carefully, he flipped the disc to put side B on the spinning turntable. He carefully placed the diamond-tipped needle on the fourth track: "Locomotive Breath," and turned up the volume to six on a scale of ten.

As the intro of classical piano wafted throughout the house, Digger quickly opened all the windows and doors on the ocean side of the house. The living room and solarium were engulfed in swirling wind and the roar of crashing surf, nearly drowning out the piano. Slowly the electric guitar began to piggyback on the sensual piano melody and took the song from baroque to more of a jazz-fusion sound. Shortly after that, the drums kicked the rest of the band into a hard-driving rock anthem. Digger, completely alone, performed an embarrassingly strenuous rock star impression with air guitar in hand, gyrating and posing in ways that flexed his well-toned biceps, chest muscles, and abs. He hopped his way back to the controls and bumped the volume to eight and then punched in the loudness button on the amp. It was like slamming a shot of steroids into Jethro's thigh. Good thing the storm shutters were still on at St. Peter's Rectory across the bay. It signaled that there were no neighbors to bother yet.

Digger loved the Port in the off-season, especially out on Ocean Avenue. It had the rugged feel of man versus nature. For the most part, man was winning the battle with his massive oceanside cottages and roaring fireplaces, butler's pantries, solariums, and feather beds with electric blankets. Occasionally nature scored some points by blowing off a roof and flooding a basement with surf.

As the song began to wind down, Digger headed to the black slimline telephone on the wall in the kitchen and punched in 4-0-1, the area code for Rhode Island, and seven more digits. Kristy Riggins answered on the first ring. "How's my Maine man?"

"I better be your *only* man! How did you know it was me?" asked Digger.

"I didn't. I figured I had a fifty-fifty chance it would be a male and they would be somewhat encouraged to be called my Maine man... even if it was Dad. I also figured you had made it to Port Talbot by now and you were calling your Maine squeeze."

"You're my *only* squeeze! But true, we did meet in Maine. Say, when do you sail for Bermuda?"

"Well, my return crew is bailing on me," she moaned. "But we shove off tomorrow from Newport to deliver the Hinckley to King's Wharf. Coming home is the problem. The delivery of the C&C 30 to Wilmington, North Carolina, is in question. It's only a thirty-footer, but I don't want to sail over 600 miles by myself."

Digger responded eagerly, "Would a landlubber do for crew?"

"What kind of landlubber? Not a mountain man from the Adirondacks..."

"That's exactly what I mean. This mountain man can read a compass and talk CB on the VHF radio! 10-4 good buddy!"

"Uh… I'm afraid we'd get lost in the Bermuda Triangle with you at the helm. Do you know how to read the Loran?"

"Loran?" asked Digger. "That's the book by Dr. Seuss, right? Yeah, I read it… twice."

"Oh, brother… that's the Lorax! The *Loran* is our navigation system! It gives us our location and helps us keep on course." Kristy corrected him with mock exasperation in her voice. "But you'll do fine. I just need an extra watch and a pair of hands to make PB and J's. Do you have time? I'd like to leave St. George's harbor around May 28, and arrive in North Carolina around the third. Then I have to be in Port Talbot by June 6." She asked coyly, "Do you know why?"

Digger stammered, unable to come up with a ready answer.

"Oh, great!" she said with feigned disgust. "You've already forgotten the town named June sixth Kristy Riggins Day, for my heroic efforts on sea and land!"

Digger kept stammering but Kristy ignored his lame jibber-jabber. "Mayor Schwarz asked that I present this year's award to a surfer girl who saved a dog fetching a ball in December. Apparently, the owner thought it was okay to play fetch in the snow and surf. The poor dog went into cardiac arrest, and the surfer brought the dog back to shore and administered first aid, including CPR, through the dog's nostrils!"

"You're kidding! That is an amazing story. Worthy of the Riggins award!" cried Digger enthusiastically.

Kristy deadpanned, "Yeah, it's perfect, considering how many dogs I've kissed in my life…"

Digger chortled, "Present company excluded, of course!"

"No, Digger, you're a dog too. You're an overactive K-9 cop dog. You need a choke chain, Fido."

"Well, if I'm a dog, you're a squeaky chew toy!"

"You got that right, Fido. Sit, boy! Back! Get down!"

"Alright, alright, Riggins, you win. Those sailing dates should work perfectly. I start at the department around the twentieth of June. Mom and Dad would be happy to know I'm doing something constructive and not turning Seaside into a frat house."

Kristy gushed, "Digger, it'd be great if you could pull this trip off. I can share some of my delivery fee with you. It'll cover the flight to Bermuda and all the PB and J's you can eat!"

"Deal, Riggins. I'll call for flight info and run it by Mom and Dad. I'll call you tomorrow around noon, roger?"

"Roger wilco, Fido. Over and out, my love." Digger howled into the phone like a lone wolf as they both hung up.

He punched the dial pad again right away. For local calls, only four digits were necessary in the exclusive neighborhood of Cape Talbot. "Dang!" he muttered. No answer at the Reynolds' house. He tried a few more friends' numbers. His part of the town was dead. The season wouldn't truly start for another month. Digger looked out to sea and thought, *It's Friday. Ship's Pub will have some local fare tonight.* He looked at his watch and decided to visit Chief Nickerson and square away his start date at the police department.

CHAPTER 10

CHECK-IN WITH THE CHIEF

Digger pulled into police headquarters on Sow Hill for his visit with the chief. When Patty, the mother hen also known as the dispatcher, caught a glimpse of Digger coming in the front door, she interrupted the caller. "Hold, please!" She hit a button on her console, ripped off her headset and ran out of her plexiglass cage yelling, "My hero! Digger Davenport! Welcome back, Officer 19!" They embraced.

"Good to see you, Patty. All quiet on the Talbot front, I trust?"

Chief Edward Nickerson entered the foyer and answered the question. "Ayuh, it's quiet on the Talbot front and…" Sticking his hand out to shake Digger's, he grabbed his hand and pulled Digger into a hug. The chief growled directly into Digger's ear, "and… it's gonna stay that way… right, 19?"

Digger pulled back from the embrace. "Aww, please, Chief, I really hope so. Parking tickets for the parents and Tootsie Rolls for the kiddie tourists. That's it. Please!"

The Chief was only half-kidding. Drama and criminal enterprise seemed to follow Digger ever since he had accepted the summer job as the Bike Cop two summers ago. In his very first season, a murder occurred out on Brigantine Beach. An embarrassing trial of the wrong suspect ensued until Digger discovered the greater weight of evidence implicating someone well-known in Port Talbot. Just last summer, Digger barely escaped with his life as he stalked a military maniac who tried to hang a wealthy heir's son over the yardarm of a schooner.

* * *

Patty spoke up in a saucy tone, "Digger didn't cause the crimes.... He solved the crimes!" She spun around and ran back to the dispatcher's cage, yelling, "Oops, I put the sheriff on hold!"

The men looked at each other and rolled their eyes. Chief Nickerson invited Digger into his office. "How was college this yeah, Diggah?" He motioned to Digger to take a seat, lighting up his signature Camel non-filter with the Zippo lighter with the miniature chief's badge glued to it.

Digger realized he had missed hearing the chief's Maine accent. "It went pretty well, Chief. But I am not sure I am cut out to be a police officer."

Nickerson wrinkled his face. "Stop right theyah, young man. You havah nose for this business like no othah I've evah known. Why you in the dumps?"

"Well, this year, I interned for the NYPD's Cadet Corps, and they had me working the transit system, and frankly, I hated it. It's not just the turnstile jumpers but the flashers and the gropers. We could only call for backup. The creeps would laugh at us and take off. So brazen! They'd be long gone by the time backup arrived, *if* backup ever arrived. Worse was if I would be with an officer and assist in subduing a violator, I would be taking my life into my hands. They were likely to slash with a knife or worse. I would hesitate and freeze. I'm not into risking my life to correct some yahoo. I feel like saying, 'whatever, dude, knock yourself out.' Or if they do victimize someone, I want to pummel them and ask questions later! Just being honest, Chief."

Nickerson took his time stubbing out the cigarette as it bought him time to respond. "Diggah, we all feel that way at one point in our careers. It is good to be honest about these feelings and let your supervisah know. Sometimes it is best to back off an assignment or area and use your talents in a different way. I have moved offisahs from the beat to admin, from admin to detective support, and so on. Also, let's face it, fightin' crime in New Yawk City is not for everyone...especially a country boy from Lake Placid and Port Talbot. Here? It is not like New Yawk. It's been the usual. OUIs, domestic violence, pot busts. Although we seem to have an arsonist torching buildings on North Street. I can't get a lead on the sicko. I'm looking forward to your help."

Digger raised his eyebrows with interest and felt grateful that he was finally being considered a resource for solving crime.

The chief continued with a rundown of what the department had been dealing with while Digger was at school. "Then the town selectmen tried to have us enforce building code violations. Can you imagine that? Poor suckahs puttin' in windows, constructin' porches… rebuildin' chimneys? I mean, c'mon! The town thinks theyah criminals because they didn't pay for the permits. I threw a hissy fit at the public hearin' and nipped that right in the bud, yessuh! I'm too busy to write up the weekend warriyah improving his neighbahood. The selectmen told me privately that I sandbagged them at the hearin' because the public gave me a standing ovation. I asked the politicians how much advance input they give me? Their ansah sounded like a meadow in June… crickets. They were the ones that sandbagged me!"

The chief continued his rant. "So, I'd rather be a cop, please. And yes, stick to the rules." The chief reached for a small red leather-bound pamphlet on his desk. "I got all the powah I need right heyah."

Digger reached into his back pocket and pulled out a similar copy mashed next to his wallet. "The Constitution is good enough for me too, Chief. It's incredible how this little book has settled so many disputes."

Patty knocked on the door and walked in. "This is an odd one, Chief. Sheriff McGeary just alerted us to an APB coming from New Hampshire State Police." Digger and the chief looked at each other at the mention of McGeary's name. Digger's history with the sheriff from previous summers was a source of stress. Patty continued, oblivious. "Sounds like one Wilhelm Harding, white male in his twenties, stole artifacts from the Hartson family collection at the Dartmouth College museum today." Patty continued as she consulted her notes. "Harding, aka Will or Bill Hardin, who is over six feet tall with blond hair, was last seen leaving the college wearing a tweed jacket and striped tie. He was driving an older military-green Ford Mustang with Maine plates. Harding presented a St. Francis College ID saying he was working on a term paper regarding Biddeford's textile mills. McGeary said St. Francis College has never had a student named Wilhelm Harding or any variation of that name."

"You got a plate number, Patty?" asked the chief.

"No plate number, just a Maine registration for an old green Mustang."

Digger piped in. "Can DMV give us a printout for every green Mustang registered in our county?"

Chief rolled his eyes and gently replied, "Digger, this may be waiting for you when you start work in a few weeks. In the meantime, let us deal with it."

"Of course, Chief. I just thought the Hartson artifacts would be of more interest to a local than some yahoo from Aroostook."

"We'll check it, Digger. When do you start?"

"Is June twentieth okay?" replied Digger.

The chief reached for his desk calendar and thumbed through some pages. "Oh boy, June sixth is 'Kristy Riggins Day.' You still dating her?" The chief didn't wait for an answer and blurted, "You want to start on a Friday? The twentieth is a Friday!"

"Oh, that's perfect," said Patty. "Just in time for the tourist procession through Talbot Square."

The chief added sarcastically, "Fah be it from me to oppose my dispatchah on personnel mattahs. See you then."

Digger stood up to shake hands with the chief. "Thanks, Chief Nickerson, and yes, I am still dating Kristy. We will be sailing from Bermuda and back in town by the sixth."

As Digger turned to leave, the chief bellowed good-naturedly, "Well, la-dee-da! Yachting and then a little blue-collah work for the town... so happy to keep you humble, Davenport!"

Digger thought to explain that it was only a thirty-foot sailboat, and the trip was being made for pay, but he let it slide and followed Patty out the door.

"Hey, Patty," Digger asked as he followed her toward the dispatcher's cage, "what is going on over at Hartson's Beach? As I drove in today, it seemed as if there were For Sale signs all up and down Route 35."

"Yeah, I guess the family is selling the landward parcels. I'm not sure about the oceanfront homes."

"Please don't tell me Royal Orchard is for sale," he lamented.

Patty shrugged. "Everything is for sale at the right price. The town's taxes have steadily increased to the point where families can't keep the homes they grew up in. Government services are great until it's your home that gets redistributed...not to the poor but to the nouveau richer!" she said with authority, butchering the French phrase. Just then, the phone rang. "Oops, gotta run. Government at your service! Be safe sailing, Digger!"

CHAPTER 11

THE WHITE HORSE

A British-style black cab pulled up to the famed White Horse Tavern down by the docks at St. George's Harbor, Bermuda. Digger paid the hackney with the colorful scrip of the island, slung his backpack onto his shoulder, adjusted his white Tilley's hat at a jaunty angle, and headed into the local hot spot. It was crowded with tanned tourists dressed in colorful pastels. Digger slid his lid on to his back, suspended by the lanyard, and looked around for his captain. He zeroed in on the back of a blonde seated at the bar and surrounded by three swarthy men having an animated conversation. The gesticulations were unmistakably Kristy's, as was her husky laugh. Digger's adrenaline spiked. He moved stealthily like a puma, circling to the right to observe more of his gorgeous girl. Her right profile came into view. The thick layers of golden hair partially covered a tanned face with perfect white teeth and a small, slightly upturned nose. Digger kept moving to the right until he was directly across the circular bar from her. He was savoring the moment.

The men surrounding Kristy were hanging on every word she said. Digger slid his chapeau back onto his head and tilted the brim down to hide most of his face. He bent over to order. "Two Dark 'n' Stormies, please. One for that pretty girl over there. Tell her it's from a secret admirer." Digger put an American twenty on the bar. Digger received his drink, took a swig, and circled around the edge of the bar, keeping his prize in sight at all times. The bartender handed Kristy the local favorite, mumbled some words and pointed to where Digger had been. Then he shrugged his shoulders at the empty spot.

Kristy shot up, standing on the foot bar of the barstool and looked around. Her fan club also began looking around, for what, they weren't quite sure. Kristy howled toward the ceiling, "Hot Diggity Dog!" The guys, having no idea what was going on, took the prompt as an occasion to start howling in support of Kristy's outburst.

Digger sidled up to them with his hat down low and slid his arm in between two of the men. In his hand, he held his Dark 'n' Stormy in front of Kristy and peeked between the men. "Cheers, Captain!"

Kristy looked down and under the arms of the men surrounding her and saw Digger hiding behind them. "Hot Diggity Dog! Get over here!" Kristy pulled his arm into her, pushing the two guys aside and wrapping Digger in an octopus hug. Digger stood up to full height to hold Kristy as she attached herself to him. He was a full head taller than the three men who had been closing in on the suntanned superstar.

The men stepped back several feet to observe the nature of the interloper. Was he family? Employee? Or alas, boyfriend? The fervency of the hug confirmed the latter.

Digger moved toward disengagement and started introducing himself, but Kristy took over. "Allow me, Mr. Davenport," she said. "Gentlemen, please meet the hero of Port Talbot, Maine, Officer 19, David Digger Davenport!"

Digger shook the men's hands and asked their connection to Kristy. They, too, were sailors and knew of her role as the first mate on the *Performer*, which was a unique schooner-brigantine rig from Penobscot Bay. Digger explained how he had met her while checking out the *Performer* when it docked in Port Talbot last summer. He stayed away from discussing the near-death experiences of that summer.

The instant bond of friendship among sailors in a far-flung port was remarkable. They seemed to be connected by knowing a distant acquaintance, or their boat, or their port. Digger found himself talking with an Aussie who knew the depth of the Talbot River at low tide and also knew Rusty, the red-haired bartender at the Ship's Pub.

Kristy and Digger deftly extricated themselves from the gaggle of guys and found a quiet dinner table overlooking the docks. "There's our ride," Kristy said, pointing at a comparatively small white-hulled sailboat. "That's the *Fortune Hunter*."

Digger looked it over and asked carefully, "It looks like a top-notch sailboat. Is it large enough to make a crossing back to America?"

Kristy paused from picking apart the blooming Bermuda onion appetizer and looked Digger in the eyes. "It is the perfect size to cross in, and we are only going six hundred miles. So, no worries, me matey."

Digger had hoped for something a little bigger. After all, he had earned his sailing chops in pint-sized punts on the Talbot River. He put his best foot forward. "Excellent word, Captain. I look forward to the adventure."

Kristy was delighted by his enthusiasm. "Tomorrow, we will check in with the weather station and get a clear sign before we head out. I've been listening to the weather band on the VHF, and it says it is clear sailing west." Kristy paused with a beaming smile. "But out here, you never know. I'm just thrilled to be on our own adventure!"

Digger reached for her hand. "I have missed you. I am psyched." After a few moments of looking out the windows onto the harbor, Digger asked: "Is it just me or is there an inordinate number of tall ships out there?"

"It's not you. It's the annual Cutty Sark Tall Ships' Race. This year the race runs from Puerto Rico to Bermuda, then to Halifax." She squinted. "Do you see that ship there with the red stripe on its bow? That's the *Eagle*, owned by the US Coast Guard. We got the boat from the Germans as war reparations in '46."

"That means it's been 'jerry' rigged. Right?"

"Oh, that's too funny. You're quite clever to tie in the World War Two terminology for Germans."

"I have more tricks. Do you want to see?" Digger offered in jest.

"Down, sailor," she teased. "Now, look at the boat next to it with the black hull and three masts. That's the *Windsor Star*. The skipper wanted me to serve as first mate on this race. There are twenty-eight aboard, twenty of whom are students. If I didn't have the Hinckley job and this C&C delivery, I'd be on that boat right now."

"Well, I am grateful to be with you, and I promise to be an obedient student," Digger said with puppy dog eyes.

"Are you kidding? I'm ecstatic we are doing this together. This will be a lifetime memory. If we can stand each other after three days confined in 200 square feet bobbing in the middle of the ocean, there may be hope for a lasting relationship. I'm psyched. Besides, I have a whole summer of babysitting rich kids on the *Performer* to look forward to. No need to double down on that gig. Plus, I'm making some bucks on these deliveries."

"When does the *Performer* gig start?" Digger asked.

"We're boarding the sailing students at Government Wharf in Port Talbot on Kristy Riggins Day, June sixth." She gave him an embarrassed smile, still not used to having a day named after her for her heroic bravery last summer. "The captain is making a bit of a spectacle over it. He put last summer's ventures in the brochure, touting how students learn to give to their community, blah blah blah."

"I hope he has given you a raise, cuz he's making bank on your bravery."

Kristy responded vacantly as she looked at her watch. "All praise and no raise.... Say, we better hustle. We will shove off early."

"How long does it take to get to North Carolina?"

She smiled and launched into her favorite subject. "Okay, so we are riding trade winds that flow from Africa toward the Caribbean. It's called the Bermuda High. We should be doing a broad reach the whole way, at hopefully around a minimum of 6 knots boat speed. At that rate we'll hit Bald Head Island and the Cape Fear River in 90 hours or about three and a half days. Or by..." Kristy looked toward the ceiling and counted on her fingers. "By June first. Plenty of time to get up to the Port by the sixth. Let's go get ready for an early departure."

CHAPTER 12

First Mate?

Digger scrambled down to check out the accommodations belowdecks. There was the captain's double bed and then a long thin bunk covered with sail bags, a toolbox, and a couple of coolers. The bow was jammed with flotation devices including a deflated lifeboat. He scratched his head as he spun around looking for a place to stow his backpack while Kristy was above deck checking the lines.

Until now, he had not pushed the physical aspect of the relationship with Kristy. He was quite content to be her boyfriend and sealing this status had taken an entire summer to achieve. He had road-tripped to Roger Williams College once last fall. Then they rendezvoused for New Year's at Times Square. On both occasions they had stayed at their respective university dorms in separate beds except for one close call.

It wasn't that Digger didn't know what to do to advance the relationship. In fact, he had witnessed such things when he was at the Whitney School. Rather, he sensed that Kristy was more comfortable not moving the relationship to a point where such intimacy would occur. After arriving back at Digger's apartment-style dorm on New Year's Eve, Digger and Kristy were engaged in passionate freefall on the couch fueled by that evening's ever-flowing champagne. Digger abruptly sat up and asked Kristy if she was comprehending where they were headed.

Digger was himself unsure it was wise to go where his urges were taking him. After all, he was still wrestling with last summer's revelation that his very existence was the result of an unwanted pregnancy and that he had been adopted at birth by the Davenports. He had thought of the pain his birth mother must have gone through. Then he would think what a loser she was; then bounce to admiring how brave she was to carry him to term. He was thoroughly confused and reluctant to commit such a mistake himself, but on nights like this with Kristy, all these warnings were so easy to forget. His parental and religious training on the subject was through the traditional Episcopal rubric: osmosis. That is, "be careful" and "be a gentleman" and other completely anemic guidelines. "Fornication" wasn't in their lexicon; too fire-and-brimstone-y.

For Kristy's part, she had been fending off boys her whole life. At dancing class in seventh and eighth grade in her hometown of Albany, New York, the battle could not have been more evident or more embarrassing. The dance instructor, looking like an aging Rocky Balboa but carrying his body like Fred Astaire, would stand in the middle of the gymnasium. On his right was a 75-foot-long line of girls seated nervously in squeaky folding chairs. They were dolled up in frilly dresses and wore white gloves. On his left, about fifty feet across from the girls, was an equal number of boys wearing jackets and ties. The instructor's wife, sporting a beehive hairdo and a twin-missile brassiere, would be at the phonograph ready to put the needle down on an innocuous Neil Diamond tune like "Cracklin Rosie."

"Gentlemen, please stand. This will be a foxtrot. Please ask your choice of partner to join Mrs. La Costa and me on the dance floor." As soon as he uttered the words "ask your," most boys were on a tear across the glossy gymnasium floor, knocking each other out of the way to get to the prettiest girls. They actually ran, shoved, and slid on their knees to the chair where a cute girl was blushing. Kristy hated it. She would look at four or five boys wrestling in front of her, reaching their hands out for her hand. The girls next to her might be overweight or sporting a prominent rack of teeth under construction. These girls would be ignored entirely by the front line of rushers. Kristy quickly learned who the gentlemen were and developed affinities for the boys who walked calmly and asked the second-stringers. When La Costa called for ladies' choice, Kristy headed for the gentlemen or the homely boys who dared not lift their eyes from the floor during ladies' choice.

Suffice to say, Kristy learned quickly what most boys wanted and the impact this had upon the poor girls who had capitulated. The fact that Kristy had issues back at home with her mother's unpredictable bouts of intoxication also caused her to shun the squeeze-fests her friends frequented. Dating on a serious level would mean that the boyfriend would come to the house. And that was not happening in Kristy's world.

Unfortunately, Kristy's mother's spiritual advice on sex was undercut by frequent inebriation. It completely sidelined her mom as a valuable resource as she undoubtedly could have been. Mrs. Riggins had told Kristy that sex was like fire, and marriage was like a fireplace. Sex within marriage was a beautiful and breathtaking fire in a safe and homey fireplace setting. Sex outside of marriage was a potential forest fire causing damage to all who got too close too soon.

* * *

On the *Fortune Hunter*, Kristy descended the ladder into the cabin. Digger was still trying to figure out where exactly he was expected to sleep. She stopped him when he faced her, put her arms around his neck, and pulled him in close for a kiss. The backpack dropped with a thud, freeing up Digger's arms to return the affection. He whispered, "Where do you want me, Captain?"

"You would be my first mate, wouldn't you?" He remained silent. He wasn't exactly sure what she meant. Kristy continued to kiss him. Finally, she spoke. "We take good care of the first mate. Throw your sack in there." She nodded her head toward the captain's bunk. She added with a grin, "When you get the idea that we are doing shift rotations, you'll see I haven't invited you into a compromising situation."

Digger whispered, "Oh, good. Who is taking the first shift here at the dock?"

CHAPTER 13
Making the Cut

Digger stirred to the crackle of the VHF radio. Kristy was at the small desk in the galley area, where the receiver was attached to the low ceiling. "Channel 2, come in, please. This is *Fortune Hunter* bound for the Carolina coast this morning, over?" Kristy spoke with such authority.

"*Fortune Hunter*, this is Bermuda Weather Station. All weather systems to the west are clear and no low-pressure fronts to our east. You and the tall ships race are clear for some great sailing weather. Over?"

"That's a 10-4, Weather Station. Jolly good show! Over and out channel 2."

"Bermuda bids you well, *Fortune Hunter*. Weather Station standing by."

Kristy spun around to a disheveled Digger. She stood up to kiss him and whispered, "Look lively, sailor." More fervently, "Time to cast off lines!"

Digger climbed the ladder to the deck and repeated the command in a loud whisper, "Casting lines!"

Kristy primed the glow plugs on the diesel engine, and when a beep sounded, she fired it up on the first crank. Digger was listening carefully to the youthful response of the motor and gave a thumbs-up to Kristy. The bow was pointed seaward. He undid the spring lines first then laid the bowline and stern line on the deck. Then he held the gunwale of the vessel at midships, awaiting further orders.

"Are we clear?" asked Kristy.

"All clear, Captain!" Digger replied.

"Okay, Digger give me a shove to port and climb on, please."

"Shoving! Climbing! Stumbling!" Digger called out his actions in a joking manner. He recalled from last summer how Kristy's students aboard the *Performer* had repeated all the orders shortly after Kristy had barked them. It was nice to know your crew was comprehending instructions, especially on a larger boat.

Kristy maneuvered the boat among the tall ships. Digger ran below and returned with a disposable camera and started taking pretend pictures of Kristy as if she were a model in an L.L. Bean photoshoot, for which she certainly qualified. He took some real photos of the *Windsor Star* and the *Eagle*.

"Digger, take the helm! Head toward that fort thing." Kristy pointed slightly to starboard as she walked toward the stern to call up to the *Windsor Star*. "Morning, Captain Coltrane!"

A man in his mid-forties with curly blond hair looked down from the poop deck and squinted. Kristy yelled up. "It's Kristy Riggins!"

"Hey ho, Riggins!" The tall ship's captain saluted. "I thought you were working!"

Kristy yelled back as the distance between the two vessels increased. "Don't I look like I'm working?" She ruffled Digger's hair as he stood at the wheel trying to find the fort on the horizon.

The captain laughed and gave a final salute. Kristy stepped into the cockpit and whispered, "So glad I am not headed to Halifax on that floating kindergarten. I hope he has some experienced talent aboard."

Digger was focused on the job at hand. "You mean that fort there on the hill to the left?"

"Yes, sweetie, over there to *the port*. It's Fort Gate, head straight for it. Then you'll see the channel markers and just head out following the markers. We are going out the cut between that fort and Horseshoe Island. It's about the width of a football field and the current rips through there. Once we get through, then we'll hoist some canvas."

"Got it, Captain Cutie!" Then Digger yelled, "We're doing it!"

"Indeed. You good? I want to go below and enter our coordinates into the Loran, okay?" Kristy pointed to the compass. "Once you get around Horseshoe, you'll be heading north by northeast out into the wide blue sea, got it?"

"Got it. Wide blue sea coming up, Captain." Digger really didn't get it. He just knew to head for the fort, and then hopefully it would become clear where to go next. He did not see a cut through the island and Fort Gate.

Kristy disappeared below. The radio crackled to life as she tuned in a channel. She appeared at the bottom of the steps. "When we're in the harbor area, I monitor channel 13 to listen to boat chatter. Once we're clear from traffic, guess what channel we go to and why?"

Digger, having had his own training in powerboating, answered like a Naval Academy plebe. "Sir! Channel 16, sir! To monitor Coast Guard and distress signals, sir!"

"Affirmative, Popeye! Nice." Kristy disappeared. A moment later, the radio chattered from the cabin.

Digger looked at the small square fort to his left. He could see two cannons pointed toward him. His mind wandered back in time as he tried to imagine what enemies these cannons had fired upon. Imperceptibly, the small boat gathered speed in the current. Digger's thoughts wandered to the War of 1812 and the possibilities of a skirmish in this very spot. He then marveled at how the greenish-blue water contrasted with the dazzling white buildings distinctive to Bermuda. He gazed off to his right, and he noticed a large white building with small windows several stories above the tree line of Horseshoe Island. *Geez, what's that? Military barracks? What a shame it is getting so built up.* Digger let his mind wander. The boat's speed swiftly climbed as the boat entered the cut. Digger glanced at the instruments. *Seven knots… whoa, we're screaming.* Digger turned around to check his wake and his position. *Perfect — right in the middle of the cut. This is so much fun.* His endorphins were coursing at an all-time high. He tried to identify the White Horse Tavern and how far they had traveled. *I wonder when I'll see Bermuda from this vantage again?*

He turned back to grab his camera for a photo and was immediately disoriented. All he could see ahead was a wall of white steel with small windows. What he had mistaken for a military barracks happened to be a cruise ship entering the cut. A horn blasted five short signals, causing Digger's body and the entire boat to shudder. The radio jumped to life at the same time that a public address speaker yelled, "*Give way, white sailboat! Give way immediately!*"

Kristy bounded to the cockpit and cranked the wheel to starboard and goosed the throttle to full without even looking at the massive cruise ship entering the cut. "Digger to the bow. Watch for rocks. We're gonna get cozy with Horseshoe Island!"

Digger scrambled to the front of the boat, never taking his eyes off of the massive ship passing a mere twenty feet from the *Fortune Hunter.* The hull of the cruise ship actually flared out over the sailboat as it passed. Kristy's eyes were on the top of the mast, making sure it would clear the side of the ship. A shadow enveloped the small boat. Digger looked down into the clear water. "Uh, Kristy! We got rocks!"

Kristy cranked hard to port on the wheel and yelled, "Hold on!" The small boat glided alarmingly tight to the seemingly endless cruise ship. Digger tilted back to view nearly ten stories of decking overhead. At the very top, he could see what looked like little faces looking over the rail above, waving and shouting things he could not decipher. Digger refrained from returning his own hand signal but instead turned to look for rocks.

The radio crackled to life "Thank you for yielding to our right of way. SS *Norway* standing by on 16."

"Digger, take the wheel! Just don't hit that ship or those rocks!" Kristy jumped into the cabin. "*Norway, Norway,* this is *Fortune Hunter,* the white sailing vessel in your shadow. Thank you for your courtesies. Standing by." Kristy hopped back into the cockpit with a stern look on her usually cheerful face. "Are we clear?"

Digger replied, "Just about. Brace yourself. We're about to hit their wake. Shall I take it straight on, Captain?"

"Affirmative. Steer into it, please."

Digger steadily turned the wheel to his left. The cruise ship's stern still hulked over their boat. The name SS *Norway* was emblazoned near the top rail ten stories up. A large red and blue Norwegian flag snapped in the wind. Digger noticed the cross embedded in the flag. He muttered to himself, "Thank you, God." The sunlight was restored as the ship glided past them, and the sailboat breasted the wake of the leviathan.

Digger and Kristy looked at the wide-open blue sea ahead of them then turned to look at one another for a long moment before hugging. "I thought the dang thing was a building on that island!" Digger apologized. "I had no idea it was moving, let alone headed our way! I'm really sorry. I was so happy cruising in the center of the cut. Man, that was a freakout. I'm so sorry."

"No apology needed. You were doing exactly what I told you to do. I can't wait to get away from here. I hate big boats when I'm in a little boat. Wow! That was super close. One, I don't think I have ever seen a cruise ship that big — ever. Two, I have never been that close to a ship of that size underway. That is one for the log." Kristy looked at her fancy navigational wristwatch. "And it's barely eight o'clock in the morning! Digger, did you see how close our mast was to hitting that ship? Yeowch!"

Digger looked at his own watch. "I know it's only eight, but may the first mate suggest to the captain that the crew has earned a wee dram?"

Kristy wrinkled her forehead briefly, trying to understand Digger's put-on Irish accent and meaning. Then a big smile came across her face "Indeed! A wee dram of rum for the crew for medicinal purposes and superior conduct in the face of certain danger! Grab the Black Seal in the galley. Ration just one dram, Mr. Davenport!"

"Aye, aye, Captain Riggins!

CHAPTER 14

A Sail Tale

The adrenaline abated as they passed Fort Gate, then Horseshoe Island, and left the Town Cut miles astern. Waiting for them was a comforting southeasterly breeze. Sails were hoisted, sheets were eased, and Digger turned northwest. *Fortune Hunter* was running wing and wing through the narrows off St. George's Harbor. It was a beautiful day for sailing. At St. Catherine Point, Bermuda's most northern shore, Kristy had Digger head up slightly while she helped the jib rejoin the mainsail on the leeward side. From that moment, Bermuda gradually became smaller, distant, and out of reach. By later in the afternoon, Bermuda had disappeared from the horizon behind them. All semblance of civilization was gone -- no vessels, no planes, no land, nothing but blue sea and sky. They marveled at the dolphins swimming playfully alongside the boat, headed in the same direction. They felt as if they had a squad of sea soldiers accompanying them to their destination.

"Just follow the sunset, Digger. I'll make us some dinner. Keep the compass around 270 degrees, and we should be fine. The trade winds are blowing us down east a bit, but we can adjust as needed. The Loran monitors our course and an alarm sounds if set correction is needed."

As darkness overcame the boat, Kristy handed up a bowl of steaming food. She climbed up into the cockpit with her own bowl and a tray of garlic bread. "This chowder is awesome, what is it?" asked Digger.

"I started with bacon then sautéed some grouper chunks in it. Then I added some onions and then stirred in some of yesterday's home fries, some milk, and peppered it generously and voila!"

"It's delish!" exclaimed Digger. "Hold on." Kristy grabbed the wheel. Digger clambered down to the galley and passed up a citronella candle and two plastic tumblers of white wine. He passed up his Sony Walkman cassette player with a small speaker attached.

Once he was back in the cockpit, and Cat Stevens had started singing "*I listen to the wind... to the wind of my soul...*" Digger raised his glass. "Here's to our first dinner alone at sea."

"Hear, hear!" said Kristy, sipping the wine and looking Digger in the eye as part of the toasting ritual. "We're not all that alone, however," she added. "The Bermuda Triangle is full of cargo ships and other travelers. Look there to the north. You can see the light of some vessel, but... we're alone enough." She raised her glass again." And I love Cat Stevens! How did you make the Walkman play through a speaker?"

"The speaker has a battery booster. It's basically earphones on steroids. Speaking of the Bermuda Triangle, what's with the hype anyway? I hear Atlantis is out there somewhere, and sailors and pilots get swallowed up in her vortex."

"It's hogwash," Kristy said definitively. "Someone is selling a story. Now I'll grant you, boats and planes go down in what they also call the Devil's Triangle. The area runs from Florida to Bermuda and down to the Caribbean." Kristy used her hand to draw the triangle in the air as she mentioned the locations. "But that's some of the heaviest traffic at sea right there. US travel, European travel, South American travel, they all move through that huge space. Does calamity happen? Of course, but no little green men are taking over the navigation."

Digger stood up and assumed a karate stance. "Not if I can help it!"

"Nonetheless, Mr. Davenport, we keep a vigilant lookout. We will cross shipping lanes and don't want to kiss a barge, or worse, get hung up on its towline."

"What?" exclaimed Digger. "Get hung up on a towline? What are you talking about, Captain?"

Kristy looked furtively left and right, signaling she wasn't sure she wanted to explain the issue, but she obliged. "Well, you know how a tugboat can push a boat around in a harbor, right?"

"Of course," Digger replied.

"Well, a tug can also pull a barge on a cable and will do so for long trips in the shipping lanes, generally... hopefully. Those cables can extend for hundreds of feet. The cable can be so long and so heavy that it is underwater. From our perspective, we see a tug here." Kristy pointed into the dark at the starboard side of the boat. "But, the barge it's towing will be over there." She pointed out into the sea on the port side. "And there is a thousand-foot or longer steel cable between them. If we were not alert, we could sail into that cable and get seriously fouled up."

"Crap! You're kidding me, Kristy!"

"I kid you not. I might as well tell you a true story about this that occurred at night on an Atlantic crossing. We studied the case in my navigation class at Roger Williams."

"Oh, great," Digger sighed.

"But first the good news, towboats or tugboats have lights on them that signal that a barge is behind and let you know to steer clear. The barge, too, has lights so you can connect the two vessels to towing activity. The towboat has a mast of three white lights and a lower yellow light. If you see that, come about immediately. It's summed up in the sailor's phrase: *Three white lights and yellow… kill a fellow.*"

Digger was silent, his eyes as wide as saucers. Kristy noticed and became more animated. "Okay, ready for the story?" Digger nodded, his admiration for this girl growing more than ever.

"It was actually an admiralty case in federal court. A husband and wife were sailing from Annapolis across the Atlantic to Gibraltar. Their boat was about fifteen feet longer than this one. In the middle of the night, they hit the tow line. The husband said he just saw the regular running lights, the red and green ones, of the tug. He said their sailboat was passing so far to its stern and that he had no idea it was towing anything. When they hit the cable, the husband fought the wheel to come about and reverse direction. Somehow the tow cable got caught between the keel and the rudder."

Kristy threaded one index finger between two fingers of her other hand. "It got hung up and lifted the sailboat partially out of the water." She raised her hands. "And the hung-up boat kept moving through the water with the towboat." She moved her hands in a horizontal direction to depict the sailboat being carried away.

Digger was silent as Kristy continued, "The bow of the boat was being dragged through the water with the stern completely out of the water. The boat was pointing down at an angle of sixty degrees. The wife joined the husband in the cockpit. They tried everything to alert the tug of their presence and predicament. They used the radio, emptied the air horn, and used up all the flares. There was no response and no change. The sailboat was bound up and had slid closer to the barge. The husband testified that they couldn't abandon ship in their life raft because they would get run over by the barge. This suspended state lasted for hours until the point where the husband decided to shinny up the cable to the barge. Can you imagine?"

"This is… this is… criminal!" Digger exclaimed.

"I know! He left his poor, terrified wife in the boat and climbed approximately 100 feet up a slimy steel cable in the pitch black with the ocean churning in a froth from the bow of the barge below him. The wife testified that she kept letting out the safety line tied around her husband's waist. At one point, she thought he had fallen when the flashlight that was clipped to his life jacket fell into the ocean, but then realized he was okay when the rope kept moving upward into the dark."

"And then?" Digger prompted.

"The husband made it to the deck and tiptoed down the catwalk to the stern of the boat about 150 yards. He went down into a small cabin and woke up two sailors, who immediately radioed the captain of the towboat. The tow turned on their floodlights and finally slowed to a near stop. The husband quickly returned to the cable and shinnied back down to the sailboat before it, and his wife, was set adrift. They fired up the engine after the cable had slipped below the boat's hull. They were able to pull away from the inertia of the approaching barge. The sailboat's rudder was inoperable, so the tug towed them to the Azores. The lawsuit in the US followed. Lloyds of London paid out several million before the jury rendered a verdict. The issue was whether the lights were properly displayed."

"Three whites and a yellow… kill a fellow," Digger repeated in awe. "Holy mackerel, what a story."

"That's why I don't rely on the boat's autopilot at night. We will always have eyes wide open up here on our three-hour shifts, okay?"

"You bet!" Digger changed the atmosphere by flipping the cassette in the Walkman, which had become dramatically silent during Kristy's story. Cat Stevens started singing about being followed by a moonshadow. Digger looked up, and indeed the moon was out. He raised his glass. "Here's to sailing in the shadow of the moon."

CHAPTER 15

TRIANGULATION

The next day, sailing alone together allowed Digger and Kristy to talk endlessly about their lives and the issues most important to them. For Digger's part, he relived last summer's shocking discovery that he was adopted. "I thought I had come to terms with it, but I'd really like to know my birth parents. All I know is that both my birth parents went to my prep school in Lake Placid in the late 1950s. I think they were nicknamed Cissy and Hutch, but my mom–Mrs. Davenport won't say any more than that, and won't confirm even that much."

"Why not?" Kristy asked.

"When I ask Mom for more details, she tells me they made some promises to my birth mother when I was adopted. Plus, there are laws in New York that date back to the 1930s that deny me access to my birth certificate as an adoptee. My only recourse would be to hire a private investigator."

Kristy whispered softly, "And let me guess. You, being Digger, have decided to do your own investigating." She reached out to hold Digger's hand.

Digger contrived a reply, afraid he might cry from Kristy's kindness. "This year, Congress looked at a federal law to open adoption records for the physical and mental health of the adoptees. They took testimony from geneticists and psychologists who urged the records to be opened so that the children could know of possible inherited medical conditions and get treatment. I could be susceptible to some freak defect and have no idea how to treat it. I'd sure like to know who my real parents are. I mean, it's my identity."

Kristy knew they were treading on hallowed ground and gently asked, "Finding your mom might bring trauma to her, right?"

"That's a possibility, but she may be relieved to know how I am doing."

"All she has to do is read the Maine newspapers to see how you're doing. In fact, weren't you recently in the *New York Times* too? She knows who adopted you and could easily watch from afar. If she was pining to know more about you, she'd reach out to your mom and dad, er... the Davenports. And who knows, maybe Mom and Dad D would be stressed out by the whole exercise."

"Kristy, you're not helping." Digger shook his head. "Okay, so it's my issue. I'm the only one who cares. I think I get it the worst in this three-way triangulation of rights and interests. Their interests are to hide their shame. My interest is to live healthily with knowledge of my genetic heritage. I aim to find out who my parents are this summer and I have a plan. You wanna help?"

"Uh, oh." Kristy gulped. "What's Digger gonna dig up now?"

"Well, toward the end of June, the Whitney School is throwing a huge party to celebrate the seventy-fifth anniversary of its founding, and all the alums are invited. There will be special reunion parties for classes celebrating their graduation years ending on the fives and tens. If my calculations are correct, I think my birth mother is celebrating her twentieth reunion and will be there. It's a hunch, that's all."

"I don't know, Digger... I'm not sure it is the best idea... to... to what? Ambush her if you did discover her identity? I see 'Danger, Will Robinson' all over this." Kristy used her best robotic voice to channel the catchphrase from the TV series *Lost in Space*.

"I wouldn't sandbag her. I would just poke around to see what I could find and then follow up at a different time when the conditions were right."

Kristy wrinkled her face. "I'm not sure you need me around for that type of operation."

"I think having you with me would be helpful for support. I don't want to do the wrong thing."

Kristy sighed. "Well, I am not convinced the entire project should be undertaken at all, and you may see me as the enemy, and I'd hate for that to happen. Another problem is I'm supposed to be on the *Performer*. Let me think about it." Kristy paused and changed the subject slightly. "Aren't we a pair? You're running toward a relationship *with* your mother, and I am running *from* my mom."

"Geez, Kristy, I thought your mom was doing pretty well last summer at Dad's birthday party. She was drinking Perrier and having a blast. Is drinking still a problem?"

"Digger, it's a disease. If she isn't drinking, she's edgy and irritable. If she is drinking, she's an absolute embarrassment. There is a little girl inside her that I love and am so sad about. The big girl I have to deal with… I hate." Kristy looked away to hide a tear falling.

Digger moved from behind the wheel and started rubbing her back, which made no sense because of the bulky life jacket she wore. He picked up her hand and moved in front of her. "I don't know all that you have endured, but I can say that what I see in you, I like — I love! You are the awesome woman you are *because* of your mom… and, of course, your dad too!"

"You like a slobbering mess like this?"

Digger put his arm around her. "I do."

"Well, I don't!" she replied stiffly. "I don't like not wanting to go home. Ducking her calls, wondering if I have the disease… I hate it!"

Just then, the radio crackled to life with a women's frantic voice calling,

Mayday, Mayday, Mayday! This is Julie Beard on the Rum Runner. *My husband is injured. Mayday! Please help we are in a gale…* [garbled]… *went below to manually crank the engine because* [garbled] *died trying to start the engine. He used a crank arm, and it snapped back and cut his thumb off. He is bleeding! This is* Rum Runner, *we're north of Bermuda somewhere! Can anyone hear me? Please!*

Digger and Kristy looked to the starboard, due north. Nothing but blue sky. Kristy spoke first. "Okay, they're out of our range for our radio. We will just monitor for a minute. We may hear responders, but maybe not. We are 150 miles west of Bermuda and 450 miles east of North Carolina." The radio started crackling incoherently. "Those are boats responding within her range."

"Grab the wheel, Kristy." Digger clambered below and started playing with the dials on the radio. As he adjusted the squelch dial, the voices began to be more coherent. A young man's voice rang out, *"SOS! SOS! SOS! Canadian Air Patrol, this is the* Windsor Star. *We are lost. Life rafts deployed. Located 36.32 North and longitude 6..."* The transmission fizzled.

Kristy screamed, "What did I just hear? Did I hear an SOS from *Windsor Star?*"

"Hold it, Kristy, listen!" The radio kept breaking up with static. Then another transmission came in as clear as a bell. A strong older man's voice, *"Mayday, Mayday, Mayday! This is* Sea Change *in distress. A gale from nowhere has swamped us. Latitude 36.31..."* The radio transmission cut out again.

Kristy was looking up at blue skies and at the horizons. "What the heck are they talking about? It's beautiful here! Was that the *Windsor Star* in an SOS? Tell me I didn't hear that!" As Kristy looked directly to their stern, she squinted. "Digger! Get up here. Check this out!"

Digger bounded up in one leap and looked where Kristy was looking. "What is that?" There was a thin black ribbon at the edge of the horizon, as if someone had drawn a flat black Magic Marker line right where the sky met the sea. It ran from the north to the south on the eastern horizon. Yet oddly, the rest of the sky was blue all the way to the western horizon.

Kristy sternly directed Digger to take the wheel, climbed below and turned down the maydays and other chatter on the radio. She muttered, "God help them" as she headed for the V-berth in the front of the boat. She pulled out a sail bag marked "Storm Jib" and a spool of blue webbing with carabiner clips and saddles.

As she was sorting her thoughts and the gear itself, Digger called out, "Captain, you may want to see this!" Kristy hauled all the stuff to the companionway. Digger pointed aft. "Check this out!" Kristy pushed the gear into the cockpit, climbed up, and looked back at the stern. The ribbon of black was now thicker... more like a two-inch brush stroke uniformly from north to south on the eastern horizon. But now it was branded with silent sparks and bolts of lightning. She peered up at the sails and sky overhead. To the west, it was still a picture-perfect sailing day.

Digger pointed toward the bow of the boat. "Look at the dolphins!" The dolphins were no longer accompanying them westward. They were swimming due south, seemingly with intention. They crossed directly in front of the boat. A powerboat would've had to turn to the south to avoid hitting them. "You think they are trying to tell us something?" Digger shouted.

"Yeah, like get the heck out of here! Okay, Digger, it's clearly heading this way, and it is coming fast. Here's the plan. We get the engine idling. I'll set the safety lines. Then I recommend you use the head. Once you get your oilskins on and this safety harness, you won't be able to go to the bathroom easily. We will be clipped into the safety lines at all times. Next, we will secure the life raft to the stern rail. We will reef the mainsail now and put up the storm jib. Any questions?"

"Uh, yeah." Digger looked up at the shiny aluminum mast and the steel steering wheel. "What about lightning and all this metal and us being kinda higher than anything else around here. How do we avoid getting zapped?"

"Great question. First, we may get zapped, but look here..." She grabbed Digger by the shirt and pulled him firmly into view of the top of the mast. "See that thing with silvery tentacles? It's a lightning rod. It draws the bolt through the mast and boat to a special metal plate in the keel. The energy passes through the boat into the water. But we still need to be careful and not be touching electronic items. In fact, I'm glad you asked, sailor. I'm turning off the radio, but I am keeping the Loran on. A major no-no is to have one hand on say, the throttle, and the other on the VHF microphone. You suddenly become a major conductor. Any more questions?"

"Can I urinate now?"

Kristy laughed and came in for a quick kiss, whispering, "We got this, Digger, I promise."

CHAPTER 16
A Sea Change

Within a half-hour, the dome of the sky turned half black and half blue. The wind changed from southeast to northeast, and rain started pelting the boat. The sails snapped to the starboard side, and the vessel heeled over in the gale winds. It was as if they were in a fancy chafing dish where the dome glides over the food. Here, the lid came down and put the sailors in a roaring black cauldron. The seas came to an instant boil as the wind increased, causing the rigging of the boat to howl. Lightning flashed and thunder blasted continuously in all directions. The Loran navigation system started beeping.

"We are being blown off course!" Kristy yelled as she slid back the cabin door and climbed down to check the course coordinates. "Digger! Steer to the south for Savannah bearing two-five-oh!"

Digger repeated the command and wrestled the wheel slightly to his left. "Kristy, we have 42 knots of wind out here!" Digger kept glancing at the instrument panel. "Boat speed 12 knots!"

The rigging howled in displeasure. The steel stay lines that stabilized the mast whistled a constant high-pitched outrage. The nylon lines to the sails voiced a soprano-pitched shriek. The blue safety line beat a tantrum on the deck, and the wind buffeting the mast caused a deeper reverberation. While the noise was alarming, the waves were the worst.

Within thirty minutes, the boat was engulfed in troughs of waves that were over Digger's head as he stood at the wheel. When in the belly of the trench, boiling black water surrounded the boat. Digger had to look up 45 degrees to see the sky. Then thankfully, the ship would climb out of the trough in time for Digger to catch a brief vision of the horizon and the tops of the crashing waves. The horizon had shrunk. Visibility had gone from twelve miles to less than a quarter-mile of angry sea and sky. Crests of waves repeatedly crashed into the side of the boat and filled the cockpit.

Digger remained at the wheel, fighting the waves. "Kristy, I can't hold this course! We're getting hammered on the starboard side."

"Fall off to the south a bit more!" Moments later, the Loran sent off another alarm.

Kristy yelled, "Don't worry about that. We're not sailing based on doggone coordinates! We're sailing based on sea conditions. I'll adjust it in a minute!"

Digger eased the boat to a more southerly heading, and immediately less water crashed into the cockpit from the right side of the ship. The bilge pump was working overtime, and the engine was keeping a steady bass groan.

Fierce gale winds and rising swells continued into the night. Kristy took the wheel and stood on the seat of the cockpit in a squat position. The footwell of the cockpit was sloshing with seawater.

Digger had gone below to grab some medication for seasickness. The cabin was in shambles with inches of water on the floor. Digger made it to the head to snatch the pills. Both Kristy's and Digger's fathers were doctors, so the supply of Phenergan was ample. Digger popped the pink pill and fought his way back to the galley for water. Queasiness was rising fast in his gut and in his mind. The diesel fumes, the confined quarters, the jostling, the moist air… everything was conspiring against his well-being. Digger abandoned the idea of seeking refuge in the cabin for his shift break. They were now down to one-hour rotations. He bolted for the cockpit, gasping, "I need air!"

Kristy kept her eyes on the instruments and the reefed mainsail. "Oh, we got air, brother! Fifty-five knots and climbing. This is a hurricane, my friend!"

Suddenly, the wind changed direction, and the two small sails whipped loudly to the other side of the boat, causing it to heel over to starboard. Kristy barked, "Clip in and hang on! Wind is out of the southeast…" In an instant, the wind was at their faces, making it feel like someone had hit the brakes. The sails slapped and snapped violently as the boat was faced directly into hurricane winds from the southwest.

The slowing of the boat speed allowed the waves, still obeying the trajectory from the northeast, to start swamping the boat from the stern. Kristy, carried by a wave from her position at the wheel, was helplessly slammed into the cabin door and left in a heap in the footwell of the cockpit. The wheel on the boat spun like a roulette wheel. They were at the mercy of the storm.

Digger dove for the wheel and yelled, "Where do I steer?"

Kristy crawled to her knees and looked at the wind directional. It was spinning like a top. "Goose the engine full throttle and head south!" She gasped as she pointed to her right. The engine roared under Digger's command. It occasionally screamed as its props surfaced when the bow of the boat was thrust forward down into a trough, exposing the stern.

Digger was trying to get the boat to head south, but the rudder and props, being in the air for significant periods, wouldn't allow for any purchase in the water to direct the boat. For what felt like an eternity, waves and wind came from all directions. The sailors looked at each other, clueless as to what to do. Digger yelled, "Gimme your hand!" Kristy lunged to Digger. He held her with one arm and held the wheel with the other and whispered into her ear. "God of the universe, hear our prayer. You control the earth and all that's in it! Help us now. Silence this storm. Give us strength and wisdom, please God! Amen."

Kristy whispered, "Amen." Then she mustered up her leadership role. "We need to get the mainsail down before it rips the mast out!" As she started to climb to the winches on the mast, a gust came from the northeast, as fierce as anything they had seen yet, and caused the front jib sail to snap and blow out. It had torn from its lines and was waving freely like a fervent flag of surrender. Kristy hauled the jib sheets into the cockpit. "Don't need these anymore." She dumped the tangled mess into the cabin.

She resumed her climb toward the mast to completely reef the mainsail. "Hold it!" Digger yelled. "The wind is returning to the northeast. It's too dangerous up there!"

Kristy looked at the instruments. "Look at the barometer. It's dropping like a rock."

Digger yelled, "Is that good?"

"We may be moving into the eye," Kristy responded. The wind speed began to drop, but the seas, which had grown to swells that towered over the mast, continued their assault.

"I can handle less wind. That's good!" Digger exclaimed.

Kristy looked up. "Digger, look! I see stars directly overhead!"

Digger looked up and exclaimed, "Thank you, God!"

Kristy clambered to the mast and dropped the flapping storm jib, then brought another shredded mess of sail back and dumped it into the cabin. She then descended into the cabin, reset the Loran, and yelled back up at Digger, "Next stop, Bimini, Bahamas, unless this breaks!"

She climbed back into the cockpit and handed Digger a water bottle and a bag of nuts mixed with M&Ms. "Here, hydrate, and eat some of this gorp! We are not out of this yet. It's your shift. I'm gonna try and rest down below. You're headed due south to ride these waves. If we try to head west, we'll bust up the boat and get wet."

At the helm, Digger was feeling better and trying to enjoy riding the swells while the wind died down. The light was appearing in the east, which allowed him to see that the swells were over 40 feet in height from trough to crest. As the boat climbed a swell at an angle of 60 degrees, the mast pointed toward the stern and the front of the boat appeared to be slowly powering up a hill of water. The top of the wave was higher than the mast pole. When the crest of a wave reached the ship, it caused the bow to launch out of the swell and slam down hard to head down into the belly of the dark canyon.

Kristy yelled up, "Don't let the boat slam like that when you crest! Crank the wheel just before the crest, so it falls to the side, and then traverse down the swell like you're skiing at an angle to the mountain. Correct your course on your way down and way up. But do not let it slam. We don't need the hull to separate from the deck or crack at the keel."

Digger pondered this guidance with dread and simply replied, "Got it, Captain. Get some rest, I got this." As the light increased, he observed angry cloud formations over his shoulder to the north. He checked the barometer. It was climbing. The rigging began to sing its threatening song again. Fighting off his exhaustion, Digger stood up and started humming a sea chanty about a drunken sailor.

Before long, he was belting it out. "Way, hey, up she rises, way, hey, up she rises! Way, hey, up she rises ear-li in the morning!"

Nonetheless, the rain and gale winds resumed.

CHAPTER 17

SINGING IN THE RAIN

The storm hovered over the *Fortune Hunter* for three days and drove them further south. The biggest concern was that the boat would start breaking apart. The size of the waves and the pounding the boat took had the sailors on pins and needles. Strange groans and sharp cracking and creaking noises emanated from belowdecks. The sailors shot worried glances to each other.

Digger allowed Kristy to take longer breaks than the one-hour shift. Both sailors were using Phenergan to ward off seasickness. Kristy's father had prescribed the medication for her sailing excursions, explaining how it was designed for cancer patients undergoing chemotherapy to calm the stomach. The side effects were sleepiness, hunger, and thirst.

When either finished their shift, they rummaged in the galley, banging against the walls. Come Hades or high water, they would make a sandwich and eat it with a ravenous appetite. Then without a care in the world, either one collapsed on the bunk and slept through the maelstrom. One time, Kristy discovered Digger sprawled on the floor of the galley, wrapped in the shredded jib sleeping like a baby. Digger was oblivious to the seawater sloshing around him.

At one point, Digger solemnly asked, "Kristy, when do we go on the radio and ask for help? I mean, our jib is gone. The mainsail is in tatters. Our fuel is getting low, and the hull is groaning like it wants to give up the ghost."

Kristy responded sternly, "We're not going to call a Mayday or SOS until it is needed. We're holding our own. If we run out of fuel and battery power is declining, I'll call out our coordinates. If the hull starts to separate, I'll be on the VHF immediately, and you'll be at the aft freeing up the life raft. Right now, we are floating, moving, breathing. When any of those stops, one of us gets on the radio, okay?"

Digger didn't like the answer nor its delivery. He respected the office she held on the boat and replied, "Yes, sir." He didn't care to correct the misgendered term. Nor did Kristy care that, when she served as the first mate on the *Performer,* students were continually calling her "sir." It came with the job.

When Kristy was sleeping, Digger thought a few times about turning on the radio and whispering their coordinates into the microphone. The lightning had died down. But he couldn't leave the wheel unattended. He wasn't sure how the autopilot worked but mainly didn't want to torque off his captain and girlfriend. *What would she do, try me at sea for insubordination?*

Digger's thoughts were becoming distorted by the duration of the storm and the side effects of Phenergan coursing through his veins and brain. As he assumed the role of a camel jockey riding up and down the swells now twice the size of their boat, he found that singing was the only way to keep his spirits up. He sang current pop songs and made up the words he had forgotten. He fired through the campfire folk tunes and spent quite a bit of time singing the hymns and songs he had learned as a choirboy in church. They made him feel the best. He felt as if God was listening to those songs more than the other ones he sang, like Frank Zappa's "I'm a little pimp with my hair gassed back." He belted them all out to the raging wind and driving rain. He yelled into the maelstrom, "I'm a crazy camel jockey! Woo-hoo, let's get it on! The Bahamas, here we come! Yah mon!" As he climbed the back side of a swell, he would sing out, "I think I can, I think I can, I think I can says the choo-choo!" He found himself whispering in the cadence of a train chugging down the tracks, "I think I can… I think I can… I think I can…"

* * *

Kristy came up the morning of the fifth day at sea to find Digger slumped over the wheel. His arms were lifeless, but he was clutching the wheel with his body. His arms and knees were wrapped around the fixture, and he was repeatedly but barely whispering, "I think I can." Kristy looked at her watch. "Oh no, Digger honey, I am so sorry! I overslept for four hours! Come here, honey." Digger didn't move from his perch. "Digger, are you okay?"

He lifted his face, and smiled weakly. "I think I am… I think I am… I think I am a choo-choo." He slid to the bench seat and keeled over on his side. "I just need some rest." Kristy straightened him out to a fully prone position and took over the wheel.

When he woke, it was mid-afternoon, and the bright sun was ablaze as they headed due west. The mainsail was fully hoisted and filled. They were on broad reach pushed by the trusty trade winds from the southeast again. The engine was blissfully silent. Digger rolled from the cockpit to his knees, clasped his hands together, and looked heavenward, much like William Bradford of the *Mayflower* must have done on sighting Cape Cod. "Thank you, Lord!" He stood slowly and turned to hug Kristy. She was beaming and had shed everything but short shorts and a tank top. "We live to fight another day, my love." They embraced for a long time as the boat quietly pushed through calmer waters. "Are you a sight for sore eyes?" Digger whispered in her ear. I thank God for you, too. You got us through this, Kristy."

"This is clearly going on my sailing resume. There will be news on this storm. I am hoping the *Windsor Star* crew is okay."

"Man, the Maydays and SOSs wouldn't quit. Should I turn on the radio?

"Can we just sail quietly for a while, Digger? We are getting back on track and don't need the radio. If you don't mind."

"I agree completely!" he replied jovially.

"Okay, we're heading due west to hit the Gulf Stream, then we'll come about and ride it due north to North Carolina. We will only be a few days late."

Digger laughed "Yeah, only a few days lost at sea. Not a problem!" He started whistling a ho-hum tune in a carefree manner.

The next afternoon, the sailors landed at Southport, North Carolina. After securing the boat at the marina, Kristy went to the dockmaster to inquire about news of the *Windsor Star* and to contact the *Fortune Hunter's* owner. Digger remained on board, making the boat shipshape and packing up their gear.

Kristy came back in tears, a newspaper clutched in her hands. "Three boats lost in the storm... including the *Windsor Star*!" She could not get her breath between the sobs. Digger jumped to the dock and put his arm around her. He looked down at the newspaper and saw a picture of the *Windsor Star* in its former glory, bedecked with flags and ribbons.

"Captain Coltrane?" asked Digger quietly.

"Lost!... his wife and children were aboard... lost. Only six students survived!" Kristy handed the newspaper to Digger and stumbled toward the cabin. "The owner of the *Fortune Hunter* will be here in a few minutes. Then we can catch a shuttle to Wilmington airport. I'm done with this."

CHAPTER 18

Ricky the Researcher

While Digger and Kristy were at sea, Rick Eaton was hard at work back in Port Talbot. He'd been busy poring over the treasure trove of Hartson family memorabilia in his walled-off garage attic. Between the peak of the garage roof and the rafters of the ceiling below was a space of six feet that ran the length of the building. In this cramped area, encased in tarps, sheetrock, plywood, and whatever he could find to hide his workspace; he set up his war room. He used an armless rolling secretary's chair to move up and down the length of the makeshift tables he had constructed in his hideaway. To the far left, toward the front of the property, he amassed Hartson social communications and photos. The slanted ceiling and the sidewall had photos stapled into crude plywood panels hammered into the rafters and studs. Rick scrawled the names and dates below each picture.

Moving to the right toward the back of the property, he put real estate documents such as deeds and mortgages. In this area were copies of Maine statutes and law books on wills and estates as well as the pleadings his father had collected from the grandfather's probate case. Further to the right along the back wall, he had business documents and pictures of factories, cotton gins, and surveys of train tracks. He hung telegraph ticker tapes from separate nails. The Morse codebook was nearby.

If anyone walked into the garage below and looked up, they would see only a ceiling made of a stapled army-green tarpaulin. This was par for the course for insulating any Maine garage that had a wood-burning stove. It was not an embarrassment; it was the sign of Yankee ingenuity or a penny-pinching Puritan.

Samson, Rick's Belgian Malinois, was penned at ground level in space against the far corner of the garage. In the dog's area was a simple step ladder casually propped against the wall. Above the ladder was a piece of plywood that would slide open to reveal the attic office. To get to the ladder, one had to go through Samson.

Rick's attention was currently on the far-right side of his war room, focusing on the business documents of the late 1850s. He held a yellowed balance sheet up to the light, trying to decipher the hand-inked numerals. He muttered aloud the title that ran across the top of the sheet, *1859 Bay V-l-t. Inventory*. His eyes scanned down the columns and saw entries for *G. Ing* and *S. Ing*. Entries also included the abbreviations, *Fr. Cur, Sp. Cur, Brit. Cur*. He followed the entries over to the far right of the page and read numbers like *10, 15,* and *30*.

Think, Eaton, think! What kind of ledger is this? Bay Vlt. Inventory... Is this the boat-building operation in Talbot.? Rick stood up to look at a tintype photo of the basin in Port Talbot, where the Hartsons had a shipbuilding operation. He banged his head on the rafter as he stood. He swore. He crouched and read the photo inscription. Hartson Launch, Talbot Basin, 1859. He sat down, rubbing his head. "Right year, but it's *Bay*, not *basin*... Bay... where have I seen Bay?" He rolled to his left and looked at the deeds that he had sorted by state. The handwritten deeds were hard to read. He picked up the Georgia pile. As he started unfolding the documents, they flaked and crumbled in his hands. Then he spied *Seven Bay Street, in the city of Savannah and the county of Chatham in the State of Georgia* in the top paragraph of the deed.

Rick went back to the balance sheet. *Hmmm... Bay Vlt. Inventory... Seven Bay Street Savannah Georgia Inventory? V-L-T? Volume? Voluntary?* He continued scanning the balance sheet. He looked in the lower right corner and tried to decipher the entry *6.8 Mille Mille*. "What is the matter with these people? Speak in English. Are these bales of cotton?" Rick rolled to his far left to the pictures of the Hartsons. A white man had his arm around a tall black man in front of a building. He pulled the tintype off the wall and put it under the light and reached for the magnifying glass. The men were standing in front of a brownstone-style building.

Rick moved the magnifying glass slowly, whispering, "That's Jonathan... and that's Tombo Lincoln, the freed slave." Rick glanced at the court document on his long table entitled *Manumission* with Tombo's name on it, confirming his guess. Rick returned to the photo and scanned it with the magnifier. "Bingo!" Rick squinted at the number of the building. "That's Seven Bay Street, Savannah." Rick looked to the left side of the photograph. He noticed an open door on the sidewalk. He looked at the roofline of the building and saw a block and tackle. He moved the light carefully and muttered, "There is a rope descending into the sidewalk cellar door." He looked up and thought, *So Bay Street had a sidewalk cellar door... so what! This is useless.* He looked at the balance sheet. "So this is a V-L-T inventory of... Ings and curs at Bay Street in Georgia." He lit a cigarette and focused. "What is *cur*? *Fr. Sp.* and *Brit. cur*?" When he said the last two words, his mind jumped. *British cur? French cur? Spanish cur? Currency! Currency?* He blurted out, "Tell me you guys have an inventory of currencies!"

He rolled over to the photo and looked at the sidewalk doors that opened to a cellar. He looked at the doors closely. They were rather thick compared to the ones he knew that existed in Boston. "Of course! Currency is kept in a V-L-T Vault! Currency and Ings... Ings... What are Ings in a vault?" Rick's eyes went as wide as saucers. He whispered a curse word and then yelled, "Ingots!" He looked at the bottom right and thought, *Hartson had 6.8 mille mille of currency and ingots. Mille in Latin means a thousand. Thank you, Professor Clough.* "Why repeat the word?" Rick asked himself aloud. He repeated the words together, "Thousand thousand." He haltingly stated the words differently. "A thousand... thousands..." He banged his fist on the table. Samson barked below. "A thousand thousands is a million!" Rick shuddered and felt sudden goosebumps.

He blurted out, "Can this be right? Slow down, Ricky." His mind was in overdrive. He lit another menthol Marlboro. *In 1860 the inventory of the Bay Street Vault had currency and ingots worth over six million.* He glanced at the upper right corner of the balance sheet. He snatched the magnifying glass and identified the symbol and exclaimed, "Dollars! Good, God-loving, red, white, and blue American dollars!" Rick continued his conversation with himself. "So, I ask you, Mr. Genius, if I am reading this right, what is the present value of six million dollars of gold or silver in the desired year of 1980 dating back to the initial year of 1860?" Rick was starting to use the postulates from his economics classes from a few years back in high school.

"Well, professor, would you like that based on the CPI or GDP?"

Rick reached for a treatise entitled *The Civil War*. He scanned the index. "Cost of the War, page 75." Jumping to the page, he began mumbling and reached for a battery-operated calculator. "Let's see, the war cost $6.7 billion in 1860, the initial year." He clicked a number into the calculator. Then he referred back to the text, "… *using a GDP deflator, the cost of the Civil War would be $153 billion dollars today.*" Quickly he looked at the copyright of the treatise, *1975*. "Close enough."

He turned to the calculator and spoke aloud as he made the calculations. "The Civil War cost is $153 billion. That's the value in the desired year… the rate of inflation… the value today would be roughly twenty-two times the initial value or…" He paused as his fingers punched the calculator buttons. "So, six million in currency and ingots in 1860 is worth…" He hit the equals button dramatically. "$136 million… today." Rick smiled and looked up at nothing while his mind raced through his findings. His eyes widened. "And that does not factor in gold's rise in value… that's inflation only!" Rick whistled.

He looked at the spreadsheet in one hand and the photo of Bay Street in the other hand. He tilted his head to the side and asked, as if the other party was in the room, "Where'd it go, Jonathan? Where'd you put my twenty percent, Ted? There it is, Pops. I told you." Rick resumed his research with renewed vigor.

Rick rolled his chair back to the deeds area of his laboratory. "Bay Street… Bay… Bay…. Here it is. *Hartson Cotton Limited, a limited enterprise formed under the laws of the State of Georgia, party of the first part, the Grantor herein and Braxton Cotton Brokerage, a sole proprietorship, party of the second part, the Grantee herein.*" Rick continued to scan the deed. "*In witness whereof signed and sealed this nineteenth day of January 1861 in the city of Savannah, the state of Georgia.*" Rick reached for the Civil War treatise and turned to a timeline and read, "*January 19th 1861…Georgia secedes from the United States.* Rick whispered, "These Hartsons don't mess around." He paused. "Man, I should go to law school. I love this stuff."

Rick turned back to the balance sheet of the vault's inventory; it was dated 1859. He double-checked the date of the deed selling Bay Street. It was January 1861. Rick whistled again. *The Hartsons moved at least $136 million dollars of gold in 1861 out of their vault in Savannah at the time Georgia was seceding from the Union.* "Ricky, where would you put that much gold?" He rolled his chair back to the photos of the Hartson properties and looked at the huge cottage on the ocean. Underneath the photo he had handwritten the note, "*Crescent Point, Jonathan Hartson Residence ca. 1860.*" Rick looked at the map of the farm and properties that dotted Hartson Beach. "Jonathan, you look like the brains of the operation and your home is being built right at the time a good heavy foundation is needed. Well, Johnny Boy, looks like it's time for a structural inspection of Crescent Point before the season starts," he added, laughing maniacally.

CHAPTER 19

HOLLY HARTSON

At the marina in North Carolina, Digger offered to fly with Kristy to Providence and drive up to Maine in her car which she had left at the Newport Yachting Center. She declined, stating she would like to be alone for a couple of days before driving up to Port Talbot on the morning of the awards ceremony. Digger reluctantly obliged and flew into Portland alone.

Back in Port Talbot, it was still pre-season; in other words, dead! Alone at his home on Ocean Avenue, Digger read the Portland paper's account of the *Windsor Star* going down. As he laid the paper down on the coffee table in the solarium, his eyes caught a small article in the paper below the fold that he had almost missed. *Hartson Beach Home Robbed.* Digger snatched the paper up, and read:

Port Talbot June 2, 1980.

Port Talbot police were called to Crescent Point, the summer residence of Jonathan Hartson, having received a call from a family member stating that their home had been burglarized and vandalized. The mansion, located on the western point of Hartson's Beach in Port Talbot, has been in the family since the 1800s.

Police Chief Edward Nickerson commented briefly. "We don't usually discuss active investigations, however, here we are asking the community to come forward if anyone has any information on activity in this area over the Memorial Day weekend. This is a remote area and the coming and going of a vehicle or person may have been noted. There are several valuables missing, including one of the first telegraphs invented and the logbook of the historic schooner, Vigilant. The Vigilant was one of the last boats built here in Port Talbot. We know Maine is a great place for antiquing and we want to get the word out about these items and seek their assistance if any antique store owners should see them. If anyone has information or comes across such information, please call our headquarters. We suggest extreme caution as the intruder may be dangerous and capable of causing harm, based on the senseless destruction done to the home." The chief refused to elaborate further. Jonathan Hartson the fourth was reached at his winter home in Florida but declined to comment.

Digger set the paper down again and whistled. "What's going on with the poor Hartsons?" He looked at his watch and the paper to double-check the dates. "While we were sailing through a hurricane, the Hartsons were getting robbed." Shaking his head in disbelief, Digger next turned to the mail that had been forwarded to Ocean Avenue from his college address. He tore into the fancy oversized envelope from the Whitney School. It was a polished invitation to next weekend's seventy-fifth anniversary celebration. Digger pored over the schedule of events. Klaus Phillips, the ancient English and drama teacher, was retiring and was being honored for 30 years of service to the school. The drama in Port Talbot melted in importance when compared to learning more about his own identity. Digger started calculating.

The old geezer probably knows my biological mother and father... wonder if I can get him to spill the beans. I think he liked me when I was there. After all, he did cast me in a leading role in Plaza Suite. *Hmmm. What's the angle I can use with this guy to find out about a previous student who took a leave of absence to have a baby? Maybe it's just the leave of absence itself? I could say I'm writing a paper about students who succeeded after dropping out. Yeah, like I'm researching for an independent study of war stories turned into success. As I recall, this teacher was a lush... drinking cough medicine in class. What was that stuff? Terpin... turpentine... terp-something.*

Digger headed for his dad's office. He reached for the fat red *Physicians Drug Reference.* Thumbing through the index, he found *terpin hydrate.* He scanned the medical verbiage. "Codeine, huh? No wonder you were loopy, Klaus." He read the *Caution* section. *Terpin hydrate has been cited in the Desk Reference on Drug Abuse, NYS Dept. Health, 1971, as follows: Street name Terp; see also Turp: cough syrup with high codeine content.*

Digger slammed the book shut. "Klaus was on Whitney's disciplinary board kicking kids out of school for pot violations while he's mainlining Turp! Ain't that rich!"

Digger looked at his watch. *Ten o'clock... time to visit Ship's Pub. Probably dead as a doornail but might as well rekindle friendships with the locals.*

The vast parking lot held only a scant number of cars. On entering the pub, Digger was hit with the whining sound of Procol Harum's "Whiter Shade of Pale." He saw his old friend, trusty Rusty, behind the bar. "Crusty! I love this place! Who else plays Procol Harum?"

Rusty rang the tip bell and yelled, "Salty Dog in the house!" That was a subtle reference to a Procol Harum album title and a good-natured greeting for his old friend.

The lobstermen at the bar turned to see who was joining the intimate setting. One of them yelled out, "The summah has officially stahted! The Bike Cop is baaack!" Another quipped, "I feel so much safah now!"

Digger patted the lobstermen's backs as he moved down the line to greet Rusty with a handshake and a manly hug at the service area of the bar. Rusty lifted the hinged portion of the bar and came out to embrace his old buddy. "Are we gonna get to do some fun things this summer, or what? We work too hard and ain't getting any younger." Rusty had been on the crew team at Bowdoin while Digger rowed for his college in New York. They had originally met as kids in the sailing school at the Talbot Yacht Club.

Digger agreed. "How 'bout we grab some chicks and party on Trotter Island?"

Rusty responded, "I know which chick you'll grab. Are you still dating the sailing girl?"

"Yeah, Kristy and I are going strong. How 'bout you?"

Rusty returned to the bar area and yelled, "Oh yeah. I got my pick of the litter!" He spread his arms wide to acknowledge the curmudgeonly lobstermen hunched over their beers.

"We'll fix that this summah, brothah!" Digger yelled back.

Without asking, Rusty placed a Mount Gay and tonic in front of Digger. "Time to kick start the summer, my friend."

Digger raised the glass to toast his friend. Rusty grabbed a glass he had hidden next to the cash register and returned the silent toast.

Digger took a tour of his old haunt. The main room around the corner was occupied by just a few tables of early birds. Digger didn't recognize anyone as he walked through slowly and started to return to the bar.

"Mister Davenport?" a female voice called out from a table. Digger stopped, squinted in her direction and went over to the table. The girl stood up and stuck out her hand. "Holly Hartson. I think you know my older sister, Agnes?"

"Of course, Holly! How are you? I didn't recognize you. Boy, you're all grown up!"

Holly was beaming up at Digger. "I'm in college now and these are my friends from Dartmouth. We are hiding out at Royal Orchard." Digger shook the hands of the trio of friends.

"How's Agnes doing?" Digger asked.

"She is in New York working for an advertising firm and loves it. Hopefully she can get some time up here before we sell... er, I mean, the summer is over," Holly chirped.

Digger didn't want to be too forward and ask about the "for sale" signs he'd seen at Hartson's Beach. "Well, I hope I get to see her when she comes up. Are you as good of a sailor as she is?"

"Oh no, she has all the trophies. I'm the powerboat type, the faster the better."

Digger turned to Holly's college friends. "These Hartson girls are the treasure of the town, dontcha know? You are in very good company. Holly, please give my best to Agnes and if I can help you in any way this summer, you know where to find me."

"Oh, thank you, Mr. Davenport."

"Call me Digger, please. I'm just a college kid like you."

Holly blushed "You're a bit more than that, sir. You're the hero of Port Talbot."

One of the friends spoke up. "We were just talking about last summer's explosion. That's a wild story!"

Digger tried to downplay the event. "Fun and games in sleepy Port Talbot. Well, great to see you all." Digger took his exit, thinking. *Gosh, that Holly is as cute as Agnes. I hope things work out for the Hartsons.*

When the cocktail waitress came to the service bar area, Digger told her he wanted to buy a round of drinks for the college kids in the big room. "You got it, Unit 19. This is their order." She spun away to deliver a trayful.

Digger motioned to Rusty. "Who's that?" he asked, pointing to the cocktail waitress.

"That's Mr. Ruge's daughter, Michelle." Rusty raised his eyebrows twice quickly, signaling his interest. Mr. Ruge was the town's pharmacist, a well-informed oracle of information on all things Port Talbot.

* * *

As the evening at Ship's Pub wound to a close, Digger was engaged in a spirited discussion with several lobstermen about the docking privileges of the *Performer* at Government Wharf, and the recent extension of police jurisdiction over the docks instead of the harbormaster. Digger remained noncommittal and distanced himself from the politicians who made such decisions.

While Digger huddled with the old salts, Holly appeared at his side.

"Mr. er, Digger, my friends and I would like to thank you for the round of drinks and we would like to invite you over to Royal Orchard for a nightcap. We have the place to ourselves and would be honored to get to know you better."

Digger looked at his watch. *It's only 11:45,* he thought. "I'd love to. Are you headed there now?"

Holly beamed, "Yes, do you need a ride?"

"No, I'll meet you there shortly. Thanks. It'll be fun."

As Holly departed, the lobstermen gave Digger a thumbs-up. He brushed it off and paid his tab.

CHAPTER 20

THE WIDOW'S WALK

Digger pulled into the tree-lined driveway and drove past the white filigree gates and matching sign that announced Royal Orchard. The expansive Federal-style mansion was dark except for the front porch light and the light at the very top of the house, four stories up, where the widow's walk was perched. Digger approached the main front door, which was big enough to drive a VW Bug through. He heard music playing inside. He gave a knuckle-knock, avoiding the brass door knocker with the Hartson family crest on it. Holly opened the door. Her hair was no longer in a ponytail as it had been earlier at Ship's Pub. It was a dark brown silky mane that flowed to her elbows and contrasted nicely with large blue eyes and bright white teeth in perfect order. Holly had the full, dark brows and tan skin of a Mediterranean movie star, but her kilt and crew neck sweater with the gold, monogrammed circle pin just below her neck was classic New England WASP.

"I'm so glad you came," Holly said, greeting her newest guest.

"We're in the little house, this way…" She led Digger into the front hall and immediately took a left turn down three stairs into a living room with a fireplace and then around through the dining room to a back kitchen where the other kids sat listening to the music. Steely Dan was singing about being "in a room with your two-timer" and "you go back, Jack, and do it again, wheel turning round and round." Digger marveled at the antiques, Persian rugs, and stately portraits of sea captains and grande dames.

Holly explained as they walked that the "little house," while completely contained within the "big house," had been a separate quarters for her great-great-great-great grandmother, who was mother-in-law to Henry Hartson. The size of everything in the little house was precisely three-quarters of the size of the rest of the house to accommodate the mother-in-law's slight frame: door openings, fireplaces, chairs, dishware… everything.

"Digger Davenport, please formally meet my sorority sisters, Shelly Brookstone and Julia Gamwell. This is Julia's boyfriend, Gary Waldmann."

"Good to be with you again." Digger nodded politely. "Are you all in the same major at Dartmouth?"

"Before you all get chatting, Digger, would you like a snifter of Hartson Rum?" Holly broke in. "It's the 1830 reserve."

"Do you have the '35?" Digger asked, deadpan. He was about to add that he was joking but Holly's earnest answer surprised him.

"I think we do. I can check in the cellar!"

"Oh my gosh, Holly… I was kidding! You actually have rum from the 1800s?"

"Kegs, bottles and jars!" Gary exclaimed. "It's unbelievable down there. By the way, I take mine on ice. It packs a punch!"

"I'll take the 1830 straight up to get the real feel of yester-century," said Digger.

"One snifter of yester-century coming up!" Holly called over her shoulder as she headed for the small alcove known as the butler's pantry.

Shelly spoke up. "To answer your question, Digger, Holly and I are pre-med and Gary is what… poli-sci?"

"He's pre-law," said Julia. "He'll take whatever label they give him when it's all over. I'm fine art with a minor in art history." Julia emphasized her point by pushing her tortoise shell glasses to the top of the bridge of her nose with an exaggerated gesture.

Gary added, "When I walk across the stage at graduation, I'll have to peek at what major they decided to give me. My courses are all over the map."

Holly, who had kept an ear on the conversation, came back with Digger's three-quarter-scale snifter and added, "*If* he graduates!… Just kidding Gare-gare. You're the smartest of the bunch."

Holly raised her glass. "Here's to our next lawyer! Gary Waldman, Esquire!"

They all raised their glasses, except Gary, who was being toasted. He sheepishly thanked them.

Digger piped in, "Pontiac rules! You can drink on your own toast."

Gary saluted everyone with his tumbler and sipped.

Holly turned to Digger. "Although you might become an attorney too, right?"

Digger responded confidently, "I'm pursuing a criminal justice degree."

Gary countered, "I thought that was a two-year degree. I did the criminal justice thing for a while, too."

"You're right," Digger agreed. "It usually is, but at the University of New York, it's a four-year forensic degree. We really drill down into the science of catching bad guys."

Shelly whispered loudly, "Hide the pot!"

Digger laughed good-naturedly. "I'm not on duty. I don't smoke it, but it's not within my jurisdiction to enforce it either. Now, that red car out there... I *can* give it a parking ticket... but that's all I got. So, no worries. Knock yourself out."

They laughed and Shelly quietly disappeared.

Digger noted her disappearance and asked, "Where are the 'rents'?"

The question seemed to make the girls scatter, one for more ice, another to find Shelly. Digger noted the exodus. "Wrong question?"

"No, Digger, you're fine. The Hartson family as a whole is going through a tough time right now. Mom and Dad are down in Boston. Dad's very sick and is getting treated for an illness that has been brewing for a long time, so it's no crushing shock. It's also something he's probably brought on himself. I am not sure when they'll be back. Mom has had to rent an apartment down there to be near him as he gets treatment. And poor Uncle Jon is hiding out in Florida waiting for the outcome of a court case. It's been a few tough years around here. I mean, it's no secret to anyone who drives by. This winter the Hartson Boys, Jonathan and my dad, Ted, got together and decided to sell the Maine properties."

Digger whispered, "I'm sorry to hear it. This place has quite the legacy."

"It's running in the red. The town refused to recognize all that land out there as being farmland because of the lack of farm income. Instead, they want to tax it all as oceanfront, or waterfront for the river and tidal creeks, and if they don't get us for that, then they want to charge it for ocean view or water view. Sale of a parcel here and a parcel there won't cut the massive bills the town is trying to levy against us. Do you know Mama Bear Stockton, the attorney?"

Digger nodded.

"She's representing us, but she doesn't seem very optimistic."

Mrs. Sharon Stockton was a plus-sized attorney known as the Mama Bear. The mama part of her nickname derived from her vigilance and fierce protection of her clients, while the bear part was due to her amazing legal shrewdness and tenacity, with overtones of bravado.

"I know Mama Bear. She's great," Digger said encouragingly. "What about putting the land in one of those land trusts... forever wild-type things?"

"It's been discussed. It comes with strings attached that the patriarchs are opposed to, as it would restrict what Hartson's Beach was supposed to be, but most importantly it doesn't solve the exorbitant taxation of any parcel we'd want to keep. So, it's like we'd give it all away to the land trust and then still have to sell the rest in due time to pay debts. If the Hartsons are anything, they're business-minded. Thus, the 'for sale' signs."

Shelly returned with a crudely rolled item perched between her lips. Holly's eyes widened. "Not in here," she protested. "Let's go up on the widow's walk. I think there's a moon out. Plus, I really don't want to tread heavily on Mom and Dad's space."

"What's a widow's walk?" Shelley asked.

"It's our deck on the roof where Sarah Hartson would watch for ships to arrive. It's beautiful up there.... Guys?" Holly yelled toward the back of the little house. "C'mon, freshen up your cocktails. Grab a sweater. We're going up on the roof!"

Holly led the entourage back through the little house into the big house, which was dark. Holly flicked on a flashlight. "I love creeping through the house in the dark. I imagine what the original Henry Hartson might have looked like stumbling through here with his cane, or the original Agnes of the 1800s."

Gary inquired, "We're gonna climb four stories in the dark?"

Julia elbowed him and loudly whispered, "Wussy!"

Holly did not answer but stopped under the sweeping stairway that rose overhead. She waited until everyone was gathered round. Like a docent in a museum, she began, "The murals on the walls are depictions of scenes from our past business interests. Here you have the Freedom Express chugging into the stockyards of Omaha on the Omaha and Republican Valley Railway started by Henry Hartson."

Holly held the light steady on the scene of hundreds of heads of longhorn cattle in the foreground, with dust rising and a black locomotive belching white smoke as it pulled into the station in the center of the mural.

"Over here you have cotton being loaded onto the schooner our family built, called the *Vigilant*. This scene takes place on Bay Street in Savannah, Georgia." Holly held the light on the painting only briefly. "Over here are…"

Digger interrupted, "Can you go back to Bay Street?"

Holly moved closer with the light and held it on the scene.

After a moment Digger asked, "Does anyone notice something odd about the picture?"

All heads drew closer.

Holly spoke first. "I know what's odd, but let's see if these Dartmouth Indians see it."

"Hey! we're not Indians anymore," said Julia. In an official tone, she added, "Use of the term 'Indian' is inconsistent with our academic objectives." Switching to a mockingly smug tone, she said, "We are Dartmouth *Greens*. Get with the program, Hartson!"

In true Hartson fashion, Holly quipped, "I don't know about you, but the last thing I want to be called is a *green* doctor. What a stupid word choice. It means inexperienced. I'm gonna forever refer to myself a Dartmouth Green? I don't think so, Charlie."

The group chuckled as the flashlight remained focused on the Bay Street scene.

"I see it!" exclaimed Gary. "They're not wearing OSHA-approved safety belts?"

"Nope," said Holly.

Digger spoke up. "I don't know if this is accurate, but the laborers are mostly white, and it doesn't seem like that's the way it would've been back then in the South."

"Right you are, Mr. Forensic Investigator!" announced Holly. "Jonathan Hartson, or so the legend goes, was antislavery in a pro-slavery city and he paid his longshoremen good wages. Had he paid blacks such wages, he would have been boycotted or worse." Holly started to move the light.

"Hold it!" interrupted Julia, the art student. "I see something else. Look at the boat. The center area there…"

Digger offered, "You mean the hold of the ship?"

"Yeah, the hold. It should be dark and shadowy. The sun is over here," she said, pointing to a side area of the mural. "It looks like light is emanating from the hold. Do you see that? That's weird. Like they had bright lights on or something. It's odd to paint it that way."

Gary ribbed his girlfriend. "You painters are in it for the toluene." He inhaled in an imitation of someone getting high off fumes.

"Well," Holly continued, "the painter was a Hartson. Sarah Hartson. She went to Mount Holyoke in the 1850s. Over here, ladies and gentlemen, we see the Biddeford mills with billowing smoke and churning water wheels in the Saco River. That's where most of the Hartson wealth was generated." Holly moved to the final mural. "This is the Dog Island lighthouse under construction. The light is located out there." She pointed toward the ocean. "Jonathan and Ted Hartson constructed it between 1861 and 1862."

"Why is the brick such a bright yellow? Did they get it in Oz?" asked Gary facetiously.

Holly responded like a true historian, "Again, family folklore is that the brick came from the South and because of the war needs for iron, which gives bricks their red color, they imported Southern brick made with lime, which causes the yellow color."

"The lighting is unusual on that lighthouse, too," Julia observed.

Shelly huffed in exasperation, "You all need a puff of this and then do your analysis! Let's start climbing!"

Holly said, "May I direct you to Port Talbot's first and only residential elevator?" She flashed the light on a door that looked like any closet door, except that it was oversized.

Holly opened the door and a light turned on automatically to reveal a large mahogany cage with beveled mirrors. Holly grabbed a handle and rolled back the collapsing crisscrossed brass door. "All aboard!" she announced. Everyone squeezed in.

"Maybe I should walk," offered Shelly, who was rather broad in the beam.

"Nonsense, Shelly! You wouldn't believe what this thing lifts. Our whole upstairs furniture was moved using this thing." Holly cranked the arm on the brass wheel forward. The elevator dropped a foot. There were screams. "Oops! sorry ladies and gentlemen. Let's go up!" She pulled back on the arm and it took off silently, climbing at a rapid rate. "Keep your hands in please."

On the fourth floor immediately opposite the elevator door there was a circular stairway.

"Gary, can you and Digger go first? That trapdoor up there needs to slide back this way."

The boys took to their duties with vigor. The girls climbed the stairway behind them and were suddenly showered with leaves and pine needles.

"No worries, kiddies. Just a little vegetation. Onward!" encouraged Holly.

Once everyone was atop the house, the *oohs* and *ahs* exploded enthusiastically. It was a clear crisp evening with a light onshore breeze. The moon and stars were out. There was a moment of silence as each beheld the beauty of the scene, and then a little scratching sound and a bright light on Shelly's face as she lit her handmade creation. She puffed on it and started coughing as she held it out to Holly. Holly passed it to Gary, saying to her friend, "You know I don't smoke that crap."

Shelly held the smoke in her lungs and squeaked out a short reply, "Sue me!"

Gary hauled on the joint and passed it to Julia, who partook and passed it back to Shelly.

Digger was alone at the rail of the widow's walk that looked out to sea. Holly came to stand next to him.

"Nice view, huh?" The ocean was a quarter-mile in the distance, lit by a silver path of moonlight that spilled across the water, all the way to the horizon. In the foreground, dimly lit by the moon, were a rolling pasture and prominent tidal creek. To their left was a small tidal river, Salmon Creek, that came up behind the house and eventually led all the way to the New Hampshire mountains. Royal Orchard had a small dock on Salmon Creek. Half of the time the dock and the fishing boat tied to it sat on mud at low tide.

Digger whispered, "You can't sell this part. This is worth fighting for."

Holly slowly sipped her rum. "Agreed, but I'm in the wrong generation to make that point or cut the check."

"So, what are we looking at here? Is that the Brigantine Hotel over there to the left?"

Holly pointed. "Yes, that's the Brigantine. That dark area there is St.

Peter's point. I don't think we can see your house. It's hidden behind the church, but you can see the tip of Whitten Point. Then coming across to the right... straight, about three miles out, you see the Dog Island Light; then over to the west, you see Boon Island light, then in the foreground you see Uncle Jon's house, Crescent Point."

"I was sorry to hear about the burglary," Digger said gently.

Holly sighed. "Yeah, it's just more of the crap we're going through. I don't know... it's like the family's being kicked while we're down. Dad's illness, Jon's SEC suit... and did you know our archives were just stolen from Dartmouth? Then there was the burglary... and worst of all, the senseless vandalism. What was the point of that?"

"What did they vandalize?"

"Someone slashed several very historic oil paintings of our family members. Not to mention they dumped and abused the books and bookshelves in the library, ripped up the oriental rugs, smashed all the drawers to Jon's desk, punched holes in walls, and ransacked the master bedroom! It was sick!"

"I am so sorry. I know a few years back that vandalizing summer homes was a sport in the off-season. But I thought that had died down."

"I was the one to call the police and walk through with Nickerson. He is such a nice guy."

"He didn't light up one of his Camels at the site, did he?"

Holly giggled. "No, not that I saw."

"Oh good. He's improving. I can remember a couple of times being at a crime scene with the chief lighting up and flicking butts anywhere," said Digger. "Drove me nuts, but what could I say? The summer hire, a Bike Cop... kinda of frustrating."

"You're much more than that, Digger." Holly inched closer and looked intently into his eyes. Digger's internal DEW line, or distant early warning bells started clanging in his brain. *Uh-oh, this is getting dicey. What am I doing? What about Kristy?*

In the distance, they heard a distinct howling noise. Digger broke the eye-lock Holly had on him and looked out toward the ocean. It was inky black, but there it was again. A haunting rhythm which sounded like crying, or no, more like a gothic howl. It stopped. And then louder, he heard it again.

"Did you hear that?" Digger looked back at the other three who were in a little cluster as if they were giving Holly space to have a private moment with him. He smashed through the artificial boundary of their odd little huddle by repeating in a louder voice, "Did you guys hear that?" The trio walked over to the edge where Digger and Holly stood.

Digger whispered, "Listen. It's out there somewhere."

Shelly whispered, "Like wow, dude, you're freaking me out, man."

Gary whispered "Shhhh... I heard it too..." All five went silent with their faces turned to the beach and the ocean beyond. A light breeze brushed over their faces. Then it happened again. A light but crisp and clear yowl permeated their ears and emotions. *Ah Ooooooo, Ah Oooooo!* The howls came in double and triple layers.

"It's a whole pack of them!" whispered Julia.

"I think the baying is being carried on the breeze from Dog Island... straight out there... where that light is. Family folklore is that you could hear the howls, but I never have until tonight. How eerie."

Gary asked, "Does anyone live out there?"

Holly paused. "There's a lighthouse keeper and he and his family before him have been Hartson employees since the old days. Way back, like in the 1880s, the Hartsons actually lived out there until the influenza passed through southern Maine. It's rich with history going back to the 1600s, with Indians living there and stuff. The government recently sent Uncle Jon a notice that the light is to be converted to solar power and the keeper position would no longer be needed. I think the island is for sale, actually."

Shelly piped in, "Solar-powered... far out, man!"

Digger added, "I suppose if it's good enough for Jimmy Carter in the White House, it's good enough for the Dog Island Light."

Julia sighed. "I think it's sad. It's such a romantic concept. A lighthouse keeper. I'd love to do that and paint to my heart's content. Would your uncle let me go out there to paint?"

Gary exclaimed, "And get eaten by those wolves? Jules... you're crazy."

Holly corrected, "I think they're wild wolfhounds technically... a mixed breed of wolf and dog. But maybe Uncle Jon would let you go out there, but I don't know much about the keeper. He's a loner for sure. A black guy that lives off the land. Although I'm sure he's harmless, he may be creepy."

Digger looked at his watch. "Holly, this has been one of the most memorable evenings I've ever had in Port Talbot. I'm sorry, but I gotta run. I have a big day tomorrow. There's an awards ceremony at Government Wharf. I heard that this past winter a surfer on Talbot Beach saved a dog in heavy surf and gave it mouth-to-mouth…or mouth-to-snout resuscitation. Anyway, I want to be there for the award ceremony. You all are invited. It's at 11 in the morning."

The other four mumbled and chuckled over the concept of giving a dog mouth-to-mouth resuscitation.

Digger gave his hostess a quick hug. "It's been great getting to know you better, Miss Hartson."

"Likewise, Mr. Davenport. I'll walk you down."

"No, that won't be necessary. I know to close the brass door. Stay here, finish your cocktails." Digger turned to Holly's friends and shook their hands and expressed a hope their paths would cross in the future.

Holly walked Digger to the roof door over the circular stairway. "Digger, do you think you could come visit again? I'd like you to walk through Crescent Point with me and see if you see anything that the police missed. I'm sure Uncle Jon would be happy for anything that might help catch those rotten crooks."

"Uh… Holly, I'd have to think about that. I go on the Port Talbot Police Department payroll on June 20, so it might be a conflict. Besides, isn't it a designated crime scene right now?"

"Well, if it is a crime scene, shouldn't Chief Nickerson have told me? I mean, Uncle Jon is paying me to get the whole house ready for some short-term renters who are coming in a few weeks. I'm gonna have to scrub it top to bottom in the next week or two. Wouldn't that destroy any evidence the burglars might have left?"

Digger thought for a moment. "How 'bout this? Call the chief and ask him if it's okay to prepare for the tenants. If he says yes, then it's clearly not a crime scene anymore and the PD has relinquished jurisdiction over the site. In such case, I, not being on any official business, and being a sailing buddy of the Hartson family, could certainly visit as a friend. Call my house number 2-2-8-7. You can leave a message on a recorder. My dad has one of those fancy new things called an answering machine."

"Yeah, I've heard of them. Okay, I'll call 2-2-8-7." Holly gave him a lingering hug. The DEW alarms started going off again in Digger's mind. He softly disengaged and thanked her again.

As he descended the circular stairway, he asked, "Do you think you can handle this sliding door?"

Holly beamed. "It won't be a problem, sweetie. We got it."

As Digger descended in the elevator to the first floor, he thought, *I gotta get outta here.* When he shut the wooden outer door of the elevator on the first floor, he was in pitch darkness. He opened the door again to cast enough light in the hall so he could find a light switch and exit without tripping over some museum piece. The light switch was a shiny brass panel containing two round black push-buttons in an over-under arrangement. The "on" button was marked by an inlay of white mother-of-pearl. Digger depressed the button. *Fancy.* The front hall was bathed in light. Digger took a moment to look at the murals again. He scanned back and forth between the schooner painting and the Dog Island Light painting. He approached them and looked closely. He lightly touched the bright areas. *That's real gold leaf paint… huh, these guys had money to burn.*

CHAPTER 21

KRISTY RIGGINS DAY

Digger walked down Ocean Avenue from his house perched high on the rocks. He passed St. Peter's Point on his left. The beach roses were beginning to bud, and the elm trees had small, pale green leaves signaling they were just reviving from the coast's harsh winter. Digger inhaled the salty ocean air. He loved this stretch of the coastline from the Brigantine Hotel to Whitten Point. His mother, Meredith Davenport, often claimed that, while she had traveled all around the world, there was nothing else comparable to the beauty of this small piece of landscape.

As he walked towards Government Wharf, he started recognizing friends everywhere he looked. He stopped at the quaint little cottage on the corner. Paula and Steve Hast were, as usual, on the porch.

"Hey Digger, welcome back! Coffee is on," Paula called out. "Steve's custom blend. Can you join us?"

Digger looked at his watch. "Hey Paula, sure! It's not Steve's laced concoction, is it?"

Paula wrinkled her pretty face that defied aging "No silly, but it's a special Kona blend from our cruise to Hawaii."

"Oh, too bad. Do you have a traveler? I want to make this event down at the wharf," he said, pointing to the crowd that was starting to gather at the river's edge. Steve came out on the porch carrying a large paper cup with a lid.

"No cream. No sugar. Just jet black, cop coffee!" He handed the brew to Digger, who grabbed it with a grin and shook Steve's hand.

"How was your winter, brother? Oh wait, I know how your winter was… Fiji? Or was it Bago Bago?"

"Close," Steve chuckled. "It was actually Bora Bora. It was nice, but Paula and I like the Mediterranean better."

"Did we hear you sailed through that storm a few days ago?" Paula asked, sipping her coffee.

"Who did you hear that from?"

"Oh, I was picking up a prescription from Ruge at the Pharmacy."

Digger rolled his eyes. "That guy has his ear to the ground, wow! But yeah, scary stuff. Say, you coming to this thing?" Digger nodded toward the wharf.

Steve shrugged his shoulders and gave a look as if to say, *why?* He nodded toward their cute porch. "We're already here in the front row."

"Thanks for the joe, I gotta get closer," Digger said as he headed for the crowd.

Steve called out, "Don't forget, Manhattans on the beach at five!" Steve pointed to the pebble beach on the banks of the Talbot River. Digger gave him a thumbs-up and could see Paula rolling her eyes over Steve's suggestion. Digger chuckled at Paula's good-natured concern for her man.

Digger surveyed the staging area for the ceremony. There was Kristy, already up on the stage, huddled next to Mayor Bobby Schwarz. They were attempting to free a package from its bubble wrap. Chief Nickerson was there talking with some town selectmen. The high school band was playing "Battle Hymn of the Republic." *Nothing like music to get the emotions stirring*, Digger thought. The crowd was of a respectable size and started to sing the familiar tune spontaneously.

Digger positioned himself at the back of the crowd. He could see Tracy Thomas from First Responder News with her cameraman, looking sharp. She waved at him and he gave a thumbs up. After the band finished playing, the mayor nodded toward Pastor Joe of the local Baptist church. Joe walked up to the microphone and, dispensing with any niceties, jumped right in.

"Would you please bow your heads and pray with me. Eternal Father, strong to save, whose arm does bind the restless wave, who bids the mighty ocean deep, its own appointed limits keep; O hear us when we cry to thee for those in peril on the sea." Joe paused. "We thank you for the heroism of your servant Tina and ask your continued protection upon her as she surfs and for your favor at home and at school. Bless also, Miss Riggins, in whose name this award is given. Watch over and protect her in her seafaring duties this summer. Finally, Lord, we pray for our town and the people herein. May we always be a beacon of light on a hill for the visitors, the residents, and the seafarers. In Jesus' name we pray. A-men"

Digger noted the distinctive "A-men," not the Episcopal "Ah -men," and thought, *You gotta love those Baptists… they don't get mealy-mouthed about in whose name they're praying.*

Mayor Schwarz stepped up. "Thank you, Pastor Joe, and welcome to you all. Today we remember just a short time ago that we rewarded Kristy Riggins for tremendous acts of bravery right out there." The mayor pointed toward the mouth of the river behind him. "Last summer, her heroic actions resulted in two of our EMTs' lives being saved. This is worthy of pausing and thanking her; but we also want to take this opportunity to recognize that there are heroes like her all around us. The town felt it befitting to set time aside each year to honor such bravery in her name and spirit. Today we recognize such a person. To confer the first ever Kristy Riggins Award, I invite Dean Morehouse of Port Surf to present the medal." As the tall man with a shock of blond hair and requisite surfer's tan approached the podium, the crowd whooped and hollered enthusiastically.

"Thank you, Port Talbot…" As the aging surfer began his speech, Digger scanned the crowd looking for a dog. *After all, it was all about saving a dog's life*, he thought. *Where's the dog?* His mind continued to wander. *Hmm. Maybe the owner's embarrassed for throwing the ball in the ocean in subzero weather and stayed home. Makes sense. I'd probably stay home too.*

The presenter continued, "… It is for these reasons that Tina, at only fifteen years of age, deserves this honor. Kristy Riggins will place the medal around Tina's neck and Mayor Schwarz will present Tina with a gift as a thank-you for her public service. Tina Horner and Kristy Riggins, would you step forward, please?" There was applause as Kristy draped the award around the honoree's neck. Kristy shook Tina's hand and stepped back into her place on the stage.

The mayor then stepped forward with an item that he carefully unwrapped and presented to the young surfer girl. It was a cut crystal statue of a curling wave with a surfer riding the curl. The mayor held the heavy item high and leaned over to the microphone to read the inscription:

Thank you, Tina Horner for your bravery. From the grateful Town of Port Talbot, Maine, June 6, 1980, KRD. The mayor added, "K-R-D stands for Kristy Riggins Day." He looked over to Kristy. "We had to shorten something. Kristy, hope you don't mind." There were chuckles in the crowd as Kristy gave the mayor a thumbs-up, followed by applause. He added, "K-R-D now puts this day on the same ranking as V Day, or D-Day!" There was a smattering of more applause, though considerably less than before. Some of the military veterans in the crowd looked annoyed.

The mayor walked over to Tina and Kristy. He whispered first to Tina, "Would you like to say anything?" She nervously shook her head *no*. Then, he looked to Kristy. "Any words?"

Kristy said, "Thank you, I do have just a couple."

The mayor leaned into the microphone. "Please welcome Kristy Riggins from Roger Williams College and first mate on the *Performer* schooner, which is the beautiful boat docked behind us." Digger's stomach tightened, for no apparent reason.

Kristy stepped up. "Thank you, Port Talbot, for this warm reception and for continuing such a great honor in my name. I ask myself how did I get here? And I really think I am much like any of you. If you see a need, you step up. I just want to say to the mayor and the selectmen that honestly, this annual celebration need not continue in my name. I release you all to rename it, so it recognizes the potential for heroism within us all…" She quipped with a cute smile, "Maybe it will save on printing costs!" The crowd cheered.

"Finally, I want to recognize an event that occurred just a few days ago. Perhaps you have read about the sinking of the *Windsor Star* and the horrible loss of life." Kristy paused, visibly composing herself. "I was supposed to be on that tall ship, but instead, I am here today standing in front of applauding people on a sunny day." The crowd gasped. Kristy teared up, her voice choked with emotion. "Part of the bravery we celebrate today is… is facing tragedy and moving forward in life with vigor despite the loss of our dear loved ones. That's bravery. We must value the fragility of life and know that we must carry on for those who are gone. There are risks to living. Prepare yourself for them and resolve to carry on for the loved one you lose. Don't hole up with a hardened heart. It's okay to be vulnerable. You will heal faster. Captain Coltrane of the *Windsor Star* was my friend. I knew his wife and ch… children. And I… I… would like to remember those who lived life fully on… the… *Windsor…*"

Kristy looked over at Pastor Joe through a flood of tears. "Pastor Joe, could you help me here?" Joe came bounding to the podium. Her whisper was caught on the mic. "Could you pray or something for the souls lost on the *Windsor Star*, many of whom were Tina's age?" Kristy handed Joe a small crumpled piece of paper. "These are their names." Her shoulders shook with sobs, and Joe had a ready handkerchief for her.

As Joe positioned himself at the podium and put on his reading glasses, Kristy dabbed at her eyes and started to retreat. Joe snapped a glance her way and reached for her.

"Oh no, sister, you got to help me up here." He brought her under his arm and his broad shoulder. He composed his thoughts for a few seconds before looking over at the band. "Do you know the Navy Hymn?" The bandleader gave a thumbs-up. "Can you play it softly while I read these names?" The bandleader gave a vigorous nod and gave the band some instructions. Joe said, "I'll read these names, the band will finish playing, and we'll observe a moment of silence, after which we'll have the dismissal by Mayor Schwarz." The bandleader held his baton suspended in air, waiting for the pastor to nod and begin. "These are the souls who lost their lives: Captain Charles Coltrane, Mrs. Victoria Mason Coltrane, Thomas Coltrane, John Paul Coltrane, Sally Coltrane…" As he read out the names, the band accompanied him quietly. The trumpeter stood off from the rest of the musicians and played a solo with a mute covering the bell of the horn. Then he stepped back into ranks and the rest of the band melded movingly into the remaining verses.

There wasn't a dry eye in the crowd.

"Please join me in remembering these people by observing a moment of silence," said Joe. As silence overcame the crowd, the sound of lobster boats plying their trade punctuated the moment with far-off signal horns and laboring diesel engines. As if on cue, a seagull capped the moment with a piercing yet mournful cry.

After a few moments, Joe's soft voice returned. "Concerning death, Jesus said this: *I am the resurrection and the life. He who believes in Me, though he may die, he shall live. And whoever lives and believes in Me shall never die.* Heavenly Father, accept these souls into your eternal kingdom and comfort those who remain behind. In Jesus' name I pray. A-men." The microphone inadvertently picked up the resolute "ah-men" from Kristy.

As the mayor returned to the podium he saw Tina signaling him. She was looking at someone in the back of the crowd.

"Can I say something before we go, Mr. Mayor, sir?"

"Of course, kid, this is all about you." The mayor reached for her hand and brought her back to the podium. "Ladies and gentlemen, please indulge us a moment longer to hear from the lady of the hour. Please welcome Tina Horner, sophomore at Port Talbot High." The crowd was happy to climb out of the emotional low and offered robust applause even as some were still wiping away tears.

"I have been really touched here today and I have something to say. I'll try to get right to it 'cause you have been standing here a long time. I mean, my legs are killing me!" There were giggles in the crowd. "Please forgive me. I don't know how to speak in front of a crowd so this may get awkward. I can stand up and ride an eight-foot wave on a sixty-inch piece of wood in forty-degree water... but standing up *here* is downright scary."

Someone yelled, "You're doing great!" and there was sustained applause.

"I have something I need to say but I would be out of order if I didn't thank you all on this podium for recognizing me today. So, thank you all." There was applause as she looked at the mayor and the selectmen. Then like a pro, she pointed to Pastor Joe and the band. "And I'd like to give a special thanks to you, Ms. Riggins." Tina looked back at the selectmen. "Please don't ever change the name of this award. She earned it all over again with what she just shared today. We need her name on this day because she shows us what we should *try* to be. And she is so darn pretty!" The crowd erupted with whistles and applause.

"I have something else I'd like to share with you about that day on the beach this past winter. I have to tell you, it is a little embarrassing being honored for giving mouth-to-mouth to a dog!" More laughter. "But then again, as my dad said, it's not much different than kissing some of the boys who are brave enough to come to my house." Raucous hoots of laughter mixed with sustained applause.

"I got to know Baxter the dog that day in 38-degree water," Tina continued. "He was lifeless and I brought him to shore and performed CPR through his adorable snout and he came to life. What should be a positive story has a dark side to it. You see, Baxter is all about a ball and will chase it to the ends of the earth. Well, that day, Bax had been retrieving the ball for his owner on the sand and for a moment the owner went to his car to get a bag to pick up after his dog. Don't we wish everybody did that? Anyway, the owner comes back from the car and he sees his dog looking in the surf for the ball. which was still on the beach. The water was 38 degrees with awesome waves. Poor Bax went into distress and the owner went in to save him. I watched the scene and saw the owner get overpowered by a wave and I, in my winter wetsuit, actually caught a miracle wave over to them and dragged the dog onto the beach with the owner following me. I closed Baxter's mouth and put my mouth over his nostrils and blew air into his lungs. The owner, soaking wet in freezing air, started crying when Baxter started to stir."

"Here is my point. This was an accident with a dog who is just crazy about chasing and finding a ball, but this owner has received nothing but criticism from the community. That's why I had to speak. If you see him or know him, please cut him a break. The owner was the first one to rescue this dog from the pound. Since I have been visiting the owner and his dog, I have witnessed nothing but love for Baxter. The owner is now my friend and I know he doesn't want any attention, but please, forgive him, okay?" The crowd applauded vigorously.

"Thank you, Mayor Schwarz, sir." Tina stepped back to stand next to Kristy. The mayor complimented the up-and-coming youth like Tina, indicating the future was in good hands, and dismissed the crowd. The band played more patriotic tunes as the crowd dispersed.

As Digger moved toward the stage, a familiar female voice to his right called out, "Hey, Digger! There you are!" Digger instinctively smiled as he turned to see who was calling him. His smile slowly waned at the sight of Holly Hartson, looking perky and dressed in pink.

"Hey, Holly! You made it!"

Holly gave him a little hug. "Gosh, what a ceremony! It was so moving! That Kristy girl stole the show, didn't she?"

Digger had to respond by putting it out there… right up front. "Yeah, Kristy is awesome. We've been dating for about a year and she constantly amazes me. Would you like to meet her? I'm headed to her now."

Holly's face registered a slight dismay but she gamely replied, "No, you go congratulate her. I'll say hello to some friends here and if there's a chance to meet her in a few minutes, I'd love to. Say, I spoke to Chief Nickerson this morning. Uncle Jon's house is not a restricted site. I can clean it. Do you want to go over before I do?"

Digger thought for a moment. "Can you give me a few days? I got to run to Placid for the weekend. I can probably come over on Monday morning. Would that work?"

She put her hand up for a platonic high-five and added, "That'd be great!" They parted with Digger thinking as he walked to the stage, *Thank God. She gave me some space. She's classy.*

That evening Kristy and Digger spent a cozy night at home at Seaside. Digger explained his plans for going to his winter home in Lake Placid and attending the reunion at the Whitney School. Kristy again declined to participate in his skullduggery to find his real parents. She planned to board the *Performer* in the morning for another summer as the first mate on the training schooner for rich kids who needed to grow up. Before going up to bed, Kristy asked, "Who was that girl at the ceremony today who gave you a hug?"

"You mean Tracy Thomas?" Digger didn't want to get into the whole Hartson thing.

"No, I mean the brunette in pink. I don't think I know her."

"Oh, her. She's one of the Hartson girls. I took sailing classes with them at the Talbot Yacht Club when I was a kid. The whole family is going through a tough time right now."

"Oh no... not another curse thing!" said Kristy, referring to last summer's escapades with Timothy Kerr.

"No, the Hartson family's oceanfront land is getting taxed out the wazoo by the town and they're having to sell everything."

Kristy didn't look very sympathetic. "She's cute," was all she said as she headed up the stairs to the guest bedroom.

CHAPTER 22

THE FAMILY REUNION

Digger left for Lake Placid early the next morning, enjoying the beautiful drive through the mountains of New Hampshire. When he reached Shoreham he boarded the Fort Ticonderoga Ferry that connected Vermont and New York across Lake Champlain. From there it was only another hour and a half drive up the Northway to Digger's family home on Humdinger Hill, just off the famed Mirror Lake Drive that skirted the lake.

He saw that their neighbor, Ed Gillis, had the lights on in his sugarhouse. *That's odd... sugaring is done by now. Then again, Ed is a quirky guy.* When Digger was younger he had worked on the Gillis' maple farm collecting sap the old-fashioned way: in tin buckets hanging from taps hammered into the trees. Digger would have to walk a bucket or two at a time down from the woods known as the sugarbush to a collecting tank, dump the watery contents, and re-cover the tank. Walking through two feet of snow carrying heavy metal buckets was not easy. The students from the nearby Whitney School would often trek and cross-country ski through the sugarbush and if thirsty, simply drink from the pails attached to the trees. Digger had helped Mr. Gillis lay out the new method of sap collection, which involved a web of flexible tubing that went from tree to tree. This system relied on gravity to bring the sap down to the collecting tank, which was then piped directly to the sugarhouse. There, the sap was boiled for hours to reduce 40 gallons of sap down to a single gallon of syrup. It seemed hardly worth it to Digger until he saw the prices the syrup was fetching.

Gillis kept a pellet gun handy and when he heard a snowmobile whining in the woods, he'd tear off like he was saving sheep from a wolf pack. The snowmobilers would cruise right through the sugarbush, snapping the sap collection tubes without a backward glance. Gillis had always talked about setting up barbed wire around the tubes to cause the snowmobiler's injury, but he never did nor did he ever fire a pellet at them, to Digger's knowledge.

"Hi, Mom!" Digger said cheerfully as he entered the huge Adirondack-style home. A chandelier of interwoven antlers and lights hanging in the center of the great room was stunning, and was balanced by a cobblestone fireplace that rose two stories high. Attached to the opposite wall was the winning four-man bobsled from the 1932 Lake Placid Olympics.

"Digger! Darling! You survived! We were so worried about you in that horrible storm last week!" His mother hugged him extra hard and extra-long.

"Aw, Mom, it was nothing. Some big swells for sure."

"Don't you downplay it to me, young man. It sank at least one tall ship and some other boats according to the *Times* and the *Boston Globe!*"

"Do you have those articles, Mom? I'd love to see them."

"Yes, of course. They're around here somewhere… in your father's office, I think. So you have come back for the seventy-fifth anniversary at Whitney? Why, you just left for Maine. We didn't expect to see you until we headed over on the fifteenth." Digger's parents always liked to wait until a couple of weeks after Memorial Day just to make sure. Even Southern Maine was known to have cold snaps all the way into the middle of June.

"Yeah, some friends are there from the upper classes celebrating their fifth reunion and I wanted to see them. Seventy-five years is a big event for my alma mater. It should be fun!"

"Of course, Digger. We're glad to have you home, son! We haven't seen you since the Olympics in February. Wasn't that hockey game against the Russians unbelievable?"

"Yeah, Mom, a miracle."

"Well, they're already making a movie starring Karl Malden. I saw him on Main Street last week. He really is a nice man."

"I look forward to seeing it. Hey, Mom, I have to change for the kickoff ceremonies at the club. Is Dad around?"

Meredith Davenport looked at her watch and shook her head. "No, honey, he should be home shortly." Before Digger turned away, his mother stood on her toes and gave him another kiss. His height in comparison to his mother's triggered a thought about his genetics. The Davenports were both tall, which is where Digger had always thought he had gotten his height. Maybe tonight he would see that this was just an odd coincidence.

"Okay, I'll see him later tonight if I get back at a reasonable time." Digger headed for his bedroom. There in his cedar-paneled room with bay windows that overlooked the woods, he turned to his built-in bookcase filled with classic books from his high school days, as well as his yearbooks. He scanned the spines until he found what he was looking for. *There it is.* Digger grabbed his heavy criminology textbook from his first year in college. He turned quickly to the chapter "Nurture versus Nature" and began speed-reading through the pages. *There it was. High School Dropouts Correlated to Increased Incarceration.* He skimmed the text, muttering to himself. *Strain Theory... blocking of an individuals' goals... leads to deviant behavior... American dream thwarted can cause one to pursue criminality....* He read on a bit more about the theory. *Okay, that's hogwash, Let's see if my old guidance counselor and English teacher, Herr Klaus Phillips, can help me demonstrate it. Hopefully, I don't need this ruse and Cissy and Hutch just show up... if that's their real names.* He slammed the book shut and got dressed for the Whitney School's cocktail reception.

On his way out of the house, he stopped by the den, which doubled as his father's office, and grabbed the portable Dictaphone his dad used for recording patient notes. Mrs. Davenport walked in as Digger was fumbling to insert a new tape into the machine. Digger looked up nervously and asked, "Hey, do you think Dad would mind me borrowing this? I'm working on a school project and want to interview some professors."

She furrowed her brow. "Over the summer? You're doing college work?"

"Yeah," he lied. "It's an independent study on teen crime. I was hoping that being able to interview a bunch of high school teachers all available at one time would allow me to get some great insight quickly."

His mother shrugged her shoulders. "I'm sure it's okay. I use the thing to record bird songs. We get such a beautiful array of birds at the feeder." She nodded toward the window. "Boy, you are a determined young man. I'm so proud of you."

He pocketed the gizmo and went to hug his mom. "Thanks, Mom. I should be back after dinner. I doubt this crowd is the partying type."

"Are you kidding? This *is* the Whitney School, after all. The Nit-Whits are legendary. How soon you forget."

"True… don't wait up in that case." Digger laughed.

He pulled into a parking spot behind the club by the tennis courts. Digger preferred to go in through the service entrance and scope the scene from afar. Having grown up in Placid and gone to the club when his family had a membership, he knew the property inside out. He had classmates who had worked here and probably still did. He was aware that a few years earlier, the resort had stopped being an exclusionary club, as it had been since the early 1900s. It was founded by Melvil Dewey, the man famous for the Dewey Decimal System used in libraries.

In Lake Placid, Dewey had become infamous, since his exclusionary policies and quirky exploits made him somewhat of a rebel. He was known for wanting to reform the spelling of English words and tried some of his suggestions at the club. Thus, an Adirondack lodge became a "loj." The club's menus in 1926 were titled, "Simpler Spelin" and offered entrees like "Hadok, Poted beef with noodls, parsli or masht potato, butr, and steamed rys." He changed the spelling of his first name by dropping the L and E at the end and had even floated spelling his last name "Dui."

As awareness of Dewey's inappropriate conduct and the unfair rules of club membership began to percolate in the minds of subsequent generations in the mid-1970s, Digger's father had cancelled the family's membership. The club also saw a general decline in memberships as the wealthy expanded the scope of their vacation plans via tourist travel by plane.

As he searched for the banquet room where the reception was being held, he noted with sarcasm, *Boy, this place is going to rack and ruin. It's doing its best to survive.* He heard the tinkling of glass and ice and the din of conversation coming from the Marcy Room. He slipped into the room through the service door and observed things from a distance. Digger identified old man Klaus Phillips immediately. *Man, has he aged.* Digger noticed that his former teacher, who was of slight frame and balding with wire-rimmed glasses, was holding himself up with a cane in one hand and holding a cocktail in the other. *Geez. I'm the youngest one here.* Then he spotted his old buddy, Fitzy, who must have made the trip from New Jersey.

He walked over and greeted his former classmate with their signature salutation. "Yo, Fitzy!"

Fitzy spun around from the bar. "Oh, thank God. Someone under fifty! Digger dude, how are you, man?" They hugged and as they did, Fitzy patted Digger down. "You packing, officer?"

Digger assumed a karate position. "These hands are registered weapons… back off, Superfly! I'm always packing."

Fitzy glanced around hopefully. "Any chicks here?"

"Fitzy, I thought you were as good as married, man. What happened to Prudence?"

Fitzy sighed, "C'mon, you knew that wouldn't last. We were so different. She was a granola mountain girl. I'm a Jersey boy. We were the odd couple."

"Pru was awesome, man!" Digger lamented.

"Yeah well, you're too late, Digger dude. She's engaged to a forester she met at the Syracuse School of Forestry."

Digger's eyes lit up. "He'd be called a Stumpy at *that* school."

"Yeah, I know what they call those jerks." Fitzy looked around, scoping the place out.

"So, let me get this straight, you got dumpied for a stumpy?" Digger couldn't resist teasing his old pal.

"Very funny, dapper dork. It's time to get schtumpied!" He drained his cocktail and beelined over to a group of girls who looked like they were still at Whitney. Digger turned to the bartender and ordered a Labatt 50 ale.

"La-bo five-oh please." While he waited for his beer, Dr. Doxsee, the headmaster, came alongside Digger.

"Officer Davenport! Thank you for coming. It's great to have some of the more recent grads. How have you been down there in New York City?"

"Evening, Dr. Doxsee. Great to be here again. Thanks for putting on the party. New York has been a great experience. I miss L.P. and Whitney for sure." The headmaster looked at the bartender.

"Dewar's, two cubes, please." Digger couldn't be sure Doxsee had heard a word he said. The headmaster seemed more focused on the dispensing and delivery of his scotch whiskey. Digger silently watched Doxsee focus intently on the drink as the bartender held it an extra second before releasing it into the old man's slightly quivering hand. As Doxsee took his ceremonial first sip, Digger pivoted, pretending to wave at someone.

"Excuse me, Doctor." Doxsee simply nodded and took another haul on his drink. Digger felt that watching him any longer would be akin to being a peeping Tom under a neighbor's bedroom window. The headmaster needed privacy with his love.

As Digger headed to rescue Fitzy, he walked by some older alums and overheard someone say, "Remember Hutch's room? He was the original beatnik, man. Right?" Heads nodded. Digger froze and pretended to pick something up off the floor and then tie his loafer as he continued to eavesdrop.

"Hutch always wore the black jeans, ankle boots and that faded checkered shirt, remember that?"

"It was like a uniform," another alum added. "I swear he wore John Lennon wire rim shades before Lennon did. Say, has anyone heard from him? Is he coming?" A third commented, "Oakland is a long way to go for a high school reunion."

"Do you think Cissy's gonna show?" asked another.

"Oh, wouldn't that be some fireworks, seeing those two together after all these years?" said the first man.

Digger's knees weakened as he walked toward an exit door. His mind was reeling. *What are the chances? I've heard enough. My real father was a beatnik? Great! I have antisocial, riffraff genes. Fireworks?*

Fitzy stepped in front of him. "Digger dude, you okay? You look like you've seen a ghost."

"Excuse me, Fitzy, I'll be back in a sec." Digger ditched the drink and drifted out the back door to the tennis courts. He leaned over, taking some deep breaths, then kept walking down the trails toward the golf course. He needed to be alone. He was lost in his thoughts until the most gorgeous sunset found him. The sun was disappearing behind the Adirondack peaks. The grandeur shook him from his trance. All he could utter was, "God, this is beautiful… am I doing the right thing here, Lord?"

Digger heard a twig snap behind him. He spun around. An attractive woman wearing a tea length floral dress with a shawl wrapped around her shoulders was walking barefoot toward him. She was carrying a pair of high heels in one hand. The setting sun bathed her in a luminescent glow. Her fine long brown hair gently lifted on the wind. As she approached, Digger guessed she was around 35 to 40 years old.

Digger spoke first. "Hello, did you know this was the best place to catch the sunset in Lake Placid, too?" Digger twisted to point at the sun over his shoulder. The woman smiled and didn't answer, but kept walking, or rather gliding, toward him. She looked familiar but he couldn't place her. She wore no makeup. She didn't need it with her beautiful blue eyes and perfectly proportioned facial features. Her calm but robust smile revealed even white teeth.

"David?" the captivating woman inquired as she extended her right hand as a greeting. "I'm Priscilla Traub. My friends and family call me Cissy."

Digger received her hand, dumbstruck as he connected the dots. Though his stomach had started to twist into a knot, he responded evenly, "Do I call you Cissy as a friend? Or, do I call you Cissy as family?"

She kept holding his hand firmly and looked deeply into his eyes. "You call me Cissy as family."

Tears welled up in Digger's eyes as he pulled his hand away. He spun around to look at the last vestiges of the sunset. "You sure I don't call you mother?"

Cissy pulled even with his shoulders to watch the sun sink below the mountains. "I'm sure…" Digger heard a sniffle but didn't look at her. She added, "There's no better mother than Meredith Davenport." Cissy dabbed her eyes with her shawl. Her lack of mascara really paid off in the moment. Digger wiped away his own tears with the sleeve of his blazer.

He faced her profile as she gazed toward the waning light. "So you are my real mother… is that right?"

"Yes, I'm your *birth* mother and I am ready to answer any questions you may have. The answers may be embarrassing to me and difficult to explain, but I'll do my best."

Digger thought for a moment as he continued to look at her profile and began to speak. Cissy turned to face him squarely. She was distractingly beautiful. "Uh… uh well… How did you know to come here, to this place, at this time?"

Cissy smiled. "When I decided to come to the anniversary in Lake Placid, because it's also my twentieth reunion, I knew I might meet you here because we are both alums. Your mother has given me pictures of you through the years, as we had agreed to an open adoption. Moments ago, just as I was about to enter the Marcy Room, I recognized you speaking to Doxsee. I stayed out of the room and observed. Then you bolted out here and I followed."

Digger had a sudden, strange compassion overwhelm him. This was his real mother thinking, speaking, smiling. He was flooded with emotions and thoughts. He paused and she paused. Then Digger began slowly, "The first thing I want to say is… thank you. Thank you for bringing me into the world." He looked around at his surroundings. "I'm really enjoying this beautiful world." Digger turned around slowly, pointing toward the woods, the sky and the mountains. His gratitude slayed Cissy. She hunched over and began weeping. Digger hesitantly put a gentle arm around her heaving shoulders and whispered again, "Thank you for giving me life."

Cissy reached around to hug Digger and sobbed uncontrollably. "Thank you for being so kind and understanding. You are a fine young gentleman." Digger hugged her tightly as she whispered between sobs, "I'm sorry you had to have this weird and confusing part of your life story. I made a mistake with a boy when I was very young, but God has turned the shame, pain, and practical difficulty of being a teen mother into a beautiful result… a handsome young man ready to help shape this world. Please forgive me for creating this conflict and pain in your life."

Digger gently pushed her a little away from himself so he could look in her eyes. "Hey, I want you to know that I completely forgive you… now and forever. I forgive you now and forever," he repeated more emphatically, "… for any and all negative ramifications or effects this so-called mistake has caused me in my life. You are forgiven. Period." Cissy wept and they just held each other until her tears began to subside.

Digger whispered, "I have to thank you for another thing." He paused so his birth mother could compose herself and receive what he was about to say. She backed away from her son and wiped her face with her shawl, looking up at his gentle smile. "I have to thank you for giving me such great genes. You are so darned pretty!"

Cissy hadn't expected this and couldn't help but laugh. "Thank you, but you actually sound like your birth father. He was suave and so kind and complimentary. I'm sure that's what led to the mi… mi… the miracle of you."

"Please, tell me about my birth dad. It was freaky. Just after talking with Doxsee in there, I heard these guys talking about a guy named Hutch."

Cissy confessed, "I watched you linger by my classmates listening, and then you bolted for the door. I wondered if something had been said. I knew I had to follow you here."

"They said he's a beatnik. Is that true?" Digger asked with a slight frown.

"He certainly was back then," Cissy answered with a touch of amusement. "Now, Henry or Hutch, is an artist out in Oakland. He has his own gallery. He never married. He's completely immersed in his painting. I heard through the grapevine that he probably won't make it this weekend, but I don't communicate with him. I haven't in almost twenty years. As for me, I married a good man; a doctor. Rod and I have a twelve-year-old son and a daughter who just turned sixteen. We're living in Greenwich, Connecticut. Rod knows all about you, but my children don't... yet. I hope you can meet them some day."

"Cissy, I'm happy to hear that you have such a stable life. When I learned last summer that I was adopted, I envisioned some scary scenarios." Digger looked at his watch. The light was fading fast. He paused, "Say, assuming we head back into the party, how do I refer to you if we're talking and being introduced? Are you just a friend? A distant cousin... a fellow alum? I don't want to let you go! I want to spend more time with you. I'm afraid it might appear that we are more than fellow alums." Digger threaded his arm through hers and helped her walk on the path of pine needles in the twilight.

Cissy thought about this as they walked arm in arm. "I have an idea. If you want to know God's honest truth, I have been praying for you since you were born. That makes me like a godmother, and you like my godson. Will that work for you or is that too hokey?"

"It's perfect, Cissy. It fits. You *are* my godmother and we are having our own twentieth family reunion!" Cissy, from whom Digger decidedly did *not* get his height, stood on tiptoe to kiss her son lightly on the cheek, for the first time in twenty years.

CHAPTER 23

THE CHOIRBOY

Meredith Davenport, relieved to finally have things now out in the open, had invited Cissy to join them Sunday at St. Eustace Episcopal Church and for brunch after at the house with the rector and his wife. Digger and Cissy knelt side by side as they took communion. Departing the church, Digger introduced Cissy to the rector as his "godmother." The rector greeted her warmly. He had been instrumental in arranging the adoption twenty years ago and was pleased to hear the new title that Cissy had assumed.

As the Davenport's live-in maid, Isabelle, served the guests eggs Benedict with asparagus and her signature cheese grits, the rector enjoyed regaling Cissy with the story of Digger when he was in second grade and part of the church's men and boys choir. He described how the whole choir took a weekend trip to sing at the World's Fair in Montreal, known as Expo 67.

"Digger, do you want to tell it or shall I, because it is going to be told!" said Reverend Cooper.

"Why don't you tell it, Pastor, that way I still have a layer of deniability."

"Okay, so approximately fifty men and boys head off to Montreal to sing at the World's Fair. It was a tremendous honor because Queen Elizabeth was attending. I negotiated a deal with the Nuns' Island Seminary to allow the whole team to sleep on cots in their dining hall. So, the boys go to sleep with their uniforms folded neatly along with their pair of black shoes placed in an orderly fashion under their cots. After a long while the men retire to the same large room and get ready for bed in the same orderly fashion. They all thought the boys were fast asleep, which most of them were." He looked with mock sternness at Digger.

"Unbeknownst to anyone, a mischievous boy gets up while everyone else is sleeping and re-arranges all the black shoes. Come morning, while everyone is dressing for the performance, utter mayhem breaks out. Nobody had the right shoes! Someone starts calling out sizes and fights break out as people try to figure out which shoes are theirs. Finally, the men and boys get shoes that sort of fit, but are not necessarily their own and they go to the concert and perform. After the concert, some free time is built for rides and in the afternoon everyone, some limping from foot pain, have to line up to take the monorail back to the seminary and board the bus to return to Lake Placid." The rector paused. "Digger, do you want to take it from here?"

Digger smiled. "Well, all I remember was that we were lined up two by two, and we were waiting forever for this fancy train to arrive. I, being so tired from the night before, stood against a pillar in the metro station and promptly fell asleep on my feet." The table guests started to giggle. "When I awoke the metro station was empty. I started wandering the station alone. I was around six or seven years old." Cissy was wide-eyed, with her hand over her gaping mouth. Digger paused for a sip of his shandygaff.

Mrs. Cooper burst out, "Don't torture us, Digger. What happened?"

Digger loved tweaking the guests. "Well, not too long after, I saw a policeman dressed like an English bobby and flagged him down and told him my predicament. He brought me to a lost-and-found play area that actually had a couple of kids in it. I started playing with Legos or something and watched tearful parents pick up their kids. After a while, the room emptied and I was alone. I don't know how long it was, but eventually, the good rector here showed up, raising his hands to the heavens either in happiness or calling down a rain of fire. As we walked back to the train, he asked me what happened. You want to take it from here, Pastor?"

"I asked the exhausted child, who was so cute in his little blue blazer emblazoned with the Choir's crest and still wearing his matching tie, what had happened," said Cooper. "He told me that he fell asleep on his feet. Then it dawned on me. I asked him casually if he had been up late. He said 'Yes' then quickly said, 'I mean no.' I looked him in the eye and said, 'You were working diligently late last night, weren't you?' His face was priceless. It said, *guilty as sin*'! I don't think the shoes ever got fully sorted out."

115

Dr. Davenport raised his glass. "I'd like to propose a toast to our rector, who never told us this story until many, many years later. To a reverend with discretion. To Jack Cooper!"

The minister shrugged it off after all had sipped in his honor. "It's nothing unusual. We call it the priest-penitent privilege. It's a sacrosanct bond between the confessor and priest."

"Uh, I confess to nothing!" said Digger. "I will admit, however, that I had no problem with *my* shoes that morning." The guests erupted with laughter.

After the pastor and his wife left, Digger hugged his dad. "See you in Maine, Pops!"

"Goodbye, son. It'd be nice if the house is still standing when we get there, please."

"Of course, Dad. The Bike Cop isn't throwing any wild parties. It would make my job more difficult. I want a peaceful summer." Digger then said an emotional goodbye to his mothers, plural. He and Cissy walked to his car and they promised to see each other again soon.

"I'd like, sometime, to have you meet my family," Cissy said as she hugged him one last time.

"No more secrets," Digger said softly. "When you're ready."

As he headed to Port Talbot, he thought about what had just happened. It was stunning, actually. He felt very good about who he was and about who his birth mother had turned out to be. She was awesome really, he thought, a warm feeling filling his heart. He recalled how he parted, telling both mothers how much he loved them for their brave roles in supporting his life. As he drove his jeep down the road headed for Maine, there were four pairs of eyes flowing with tears. With a few mountains and many miles under his wheels, he resolved, in due time, to meet his real father, the *artiste*.

CHAPTER 24

An Inside Job

Digger was happy to be back at his house in Maine. Seaside was his favorite place on earth and his true home. The variety of seascapes shaped by weather, seasons, and celestial positions was as manifold as the different faces of humanity. Digger would often zone out just watching the crashing waves from the solarium. He loved the early season before his parents arrived, as it was the only time he could blast his music freely and go wild. On Sunday afternoon, a week after he had returned from Lake Placid, he cranked up Stanley Clarke's *School Days* album. As the legendary jazz fusion bassist was spanking the guitar with an infectious upbeat, Digger juked and jived his way into his father's study. The little red light was blinking on the answering machine. Digger hit a button and heard Holly's voice.

"Digger, old friend, I hope you'll be able to come to Royal Orchard on Monday morning. We can take the horses down to Uncle Jon's house and check things out. Please let me know if that works for you and I'll have Gaston and Lady saddled and ready to go."

Digger hesitated slightly before calling Holly back to let her know he was coming.

"Hey, it sounds like you're having a party over there, Digger, and I wasn't invited. I'm bummed!"

"No, Holly. No party. I just like blasting the music when I'm here by myself. I open the windows and let the ocean and wind mix with the musical mood of the moment."

"By what I can hear, you are in a jamming good mood!"

"Yes, a little funky jazz. Say, I am psyched to take the horses for a walk tomorrow morning at what, nine?"

"Yes. nine is perfect. We'll be riding the beasts, so wear jeans, okay, cowboy? You up for that?"

"Sure, Holly, I'll give it my best. I haven't ridden in a while, but I'll try not to humiliate myself. This will be very special. Thank you." She laughed and clicked the phone in his ear. *She's kind of flirtatious,* Digger realized. *Better watch it,* he warned himself. *Let's not mix business with pleasure.* He pictured not Holly, but Kristy, as he went back to rocking out, but suddenly he wasn't in the mood anymore. Digger left his dad's office rubbing his forehead. His juke and jive got nuked and dived. He turned down the music. *What am I doing? Riding horses on a beach with Holly and checking out a crime scene ex officio.* He looked in the hallway mirror framed by a hand-painted scene of lobsters crawling into cute wooden traps. *It's what you do, Davenport. It's the edge.* He walked away from the mirror and muttered out loud, "Not the edge, again…"

* * *

When Digger arrived at Royal Orchard in the morning, he looked toward the barn and saw two horses, one black and one white, saddled and tied to the fence. The beasts' ears rotated and pointed his way as soon as they spotted him. They were already communicating. Digger grabbed his backpack from the back of the jeep. He hopped onto the porch and used the brass coat-of-arms knocker. Holly was quick to open the huge door. She was wearing an English-style riding uniform complete with a black velvet helmet from which a tight, thick braid of dark hair looped over her shoulder and dangled down the front of her blue riding blazer. She thrust a second helmet at Digger.

"Perfect timing! Here you go, Billy Shoemaker, wear this. You'll be on Lady. I'll ride Gaston. He can be particular about visitors and I don't need him copping an attitude with you. Lady, however, is as her name implies, a lovely lady."

As they approached the barn, a woman in her forties came out with a pair of crops in her hand.

"Miss Holly, will you need these?" she asked in a southern accent.

Holly looked at Digger, who shrugged his shoulders.

"No thanks, Annabelle. We're just taking a mosey down to the beach."

"Lady has a western saddle for the gentleman. Gaston has your English show saddle," Annabelle said, pointing to the horses.

Digger reached out to shake Annabelle's hand. "Digger Davenport. Nice to meet you, Miss Annabelle. Thanks for your help today."

"The plezha is all mine, suh." Annabelle nodded deferentially.

Holly mounted Gaston in one smooth move. Digger was still climbing, hopping and dragging as Lady started moving, leaving him momentarily hanging from the horse's side. Annabelle intervened and grabbed Lady's reins just behind the bit.

"Hold on, girl," she said firmly to the beautiful white horse. Lady rocked her head in the air as if to say *lay off*. Annabelle held firmly until Digger was in position in the saddle. Annabelle patted Lady's forehead. "Good goober! Have fun, you two."

Holly was waiting out by Hartson's Beach Road, the tree-lined road that led to the beach. Digger kicked Lady into a canter in an effort to catch up to Holly.

"I guess you do know how to ride, Mr. Davenport! Nice gait. I haven't seen Lady canter in a long time. Let's just walk them on the road. They're both barefoot. The darn farrier is so expensive, but Annabelle does a great job keeping the horses tuned."

"Has Annabelle been with the family for a while? I can remember, years ago, that there was a boy our age that always hung out in the barn."

"The boy was Richard Eaton. His dad worked here until he got ill and passed on. The son didn't want to stay. It wasn't the right fit. They called him Ricky. He was the valedictorian for his class at Talbot High, and now I think he's pre-med at St. Francis College. He lives in the woods over there on a parcel of Hartson land given to their family."

"Sounds like a nice setup for the young man."

Holly picked up the pace when the road turned to gravel down by the beach. "Who knows? I don't see them or go down their driveway. It could be a scene from *Deliverance*, for all I know."

* * *

Down on the beach, it was clear the horses loved the packed sand. It was firm but comparatively soft for them.

"These babies want to run!" Digger called out.

Holly rode over toward Digger. "Family folklore is that the first

Jonathan and the first Ted Hartson raced their horses to Crescent Point. The first to reach the rocks won the point itself."

"Let me guess. Jonathan won?"

"You're brilliant. By the way, Jonathan the fourth said we're free to enter the house and do whatever we need to do to find the jerk, or jerks that did this." Holly's eyes flashed and she blurted out, "Last one to the rocks buys lunch! Gaston, ha!" And she was off.

"C'mon, Lady Luck!" Digger yelled. "Let's beat that big bad boy! C'mon! Ha!" Digger assessed the angle of the beach just as Jonathan had done in his race against his brother Ted, 120 years earlier.

The beach hadn't changed much since the Civil War era. There were still areas of sand that looked packed and hard but, when tested, allowed a rider to sink four inches down in soft aerated sand. Holly and Gaston hit such a patch as Digger cut toward the water. Digger tried assuming a jockey position for the quarter-mile race but the horn of the western saddle made that impossible. He looked over at Gaston and Holly and saw the soft sand flying under Gaston's feet. It was a whole lot of activity but not much speed. Digger backed Lady off and swung higher up on the beach to intersect with Holly's trajectory. Sure enough, Holly came on strong after getting through the soft sand and was neck and neck with Digger and Lady.

"Now!" Holly yelled, and Gaston started pulling away.

Digger judged that the rocks were coming up too soon to push his Lady. He conceded the race and complimented his horse. "We had 'em, girl, down by the water. Good job, Lady!" He let her slow down to a jog as he patted her neck and encouraged the hard-working horse.

Holly was circling on Gaston by the rocks. "You had me down by the water! Gaston and I got bogged down back there!"

"Holly, you won that fair and square. Gaston has some afterburners. That was thrilling to see him add another burst like that." They kept the horses circling a bit to cool them down.

"Let's walk them up through here for a few minutes and then we can tie them up at Jon's where there's a water trough."

As they approached the shingled mansion, Digger marveled at its size. "This is bigger than the rectory at St. Peter's Point."

"I think Uncle Jon said it's 6,000 square feet, not including the garage apartment."

Digger whistled, "That's got to be hard to heat."

"There is no heat. It's not winterized," Holly said.

When they had watered the horses and tied them to branches of the scrub pines, Digger slipped off his backpack and pulled out a Leica 35-millimeter camera and a pair of doctor's rubber gloves. "Do you mind if I take some pics while I am here?" he asked as he pointed the fancy gizmo at his wrist and took a photo of his own watch.

"Go ahead, Digger. Maybe you want me to stay outside?"

"No, you can help me. Let's walk around a bit." Digger wrestled the tight latex gloves on. "What is this driveway material, shell?"

"Yes, Uncle Jon has shell delivered and, of course, harvests the beach too as a little hobby."

Digger continued surveying the area. "So, there are two roads in here, correct? But they all culminate in this loop here?"

"Correct."

Digger continued, "If you come down Hartson's Beach Road, you drive by Royal Orchard and then a few houses on the beach, Right? Any of them occupied now?"

Holly thought for a moment. "The Barclays are here year-round in that newish-looking cedar home."

Digger nodded.

"And then that home right there." Holly pointed through the grove of scrub pines. "We have a distant cousin there year-round. I think the cops spoke to both families."

Digger pointed to the second entrance to the beach from the southwest. "How about coming from there?"

"There are three houses that have year-round residents and they are very observant regarding cars going down there."

Digger walked to the west side of the house, which faced another expansive, desolate beach bordered by seagrass and woods on the right. He looked down the beach toward its end at Little River, which was a favorite place for kids to ride the outgoing tide, warmed in the estuary.

"What's beyond Little River, again?"

"Well, that hill right there and the yellow barn is another seaside farm which sold, also because of taxes. They say it's abandoned. The town is going to try to resurrect it as a park."

Digger used his telephoto lens to scan the far hillside. "Let's go down on that beach a second." Digger walked toward the crude stairway built from large ocean rocks. "Did the police come down here when they came out to investigate?"

"No, they stayed up here at the house," Holly said.

"Good. Let's go over here." Digger avoided the stairs and walked along the seawall, looking down. He jumped into the sand. Holly followed suit. He came back toward the stairway and turned back toward Holly. "We're looking for anything weird. A fresh cigarette butt, a shiny thing that dropped from the thief's pocket, a fresh footprint. Stuff like that."

"Got it," Holly confirmed in a serious tone.

"When we were on the widow's walk at Royal Orchard that night, it was a full moon, correct?" Holly nodded. "Okay," Digger said. "So we had moon tide, but after that we haven't had really high tides, have we?"

Holly shrugged. "I don't think so."

"Tell me, these stone steps... does the tide ever come up to them?" Digger approached the steps slowly.

"Not that I can remember. Maybe in a moon tide."

Digger got down on his hands and knees and crawled to the steps. Pausing for a moment, he then started taking close-ups of the stone steps. Looking back toward Little River, he asked, "At its lowest level, how deep is Little River, at dead low?"

"Geez, Digger, I'm not sure. Sometimes it spreads across the beach pretty shallow at the mouth there where it meets the ocean." Holly pointed to the west. "But I would always say it is knee-deep. Why?"

"Because these sand impressions in the stairs look like the tread of a wader boot." Holly got on her hands and knees next to Digger to take a look. He got a whiff of her perfume. "You see those three half-inch bars of sand there? And then again the next step up?"

"I do!"

Digger took another photo. "Right foot...left foot..."

"How do you know which direction the person is going?" Holly asked.

"The size of the step, and the fact that the print is the front of the boot, and the fact that it's sand. Coming down from the driveway, there wouldn't be this much sand in the tread."

Holly had to ask. "Why do you say it's a wader boot?"

"Because I have boots like this. It has three distinctive bars of tread under the ball of the foot, but who knows, honestly. We just gather theories.

I like the fact that these steps are in an alcove out of the wind. This could be a good clue."

Digger stood up and started walking toward Little River. He verbalized his thought process out loud. "If so, the intruder could have walked in this soft sand and arced toward the hard sand to get traction on his way back and vice versa on his approach." Holly stayed by the stairs and watched Digger veer up into the soft sand and then come back toward her with his head down, scanning left and right. He spied something and pulled his backpack around to his front, pulling out a plastic bag. He picked up a cigarette butt.

"It's pretty fresh and it's not the chief's!" Digger said, smiling. "I think it's a Marlboro menthol. Those are kinda unique!" Holly looked like she was wondering if Digger was a little crazy or if he was a genius. She sat on the seawall and waited patiently.

"Let's take a quick look at the ocean approach from the east." Digger climbed the seawall, avoiding the stairs. He offered Holly a hand up. As he lifted her toward him, her inertia brought her squarely into Digger's broad, muscular chest.

She looked up into his eyes and said, "Oops. Thank you."

Digger released Holly's hand and backed up a step. "If I were a smart robber, I would avoid driving here. I'd come from the beach on foot with a backpack." Digger walked toward the part of the seawall that overlooked where they had ridden on the horses. "You see, if the perpetrator came from that direction, he would have had to have walked in front of those houses there; but if he came from Little River, he would've been completely out of sight. Let's go with that theory for a moment." Digger began to circle the large home. Holly literally followed in Digger's footsteps as they rounded the last corner of the house closest to the desolate beach and the stone stairway. Digger looked at the large angled metal box situated next to the exterior wall of the house.

"Do you know what this metal box is?"

Holly replied, "All I know is that it leads to the basement."

"Correct. It's called a Bilco door." Digger thought for a moment. "Can you access the basement from the house?"

"Not really. Only by a trapdoor in the pantry."

"Okay, good. Did the police go through these Bilco doors?"

"No, they went up on the front porch where the door was broken open."

Digger dropped to his knees by the Bilco doors. "No one used these doors to your knowledge?"

"Nope."

Digger took a photo of the Bilco door, stood up and said, "Okay, let's go in." Holly seemed to be relieved. She didn't appear to have the patience needed for this work. As Digger approached the front porch, he asked Holly to stay off the porch for a moment. He climbed onto the porch using the far-left side, taking three steps at a time. As he photographed the spray of shattered glass on the deck of the porch, he also took a shot of the exterior handle that had traces of white powder from police fingerprinting activity. Digger pushed the door open slowly. It glided freely inward. On the floor behind the open door, he noticed a small amount of glass in a perfect line caused by the inward sweep of the door. He took a photo of the glass and the inside knob. He motioned to Holly to join him. She tiptoed up the steps and came into the large foyer. Digger closed the door slowly and examined the frame where the window had been.

"Were any other doors broken?" he asked.

"No, just this one."

Digger pulled another pair of gloves from his backpack. "Doctor? You better get used to these things in your profession."

"Yes, indeed," Holly said, accepting the gloves. "We wear them in the lab all the time." She put them on with a snap and a smile.

"Can you bring me to the pantry, please?" Digger was working out a theory as they walked through the dining room, which was littered with broken chinaware and slashed paintings. Holly didn't have to point out the giant holes in the walls. Digger ignored the mess and followed her through the grand kitchen into a room containing shelves and wainscoted walls in a dark brown natural wood.

"I love these cottages. The wainscoting is so cool." Digger had stopped at the threshold to the pantry and turned on the light. He reached in his backpack for his flashlight and flicked a beam on the floor. "Where's the trapdoor to the basement?"

Holly, still on tiptoes, came close to Digger and put one hand on his back to steady herself. She pointed with her other hand. "You see that hole over there? That's where it is. You use the hole for your finger to pull up on the door."

Digger flashed his light in the direction of the door and walked in slowly. "Is the door on a hinge or does it just come out?"

"It just comes out."

He knelt and pulled a flash kit for his camera from his backpack and muttered, "Of course it does…"

"What do you see?"

Digger pointed at fresh scratches in the floor. "These are fresh impressions." He took some pics. "Okay. Let's go back to the front hall."

"Don't you want to see the other parts of the house?" Holly offered.

"Yes, I do, but let's review some things and see how it helps us piece together what's going on here."

As he walked slowly through the dining room, he stopped at the curio cabinet that had been smashed. He reached and grabbed a silver saltshaker and turned it upside down. "Tiffany…sterling silver…nice, small piece." In the front hall he had Holly's undivided attention. "What was taken again?"

"All I could tell was that the antique logbook and a telegraph machine, one of the first in the country, were taken from the library upstairs."

Digger had been about to speak, but paused to think. "I should look at the rest of the house before saying anything."

"Aw c'mon, give me something, Digger!"

"Be patient, Holly. I don't want to launch the wrong theory. Show me the library, please."

A huge oil painting of the original Jonathan Hartson still hung on the stairway, but the canvas had been slashed from the upper right corner to the lower left. Digger snapped a photo and muttered, "Left-handed."

In the library, the built-in oak bookcases had been emptied. Beautiful cloth- and leather-bound books were strewn everywhere. Every painting had been removed from the wall and smashed. Holly brought Digger to the side table next to the picture window that looked out to sea.

"The logbook sat in this brass book stand and the telegraph was right next to it."

Digger took a photo. He looked out to sea for a moment. "Boy, you get a great view of Dog Island from here, don't you?"

Holly was picking up books and putting them back in the bookcase. She seemed to be tiring of the sleuthing. "Yeah, you do," she answered half-heartedly. "Do you mind if I put these books back on the shelves? I gotta start somewhere before the renters come."

Digger took a picture of the books covering the floor. "Sure, you can put 'em back. Can you point me to your uncle's study and the master bedroom? I'll check them out, then I'll help you with the books."

Digger saw the drawers of the desk strewn on the floor and the file cabinet tipped over. He looked at the files on the floor. They appeared to be titled with names of companies and investment funds. He leafed through a few more. *Hmm… prospectuses and balance sheets of various companies.* He took some photos of the study and the holes in the wall before entering the master bedroom, which was also in shambles. He slid the mattress off the box spring, which had been slashed open. His camera shutter clicked.

Digger returned to the library and saw that Holly had made a lot of headway. She had picked up and re-shelved most of the books. He couldn't help but notice a large compass inlaid into the center of the floor that had previously been covered by the books. "Wow, that's cool. The compass must be eight feet in diameter!"

Holly was stacking the books with her back to Digger. "Yeah, it was built into the floor when the house was built. Uncle John says the coat of arms is real gold."

"What coat of arms?" Digger asked.

Holly spun around and walked over to the compass. "The Hartson coat of arms was inlaid right here! You can see it's been gouged out. Right here!" Holly fumed, "Now that was valuable, if it was truly gold." She quickly ran out of steam. "I had my doubts," she sighed as she returned glumly to the bookcases. "Add that to the list."

Digger kept looking at the compass inlay. He walked around it and pointed in the directions indicated on the compass. "This thing is weird. It's off, like way off."

"That sounds like the Hartson family in general, weird and way off," Holly shot back.

Digger ignored her comment, "So, you know how on a compass on a map the symbol for north is up and it's usually the biggest symbol… like a large N?"

Holly responded hesitantly, "Yes…but I'm not the sailor of the family, remember?"

"Well the symbol for north isn't even marked. Actual north is that way." Digger was in the center of the compass pointing away from the ocean. He spun 180 degrees. "This is south," he said, pointing out to the ocean. He then rotated slightly to align with the scarred flooring where the coat of arms had been the most prominent feature of the compass, and pointed out the window. "This is southeast."

Holly watched Digger spin around in the compass. As he was looking down and pointing in the direction that the missing coat of arms indicated, she said, "Digger, look up. You're pointing at Dog Island."

Digger squinted as he looked out the window. "You're right! That's not so weird, Miss Hartson. Don't rag on the family too harshly."

"Whatever! I need a cleaning team for this house. I'll never get it done on time. I'm gonna call Jon and get him to hire someone. This is too much. Maybe Anabelle can help."

"What does the coat of arms look like again?"

Holly pointed to a wall. "It looks like that. Agnes calls it a bunch of horny deer." Digger went over to the wall and examined the symbol, and then stepped back into the center of the compass mapped in the floor.

Digger and Holly were tuning each other out as they focused on what mattered to their respective interests. Digger placed a white sheet of paper on the floor where the crest had been inlaid.

"Holly, could you pull the curtain back as I take a shot of Dog Island with the compass in the foreground?" She complied without a word and held the curtain open like a model turning letters on a popular game show. Digger thought she looked sharp in her riding attire *sans* blazer. "Okay, I am almost done. I'm gonna run to the basement, okay?"

"Sure, Digger, I'll see what I can do in my uncle's office. I'll meet you downstairs in a few minutes."

Digger went outside and opened the Bilco doors. He noticed sandy tracks on the wood steps leading down into the basement. The lock on the bulkhead door at the base of the stairs had been forced open. He took a picture, and walked into the basement, where a sledgehammer lay on the floor. He flicked on his flashlight and scoped out the half-finished basement. Most of the area was rock ledge and pillars. Only a room the size of a single-bay garage was walled off and had contained a worktable. Digger went over to where the trapdoor was. An upside-down metal garbage can was directly under the trapdoor. There was a slight residue of sand on the base of the can. Digger took photos and continued to look around. *Either this guy was very angry or he was looking for something.* Digger took photos of the walls with smashed holes spaced uniformly every six feet. *This is not rage.* Digger heard Holly walking overhead. He climbed out the Bilco doors and went to the front hall as Holly came around the corner.

"So, what's the prognosis, Doctor Davenport?"

Digger looked down and began to pace. "First a few questions, Miss Hartson, and think carefully before answering as I am a cop and, come what may, it may impact the Hartson family"

"Stop it, Digger. You're scaring me! Why would the Hartsons be at risk? We were robbed for gosh sakes… but go ahead, ask away, copper!"

Digger smiled. "I'm just alerting you to possible weird turns in theories as to what happened here. Let me ask you, what is the case against your uncle about? You mentioned something about the SEC the other night."

"He's being accused of insider trading on news concerning some mining company in Brazil. Don't tell me Uncle Jon did this to his own house! That's ridiculous."

"Holly, give me a minute. This appears to be an inside job done by someone angry and looking for something specific. Come to the front porch. Did the police say this was where they broke in?"

Holly looked like she was copping an attitude. She had her arms folded on her chest and spoke with her head at an angle. "Yes. That's why they dusted the door for prints. Don't you see that white stuff?"

"Yes," Digger said quietly. "This door was the exit door, not the entrance. It was smashed from the inside out. Had the police wanted to dust the door properly, they should've dusted the inside knob. If the attack had come from the outside, which it didn't, the assailant would've reached in like this." Digger demonstrated how a smash-and-enter would have more likely played out. "The doorknob that should've been dusted is on the inside because, I believe, the robber smashed the window as part of his exit and actually used this doorknob. May I continue?"

Holly's stance was softening. "Yes, please, Digger. I'm sorry I got upset."

Digger nodded and plowed ahead. "It has the makings of an inside job. That is, someone with superior knowledge of the home did this. The entry was through the Bilco doors and up through the pantry. If you go down cellar there you'll see a garbage can upside down under the trapdoor. One would have to know that the trapdoor was there. One would've had to move a can into place to climb in. That's why there's sand on the can and more going down the Bilco stairs. This broken glass on the front porch was for show only, in an attempt to divert us."

Digger took a long breath and continued, "Next, this was not a robbery in the strict sense. This person was looking for something or trying to make it look as if he were looking for something. The walls were smashed uniformly behind where paintings were hung, and in the basement, holes were smashed in the cement blocks every six feet. It was a systematic search. If it were a smash-and-dash robbery, the curio cabinet in the dining room would've been emptied of its silver. The items taken, except for the family crest, are pound-for-pound stupid things to steal. Things that can't be sold or traded easily."

Digger concluded, "Finally, the person who did this hates your family. Take the painting in the main stairwell. It was removed, then slashed, then replaced on the hook. Either that, or a ten-foot ladder was brought up the stairwell, but I don't think so. I think it was someone venting against the family. You see it elsewhere. Like in the master bedroom. If you're robbing or merely looking for something, why smash a wedding picture? Or throw a family picture in the toilet? Someone's gotta be connected to your family somehow to do something like that, or, I suppose they could be a wild vandal, but I don't think so. They're pissed off."

Holly visibly shuddered at the thought.

"At first, it made me think that maybe your Uncle Jon was building a defense for his SEC problem, so he could cite missing records due to a robbery." Digger put up his fingers to form quote marks around the word "robbery." "But the senseless destruction of family heirlooms doesn't fit, nor the extent of the search. Someone was really looking for something and that kind of rules out Uncle Jon. It has me settling on an insider and that usually means a family member or a contractor-type who has a real bone to pick. Maybe a cousin got ripped off or something. That's the best I got. I'm done."

Holly had been listening intently with her head down while she paced in a circle in the front hall of Crescent Point. She lifted her head. "If you're right, and I do think you're onto something, I bet the Dartmouth heist is related. Maybe there's more to Hartson family history than meets the eye…or meets *my* eye."

Digger cautioned Holly, "The SEC suit is also a wild card. For all we know, there could be powerful corporate interests at play. Some of those corporations play for keeps. Please be careful, Holly. Whoever it is, is strong and angry." Digger paused to think. "I'm not sure of the play with your uncle. He could be in on something, but I doubt it. Maybe you start with your father and get some history or, better yet, check the county court and probate records and see what they show before you get your dad and uncle in the middle of it."

They mounted the horses and returned to Royal Orchard. The horses were literally chomping at the bit to get home for some oats. Digger asked for a raincheck on the lunch he owed Holly for losing the horse race. He left Holly and headed to the photo shop to turn in a roll of film to be developed. He had maxed out the roll with 36 shots. Because it would take a week before the photos were ready to be picked up, he wanted to get them in as soon as possible.

CHAPTER 25
SMELT IT, DEALT IT

That same Monday morning, while Digger and Holly were riding horses on the beach, Rick Eaton, just a mile away in the woods, had locked himself into his garage. He started a wood fire in the stove to provide cover for the anticipated odor of the operation. He unzipped his backpack and pulled out the ten-inch gold coat of arms. Samson watched with curiosity. Rick placed the gold ornament in the jaws of the vise bolted to the workbench and cranked down tightly. Next, he placed a black iron skillet on the floor under the vise. He plugged in his Sawzall with the hacksaw blade, then cut through the coat of arms like a hot knife through butter. He cut the artwork into multiple chunks that fell to the floor. Most of the gold dust fell into the skillet, which he put on the woodstove.

Firing up the propane torch, Rick began melting the gold in the skillet, one piece at a time. He put the yellow flame tip of his propane torch directly on each piece of gold. Once a piece broke down its form and could not be recognized as an antler or a deer head, Rick would let it cool. He knocked each finished chunk out onto the table and set to work on the next one. He put all the gnarly nuggets into a soft purple Crown Royal bag and pulled the golden drawstrings tightly shut. He turned the dampers closed on the wood stove and left the garage. He threw the bag into his car, and went into the trailer.

"Brenda, I'll be back in a few hours. We'll go out for dinner tonight, if all goes well."

Brenda responded from the bedroom. "Whatever!"

Rick pivoted and headed for his newly painted Mustang. *She's too much.*

Rick headed in the direction of a Boston jewelry buyer with a Russian name.

* * *

After Digger left Holly at the barn of Royal Orchard, she approached Annabelle, who was washing down the horses.

"Say Annabelle, Davenport and I had a chance to walk through Crescent Point..."

"Oh yeah, any leads?"

Holly nodded her head in disbelief. "I'll tell you what... that guy is unbelievable. It's freaky. In fifteen minutes, he had figured out where the person came from and, in an hour, a profile and a motive. I'm actually pretty scared... to be honest with you." A tear fell down Holly's cheek.

Annabelle stopped sponging down Lady, wiped her hands and came over to Holly. She put her hand on Holly's shoulder. "Calm down now, dear. What did the officer say?"

"He said it's someone who hates our family and is looking for something." Holly started to cry. "He... he... said they were strong and... and maybe tied to... like corporate thugs!" Holly's expression was distraught, and she shook as she sobbed. She couldn't hold it back.

Anabelle patted her on the shoulder. "Don't you worry, child. Let me show you." Annabelle walked confidently into the tack room and came out moments later wearing a shoulder holster with a white pearl-handled pistol the size of a small cannon. If that wasn't enough, in her hands was a Winchester "Repeater" rifle. Annabelle assumed a stance like Chuck Connors' in the TV series *The Rifleman*. She cocked and swung the rifle around, ready to mow down anything that moved. "Miss Holly, we are ready!"

Holly covered her gaping mouth with both hands. Her eyes were wide as saucers.

Annabelle pulled a spinning stunt and the rifle ended up under her armpit with the barrel pointing safely at the ground. "What do you say I move into the guestroom in the big house?" Annabelle asked.

Holly slowly and carefully inched toward the heavily armed woman. "Annabelle, I am so glad you're here. I have no idea when Mom or Dad is coming back. It's you and me protecting Royal Orchard. Are you up for this?"

Anabelle smiled. "Missy, I'm from West Virginia. I was born for this!"

"Okay then, yes, please move into the guestroom." Holly looked at her watch. "I have to go to the county clerk's office. I'll be back in an hour or two. Please don't scare friends who might visit, but also, be prepared."

"Yes, ma'am. You got it. Tomorrow we start you on some target practice!"

Holly rolled her eyes as she headed for the house to change into an outfit more appropriate to sweet-talk the court clerk into letting her access the old court records.

* * *

Rick Eaton returned to the trailer around six p.m. He had a bounce in his step. Literally. The trailer flexed as he walked.

"What're you so happy about?" asked Brenda as she crocheted a yellow baby bootie. Rick reached into a brown bag and put a banded stack of hundred-dollar bills in the middle of her knitting.

"That's just for you. Hide it away. Nurse it like you're gonna nurse our baby."

Brenda beamed. "It's all mine?" She jumped up, giddy with delight and started hopping up and down. A mirror fell off the wall of the shuddering trailer and smashed as it hit the floor.

Rick looked at the mess. "Who cares? We'll get another mirror. A better mirror!" He reached his hand into the brown bag and pulled out several more stacks of banded hundred-dollar bills and held them up like a victory medal.

Brenda's eyes widened. "Ricky, where'd you get that?"

Rick put the money back in the bag and set it down. He then assumed a rock star pose with an air guitar in hand and commenced singing a Lynyrd Skynyrd song. "Ask me no questions… and I won't tell you no lies. Don't ask me about my business… and I won't tell you goodbye!" Rick skittered up and down the trailer as he repeated the refrain and swung his guitar-picking hand in large circular motions.

Brenda rolled her eyes and conceded. "Okay, Ricky Van Zandt. Take *us* to the Wharf for dinner, Mr. Rock Star." Brenda rubbed her belly in a reference to the other person joining them for dinner. The Talbot Wharf was a favorite restaurant of the locals. That evening they had the specialty of the house, baked stuffed lobster. The secret ingredient wasn't so secret; it was hunks of haddock embedded in the stuffing.

CHAPTER 26

By Hook, Crook, and Logbook

Once back at home, Brenda rolled into bed, fully satiated. Rick was buzzing with the whiskey coursing through his veins. After taking Samson for a walk on the trails through the woods, Rick climbed up to his research laboratory in the garage. He hid the rest of the money he had "made" by selling five pounds of pure gold at five hundred dollars per troy ounce or $36,000. As he tucked the banded stacks in the eaves of the garage, he muttered to himself. "Now we have legal fees. We can convert this operation to a legitimate litigation-fest, if needed."

He sat down and opened the *Vigilant* logbook and started perusing the thick yellow pages covered in neat handwriting. He backed up to page one and read:

The Launch of Vigilant, May 14, 1859, Port Talbot, Maine

Fair skies and 62 degrees. Reverend Bidwell, Henry Hartson and Agnes Hartson climbed the launch pulpit and waved to a crowd of about one hundred onlookers including those who built the eighty-foot schooner as well as family and town officials. Rev. Bidwell...

Rick reached for his cigarettes and lit one up, exhaling as he looked back at the log. "Blah, blah, blah!" Then Rick erupted into a song by Chaka Khan and Rufus, "Tell me something good! Wat wat! Tell me something good!" He started flipping through the pages. "Here we go!" He spied the word *Savannah* and started reading.

Savannah Georgia, Sunday, January 20,1861
Jonathan Hartson, Captain
Tom Lincoln, First Mate and Log-Keeper

Cargo Report:17.5 tonnes; load completed yesterday. Inspected and taxed today. Building materials include: Milled Georgia Heart of Pine........ 2.5 Tonnes (18) 20' X 6"; Southern Yellow Brick 14 Tonnes (708 bricks); Milled Cotton Bales 1 tonne.

Draught: 10' fully loaded at waterline.

Crew: Samuel Saltus, 2nd Mate; Geo Walker, Able Seaman and steward; Kurt Thomas, Ordinary Seaman

Destination: Port Talbot, Maine

Course: East by Northeast; Lv on outgoing tide, sail port tack to Tybee Island; broad reach on trade winds North.

Narrative: Captain and crew attended Sabbath services at Christ Church and returned to a crowd of friends of the captain. A band played as locals showered captain and crew with baskets of foodstuffs and liqueurs. Vigilant cast off from Bay Street docks at high noon to catch falling tide. Uneventful exodus from challenging Savannah River. Union naval presence at Tybee Islands. Captain ordered the raising of the Massachusetts maritime ensign (pine tree flag) as Maine has not yet adopted an ensign.

Wednesday, January 23, 1861
Course: North

Narrative: Sunny skies 14 knot winds out of the SE. Crew working well together. Captain setting sails with seamen. Generally positive outlook of crew. Gained extra knots north of Charleston by staying in Ben Franklin's ocean river.

Thursday January 24, 1861
Course: Northwest

Snow squall engulfed ship. Rigging frozen before able to reef sails. Working jib lost. Captain ordered it cut away. Wind gusting to 40 knots. Course change for Cape May, NJ. Anchored in Cape May Sound. Naval Marine patrol boarded Vigilant and inspected cargo. Captain convinced naval personnel that cotton was not benefitting southern interests and was in fact in support of contracts to supply Union war preparations. Hartson name and Dartmouth connection meant more than paperwork. Naval personnel disembarked without incident.

Rick thumbed forward a few pages.

Monday, February 4, 1861
Course: Down East
Weather: 45 degrees f, Wind 8 kn, NE, Clear

Tacked into Dog Island. Brought Vigilant into the wind. Captain ordered three canon reports toward Royal Orchard. Family waved flags from widow's walk at Royal Orchard. The canon reports caused wild dogs to scatter on the island. Crew members' requests to fire the musketoons at the wild dogs were denied by the captain. Captain brought vessel to wind and headed directly to Government Wharf. Greeted at dock with much fanfare of family and friends. Off-loaded cotton into covered wagons bound for Biddeford mill. Captain Jonathan Hartson relinquished his office to Theodore Hartson and became Lieutenant Commander. Captain Theodore Hartson dismissed all crew except for LC Hartson, First Mate Lincoln, and Sarah Hartson, whom he welcomed aboard. Miss Hartson notified the captain that she received a telegraphic transmission saying that the southern states had formed a government earlier today in Alabama. It called itself the Confederate States of America. The limited crew used outgoing tide and north wind to leave Port Talbot and sail directly for Dog Island with an anchorage off Hartson's Beach. Set anchors at bow and stern. Hartson family were rowed to Royal Orchard in lifeboat. First Mate returned with lifeboat and remained aboard Vigilant to keep watch.

Rick lit a cigarette and rocked back in the secretarial chair. *So, Sarah Hartson is the telegrapher,* he thought to himself as he looked at the freshly acquired antique machine and the ticker tapes draped over the nail in his attic war room. He made a note on a pad: *Translate telegraph messages.* He rolled his chair over to the photos of the family members and examined the photo of Sarah. *Aren't you just the grande dame, honey?* He rolled back to the logbook and read the entry for February 4, 1861 again and thought. *Why not leave the schooner at the wharf? Why is Tombo staying on the boat in the middle of winter off Hartson's Beach?* Rick kept reading.

Tuesday, February 5, 1861 8 a.m.
38 degrees f, Wind 4 kn, NE, Sunny
Mid tide falling

Captain Ted Hartson arrived in punt from Royal Orchard with Jonathan and Sarah and provisions for three days at the island. Orders given to make way to Dog Island and reestablish livable quarters at the Life Saving Station on the island and commence siting of Dog Island Lighthouse in accordance with engineered plans provided by the captain and specifications issued by U.S Revenue Department. Rear grapnel anchor lifted. All hands at capstan to lift bow anchor. It would not budge. We could not lift anchor. Captain ordered the raising of the mainsail. This caused the boat to start to move which dislodged the admiralty anchor. All hands then operated the capstan in the bow to lift the anchor. It was weighed and secured as ship made headway. Sarah was at the wheel during the anchor operation. Crew added sail and set course for Dog Island.

Island is a mile long and a quarter mile at its widest. Surveying from Vigilant revealed a pond partially covered in ice. Hilly and forested terrain on the western side. Except for seabirds, no other signs of life. Structures on island seem intact. Anchor set when Vigilant was in the lee of the island and out of the wind. Surf was only at one foot. Landing rails on island seem intact and low tide afforded thorough examination of the rails and the ability to square up on the rails that run up the rocky shore to small boathouse.

Landing party and provisions assembled in the punt and rowed to the rails. Timed its stroke to meet the crest of the swell. Ted at rudder and Jonathan and I pulling on the oars. Sarah at lookout in the bow. Swell successfully brought boat up the rails. All hands disembarked. Boat was attached to a block and tackle and hauled into the boathouse with the various provisions. Ted distributed pistols in case of wild dog attack.

Party crossed windswept lawn between boathouse and the saving station quarters. Door was unlocked, party entered and inspected the five-room shelter. I started fire in the main room. Sarah set up kitchen. Ted cleared table in dining room for laying out of building plans. Ted explained that brick would be offloaded to the boathouse and timbers to the drying racks on south side of boathouse. Ted outlined the fortification of boathouse as first priority then establishment of signal light and flagpole for communication with Royal Orchard. Sarah added righting of the outhouse as top priority. Captain acceded to the request.

By 3 p.m. the boathouse was cleared. Bay door and back door secured with iron hasps and locks. Hinges re-bolted from inside. The rails were greased with sperm oil and bear grease. Jonathan and Ted returned to Vigilant to get first load of [there were two words crossed out] *materials to shore.*

By sunset, first load was secured in boathouse. Then a howl was heard from the east end of the island. Sarah in trepidation of wild dogs requested to stay in the Captain's quarters on Vigilant. Discussion ensued. First mate dispatched to accompany Sarah safely back to ship to keep watch. From Vigilant, howling was heard through the night. Several pistol shots rang out through the night as well. Howling reached a fevered pitch in response to shots. The new signal light in the second story of the saving station's window was tested. Rudimentary communication occurred between Vigilant and Dog Island using Morse code. One word clearly deciphered, WOLFDOGS.

Wednesday, February 6, 1861 8 a.m.
45 degrees f, Wind 6 kn, NE, Sunny
Low to mid tide falling

Sarah and First Mate loaded brick in punt using block and tackle and rowed to rails and boathouse. Greeted by Hartson brothers. Ted had arm in a bandage. He suffered dog attack last night as he retrieved wood for fire. May require medical attention. Party agreed to focus on offloading building materials in order to return to Royal Orchard for medical attention for Captain. Four runs to the boathouse completed the brick (708 bks) delivery. Anchor lifted at 4:30pm. Wolfdogs were seen roaming the lawn and the sniffing the boathouse as Vigilant departed at dusk. Ted was lying down in captain's quarters when Jonathan made the call to sail to Port Talbot Government Wharf. Jonathan ordered a canon report to be sent to Royal Orchard. Request for Sarah to send an SOS light signal to Royal Orchard. We were met at wharf by Agnes Hartson and George Eaton. Eaton rushed Ted to Dr Eastwood's house office. Vigilant secured. Sailing party returned to Royal Orchard.

Rick banged his fist on the table. "Eatons to the rescue…again!" He stood and stretched at the peak of his garage attic hideaway, grabbed his notebook and sat down. He started to reread the log entries for the Dog Island light operation.

"Let me get this straight, Hartson boys..." Rick began to think out loud as he consulted a calendar stapled to the wall. "You sell Hartson LTD on January 19, 1861, the day Georgia secedes from the Union, and the very next day you have a send-off party from Savannah?" He thumbed through the logbook and looked at the entry on the day of departure. "You're not coming back! So where's the currency and the ingots, boys?" He wrote on his notebook under the word *Library Research*: *Southern Yellow Brick weight?*

Rick stood and paced. "You're boarded by union officers in Cape May, New Jersey, and they just object to you carrying cotton? Where's the gold? You should've been busted, you slave traders!" Rick made another note: *Hidden gold in boat?* He kept pacing and thinking aloud. "Then in the middle of winter you decide to unload building materials out on an island? Are you nuts? That's not a job fit for a bilge rat. Bilge...bilge." Ricks eyes widened. He wrote under *Library Research* the words *bilge and ballast removeable.*

Rick looked at the entry for the first arrival at Port Talbot February 5, 1861. "They unload cotton and get rid of the crew and return to sea? To anchor off Royal Orchard? But where's the sister? The virtuous Miss Sarah Hartson? On the boat? Tombo sleeps on the boat." Rick's finger was tracing the lines of cursive writing in the logbook. "The next day they head to Dog Island for three days in February to unload building materials themselves? A job fit only for bilge rats! Are you kidding me?"

Rick kept reading the entries over and over again trying to make sense of things. "This brick is special. Who puts bricks in a building and reinforces the doors. *They* do that because this ain't regular brick!" Rick crowed, holding up the page that had scratched-out words. He looked at the area on the other side of the page and brought a flashlight and a magnifying glass to further investigate. "I believe that used to say *gold ingots*, Mr. First Mate, not just yellow bricks. Thank you, Tombo. Do I read this correctly, Mr. 'Free Man'? And what's more," continued Rick incredulously, "You, Tombo, a freed slave, spent the night on the *Vigilant* alone with Miss Sarah? Scandalous!"

Rick closed the books and tidied up the office as he muttered his resentments. *Next stop: Dog Island. I need a boat with at least a ten-horsepower engine and a trailer. I need a trailer hitch for my pony. I need some doggy-doze tranquilizers. Extra strength!* As Rick climbed down from the attic into the dog's pen area, Samson didn't move from his prone position. He just looked at his master as if to say, "You done for the night, bub?" Rick looked at Samson and asked, "Are you ready to meet some werewolves, Sammy boy? We're gonna go meet your cousins." The dog returned his head to his plush mat and heaved a sigh.

CHAPTER 27

Reporting for Duty

Four days later, on Friday, Digger started his first day of work. It was the usual, getting called on the carpet for investigating cases beyond his authority. The chief shut the office door behind Digger. It wasn't even 9 a. m., and Chief Nickerson was already busting his chops.

"Diggah, my sources tell me that you were out at Crescent Point with the young Holly Hahtson conductin' an investigation." The chief lit up a Camel and squinted at Digger through the blue smoke spiraling up from the tip of his cigarette.

Composing himself, Digger walked over to the window and looked up. "Chief, are you with NASA? Is that satellite yours?" Digger nodded toward the clouds. "The Hartsons and the Davenports go way back. Did you know that my dad was the doctor for Ted Jr.? I sailed with his kids at the yacht club. Am I not able to visit family friends and..."

"Diggah, stop it, okay, Mistah family-friend. What did you find?"

Digger thought momentarily about telling the chief what he did not find, namely Camel cigarette butts, but he declined to be disrespectful toward his boss and played it straight. He reached in his shirt pocket and pulled out a folded-up typed paper.

"Here are my findings. Use 'em as you see fit, or don't use' em. I was just visiting a friend, remember?" He gently placed the paper on the chief's desk and backed up, nervous that he had overplayed his hand. He had too much respect for Chief Nickerson to start the summer off on the wrong foot.

"My bottom line on the Hartsons, Chief, is that someone is looking for something. In my opinion, Jonathan is in deep doo-doo with the SEC and who knows what type of thugs he's dealing with… the burglar or burglars were on a mission, for sure. Did you notice that portrait sliced in the stairway? I mean, someone had to lift it off the wall, slash it, and then return the huge thing back to the wall. That's effort. Not some drug-addicted robber."

"I'll grant you that someone's looking for something," Chief Nickerson affirmed. "Otherwise, why just take the telegraph machine? And a ship's log, and then leave valuables behind?" The chief looked up to the ceiling and thought as he took a drag on his nearly finished cigarette.

"That's not all they took. They pried a gold family crest out of the floor."

"A what?" the chief asked, jerking his head down to meet Digger's gaze.

"Upstairs, buried under the strewn books, was a floor decoration that had an inlaid ornament made of pure gold. The thief wanted it enough to literally gouge it out of the floor, which must have taken considerable effort!"

The chief pointed at the paper in front of him. "Is that in here?" he asked, scanning the notes.

"Yup, it's in there, sir."

"How'd they get there, Diggah?"

"Judging from the estimated time of the break-in and the sand tracks and footprints, it appears they came from Wells across that desolate beach."

The chief thought for a moment. "There's a river though… doesn't make sense."

"Correct sir. That's Little River. It's only knee-high at low tide. Our visitor wore waders, as evidenced by the footprints I photographed, entered the house through the Bilco doors and climbed in through a trapdoor up into the butler's pantry. Did you check the basement?"

The chief stammered, "Uh, no. Is that in your report?"

"Yes, sir." Digger looked at his watch. "Chief, I have to hit the beat. If you need anything further on the report, just ping me on the radio."

"Well now, just hold on, take a seat. The jaywalkers can wait. I want to read this and see if I have any questions." The chief rocked back in his chair and read intently. "You say this appeahs to be an inside job?"

Digger nodded. "Yes, sir. It all adds up. The entry through a completely concealed trapdoor. The making it look like an entrance through the front door rather than an exit, which it obviously was. The approach from the west. The vicious, targeted animus against Jonathan Hartson's portrait. Whoever broke in was connected to this house, to this family… no doubt about it, in my humble opinion."

"Of course!" the chief exclaimed, throwing Digger's notes down on his desk. "You think the Dahtmouth heist is related?"

"Yes sir, I do. I don't know how yet, or why."

"Okay, Diggah. Good work. Am I gonna see an overtime request for riding horses on the beach?"

The young sleuth just smiled and shook his head.

Digger slipped out of the station before Patty arrived. He hopped on his cop-bike, a souped-up Raleigh, and pedaled energetically toward Talbot Square. The summer beat had begun! His first stop was at the small quay by the hardware store. He could lock his bike out of the way and walk around. He ducked into the pharmacy and saw Mr. Ruge in his raised work area in the back of the store. The pharmacist, wearing his standard light blue clinic shirt, waved Digger over as soon as he saw him.

Ruge asked, "Digger, are you okay? That hurricane must have been a real fright!" "Yes, sir. It was a total shocker. How'd you hear about it?" Digger asked.

"Well, I talk to your mom and dad all the time. Your dad called. He had a question about some meds and told me. You're lucky to be alive, son!"

"That's true. I'll tell you what saved my life was that Phenergan… that truly saved my life." Ruge, who was a member of Digger's church, discreetly pointed heavenward and mouthed the word *God*. Digger quickly conceded, "And of course, the good Lord, absolutely!"

The front door jingled, signaling a customer. The two of them looked to see Holly Hartson, looking immaculately casual.

She waved and called out, "Hey, Digger, I gotta talk to you!"

Digger turned to Mr. Ruge. "Duty calls, sir. Please excuse me."

The pharmacist whispered, "Boy, the Hartsons sure could use you. Go get 'em, Digger."

Digger walked over to Holly, who closed in quickly, whispering, "I know who's after us!"

Digger put his finger to his lips and slightly pivoted to see that Mr. Ruge had quietly followed them and was dusting the shelves one row away.

Digger pointed toward Ruge with his eyes and simply responded, "So good to see you, Miss Hartson. Are you done with school?" Digger started walking toward the door.

Holly played along. "I'm here all summer until I head to South America to help the Chuck-Chee Indians improve their water supply. I'm so excited. Say, I'll catch up with you outside in a minute. I have to grab something." Digger exited the pharmacy, rolling his eyes at Holly's obvious whopper to throw Ruge off with a wild rumor. He also wasn't sure he wanted to hear what Holly had to say. He headed toward the coffee shop. It had a back deck that looked over a tidal creek and the other tourist shops snuggled together in that area of Talbot Square.

Holly brought a cup of coffee to Digger, who was giving directions to Brigantine Beach to a young couple with a child in a stroller. The couple thanked Digger and rolled along.

"You fit this job perfectly, Officer Davenport," commended Holly as she handed him the coffee. Digger thanked her as he cracked the lid and smiled at the black coffee. Holly held up a fistful of accoutrements. "Cream and sugar?"

"No, this is perfect, thanks." He led her to the rail and asked what she had found out.

Holly replied, "I found out that the court clerk doesn't like opening up files even if you're family."

"Probate files?" Digger clarified.

"Any files! I had to get a letter from our family attorney saying I was working on behalf of the law firm to research legal issues. To get that letter, Mrs. Stockton had to confirm with both Uncle Jon and Dad that giving me access was allowed. I lost two days just waiting for that. Anyway, Wednesday and yesterday I poured over some very interesting and ancient documents. The most relevant thing is that in 1960 when my grandfather's estate was being probated, a cod... codi something dating back to 1925 gave a bequest to Royal Orchard's property manager, Thomas Eaton."

Digger helped her out. "Codicil...it's like a mini-will. What did it give?"

Holly's eyes widened. "Twenty percent of the Biddeford Mill!" Her voice became shrill and some heads turned toward them. She glanced around furtively and whispered, "Excuse me. I'm sorry, I'm emotional. I don't like the thought of this whole thing. It's not my issue but it *is* my issue because I'm a Hartson and we've turned Royal Orchard into a fortress. Annabelle has me practice firing her pistol in the morning and playing Chuck Norris in the pasture in the evening."

Digger spurted a sip of hot coffee over the rail, then recovered his composure. "That's too funny, I'm sorry. Go back, what happened to the bequest of shares in the mill?" he asked.

"Well, I brought the court order to Mama Bear Stockton. She said because the mill was worthless in 1960, that the bequest was determined to be worthless. She said the court wrestled with whether other assets in my grandfather's estate were held by the mill or in some other entity. She did say that if other assets could be found that were clearly connected to part of the mill, then the Eatons may have a valid claim to them, and that the statute of limitations on bringing suit against us would start on the day the assets are discovered, especially if the assets had been deliberately hidden. I think the Eaton boy is after something. Funny thing is, he can have it! We're broke! Why bust up stuff?"

Holly's voice was getting louder again. Digger looked around. Holly whispered, "Sorry. I just don't get it. Can you go over to Rick Eaton's trailer and ask him what is going on?"

Digger put both hands on Holly's shoulders. "Absolutely not. And don't you breathe a word of your thoughts to anyone for now. Do you understand me?" Holly inched closer as if to see if big brother in blue really cared for her. Digger held firm against her nudge. "Your research is good, but it is totally inconclusive. Besides, didn't your family give them the property in the woods?"

Holly stepped back and Digger dropped his hands. She started to gesticulate. "Exactly! That's what I told the attorney. My dad signed a settlement agreement with the Eatons on giving the home and land to them forever. Case closed. Settled. Right? Wrong! Mama Bear says the settlement could be set aside if there were facts kept from the Eatons. It would not have been a…" Holly looked up, searching for words. "…a meeting of the minds."

Digger nodded with understanding. "Or, even a mutual mistake."

Holly shot Digger a look like *whose side are you on?* She railed, "I mean, who is on our side? The Hartsons need some good news for once."

Digger replied, "Stockton is just explaining the angles. That's the attorney's job." Digger paused and looked over the little inlet. "If, and

I mean *if* it is Eaton searching for assets, the assets would have to date back to the time of the mill. It may be good news. I think, however, this activity has more to do with Jonathan's SEC problems. I can't imagine some local-yokel kid digging into something like this. That's too much."

Holly tilted her head to the side. "I resemble that remark!"

Digger defended his dig. "You're not a local. You're from Massachusetts somewhere. But you get my drift, right? This doesn't look like the activity of some Mainiac in the woods… I think it's corporate bullies, maybe."

Holly responded flatly, "That Mainiac in the woods was valedictorian and has a free ride to college, pre-med… just an FYI. He was commended in the newspapers a few years back for a perfect score on the SATs!"

CHAPTER 28

THE ZODIAC

Later that same Friday morning, Brenda dropped Rick off at the mouth of the marina's parking lot in Wells, the town to the south of the Port. Rick finalized the purchase of a new-to-him used twelve-foot skiff with a twenty-horse-power engine. It was an unusual purchase in that it was a battleship grey Zodiac inflatable tender, something most boaters were still getting used to in terms of the size of engine that could be put on a well-tailored balloon of a boat and still be safe. The odd-looking boat had been made famous by the popular TV series featuring red-capped oceanographer Jacques Cousteau.

The marina's sales manager went over the particulars of the boat with Rick. "You got yourself a honey of a deal, Mr. Richards. As I said over the phone, the former owner used it as a lifeboat on his yacht and she just sat on the aft deck. He never moved her into the water. You just have to keep the rubber skin conditioned and don't let it just bake in the sun. Cover it up." Rick was a little distracted. He hated assuming a different identity so close to home. The chances of being greeted by someone from high school or an acquaintance from the Port were annoyingly high.

Rick pushed the meeting along. "Sounds great. anything else? Can we load her into the water? I'd like to take her home to Drakes Island and outfit her for some fishing today."

The salesman looked at the skies. "Should be a good day for it. Sure, I put the registration number on it and the paperwork is in that cubbyhole. Let's get her in the drink. What do you want to do with the trailer?"

Rick looked at the parking lot. "Can I hook up later this evening?"

The salesman replied, "Sure, we'll leave it over there on the other side of the boatyard gate."

As another marina employee was operating the crane and saddle to lift the Zodiac, Rick asked, "Any good fishing out by Dog Island?"

"Oh yeah, there's a deep ledge to the north side of the island. Big fish down there."

Rick pressed, "Is it inhabited?"

The salesman replied, "Yeah, just by a guy named Link. He's a single black fellah out there...as far as I know. His family has been tending it forever. He comes here every Tuesday to get provisions... like clockwork. I guarantee yuh, I'll see him next Tuesday. It's a little farther than the Talbot River but he can get food cheapah here than in the Port."

Rick sighed. "You got that right!"

Once the boat was floating and idling, the salesman went over the Coast Guard-required items and their locations in the boat. Rick asked if he owed him anything further for the launching service. The salesman declined any additional monies, indicating everything was included. Rick thrust the salesman a ten-dollar tip. The man replied, "Thank you, Mr. Richards!"

* * *

In his new Zodiac, Rick steered for Salmon Creek on the east side of Hartson's Beach. His plan was to make the tide correctly, so he had enough water depth to take the creek north and get very close to his trailer in the woods for provisioning. As he left Wells Harbor to his stern, he spun the wheel to the port and headed up the coast toward Hartson's Beach and Salmon Creek. He could see the majestic Brigantine Hotel in the far distance. He looked to his left to survey the coastline as he progressed, glancing at Little River and the desolate beach that led to Jonathan Hartson's huge cottage on Crescent Point. He smiled as he recalled his raid on the home using the desolate beach approach and exit. "You *are* a genius!" he said to himself and spanked the taut rubber side of the boat in recognition of his tangible gain from the gutsy operation.

He squinted toward the mansion on the point and slowed down. A black and white police car with its trunk lid up and all doors open was parked in the driveway. Rick swore. He looked everywhere in proximity to the cruiser. Then he noticed a man in uniform on the beach. Rick carefully scanned the beach that he had been so happy about just moments before. He saw another officer headed toward Little River. Rick's mind began to race as he increased speed and veered out toward the open sea. *What the heck! Why are they tracing my route? How can that be?*

Rick mentally retraced his steps on the night he robbed and vandalized Crescent Point, trying to figure out if he had made any mistakes. "Little River is their dead end. Even if they search parking areas in Wells, they'll find nothing! The jerks!" He punched the throttle to full speed and yelled into the wind, "*Lex talionis,* you thieves! *Lex talionis!*"

In no time he was at the mouth of Salmon Creek on the eastern boundary of Hartson's Beach. The tide was favorable and he plowed through the rip current at the mouth and headed up the creek. Rick noted the stately presence of Royal Orchard on the hill on his left as he rounded behind it and sped up the creek another mile. He peeled off on a small tributary to the left in the direction of his home and beached the boat in the seagrass. He heard a whistle from the tree line further to the left. Brenda was in a beach chair wearing a bikini and waving at Rick.

As Rick approached, she asked coyly, "You like my cover?"

Rick replied, "I'm not sure I'd call it cover. In fact, it is quite the opposite. I didn't know they made maternity bikinis. But don't get me wrong. I'm glad you're here. Do you have the duck blind netting?"

Brenda pointed toward the car near the tree line and returned to perusing *Cosmopolitan* magazine. "It's still in the trunk. Say, can we go to the beach? This is a true summer day for June in Maine."

Rick barked, "No! Stay away from Hartson's Beach for a while. If you want to go, go to Talbot beach but drop me at the house first. I want to organize provisions for my camping trip next week and run Samson."

CHAPTER 29

CONFLICT OF INTEREST

Digger returned home from his first day of work. Fridays were always filled with a flood of tourists streaming into town. Digger's cheeks were sore from jawboning all day and smiling. He was Port Talbot's walking information booth.

He put his bare feet up and looked out to sea. As he thought over the day's events, he kept coming back to Holly's words about Rick Eaton. He rocked his head slowly back on the couch with his eyes closed. *This cannot be happening to me. Has Port Talbot always had this criminal activity below the surface? Or, is it just following me? Stop it. you crybaby. Deal with it. Dig, dig, dig.*

Digger ran his fingers through his dark hair and continued to process. *Get news articles on Eaton. Get a possible picture of Eaton and his vehicle telefaxed or driven to Dartmouth for a positive identification. Get a witness statement, probable cause affidavit, then arrest warrant. Bada-bing, bada-bang.*

The telephone rang. *Kristy,* he instinctively thought. He picked up the phone and answered with a cheery voice "Seaside!"

Kristy's sultry voice was on the line. "Hello, Digger, dear, how was your first day at work?"

"Exhausting. My feet are killing me and my jaw aches from talking to tourists. But it beats digging ditches. How 'bout you, beautiful? How goes the *Performer?* Are the kids on it yet?"

"We have only three kids that came on in Belfast. The captain and I and these three crew members are gonna sail to Boston this weekend to pick up seven more students. Then we'll return to Talbot on Wednesday or Thursday. You gonna be around, sailor?"

"Absolutely, Kristy. I can't wait. The 'rents will be up by then. So, there'll be some good home-cooked dinners waiting for you. Will you get some leave or are you the babysitter like last summer while the captain left the boat?"

"Yeah, it's pretty much the same. I'll get a couple of shifts off. It's the best I can offer ."

"Any time with you? I'll take it! I miss you so much. Maybe we can go to Little Ri…" Digger choked on the words but pushed through. "… I mean, Little River for a picnic."

There was a pause. Kristy asked, "How are the Hartsons doing?"

Digger hesitated too. "Not great. I ran into Holly Hartson at the pharmacy this morning. The family is scared that they're being stalked and…"

Kristy pounced. "Is this case something Chief Nickerson wants you to get into?" Before Digger could wordsmith a response, Holly upped the ante. "Did Holly ask you to come over?"

Digger felt like he was being lowered into a lion pit. "Kristy, I love you and I am not going to play. Can we talk about something else? Because if you are going to infer that me dealing with a case involving a pretty girl is a challenge to our relationship, I don't want to engage in the discussion."

Kristy asked point-blank, "Is Holly a challenge to our relationship?"

"Not at all, I promise. But I can foresee spending time on whatever is going on over there and I'd like to know that my girlfriend is okay with that and trusts my professionalism in doing my job."

"It's not so much your professionalism I'm worried about. It's hers! I told you last summer. I don't do relationships well. I get sucked in then I start getting these doubts, especially when there is a distance involved. I'm better off staying friends… because of my own psycho-schizo issues."

"No, Kristy, there's nothing psycho about wondering if a boyfriend is trustworthy, especially when there is distance involved. To be honest, Holly can be a flirt. But I'm not interested. I have the best girlfriend in the world. Please don't sully our relationship by inferring unfaithful behavior. I can't prove to you something that is *not* happening. Allow me to prove what *will* happen next week when we get together. Think good thoughts, okay?"

Kristy was sniffling on the other end of the phone. She whispered, "Okay… I gotta go… I do trust you. I love you." The phone went to dial tone.

He looked at the phone and exclaimed, "Women! Can't live with them, can't live without them." He slammed the phone into the cradle. It instantly began to ring. He held his hand above the phone waiting for the second ring, thinking maybe he caused the first ring. It rang again. Digger answered, "Hello?"

A peppy voice piped up. "Digger, it's Holly. You gotta second?"

Digger freaked. "Uh, no… Holly, I'm sorry. I'm tied up in something. Can we talk Monday? I'm swamped."

Holly hesitated. "Sure, Digger. Is everything all right? Is there something I can help you with?"

"No thanks, Holly. I have to speed clean the house, do the laundry… my parents and my girlfriend, Kristy, are arriving soon."

Her voice sinking by several notches, Holly replied, "Sure. I completely understand. I just wanted you to know that I have some good pictures of Richard Eaton."

Digger thought quickly. "Can you drop them off at headquarters up at Sow Hill, please? And see if you have a picture of his car. But do not go near him to get it. It could blow the case or worse, put you in danger. Okay?"

"Okay, *Officer Davenport*. Have a good night." A second girl hung up on him, also not very happy.

Digger looked at the phone accusingly. "Women! Can't live with them, can't live without them!" He headed to the closet to find his new Allman Brothers album, *Live at Fillmore East* and carefully selected his song. He laid the needle down on the twenty-three-minute-long song "Whipping Post." As the guitar riffs filled the house, he headed toward the fridge for a Lowenbrau. He plugged into the engaging music, occasionally breaking into air guitar poses, hopping and skipping through the kitchen into the living room onto a couch and down again. Being a jamming rock star pushed the conflicts of interests behind him for the moment.

CHAPTER 30

ASSAULTED SAILOR

Rick checked his watch as he loaded up the Zodiac. Samson sat motionless to the side, watching. Brenda sat in the driver's seat of the car, thumbing through yet another glamor magazine, oddly enough. Rick wanted to try to beach the boat at Dog Island while the keeper was away getting provisions as he did every Tuesday at this time, according to the salesman at the marina. This would allow Rick to set up his camp unimpeded by the keeper.

"What's the pickaxe for, Ricky?" Brenda cackled from the car. Rick looked around the marsh and creek area for fishermen. He replied by putting his index finger to his lips, signaling *silence*.

The high tide was on its way out and the boat slowly lowered itself down the side of the creek bed as time ticked away. He knew he had to go, otherwise getting the dog in would be difficult. While Samson was quite nimble, being a Belgian Malinois, the kind used by the military, Rick didn't want Samson to scratch or worse, puncture, the boat with his specially trimmed toenails. As it was, Samson was wearing his leather booties to protect the boat.

Once the dog was situated, Rick went back to the car. "Okay, Brenda, I'll see you in a few days. If all goes well, I will find my family's inheritance." Brenda climbed out of the car to hug him. He stepped back to keep the moment serious. "Hold on. Let's go over the plan. Where are you headed right now?"

Brenda recited in a monotone, "Wamsutta Trailhead just north of

Conway. I will sign you in on the trail board for a week of camping using the name and my favorite signature *Richard Eaton*."

Rick replied, "Good. If someone comes to the house and asks when I am coming back? What do you say?"

Brenda dutifully answered, "One week, weather and fish permitting."

Then, Rick assumed the persona of a visitor to the home. "What if they say, 'Can we look around?'"

Brenda looked at her ragged nails nonchalantly. "I am sorry, sir, but you can't. This is private property."

Rick continued playing the nosy investigator. "Does he own a green Mustang?"

Brenda smiled. "Who are you, Joe Friday or something? Talk to our lawyer, Mr. Sanford Beach!" Then Brenda pretended to slam a door shut.

"Perfect, Brenda! Okay, I got to go. If I'm right, I think our life is about to change."

Brenda looked heavenward, hands pressed together. "Lord, protect our Ricky-daddy." She leaned forward to hug him. They embraced briefly.

He looked sternly into her eyes. "There's more money in the rafters of the garage and there's a quitclaim deed to the property in your name up there too, if I don't make it back."

Brenda's eyes flared with fear. "Ricky, no amount of money is worth risking your life. Please stop now. We'll make it!" She teared up and held him back from turning to go.

He shrugged off her hold. "It's not just money. It's justice! Don't worry, you'll see. You'll be proud to be an Eaton and so will... he... she... it..." He pointed to Brenda's belly and turned and trudged toward the boat.

She called out, "I love you, Ricky Eaton!" He threw up his hand to wave without looking back.

As he headed out Salmon Creek toward the ocean, he had an unobstructed view of the big house of Royal Orchard on his right. He pretended not to look as he examined it very closely with a sideways gaze. There were two women firing pistols and rifles at targets in the field. He couldn't help himself. He reached for the binoculars and watched them as he motored out. He instructed Samson to lie down. The dog obeyed instantly despite his desire to see the wet world around him. When Rick saw the blonde girl pivot to look at him and start to raise field glasses of her own, he dropped his glasses and started fiddling with something to his left to keep his face out of her scope and goosed the throttle. *Hartson girls are hunters? I don't think so... That is odd.*

As the small but spunky inflatable met the ocean at the mouth of the creek on a falling tide, Rick encountered a rip current of three-foot waves. He had no choice but to take them head-on with a firm driving speed. From the land, it would look at times like the small boat was completely consumed by the rip. But then like a cigarette butt that refuses to flush in a toilet, the Zodiac kept bobbing to the surface, undeterred from its mission to Dog Island.

Three miles of open ocean in a twelve-foot inflatable boat was a bit ambitious, Rick realized. He reminded himself of the Navy Seals. *Nothing different... except a little training.* "We got this, Samson." The dog, who was now sitting up like a sentry in the bow of the boat, either didn't hear his master or was deep in dog thoughts as he looked out to sea. Rick consulted a clipped portion of a chart covered in plastic. In the center was Dog Island. On the right side of the island were all the buildings: the boathouse with its rails extending across the rocks, and the "soul saving station" (aka the keeper's quarters) with its long, covered walkway leading to the light itself. Rick looked to the left side of the island, where the chart depicted brush and vegetation only.

He steered a bit in that direction and slowed to a stop. He was about a mile from the island's north shore. He pulled out his dad's *Fishin' Magician*, a K-tel "as seen on TV" gizmo that enabled a fishing pole to collapse down to the size of a hammer. Rick slid the pole to its full length and just held it up as a prop. With his other hand he held the binoculars to his eyes. He kept his focus trained on the boathouse. After a few minutes, long enough for the dog to lie down, Rick whispered, "Hello, Mr. Link." He looked at his watch. "Right on time." Rick observed how Link singlehandedly rolled out the launch boat and pushed it down to the water's edge and climbed in.

Something moved on the island to the left. Rick trained his glasses in that direction. "What was that?" He saw nothing and went back to watching Link. He observed Link back the boat off the rails and spin it around in the ocean foam to head due west toward the town of Wells. He watched as the boat gained momentum. *Good.* He scanned to the left again. "What was that movement over there?" He instinctively felt for his sidearm. "We'll see soon enough. Won't we, Samson?"

As Rick approached a beach covered by smoothly rounded small boulders, Samson started jumping and barking, eager to hit the beach. "Sit." The dog sat and looked back at his master as if to say "When, boss, when?" Rick gave a blast of power and used the trim button to lift the engine. The boat coasted swiftly toward the rounded rocks. Rick firmly said, "Go." Samson leapt onto the rocky beach, slightly throwing off Rick's perfect landing. Rick too jumped out, and grabbed the painter and pulled the boat up the beach. The fiberglass shell under the boat allowed it to skitter easily over the smooth round rocks. Samson stood high on craggy rock near the tree line of the island. Rick barked, "Sit." Samson obeyed. The scene of the dog poised on the rock surrounded by pine trees looked like the label on a can of dog food.

Once the boat was above the high-tide watermark, Rick pulled out his pistol and checked the clip and the action. He took the safety off and returned it to his underarm holster. He pulled his jacket across his chest and zipped the first three inches, then he grabbed the clipboard from the backpack along with a dog leash.

He walked up to where Samson waited. He could see about forty feet into the dense pine woods littered with driftwood and a stand of bare trees barely standing. He turned around to look back from whence he came. To the far east, he could see boating activity by the mouth of the Talbot River. He lifted his glasses and scanned that direction. He noted a few power boats were headed his way.

He needed to camouflage his boat. "Samson, fetch stick!" Both he and Samson waded into the hip-high ferns covering the forest floor, searching for sticks. Rick grabbed a large bare sapling and ripped it from its decaying base and returned to the boat to start the camouflage process. Samson surfaced from the woods carrying a piece of driftwood, ready for games. "Good boy!" Rick laid Samson's branch on Rick's small tree and pointed toward the woods. "Fetch!" Samson looked toward the woods briefly, then went to the stick that was now on the pile and barked as if to say, *I did fetch and here it is. Throw it. Let's play!* Samson was prancing and hopping vertically around the stick. Rick said, "No," and pushed the stick harder into the pile. "Fetch again." Samson tore off toward the woods in search of another stick as did Rick.

In ten minutes, the boat was completely shielded from view from any angle. Rick sat and poured some water into a collapsible bowl for Samson and took a swig from the water jug himself. "Let's explore." Rick decided to take the coastal route to the south side of the island, which looked out to the open ocean. He calculated it would get him within view of the light and buildings the quickest. He also wasn't sure what was in the hilly and forested area and did not want to be outflanked by man or beast.

As he came around a corner only a few thousand feet from his boat, he saw the majestic black and glass crown of the lighthouse. It was sending out its beam every five seconds. Samson was interested in going into the woods, but Rick kept him closely heeled and kept picking his way toward the lighthouse. Soon he found himself on a path that led toward the center lawn of the civilized area. In the center was a tall flagpole with spreaders that allowed for additional flags to be flown on the sides of the main pole. The American flag and the Maine flag underneath were snapping easily in the mild breeze. Rick walked to the pole and surveyed the area. He went to the only door of the house that he could see. He knocked loudly. He tried the handle. It was locked. He backed up quickly and looked at the second story windows to see if any curtains moved. Nothing.

He turned around and headed for the boathouse. The doors on the water side were wide open. Rick began looking around for clues as to storage or hidden trapdoors in his quest for gold. He noted no VHF radio or antennae in the boathouse and headed toward the base of the lighthouse. He skirted around it looking for anything odd. He simply noted a cornerstone that had the year 1862 etched in it. He kicked it and kicked to the left and right of it, trying to hear a difference in density. *I'll tear this thing down if I must.*

Rick kept moving around the perimeter of the tower and its long, covered hallway coming from the main house. On the south side of the tower were mechanical components like the fuel house, which housed an aboveground tank for diesel fuel. There was a generator the size of a storage shed, and several black glass panels tilted toward the sky. Rick muttered, "You're gonna need a lot more of those things if this is ever going to be solar-powered. These wouldn't keep a car battery topped off."

In the crook formed where the tower met the structure coming from the house, he spied what he was looking for, the VHF radio antenna cable. He spun his fanny pack of tools around to his front and pulled a serious pair of wire clippers from the zippered pouch. He looked for a hidden area to clip the wire. There was none. "Samson, we don't want this to be obvious." The dog cocked his head and watched. Rick went to where the round cable-style wire disappeared into the building. He knelt at the spot and firmly pulled the wire toward himself. It came out a few inches. "Good" He clipped the wire at the point where the excess had been pulled out and then threaded the cable back in the hole. "Goodbye, cruel world."

Rick continued to walk slowly around the house and came upon a window that looked into the kitchen. It was ajar but the screen would have to be manhandled and it was neck-high. He moved on. He started climbing the rock ledge and came upon an affixed plate glass window that looked on the living room. *No good.* Finally, a window with a break in the screen at waist height. It looked in on a desk neatly organized with office implements and papers. He slid the screen and window sash up and crawled onto the desk and slithered onto the floor. Samson was doing the vertical hop, eager to join in. "Sit!" The dog disappeared below the windowsill.

Rick shut the window and returned things to their proper order as best he could remember. He spun around and looked at the photos on the wall. He pulled the pocket-size Instamatic camera from his pouch and took a picture of a family photo on the wall. "Well, I'll be a monkey's uncle..." The old tintype photo showed a tall, beautiful blonde-haired woman with her arm around an even taller black man, with a dark-skinned child in the foreground. "Looks like Sarah had to live out here..." Rick turned his focus to the walls and floors as he continued looking for compartments or hatches in which someone might hide ingots of gold.

He ran up the severely angled stairs with the shallow treads. There were two tiny bedrooms with commanding views, but nothing in the way of closets or panels or different or uneven flooring.

He hiked downstairs and began meticulously flipping rugs, paintings, couches and chairs and restoring them to their original positions. He examined the front door. It was not dead-bolted, only locked at the knob. This would make for an undetected and quicker exit. He searched through the small kitchen. Nothing except static coming from the VHF radio on the shelf. He checked the other channels for any sign of life. It was the same modulation of static. He returned the radio to channel 16 and turned it down. *Good.* He opened the door to the long hallway to the lighthouse. He looked at his watch. It was pushing one p.m. "I gotta hustle!" The elongated hallway looked to be newer construction and did not show up on the old photos. He stopped searching and bolted for the other end where the door to the lighthouse was half-opened.

Once at the base of the lighthouse, he could see through the iron stair structure two stories up to the flooring of the light itself. The circular wall of the structure was made of red brick. Hundreds if not thousands of red bricks. Jutting out from the brick were simple black iron stair treads. They were wider next to the wall on the left as one would climb in a clockwise fashion. All treads met at a center iron pole to the right as one climbed. While it looked like a circular black iron stairway, it was unique in that the stair treads were countersunk into the brick wall itself.

Rick climbed quickly, looking for imperfections in the wall surface. He was halfway up when he came upon a four-paned window that looked south. The casing for the window, all trimmed in brick, must have been two feet thick. On the windowsill, a beautiful cotton doily was arranged under an ornate kerosene lamp. It was like a diorama from 1862. Rick lifted the lamp and doily. A faded gold plaque with the Hartson family crest, just like the one at Crescent Point, was mortared into the sill of the window. "Bingo! I'll be back, my beauty!" He snapped a picture. Rick then lifted his head near the ridge of the glass to peek toward the west. He saw a skiff plowing through the waves, headed directly for the island. He lifted his glasses and peered again. It was definitely a black male in the open-hulled launch. He was wearing a black and red plaid flannel shirt, a Maine staple recognizable from a distance. "Welcome home, Mr. Lincoln."

Rick retraced his steps, straightening things as he backtracked. He paid special attention to the office. Then he opened the kitchen door, unlocking and then relocking it once he was on the outside. He skirted the building to the east and rounded the far end of the building. Samson was lying in the sun under the window. Rick slapped his thigh. Samson looked up and rushed to his master's side. Both visitors retreated to their boat to set up camp.

* * *

Link could land the boat on the rails in a storm. Today was nothing, a gentle breeze from the south in a rising tide. He would have to hit it hard and get up the rails in time to jump off and grab the hook and attach it to the bow. Then he'd start winching the boat up the rails quickly before a wave of rising tide knocked the boat off the rails onto the rocks. He'd dealt with that calamity, too.

After performing a perfect landing, Link hopped out and ran like a cat straddling the rails and returned with the rope and hook. He disappeared into the boathouse and there was the sound of an engine starting up. The boat moved up the ramp into the boathouse in mere seconds.

Link grabbed some of his provisions and started walking toward the house. He looked to his left up on the ridge. There was Proto, the leader of the wolfhounds. Link squinted. He could see Lupa a few feet behind him in the shadows of the trees. He smiled, carried his provisions to the door, and set them down on the stoop. He returned and hauled out a black garbage bag on his shoulder, walked toward the flagpole and dropped the bag with a thud. With his knife, Link cut the bag open to reveal a side of beef from the butcher in Wells. Using a small silver whistle, Link blew three short high-pitched blasts and returned to the house to put his provisions away.

Slowly Proto and Lupa crept forward. As they did, Link saw nearly twenty pairs of eyes glinting in the dark of the woods. The pack came forward out of the shadows and hesitantly looked at the red carcass at the base of the flagpole. Link looked up from fidgeting with his keys. "What is the matter with you guys? You normally haul that off in seconds." Link examined their positions; it looked like they were in a defensive formation. *What the heck?*

At last, four he-wolfhounds came down off the ridge and dragged the carcass back up the hill. The pack disappeared into the woods quietly.

Link commented aloud, "Well, I'll be. How 'bout, 'Thank you, Link, for the prime rib. Would you care to join us?' But no… They're sulking for some reason. Normally they'd be hootin' and howlin'."

Ever since his wife had left with the kids and moved to Washington. DC, Link had fallen into the habit of talking to himself and the wolfhounds. He thought he was great company, rather entertaining, in fact. He unlocked the door and immediately sensed something. He sniffed. He walked toward the hallway to the lighthouse and sniffed again. "What you smellin', you old fool?" He looked at the door to the lighthouse at the end of the hall; it was wide open. He normally kept it half open. He shrugged his shoulders. *Wind.* Link began unloading his groceries and cooking some bacon on the stove. He had been looking forward to a BLT in the worst way.

* * *

As dusk began to settle over the island, Rick took Samson the other way around the island, the north side facing Hartson's Beach. He needed to get to Link's boathouse undetected. They traversed the rocks in the low light. Samson kept pausing and putting his nose into the wind. On one occasion Samson looked into the dark woods and snarled his lips. Rick felt the hair on his own neck rise.

Rick paused. "I know, Samson, they're out there. I know. Let's keep moving. C'mon, boy." As they rounded the island and could see the house, the lawn, and the flagpole, they needed to move to their right to get lower to the waterline to avoid being seen. At last, Rick slipped into the boathouse. He climbed into the open-hulled boat and turned on a flashlight for a second to look at the instrument panel. He pulled the wire cutters from his fanny pack. *Radio first.* Several snipping sounds ensued. *Ignition next.* More snipping sounds clicked out in the boathouse. Rick flashed the light toward the engine. It had a pull cord. He picked his way to the engine and pulled the cord out about six inches and snipped it. The spring inside the engine rang out an with an intense buzzing sound for two seconds, then silenced. Rick tossed the rubber handle into a dark corner of the boathouse and knelt down to snip the gas line for good measure. He climbed carefully from the boat and slipped out the doors to where Samson waited on the deck and rails that led to the water.

The two of them walked boldly toward the house. Rick turned to Samson and whispered, "You stay." Rick rubbed the dog's ears, and unsnapped his pack and laid it to the side of the door.

* * *

Inside the house, oblivious to what was happening on the other side of the door, Link walked through the dining room and living room and into his office. The items on his desk seemed to have been rearranged. He looked at the window. *That screen was not open before.* His brow furrowed as he looked around the room. Then a bold knock at the door rang out. Link hunched down like a bomb went off.

He went to the kitchen and yelled at the door, "Who is it?"

Rick responded, "Hi, Mr. Lincoln, this is John Schreiber with the Massachusetts Life-Saving Station Historical Society. I am sorry to bother you this evening. I came up from Boston to do a site visit and had no idea it would take this long to get here. We are surveying the lighthouses that we helped establish through the years and Dog Island is one of the crown jewels."

Link unlocked the door and opened it. "You better come in immediately." Link looked over Rick's shoulder. "Anyone else out there?"

"No, it's just me and my dog," replied Rick.

"Your dog?" Link prepared to rush out the door. "They'll tear him up in a heartbeat! Where is he?"

Rick replied calmly, "He's a Belgian Malinois. He'll be fine." A howl rang out.

"Oh no, he won't! Get him in here now!" Link insisted.

Rick persisted, "I didn't want to impose. I just wanted to introduce myself and see if it would be all right to conduct my survey in the morning and we would be on our way."

Link looked sternly at the man. "Call your dog, sir." Rick brushed by Link at the door. Link sniffed the air and thought, *I think I smelled this earlier.*

Samson trotted obediently into the house like it was his own. Rick pointed to a corner and said, "Lie down." The dog looked to where his master pointed and walked over there, making a distinct clicking sound with his nails on the linoleum.

Alarm bells were ringing in Link's brain. He did not like this situation at all. Here he was in his comfy camp moccasins, grey sweatpants, and flannel shirt, looking at a possible intruder and his sidekick, Superdog. He had to keep his cool. "Wow, that's some dog. Here, sit down at the table. Can I offer you some coffee? Or, uh, water? I keep it pretty simple out here."

"A glass of water would be great. Thank you," replied Rick. Link reached for a glass and a bowl. He filled a bowl of water for Samson and handed Rick the glass. Rick thanked his host and handed Link a letter on the letterhead of the Massachusetts Life-Saving Station Historical Society. Link sat at the table as he read it.

May 25, 1980
To: The Lighthouse Keepers of Massachusetts and Maine
From: Edward Tremaine, Rear Admiral, Retired

　　As you know, Maine and Massachusetts were under one state

authority in Boston prior to 1820. Our organization built life-saving stations and lighthouses along both states' coasts.

Please accept our lighthouse surveyor, John Schreiber, to take vital statistics and information from the site. Mr. Schreiber is trained in site evaluation, safety, and historical sensitivities. His work will go a long way toward ensuring our mission to support stations and lighthouses along our coasts well into the future.

If you should have any questions, please do not hesitate to call or write.

Cordially,

Ed Tremaine. RDML, Ret.

When Link was done reading, he looked up at Rick.

"So basically, what I do is take a survey of the buildings here, since we constructed this house over a hundred years ago. You know that we built this house, correct?"

"I know the history of the island," Link replied evenly.

Rick continued, "Well since then, all sorts of things have developed here like that long hallway to the tower, for example. We just take stock of the condition of things, update our maps, and make sure the buildings are sound. We send you the survey with the items highlighted that need attention and we offer ways to help, from financing to material delivery and so forth. How's that sound?"

Link fumbled with the letter in his hand. "Uh, well, Mr. Schreiber, it sounds nice but this land..." Link purposely dropped the letter. Rick bent over to pick it up. Link saw the shoulder holster packed with heavy metal and flinched slightly, a reaction that did not escape Ricks' notice. Link did his best to continue with a steady voice, "... this land is private property and is posted and because of the wild wolfhounds on this island, it is quite dangerous here. A person or animal won't survive out here after sundown for more than a half-hour. This breed of wolfhound is bigger and more aggressive than the grey wolf. They don't run in packs. They herd. That is, they herd their prey and they kill it. It's most effective."

Link continued calmly, "I couldn't consent to this request without communicating with the Hartsons, who own the island. But I may be able to reach someone." Link moved toward the VHF radio on the shelf next to the kitchen window. "Let's see who I can contact..." As he reached for the mic on the radio, he watched Rick in the reflection of the window. Rick was releasing his pistol from the holster. Just above the radio shelf were three neatly arrayed black cast-iron frying pans. Quick as a flash and in one fluid movement, Link lifted the closest heavy pan off the wall, swung it around and smashed Rick on the side of his head and knocked him to the ground. The gun skittered toward Samson, who was now up on all fours growling at the tall black man.

Rick lifted his head from the floor, spitting out teeth and blood, and yelled, "Tear him up!" The dog went airborne, but Link deflected the full impact by swinging a kitchen chair at the dog in midair. It sent Samson toward the window, which shattered upon impact. The dog yelped briefly and landed in a lump on the floor as he struggled to regain his footing.

Link saw Rick crawling for the pistol, so he grabbed the second chair and kept the dog at bay while backing out of the room. Then he ran into his office and barricaded the door. Link had time to witness the dog come busting through the top half of the cheap wooden door. The dog's sharp claws had pieces of wood pinned to them. Samson was lunging and snapping his long white teeth inches from Link's face. Link made sure the door held shut. Samson was hung up, half in the door, and half on the other side. Link seized the moment to leave the door latched and throw open the window sash. He dove Superman-like with his fists out front and "flew" across his desk and out the window. He got up from the ground in time to slam the sash down on Samson's neck as the dog tried to clamber out the window. Link felt the heat and reverberations of the snapping jaws on his forearm as he held the heavy window on Samson's neck. Link let go and disappeared around the left side of the house.

Rick stumbled into the room and lifted the sash off Samson's neck. Through broken teeth and blood, Rick yelled, "Seek!" and pointed out the window. Samson scrambled out of the window and tore off to the left into the dark.

Shortly afterward, Rick heard animal sounds from the woods. With his pistol in firing stance, he crept out the door to listen. To his left in the dark toward the boathouse, he heard the thundering of several dogs headed toward the woods off to the right. *What the heck are they doing over there?* Then he heard a man screaming above the din of the growling and snarling dogs coming from the woods. The human's screams went silent. This was followed by a crescendo of growls and wails from the wolfhounds.

"That's it. Time to get Samson back." Rick contorted his mouth and whistled three very loud and very shrill tones. Moments later, Samson trotted towards him, limping badly but with an excited gleam in his eye. Rick kept his gun trained on the tree line. He could see wolfish eyes piercing through the darkness. He squeezed off a shot. The eyes vanished. Samson didn't even flinch. He trotted right past Rick into the kitchen and collapsed in front of the water bowl and started lapping it up.

Rick came in behind the dog and began praising him. "Good Samson!" Rick ran to the office and shut and locked the window. He came back to the kitchen, turned the kitchen table on end and propped it up to barricade the broken window. Looking over at Samson, Rick noticed there was a puddle of blood seeping out from under the dog. He rushed to the dog and rolled him over. He had a nasty slice right where the rib cage met the stomach. "It's from the window, poor boy!" Rick reached for a clean dishcloth and applied pressure to the wound. He examined the other bloody spots on the dog's body. Complete patches of fur were missing where there were gaping pink flesh wounds. Little blood oozed from the wounds but they were everywhere.

Rick scooped the dog into his arms and brought him to the couch in the living room. He grabbed towels and supplies from the bathroom and administered first aid as expertly as a young medical intern would. The island's first aid kit was well-stocked with sutures, alcohol, oxycodone, rolls of gauze, and bandages. With an ear on the outdoors, Rick ministered to his faithful friend. The howling continued through the night. Rick slept on the floor next to Samson, who remained on the couch.

CHAPTER 31

THE *JUG TUG*

Rick woke to the sound of an air horn blasting outside the keeper's house, suddenly remembering that he and Samson were on Dog Island. He stumbled to his feet and ran to a window to see a fuel supply boat hovering off the western boundary of the island. Apparently, they were waiting for Link to come out. Rick put on a hat hanging by the door and went over to the rock line to wave off the service. Rick positioned his hands over his head in a crisscross pattern. It universally communicated *no thanks, no go, cancel, no touchdown,* etc.

A man on the deck of the boat went into the bridge and came back with a bullhorn. "Is Link there? Do you want fuel?"

Rick yelled at the top of his lungs. "No thank you! Link says no fuel! No fuel please!" In a regular voice he said, "Go away. Get the heck out of here."

The helmsman at the wheel on the bridge of the fuel barge had binoculars trained on Rick as Rick did his hand signals.

The mate with the bullhorn returned to the bridge. "The guy doesn't want any fuel."

Still looking through the glasses, the helmsman asked, "Where's Link?"

The mate replied, "Taking a leak! How should I know? But that man doesn't want fuel."

The helmsman handed the glasses to the mate. "You wanna tell me why that yahoo has a shoulder holster and is wearing a bloody shirt?"

The mate steadied himself against the steering column and rotated the dials on the binoculars. "That's a holster, sure as shootin'… and he looks like a mess. That could be blood. I can't see his face."

The helmsman tooted on the air horn and waved in a friendly manner, then fell off to the west and applied speed. He reached overhead for his radio mic. "Talbot Harbormaster, Talbot Harbormaster, this is *Jug Tug*. Come in please?"

A female voice responded, "Go ahead, Ronnie."

Ronnie replied, "Hi darlin'. Is Hatch around? I think a safety check on Link out at Dog Island is in order. Some guy just refused our monthly fill-up. Waved us off."

The woman responded, "I'll let the harbormaster know, Ron Jon Don Juan! Harbormaster out."

"Ten-four. *Jug Tug* out," Ronnie replied.

The mate encouraged his boss, "She likes you, man!"

The helmsman looked at the compass. "Whatever. Next stop? Boon Island kiddies!" The helmsman applied more speed.

* * *

Once he was sure the fuel boat was leaving, Rick returned to the house. He checked on Samson, who was still sound asleep. Rick walked into the bathroom and saw himself in the mirror for the first time. The bloodstain on his shirt from the shoulder to the stomach looked ghastly. He noticed he was still wearing his shoulder holster, too. He examined his mouth. The upper rack of teeth on the left side of his mouth was jagged with missing teeth. *Lovely,* he thought. He peeled everything off to take a shower.

Rick ditched his bloody clothes in the fireplace and torched them immediately. He'd borrow some clothes of Link's until he could get back to his campsite. After the shower, he put some coffee on and resumed normalcy as best he could. Rick prioritized the matters at hand. *Ascertain status of Link. Confirm gold is in fact on this island. Clean up blood and any signs of altercation. Leave the island intact as soon as possible.*

CHAPTER 32

PICNIC ON DOG ISLAND

"Port Talbot Police Department. This is Patty. How may I help you?"

"Hi, Patty. This is Darla at the marina. The harbormaster asked me to call you to see if you have anyone who can check on Mr. Lincoln out at Dog Island. The fuel boat guy thinks something's wrong and is recommending a safety check. Apparently, the lighthouse keeper is missing."

"Sure thing, Darla. I'll let the chief know. We have it from here unless I call you back." Patty marched into the chief's office. He was standing in front of the mirror adjusting his tie.

"Chief, time for a boat ride. Harbormaster is requesting a safety check on Dog Island…"

The chief cut her off. "No, he's not. Hatch knows I am speakin' today at the Rotary. He is knocking us for takin' away his jurisdiction last summah. Safety check on an island three miles away? I know what he's up to."

Patty couldn't care less. "What do you want me to do with this?" She held up the pink phone slip. The chief read the slip. Handed it back to her.

He replied, "The town's boat is still at Booth's for repair. Make a note to call Booth and see if the lower unit is fixed, please."

Patty thought better of it but said anyway, "Davenport has a nice boat. It has a radio and it's fast. You want him to check it out?"

The chief looked at his watch. It was still before noon. Then his eyes lit up. "Yes! Brilliant, Patty. Hatch thinks he's gonna bankrupt the depahtment for taking over jurisdiction of the docks and watah. But…" Nickerson's eyes were gleaming. "…not at three dollahs and fifty cents an houah! Tell Diggah no overtime… to get theyah and get back before five if possible."

"Yes, sir. I'll tell him. Sir, do you want me to tell him that you gave him a raise, too? Digger makes less than three and a quarter an hour."

"Oh, forget that. I'll reimburse gas, though!" The chief put on his dress blue overcoat and headed out to the Rotary Club.

"Come in, Unit 19. This is dispatch."

To respond, Digger mashed the button on the transmitter attached to the epaulette of his dark blue uniform shirt. "Go ahead, Patty. This is 19."

"Well, I hope it is sunny and warm out there because the chief wants you to take your boat and do a safety check on Dog Island and be back by five p.m., over?"

Digger excused himself from the group of tourists asking questions. "Come back on that, dispatch?"

Patty replied, "The Chief wants you to go out to Dog Island now and make sure the lightkeeper is okay and be back by 5 p.m. He does not want to incur OT, over?"

Digger clarified, "And he wants me to take my boat, *Seahorse*, correct? Over?"

"That's correct, Digger," confirmed Patty. "Over."

Digger looked at the skies. "Dispatch, you were wondering from your cage whether a picnic could be built into the trip on such a fine day, given that the chief does allow for lunch breaks."

"Affirmative 19. I believe you copy."

"Alright, I'll gas up the *Seahorse* and head out momentarily, But wait, how did this item get called in?"

Patty replied, "Darla at the marina got a call from the fuel boat saying there was no one to receive the fuel on the island and they recommended a safety check."

CHAPTER 33

BRICKS AND MORTIS

Rick felt much better with a cup of coffee and clean clothes. He fixed a breakfast for Samson courtesy of Link's refrigerator, franks and beans. The two of them stepped out into bright sunshine with a steady breeze. "Let's find out what happened to Link." Rick pulled out a tee shirt that had been in Link's laundry basket. He rubbed it around Samson's nose and commanded, "Seek!" Samson took off on a wobbly gallop in the direction of the woods. Rick yelled "halt" when the dog was more than 50 feet ahead of him. Samson just sat and didn't even look back. When Rick caught up to the dog, Rick would say *seek*. Rick had his pistol ready. They were deep in the woods and could easily be outflanked by the wolfhounds. Rick recalled Link's words about some evolutionary development where the beasts herded their prey. Rick shivered.

He noticed that Samson was sitting at a clearing looking up in the trees. He had discovered the end of the scent trail. As Rick came into the clearing he lifted his shirt to shield his nose from the smell emanating from the scene of mutilation. Rick pulled out the camera. He took a shot of the shredded red and black plaid shirt. He snapped a photo of the grey sweatpants, now nearly all red. A half a moccasin was among the remains. Rick exclaimed, "They ate his shoes!" He stepped back and picked up a long stick to push the bones around. Rick had a special penchant for anatomy. "This guy was built like an ox."

He threw the stick on the pile of bones and shredded clothing. As he turned to go, he noticed scratches on the nearby trees; they were six to ten feet off the ground. He called Samson over. Well aware that his dog could use his sharp claws to do some climbing, Rick said, "Those scratches are yours, aren't they, boy? Must have been quite a scene."

They both walked slowly back to the keeper's house. After a brief time of tidying up, Rick and Samson headed directly for the boathouse. Rick had seen some tools out there and did not want to take the time to go back to his own boat to get tools. The thought of a gold deposit being within his grasp caused adrenalin to course through his veins.

Rick assembled a bucket of tools and headed for the Hartson family crest embedded in the sill of the tower window. Once at the base of the tower, he unlocked an exterior door that led out to the area where the solar panels reclined. The open door allowed for fresh air to waft through the tower. Plus, it was a quicker exit if he needed more tools from the boathouse, instead of going through the long hallway into the kitchen and out through the house. Rick quickly set himself up to work at the windowsill. Carefully, Rick chiseled up the crest made of pure gold and put it in his backpack. *If I find nothing else, the mission is already a success.* He climbed a few steps up and looked out of the tower before he began in earnest to remove the brick. "This is a beautiful day!" He returned to the windowsill, put on safety glasses and went mad dog on the brick sill.

Pieces started flying and falling 20 feet to the ground below. Samson lumbered into the hallway to avoid the noise and debris. Once Rick cleared a brick, he had a starting point and used a chisel to pop the next brick. He carefully stacked the bricks on the stair treads to his left and right. Two courses down into the horizontal plane of the brick windowsill, his chisel hit a hollow-sounding object. He popped the bricks up to reveal a basic wood platform that was countersunk at the sides into the brick wall. Rick muttered, "A header. Let's see how strong it is."

He picked up the small sledgehammer and positioned himself on the stairs for a good swing fest. Bam! At the first strike, the board began to crack along its grain. Rick kept at it furiously until he could remove splinters by hand. There clearly was air space below the wooden board. Rick got enough of an opening to reach his arm in. Nonetheless, he continued to smash and pick away more splintered wood, then got his flashlight and aimed it in the hole. He peered in as he turned on the light.

The opening radiated with bright golden light. He looked closely and saw individual gold bricks lined up perfectly. Each brick was stamped with the Hartson crest. He exclaimed, "I told you, Brenda!" He sat for a moment and thought. *This is mine. All mine. I discovered it. At the very least, twenty percent is the Eaton share. This has become a legal operation… totally aboveboard from here on out. Mr. Beach, Esquire, will be rich too.*

Rick reached in to grab a brick. At first, he thought they were mortared in place. But no, it was their weight that made them nearly impossible to move. His research had indicated that they were about forty pounds each. He grabbed only two ingots and put them in the backpack. Samson walked in and looked up from below. Rick noticed the dog and sensed something too. In the distance, he heard a powerboat. Rick slipped up to the top floor of the tower and peered out. What appeared to be a sport fisherman was coming toward the island in a center-consoled white fiberglass boat.

CHAPTER 34

THE WELCOMING COMMITTEE MAKES READY

Rick shrank down and whispered, "Move along... move along... please move along..." He looked at his mess on the steps below and began calculating. As he was about to raise his head, he heard Samson shuffling down below. Samson was about to exit the tower and check out the boat. "Samson, sit!" Rick raised himself to watch the fisherman. The boat was approaching on the northern side of the island in a direct trajectory for the boathouse. "This guy is on a mission." Rick raised his binoculars and examined the driver. He swore. "Digger Davenport. Port Talbot's bike cop. In uniform, no less."

Rick sped down the stairs and shut the exterior door at the base of the tower to make sure Samson didn't wander out and draw attention. He then climbed back up to the windowsill of the tower and started reconstructing the area as best he could. He filled the opening with red brick and then laid more brick on top of the busted wood and made it look as neat as possible. He used the doily to brush the dust away and then spread it nicely over the uneven brick. He put the lantern on top and backed down the stairs with his tools and extra bricks. He swept up shards of brick and wood as he backed down the stairs and put the tool bucket behind the door. Rick could hear the sound of Digger's motorboat just outside the door. He sprang up the circular stairs and peered out. Digger seemed to be circling the island now, cruising along the southern shore.

Rick took a moment to think through the options. *Link is dead of natural causes. Eaton on island discovers gold. Pesky cop discovers Eaton. Eaton proves gold is his in court. Cop noses around site. No, that's no good... don't like cop and Eaton together at all.* He continued to think. *Link is dead from natural causes. Cop dead from natural causes or survives but never sees Eaton. Eaton sneaks off without being detected. Cop prevented from pursuing or calling. Hero Eaton shows up weeks later in court totally unrelated to those menacing wolves. Perfect.*

Thinking of the wolves, Rick looked at his watch. *They won't help me until later.* He looked at Samson. "Are you ready to go home?" Samson started swirling in circles like he was going to the beach to play fetch. Rick spoke sternly to Samson. "But we must sneak." Samson cocked his head to the side. Rick pointed down the long hallway and whispered "Crawl!" Samson proceeded to crawl on his belly. "Good boy. C'mere, pup. Stay."

Rick climbed the tower again to assess what the cop was going to do. Rick surveyed an exit route on the north side of the island facing Hartson's Beach. The wild rose bushes on that part of the island blocked the view of the rocky shoreline, even from this angle in the tower. Rick was calculating as he started putting on rubber gloves from his fanny pack. Digger was still on the south side of the island, driving his boat in a figure eight pattern as he examined the island. Rick watched as Digger reached into the boat's console, pulled out an air horn and blasted it three times.

He saw that Digger had a radio mic to his lips. Rick muttered to himself. "That is gonna stop. There's only one way on this island in that boat, and you have to come up those rails. I'll be waiting for you, copper..."

Rick ran down the long passageway toward the house. He grabbed a rag and a bottle of alcohol from the bathroom and scooted back to the tower, where he wiped down the tools and railing, and anything that might have his fingerprints. He returned to the house and began wiping all the surfaces and knobs.

He watched Digger continue motoring down the southern coast of the island. *He's looking for an easier landing.* Rick ditched the cleaning products, opened the windows and called Samson over. "You ready?" Then Rick paused. "Wait a minute! Good dog! You just reminded me. It's feeding time." He spun around, opened the fridge and freezer, and started grabbing boxes of pre-made hamburger patties and anything else that looked like meat. Rick went on a tear around the house. opening and, where possible, removing windows and pitching meat in hidden areas. He ran down the hallway to the tower, hiding the burger discs intermittently as he went. Rick was careful opening the exterior door of the tower because Digger's boat could be just outside. Rick threw some frozen chicken breasts into the grass. Then he stuffed dirt into the door catch and placed a rock at the back heel of the door so that it would not be able to close properly.

Rick closed the door just in time to see that Digger was headed back his way. "Let's go, Samson!" They both ran the length of the hall, out the front door and booked it straight for the boathouse. They entered the boathouse door facing the lawn and the flagpole. Rick secured it. He commanded Samson to sit in a corner and he did. Rick bolted the barn doors shut and tested them for gaps and swing-ability. He could hear the motorboat outside. Rick grabbed a tarp, and sat next to Samson and pulled the tarp over them both. He waited.

On the *Seahorse*, Digger was jockeying into position to ride up onto the rails. He lifted his left engine completely out. *No sense in destroying both props. At least it's high tide. No time like now-time!* He goosed the engine to ride the wave up the rail. He immediately power-lifted the second engine. Upon landing on the rails and riding them up for about ten feet, he looked at the surf at his stern. *I may need to winch this baby up or my stern is gonna get hit by the waves.* Digger jumped to the rails and went to the double barn doors of the boathouse and pulled. Locked. "Come on!" He looked back at the sea roiling at the rails. Digger checked his watch. *Tide should be turning soon.* He went around to the other side of the boathouse. Rattled the door. "Great. No winch!"

Digger ran around the building back to the bow of his boat and grabbed the bow line and secured it to a cleat on the deck. He reached in for the anchor line and tied his stern to the rails directly. "That has to do. I shouldn't be here that long." Digger grabbed his backpack and went to the dry cooler and grabbed a handful of flare sticks from the full box he had just purchased at the marina. "Never know when it's fetch time on Dog Island." He picked up the radio. "Talbot Marina, this is *Seahorse* again, come in, please.

"This is Darla, go ahead, Digger. What you got?"

"Okay, I'm on the island and so far, it's all quiet here. I am about to go into the house. The place appears abandoned and locked up. Please let dispatch know."

Darla replied, "Will do, officer. Out."

Darla called Patty at the Talbot police department right away. "Patty, this is Darla. Digger checked in from Dog Island. He said that it is all quiet out there and that the place appears abandoned. Okay?"

"Alright, Darla, thanks for the report. I'll let the chief know."

As Digger began trudging toward the house. Rick sprang to his feet and watched through the crack in the door as Digger approached the house. Rick pulled out his wire cutters and went to the other doors. He slid one barn door open and snuck onto the *Seahorse,* where he opened the battery compartment and clipped twice on the black line to create a gap in the negative feed first. Then, making sure he was not touching metal, he did the same thing with the positive red line. The boathouse completely blocked the view of Rick's activities, unless someone was in the lighthouse tower. Rick checked the radio. Dead. He pulled the ignition keychain and threw it into the surf. "Enjoy your stay, Fuzzicle."

Making his exit from the boathouse, Rick shut the barn doors and brought Samson with him to the brush line on the north side of the island. Rick gave Samson the hand signal to stay. Then he crawled his way toward the east end of the island, making sure his head stayed below the brush line, out of sight. Once he had made a distance of 100 feet, he then signaled Samson to crawl to him. The two of them did this leapfrog, tag-team crawl until the angle hid them from the tower. Rick stood up and whispered "Boat!" They both started juking and jiving across the rocks, circling ever closer to their departure ticket.

CHAPTER 35

SOS!

In the lighthouse keeper's home, Digger was scratching his head. There was too much to process. One thing was clear. Mr. Lincoln was not in the house. Digger tried to reason through the circumstances. *He could be across the island somewhere and left the home open to the beautiful breezy day. He could be out in his boat or someone else's. Perfectly explainable.* Digger did not like the broken window in the kitchen. He liked the VHF radio in the kitchen, however. As a precaution, he put on rubber gloves and then began taking pictures. Specifically, he took pictures in the office of the family photos. He examined the photo of a white woman and a black man and a child. It was captioned, *Sarah, Tom and TJ, ca.1870.* "Hmmm. There's serious history on this island." Digger shrugged his shoulders and turned to walk through the kitchen and down the hallway toward the lighthouse.

He stopped at the living room and looked at curtains blowing. He paused. An eerie feeling came over him. He shuddered. An insistent thought said *flip the couch cushions* so he did. Stunned, Digger saw a large, red oval-shaped stain on the bottom side of the cushion. He picked up the cushion and sniffed. "Blood, for sure." He pinched the cushion's stain. It oozed onto his gloves. *This is fresh. Time for backup.* Digger ran to the VHF radio on the kitchen wall. He clicked the power on but only got static. He knew that sound. Either there was no antennae or it was broken. He could not raise anything by adjusting the RF gain knob. "Uh-oh, this may be cut!"

His heart rate began to climb; he ran out the front door toward his boat and its radio. Over his right shoulder he heard the bloodcurdling howls of dogs. He stopped and returned to the house and grabbed his backpack, speaking aloud in a resigned voice, "I've seen enough. Time to go. We have a crime scene. Time for the big boys. Little copsicle can go home now. Time for the heavy artillery."

Digger scrambled into his boat, reached for the radio and went to turn the key to AC power to fire it up. The key chain was missing from the ignition. He patted his pockets, looked around the boat, and rummaged through his backpack. He yelled, "Shoot! What the heck?" He looked at his battery box as he thought to hotwire the boat and the radio. The watertight lid on the battery box was askew. The straps were undone. He rushed to the battery box and opened it to find six inches of positive and negative cable missing. *Sabotage! Someone else is on this island.*

Digger pulled his backpack open and grabbed the Smith and Wesson pistol as he jumped from the boat and then gently tried the barn doors. *Odd.* They opened now with the slightest touch. Cautiously, he entered, walked around Link's boat and immediately smelled gas. Digger saw the cut gas line at the stern of Link's boat. He looked at the radio on the console but didn't bother climbing in the boat because the snarl of wires under the console had clearly been snipped.

Digger dropped his head and paced in the boathouse thinking, praying and talking his way through the scenario. "Okay, so the keeper wouldn't sabotage his own boat. His house has clear signs of foul play. Someone else is on this island. There are at least three of us on the island. Where's the keeper? Someone was in here when I landed. He disabled my boat while I was in the house." With his pistol pointed in front of him, Digger examined every corner of the boathouse. His thoughts shifted from where the saboteur might be located, to how to get a signal for help to the world... even if the bad guy was watching him. He opened the door looking toward the lawn, the flagpole, and the house. All was eerily quiet. He focused on the flagpole. It had spreaders for signal flags.

He turned back toward the boathouse and began searching. He looked up in the rafters of the boathouse and saw what he was looking for, a decorative array of nautical flags. He climbed into the boat so he could reach the rafters, snatched the flags down and began threading his way through the linked flags. There, at the end of the chain was the flag he needed. It had an orange background with a black square and a black circle on it. He jumped from the boat, and exited the boathouse slowly, still with his pistol at the ready. He searched and spun and then with his head down, he dashed across the lawn to the flagpole, lowered the American and Maine flags, and began hoisting the orange and black flag, the international symbol for *SOS*. He then re-raised the American flag, this time upside down. "Maybe someone will see that," he muttered to himself.

Another cacophony of howling on the east end of the island rang out. Digger froze. *Those wolfhounds, as Holly called them, may be an additional issue if I can't get out of here before nightfall.* He returned to the boathouse to salvage a radio, battery, antenna, the rest of the flares, wire, and more. Digger thought as he prepped, *If someone is after me, they had a prime target at the flagpole. Why wouldn't they engage? What the heck is going on here?*

CHAPTER 36

DODGING THE DOGS

On the east side of the island, as Rick and Samson had rounded the spot where their boat was hidden, they were met by a welcoming committee of wolfhounds who started to sound off in a frightful orchestra of ever-building screams and howls. It was deafening and made it hard to think. It was like what happens to a basketball player at the free throw line.

Rick knew he could start blowing away the beasts with his pistol, but that would have the cop come running. He needed a clean and hasty getaway.

"Samson, heel." Rick said reassuringly as the dog began to bristle and growl low in his throat. Rick recited his plan aloud to Samson like he was a squad leader and Samson his soldier. "We are going to outflank them to the left...even if we have to swim." Rick looked around for sticks. He picked up an eight-footer. He pulled off his shirt and tied it to the end of the stick. Then Rick opened his pouch and got the lighter ready. As he was doing these things, both he and Samson were moving stealthily to their left. Rick picked up another small stick and shoved it in his belt. "You like to fetch, right, Samson?" he asked in a friendly tone. They both kept their eyes on the pack, which was slowly rotating as the prey, man and dog, moved slowly across the rocks.

Finally, Rick saw a clear pathway to the boat up the stone-covered beach but about twenty wolfhounds on the ridge were now about six feet away from it. The pack seemed to know what the goal was. Rick turned to Samson. "Stay, boy," he said as he advanced toward the line of wolfhounds, his face menacing as he locked in on the apparent leader. The pack began to snarl and pace, their heads down in attack mode. Some crouched as if ready to spring the twenty feet between them. Rick kept inching closer to the stern of the boat. On the edge of his vision, he saw a wolfhound moving on the ridge to his right. Rick lit the shirt tied to the end of the long stick with his lighter. The smoke and flame produced an instant reaction. The hound on the ridge to his right receded into the pack.

Rick took this opportunity to advance toward the pack forcefully and shouted at them. They backed down on their haunches and growled more. Rick had made it to the stern of the boat, which was covered in its camouflage of tree branches. He carefully used his torch to touch off a branch resting on top of the pile. He reached the stern and grabbed its dock line. While resting the burning torch on the pile that rested atop of his skiff, Rick dropped his backpack and fanny pack in the boat and tied the stern line around his waist. He looked at the gas tank in the stern and grimaced. He took one of the sticks from the fire and threw it at the dogs, which caused some to run to the back of the pack.

Feeling like Atlas pulling at the Earth rather than holding it up, Rick began to tug the boat, and the burning pile of wood on top of it, backwards down the beach toward the water. It looked like a mobile beaver dam on fire and glided remarkably easily over the round stones. The large wolfhounds inched forward as Rick receded toward the water. The fire on top of the wood pile was starting to take on a life of its own and an errant spark falling on the rubber boat or the gas tank below could spell doom.

Rick moved up alongside the boat and started offloading the fiery sticks into a pile in front of the boat. He continued to throw sticks from the boat onto the firewall he was forming as he continued to pull the boat back into the water. The flames kept the wolves at bay. At last when he reached the water's edge, the boat took on its own buoyancy. He took the stick from his waistband and shook it a couple of times in front of Samson, who had been patiently seated at the waterline. Samson's eyes were glued on the stick. Rick turned and threw the stick as far out into the water as he could and said "Fetch!"

Samson took off bounding in the shallows then swam with his head out of water, pursuing the stick and leaving a significant wake behind. Rick steadily pulled the boat into deeper water and quietly slipped out of sight underwater and flutter-kicked away from the beach, hidden by the boat.

The hounds on the beach cried out in outrage. Many came to the water's edge and ran up and down the beach but were hesitant to enter the water. Some wolfhounds jumped out on the rocks that bordered the beach, but they refused to jump in.

Samson was still in pursuit of the stick as Rick climbed up the transom, using the engine as a climbing aid. He lowered the engine, fired her up and spun the wheel toward Samson, who was now headed toward the boat snorting and grinning with the stick held between his teeth. Greatly relieved, Rick looked back at more than twenty wild wolfhounds baying on the rocks with the sun setting through the undisturbed pine trees. "Now that's a picture!" he remarked, mentally and physically exhausted.

Rick stopped the boat to lift Samson in. Samson had naturally been doing the doggy paddle with all paws flailing. As Rick lifted him by the scruff of the neck, one of Samson's claws, which were specially trimmed by Rick for climbing activities, grazed the side of the rubber pontoon boat and punctured it. Rick swore. He secured Samson, applied pressure on the small slice in the rubber and immediately turned the boat toward Hartson's Beach and Salmon Creek. The leak squealed a sharp pitch as he tried to keep his hand on it. Originally, Rick had planned to head toward Port Talbot then swing around toward Salmon Creek, so that when he passed in front of Dog Island Light, he would be at least a mile in the distance. The punctured pontoon changed that. Rick knew he had to head for the nearest coastline immediately and that would be Hartson's Beach.

Too soon, Rick came into view of the lighthouse. Rick put on a slicker with a hoodie and held a fishing pole in one hand, while his other hand pressed on the shrieking leak. He sped across the water, steering with his knees. Though he heard an air horn sounding behind him, he didn't look back.

CHAPTER 37

Find the Keeper, Who's the Reaper?

On the west end of the island, Digger knew if no one came for him soon it would be dark and that he would have to make a stand for the night. Against what he couldn't be sure. A saboteur? Wolfhounds? The keeper himself? He figured it would be best to do so in the keeper's house to have the advantage of the tower and sturdy walls. He immediately set about securing the site. Leading with his pistol and moving room to room, he swept the site quickly, looking for the saboteur. Next, he secured the broken kitchen window by propping the table up against it. Then he heard a high-pitched squealing noise in the distance. He went to the front door and saw a small inflatable boat cruising at full speed not too far from the island. Digger ran to his box of supplies, pulled out the air horn and blasted it, waving his hands frantically. The boater didn't respond. Digger checked out the boat through the binoculars. "Fisherman... idiot... oblivious!" Digger felt despair as a potential rescuer moved farther and farther away.

Nonetheless, Digger continued to prepare for a night on the island potentially spent fighting against man and beast. He went down the long hallway that led to the lighthouse. A breeze was blowing through the exit door. He pulled the door shut but it bounced open. Digger ignored it momentarily and began climbing the tower. As he looked out the only window on the tower stairway, he noticed the doily and lantern on the brick sill and thought nothing of the dirty decorations. Digger climbed into the glass cage of the lighthouse and put his binoculars to his eyes.

Now he could barely see the small fishing boat that was headed toward Hartson's Beach. In the distance to the east, he could see sailboats off the Talbot River. They were of no help. He looked to the west. The only thing he noticed was that the sun was setting.

He thought of his options at this hour. *I got to get a radio working, but no one is going to want to land on this rock at night. Plus, it's a stretch that it will even work.* Digger continued to think, his brain reeling through possible ideas. *Hmmm. A bonfire! That's it. It's a signal and possible deterrent to the howling beasts of the island. I'll build a bonfire in the remaining light then work on the radio.*

Digger clambered down the circular stairs and ran down the hallway to the kitchen to grab his backpack. He circled the property, looking for the best place for a bonfire. He picked a high spot that could be seen from the south, west, and north and still be a safe distance from the house itself. The east, toward the Talbot River, was completely shrouded by the forest.

Digger cocked the pistol to put a bullet in the chamber and then headed into the woods to gather firewood. He heard the pads of running feet in the woods and in his peripheral vision, he saw flashes of grey fur. He felt like he was being watched. He repeatedly spun around in a crouched firing position only to see a shadow melt away. He came to a clearing where several seagulls were feeding on something. Dread spilled through his veins as he watched the birds pick at a pile of bones and clothing soaked in blood. Nausea overcame him as a familiar sickly-sweet smell filled his nostrils. The bones and clothing, including portions of an unmistakable red and black flannel shirt, were covered in flies. It explained the cadaverine smell and the possible whereabouts of the lighthouse keeper.

CHAPTER 38

JUST A WALK ON THE BEACH

Meanwhile, Rick was in the battle of his life to get the deflating boat and Samson to shore as darkness descended over the water. He shifted all weight to the front of the boat while keeping his hand on the hole. The pontoon was clearly failing. Thankfully, other parts of the rubber boat were remaining firm. Samson had only punctured one chamber, but it was a critical one. Rick began throwing tools overboard. He knew there was no way to swim with the gold bars in his backpack but resolved that they would be the last to go. As the wall of the pontoon weakened, it made the vessel hard to steer because the outboard motor started caving toward the weakened side. This had Rick fighting the wheel and making the boat go forward at a cattywampus angle which, in turn, caused the waves to breach the gunwales and fill the boat.

In the fading light, Rick could see the nervousness in Samson's eyes. "It'll be alright, boy. Just a football field to the beach!" Samson looked toward shore and put his nose in the air, searching for familiar smells of home. Rick began counting down the yardage like a game announcer calling the play of a football running back headed for the goal line. "Samson's at the 80-yard line… the 75… 70… Ladies and gentlemen, Samson has a wide-open field. He's at the 60!"

Rick dug through his fanny pack and backpack. With one hand on the hole in the boat, he used the other hand to awkwardly put his Instamatic camera in a plastic bag and spun it to seal it. He pulled out a large pocketknife and used his teeth to unfold it. He cut a line from the boat and tied one end around his belt. Next, he tied the other end of the line to the backpack, and slung one strap of the backpack around his right shoulder. He figured if he had to bail out of the boat in water that was over his head, he could drop the backpack another ten feet to the seabed and not be pulled down by the gold.

"Twenty yards, Samson. When I say *jump*, we go!" The waves were starting to become pronounced and form into two-foot curlers that would be enough to roll the boat. Rick timed his bailout between waves. He called out, "Jump!" Samson obeyed. Rick put the knife between his teeth pirate-style, clicked the throttle into neutral and jumped into the water as he held onto the bow line. Rick was in about twelve feet of water and began to sink quickly. He slipped the backpack off and it dropped to the sandy bottom. He pulled himself to the surface by tugging on the boat's bowline and started flutter-kicking toward shore, dragging the boat and his backpack. Samson knew his part and was already coming out of the surf onto terra firma.

Rick observed the curlers and the position of the boat. He kept the bow pointed into the waves to avoid having it overturn. Finally, he was able to stand on the sand below. With relief, he positioned himself next to the boat and opened the gas tank cap and then took the knife and put small slices in all of the other air chambers of the rubber boat. He reached over the side, straightened the wheel, put the boat in gear and pushed the throttle to full. He jumped back as the roaring propeller nearly grazed his stomach. The boat took a wave head-on and continued driving toward the open ocean.

Rick turned to get out of the surf and the rope on his belt tugged him back. "Oh yes, my bait." He hauled the heavy backpack to his feet, picked it up and walked out of the surf to where Samson was sitting, watching his master's every move. On the beach, Rick quickly untied the rope to the backpack and put it loosely around Samson's neck. "Ready for a boring stroll on the beach like a normal man and dog?" They walked at the water's edge and watched the rubber boat literally disappear into the ocean. Rick knew it was a fait accompli when the engine let out a death scream before it subsided into silence. On Hartson's Beach Road it appeared that a man and dog were heading home at dusk, having just had a pleasant swim at the beach. No matter how commonplace Rick wanted it to seem, the still-cool late-June air, the still-frigid Maine water temperature, and the evening hour made their activity appear highly unusual.

CHAPTER 39

FEEDING TIME ON DOG ISLAND

Back at the clearing on Dog Island, Digger gagged repeatedly as he viewed the shredded clothing and bones. Digger was in his element, but, he had to admit, also in way over his head. He pulled out his camera and attached the flash. He snapped some photos and immediately heard howls ring out. They were coming from unseen creatures hidden maybe fifty feet away in the brush. As Digger backed out of the area, he noticed the streaks of claw marks in the trees. "Don't tell me these beasts climb trees!"

Digger continued to build the fire and stockpile wood. While he was kneeling at the unlit bonfire shoving in paper and a flare stick, he looked through the falling darkness toward the woods. Pairs of glowing eyes illuminated the wood line from the south end to the north end of the island. "Oh my God, it looks like there are hundreds of them! And they're sure interested in me." Digger retreated to the house. The wolfhounds advanced.

Digger checked his backpack for more rounds of ammunition for his pistol. He was out of luck. The six shots in the revolver were all he had. He shoved the pistol back into his waistband. Digger tried to make sense of it all. *Were the remains in the woods those of the lighthouse keeper?* The bloody clothing reminded him of something he had seen. He ran into the office where the photos hung. He immediately recognized the plaid pattern worn by a tall black man with his arm around an attractive black woman with the lighthouse in the background. Digger's stomach twisted another knot. *That was the keeper out there... killed by the wolves!*

He looked back on the wall. A picture of a large white wolfhound bore the inscription, *Proto 1978*. Digger thought, *Mr. Lincoln seemed to like these beasts. I don't get it. I know this, no wolf sabotaged his and my boat. They didn't cut the radio antennae.*

Forced now to reconstruct a radio using a twelve-volt battery, Digger continued to piece the facts together as best he could. He looked at the books on the shelf of the small office and reached for a plain leather-bound book. The front cover was embossed with the Hartson crest. He opened it and on the inside title page was inscribed in calligraphy, *The Dog Island Diary*. Digger began to read. After a few minutes of skimming back and forth through the pages, he thought, *This island plays into Hartson history. This book may have clues to the events going on over in Hartson-world. I cannot connect the dots… yet.*

Digger brought the book to the kitchen where the radio and his supplies were located. He opened the fridge, thinking he better carb up for a long night if he couldn't get the radio to work. He noticed freshly purchased groceries and pulled some bread and cheese slices out. There was no meat anywhere. He went to the coffeemaker. It was still on. Digger shook his head, wondering how he had missed that. As he poured himself the last cup of burnt coffee, he wondered who had made it. He sipped the bitter brew and winced. He returned the empty carafe to its place and stared at the automatic drip coffeemaker. He looked at his hands. He was still wearing his gloves. His eyes lit up as he quickly grabbed the coffeemaker, unplugged it and stuffed it into the back of the highest shelf of a kitchen cabinet. "Let's save this for a rainy day. It may have prints."

Suddenly, he heard a thundering noise of animals running past the broken kitchen window. He peered through the propped-up table and out the window. It was pitch-black with the backdrop of crashing surf in the distance. Digger was struck with fear. He remembered the door at the base of the lighthouse, and that he had not secured it. He opened the kitchen door to the hallway and lighthouse beyond. He flicked on the lights. Approximately fifteen wolfhounds were busy scarfing up food scattered on the floor. They looked up, as shocked as Digger. He hesitated as he beheld a hallway of hounds with glowing eyes looking at him. In that moment of hesitation, a large wolfhound leapt from four yards away and got his neck in the crack of the door. It knocked Digger back several inches momentarily, but he responded in kind with a football tackle against the door, pinning the snapping wolfhound in the door jamb. He applied more pressure and the wolf-like dog yelped. Digger eased up slightly on the pressure and the wolfhound fell back. He slammed the door and locked it.

The howling recommenced with repeated thuds against the door. Digger cocked the pistol and ran out the front door, then circled around the house and ran down to the lighthouse exterior door. He pushed against the exterior tower door to capture the wolfhounds in the hallway. The door would not latch. He reached over and grabbed a solar panel and yanked it over, cords and all, to where he stood with his shoulder to the door. He propped the panel under the doorknob, preventing the door from opening. He heard scratching on the door and howling. When he was sure the door was holding, he rounded the base of the lighthouse and walked along the outside of the long hallway to the first window. He peeked in at his collection of wolfhounds locked in the long narrow chamber. As he looked more closely, he was taken aback by the realization that they were chewing on bones and burger patties. He blurted out, "That looks like a T-bone steak!" He shook his head in amazement. A wolfhound heard him, looked up at the window and growled. Digger ducked out of sight and returned to the front door of the house.

As he entered the house, he felt a breeze blowing through the kitchen. He turned to the left and saw billowing curtains where he had previously shut the windows. Three wolfhounds sat on their haunches, contentedly chewing at meat bones in the living room. He leveled his pistol at the closest wolf. It looked like a very large dog and cocked its head to the side in a totally nonthreatening gesture. Digger couldn't pull the trigger. The other two looked more threatening. Digger grabbed the air horn on the counter next to him and blasted it while he held the pistol at the same angle. The three oversized wolf-like creatures jumped out the window single-file and Digger slammed the window shut behind them.

How did they open that? He looked at the window carefully. There were smudge marks on the glass. He opened it slightly to feel the bottom edge of the window. It had been chewed. As he was deducing that they had lifted the window with their noses and teeth, a wolfhound lunged at the slightly open window and grabbed Digger's hand. The wolfhound clenched its jaws and pulled Digger's body into the window. When Digger did not come through the window, the wolfhound, showing more of a bulldog trait, remained hanging on Digger's arm. As Digger screamed in pain, he took his free hand and blasted the airhorn out the gap in the window. The wolfhound let go and Digger fell back on the floor, writhing in agony. His left hand and wrist were bleeding profusely.

He staggered to his feet and slammed the window shut again, then propped the fireplace poker between the lower sash and the upper trim of the window to prevent the wild dogs from opening it again. He went to the bathroom and washed the wounds and wrapped his hand in a towel. The wolves were scratching and banging at the front door and the kitchen door to the hallway. The howling sounded like it was coming from every corner of the house. He looked at the towel. Blood was starting to seep through.

Then glass broke in the living room. He looked up in time to see teeth, red with blood, chewing at the window and its trim. The tall wolfhound broke another pane of glass with its teeth. Digger grabbed the gun and fired at the window. The howling ceased. Digger could barely hear the crashing surf above the ringing in his ears from the gunshot. As his hearing returned, he heard in the distance a lone cry of a wolf, which caused the rest of the pack to start howling again.

Digger thought about his predicament as the howls and growls increased. He looked up the steep stairs. He grabbed his backpack and stuffed it with more flares, the pistol, the air horn, and the leather-bound book on the kitchen counter. Then he dragged himself up the stairs to the second story. He dismantled a twin bed and moved a box spring next to the stairs. He kicked the railing down and slid the box spring into the stairwell opening. It formed a perfect seal at a slight angle. He pounded at the high end of the angle of the box spring, causing it to jam more tightly into the stairwell. He got the other box spring from the other bedroom and did the same. Then he layered both mattresses on top. *That's gotta stop 'em and they better not start climbing on the roof, please, dear God!*

Digger peeled back the towel. The blood was oozing unabated. He removed his belt, put a tourniquet on his left arm, three inches below the elbow, and re-wrapped the wrist and hand in torn bedsheets. He muttered to himself, half in shock. "Just doing a safety check on Dog Island!" He looked around. "Looks safe to me. How 'bout you? I think we'd be safer with a bonfire." He responded to himself jovially. "Capital idea, Unit 19!"

Just as he headed toward his backpack to get some flares, he heard more glass break and the thundering of paws pounding on the floor below. He froze and listened to the clicking of nails on wood as something climbed the stairway. Then he heard the clickety-clicks retreating back down the stairs. Digger went to the dormer window and lifted the sash quietly. He could hear the wolfhounds scampering on the ground below. He looked toward the woods. To the right on the edge of the woods, sat a large, lone, white wolfhound sitting on his haunches like a general on the edge of a battlefield. *It's Proto. He is directing this melee!* Occasionally a dark wolfhound would run to Proto and circle him and lie down. Digger thought of trying to pick him off with the .38. *Too far, but I'm not ruling it out. I need to conserve bullets for sure shots.*

Digger craned his neck to the right to try to see the stack of wood he had assembled for the bonfire. His sight distance was limited by the roof. He was sure the woodpile was just beyond the roof line. He stuck three flares in his waistband and climbed out the roof. The pitch of the roof was steeper than he was accustomed to climbing, and having an injured hand didn't help. When he tried to toe his way up the roof, his shoe kept losing traction against the asphalt granules of the shingles. He remembered Fitzy teaching him how to "French-climb" such angles by keeping the entire shoe on the surface and absorbing the angle at the hip and ankle and not bending the knee or foot.

Digger French-climbed the roof to the peak and straddled the roof ridge. He was hit with a blast of ocean sound and wind. The white wolfhound came out from the shadows of the forest and howled directly at Digger. Digger stood up at the peak and steadied himself against the winds. He pulled out a flare, pulled its cap off, and struck the flare against the cap's friction pad that he held tightly in his bloody hand. The flare immediately fired up with a bright red glow and spewed sparks. Digger held the flare high over his head and howled back at the wolfhound in the meanest wolf call he could muster. He looked over at the ghostly white wolfhound and, borrowing a line from the Wicked Witch of the West, called out, "Proto! Want to play ball?" Then he threw the lit flare onto the woodpile. It fell through the tangle of kindling. Digger noticed six wolfhounds run to where the white wolfhound sat motionless. Digger suddenly felt powerful, howling like a wolf with a flare in his hand. He pulled another from his waistband and stood up again. He struck it and raised it over his head and yelled, "Hey, Whitey! What else you got? The Coyote never wins! You hear me, Wile E. Coyote?" Then Digger yelled the sound the Road Runner makes at the Coyote in the cartoon.

"Meep-meep! You loser!" Digger howled again and arced the second flare into the slowly growing bonfire. Digger sat down quickly. A bout of dizziness had come over him. He was starting to see spots. *Not good. Losing blood. Gotta get in.*

Digger knew he had to French-climb in reverse, but now he could hardly stand. He scooched his way down the roof ridge toward the center of the house. When he was above the roof line of the dormer of the window that he had climbed out, he slid down the shingles to the ridge of the dormer. Then he slid off the dormer to stand on the main roof only two feet from the window opening. He was wavering. Six wolfhounds came trotting over and stood attentively under the window, as if they sensed Digger's weakness. Digger held on to the soffit of the dormer and walked himself around to the window and fell into the bedroom. Before he passed out, he heard and felt the large canine creatures jumping through windows below. He crawled to the bedroom door and pushed it shut and blocked it with his body. Digger curled into the fetal position around his backpack and his Smith and Wesson.

CHAPTER 40

Regulation 33: Obligation to Respond

The next morning, Kristy was at the helm of the *Performer* on its way back to Maine from Boston, where they had picked up more students for the unique summer semester at sea. Her position as first mate required her to make sure the orders of Captain Von Hans were faithfully executed by the crew, or herself if necessary. They had moored for the night in Newburyport and, while getting all hands on deck at 5:45 a.m. was no easy task, they were under sail by 6:15. By 9 a.m., they had rounded the Isle of Shoals, passed Nubble Light, and officially entered Maine waters.

"Jimmy, take the wheel, please," barked Kristy.

"Yes sir, ma'am, er, Kristy, I mean first mate, ma'am." The red-haired freckle-faced teen was botching his first morning at sea. His fellow seamen were at the rail, some hiding their laughter at his awkwardness, others looking green with seasickness. Kristy was used to both the confusion about her authority and the mislabeling. She preferred being called Kristy, but the captain insisted on "First Mate" or "Madam" or "Ma'am." Kristy was uncomfortable with the southern twang of ma'am and instructed that she would go by First Mate or Madam.

She looked up at the sails and down at the compass. "Jimmy, you're doing great. You are sailing a seventy-five-foot square-rigged schooner. You're doing it!" Jimmy beamed. Kristy pointed straight ahead. "Do you see that spire?"

Jimmy bobbed and weaved to see through the rigging. "Yes, First Mate, I see the spire."

"Good, Jimmy. Sail for it. Keep the bowsprit lined up with the lighthouse of Boon Island."

"Yes, First Mate," Jimmy replied dutifully.

The captain came to the wheel and commented on the weather being unseasonably nice. Jimmy was nervous when the male authority figure was around because of his own past. He remained quiet.

After they had passed Boon Island on the starboard side, Dog Island was visible on the port side.

A student pointed toward the island. "Captain, there's a lot of smoke rising over there."

That captain reached for his spyglass and pulled it to its longest length. "Indeed, sailor! First Mate Riggins?"

"Yes, Captain? " she replied instantly. The captain paused as he looked at the island further then glanced at his watch. He looked at Kristy with a smile. "Let's set a course for Dog Island, please."

"Aye-aye, Captain. Setting a course for Dog Island." She stepped away and began shouting orders. "Marvin get my chart please. All hands to the sheets! Prepare to trim for a broad reach on a port tack!" The students yelled back some form of the instruction. Kristy, looking at the chart, the sails and then at the compass, barked, "Helmsman, bring her to 3-3-5 please!"

"Steering to 3-3-5, First Mate," replied Jimmy. The nose of the schooner started inching to the left and the sails started rattling.

"Trim sails!" bellowed the first mate.

Some students knew what to do, others were clueless. Essentially the students on the left or port side of the boat were to pull in and those students on the right side were to let out so the square-rigged sails would angle properly to remain full. Kristy ran from station to station patiently explaining the process. In short order, the boat was trim and quietly steaming for Dog Island Light.

Kristy went below and returned with a large pair of military-grade binoculars. She went to the bow of the *Performer* and examined the island. She focused on the billowing smoke to the east of the house. She moved to the west and examined the tower and saw no sign of human activity. She could see a dry-docked boat and the boathouse. She moved slowly back toward the column of smoke. She stopped. It appeared as if a flag was flying from the roof of the house. She tuned the dial on the binoculars. No. The flags were on a pole beyond the house. The flags were odd.

Kristy called out, "Captain?"

The captain, concerned, had quietly come alongside Kristy. "What do you see?"

Kristy handed him the glasses and whispered. "I'm not sure that I don't see an SOS flag and an upside-down American flag right over the center of the roof of the house." The captain squinted and then put the glasses to his eyes.

He whispered, "That's the SOS… and… that's a flipped flag. I'll call it in immediately." He handed the glasses back to Kristy and looked her in the eye. "Can we make this a calm and controlled teachable moment on flag usage and rendering aid at sea?"

Kristy nodded. "Yes sir, we can. I'll assemble the crew."

While the captain headed below to the radio, Kristy called the crew to the foredeck. She asked them to get binoculars and reassemble in five minutes. She asked Marvin to fetch the laminated flag chart.

"Okay, sailors," Kristy began after they had assembled. "Examine Dog Island over my shoulder here and tell me what if any signals you see. Raise your hand when you think you have identified something." Half of the kids were weaving around on the deck still trying to gain their sea legs. One girl, with her elbow planted on a ratline to hold the binoculars steady, raised her other hand. Kristy called on the green-eyed blonde beauty. "Gretchen?"

"First Mate Riggins, I see an upside-down American flag. Is this a commie compound?" Gretchen asked. Other students started commenting that they saw the flag too. Kristy held her tongue. One student went to the chart and raised his hand. Kristy pointed at the young man. "Robbie?"

He responded, "First Mate, I believe the top flag is an SOS flag. It has an orange background with a black square and a black circle."

Kristy nodded affirmatively and then called out, "Fall in!" The students assembled in front of her in a straight line. Some students were still resistant to the military hoopla and slouched casually but in line. Kristy took one look at the slackers and bellowed, "Ten hut!" Everyone snapped to attention. "Ladies and gentlemen, Robbie is correct. An SOS is being called out from this island. Your captain is below at this very moment calling in the coordinates to the Coast Guard. The upside-down American flag is not a disrespectful gesture of a Communist compound as offered by Gretchen." Snickers circulated down the line.

Kristy continued, "Article 8 of the United States Flag Code indicates the flipped flag is a signal of dire distress where there is extreme danger to life or property. In a moment our Captain will be asking us to take positions in regard to this emergency. Please remember that this is not a drill; this is what sailors do to help fellow citizens on the sea." Pointing to the crew, Kristy said, "You four will man the starboard lines. You four will man the port side. Marvin, you and these two will stand ready for lowering the lifeboat. Any students with medical experience?"

Gretchen raised her hand. "I am a trained EMT and certified in CPR, First Mate."

Kristy replied, "Okay, Gretchen, you're on lifeboat detail with Marvin. Stations everyone!"

Marvin, a tall curly-haired boy from Texas, was back for his second summer and served this summer as second mate. He approached Kristy and whispered, "There's another flag you should see. Look to the stern of the boat dry-docked by the boathouse."

Kristy walked to the gunwale, steadied her arm in a ratline and brought the military binoculars to her eyes. She whispered, "Oh Lord! That's Digger's boat! That's the Talbot River Club burgee for sure and his double Mercs. That's the *Seahorse!*" She went quiet and kept searching the island for signs of Digger.

Marvin was nearby and put his hand on Kristy's shoulder. "If there's anyone who can handle distress, it's Davenport. He will be fine." Kristy kept the glasses to her eyes but couldn't see a thing. Tears welled up and escaped from under the binoculars. She sniffled and wiped her nose.

The captain came over to the quiet huddle of young officers. "Are we on track?"

Kristy lowered the glasses and looked at the captain with bloodshot eyes and tear-soaked cheeks. "Request permission to lower the launch and take a rescue party to the island, sir."

The captain was taken aback by the sudden change in her demeanor and by her request. His jaw dropped.

Marvin pointed to the island. "That white boat there, sir, is Digger Davenport's boat... the bike cop from Port Talbot who..."

The captain interrupted as he peered through his own binoculars. "I know who Digger is, Marvin! I recognize his boat from last summer... Uh, well, Kristy, the Coast Guard has been informed and... "

Kristy interrupted, gritting her teeth and nearly spitting her words. "Captain Von Hans, I respectfully request, pursuant to Regulation 33 of the International Convention on Maritime Search and Rescue, that we fulfill our obligation to respond. We are in the closest proximity at this time."

The captain continued to scan the island, considered her point, avoiding eye contact with his suddenly emotional first mate. Finally he spoke. "Tell me the teams."

Kristy swallowed before speaking, as Marvin was behind the captain, signaling that he wanted to be part of the rescue. Kristy spoke as calmly and professionally as possible, a difficult feat given her fear and distress. "The landing party would be Marvin, Gretchen, who is an EMT, and me. On the *Performer*, it would be you, sir, and the remaining crew."

The captain blinked his eyes at Kristy as if to say, *does not compute.* The captain turned to his second mate. "Marvin, I need you on board. We will not be dropping anchor. We will bring her into the wind and lower the tender. Then, we will hover and maneuver off the west shore near the boathouse... waiting for word." He squared up with Kristy in front of him and added, "Kristy, you take Gretchen and two strapping young men to handle the oars and get you on those rails. They look tricky. I love that tender more than anything. I don't want it smashed on Dog Island. Pick your team, Kristy....make sure they are over eighteen years of age."

"Yes, sir. Thank you," the first mate replied gratefully.

CHAPTER 41

THE LANDING PARTY

The captain pivoted and headed to the wheel. Marvin leaned in and whispered, "Robbie knows martial arts and Ken is a hunter."

Kristy whispered back, "I tried to get you on the mission."

Marvin winked at her. "The captain needs a real sailor to stay back. I get it. Thanks for trying." He headed to the davits holding the launch.

Kristy turned to the crew and bellowed, "I need the following, front and center, for the landing party! Gretchen, Robbie, and Ken! The rest of you will be receiving orders from the captain and the second mate. You will be maneuvering off the island until we return. Please stay professional and attentive. Lives could be at stake here!"

Kristy now focused on the team in front of her. "Gretch, raid the first aid box and put it in a waterproof carry-on. Now."

Gretchen replied, "Yes sir," pivoted, and ran to the cabin.

Kristy quietly continued. "Ken, do you know how to handle a Beretta pocket pistol?"

"Yes, ma'am, I am a certified sharpshooter," Ken replied.

"Robbie, do you know how to fight if we get in a jam?"

"I'm a black belt, ma'am." He bowed as if Kristy was his sensei.

"Okay, good. You are both over 18 and are you volunteering for this mission, correct?"

Both square-jawed boys grinned. "Affirmative!"

"The most immediate and important skill we need is rowing. Please tell me you know how to row a boat?" Both boys gave a thumbs-up. "All right, let's assemble in three minutes at the lifeboat." The team scattered for final preparations.

The captain remained at the quarterdeck next to a student serving as the helmsman. "Jimmy, get ready to come about, but you're gonna only come halfway. We're gonna bring her into the wind and hold her. Okay?"

"Yes, Captain. Halfway and hold into the wind, sir."

The captain yelled up to midships. "Riggins! Landing party ready?"

She yelled affirmatively back to the captain and instructed the team to line up by the gunwale where the lifeboat was rocking from davits over the side of the *Performer*. Kristy checked the life jackets on her team by going down the line, pulling them by the openings at the arms and shaking the entire body. It was more like a tough-guy salute than a safety check.

The captain yelled, "Ready about?"

The entire team yelled, "Ready!"

He responded, "Hard-a-lee!" The boat spun like a merry-go-round. "Hold it right there!" he shouted. The rigging and the sails were rattling and snapping and the forward motion of the boat came to a halt. The captain gave a hand signal to Kristy to load up. Kristy gave a thumbs-up and the landing party climbed into the launch while Marvin manned the dual davit electrical winches. The party slowly descended the side of the boat with some crew members looking enviously overboard at them. Finally, they were able to disengage and row clear of the flapping and rocking *Performer*. The captain ran to the side to check the clearance. He signaled the helmsman by pointing to the port side and yelled, "Fall off to a broad reach, Jimmy!" The crew repeated the order and trimmed the sails. The boat responded instantly and headed to the south side of the island.

In the tender, the two boys were rowing midships and Kristy was on the tiller at the stern calling the cadence of strokes and directions to the starboard and port oarsmen. Gretchen was in the bow, looking for rocks below. Kristy squared up the launch with the rails and gave the command to stroke with ramming speed. The boat caught a wave and rode onto the left rail. Kristy yelled, "Lean starboard!" The captain's prized boat was teetering on disaster. "Gretchen! Bail out. Grab the bow line!" Kristy jumped into the surf at the stern. "Boys, hang on that starboard rail!… Gretchen, on three you're gonna pull up and to our right."

Kristy watched the waves for the right timing. "One…two, and three!" The wave lifted the stern at first and Gretchen started hauling up the rails to the right. Kristy was completely submerged, putting her shoulder into the transom and pushing up and to the right. When the wave receded, the boat was centered on the rails.

Kristy pulled herself up at the stern, looking like a drowned rat. The boys looked at each other and smiled. Ken asked, "Could you push us up a little further, please? It looks wet on that rail there."

Kristy barely smiled at his attempt to lighten the moment. "Let's pull it higher and secure it to the rail. Hustle and focus, please."

As they headed to the lighthouse keeper's quarters, Kristy's radio crackled to life. "How's my tender, Miss Riggins? Over."

"We're wet, but your boat is high and dry, Captain. We're going radio silent now. Over and out." She turned the knob until the radio clicked off. Then Kristy pulled a small pistol from her pocket and handed it to Ken. "No cowboy antics, please." Ken nodded and checked the pistol's mechanics and number of rounds as he walked.

Robbie held his hand up "Look at that! It's a wolf or some funky dog! It just jumped out of that window. See it running up there into those trees? It must have heard the radio." Robbie paused and pulled a pair of nunchucks from his backpack and pulled off his white collared *Performer's* uniform shirt and stuffed it into the backpack. He started flipping the nunchucks around his shoulders and his bare chest as he walked. A tense silence came over the team as they approached the house.

Out of the blue, Kristy took off at a run toward the front door, yelling Digger's name. The rest of the landing party looked at each other wide-eyed and mouthed the word, *Digger?* Ken sped off after Kristy. "Kristy! Kristy! Hold it!" He grabbed her arm before she entered the front door.

Kristy spun around and hissed, "My boyfriend is on this island somewhere! We've got to find him!"

Ken put both hands on her shoulders. "Okay, we will! But hold up. I'm here for a reason." He held the pistol in the air. "Now get behind me." As he slowly opened the front door, he chambered a round in the pistol and led the way into the kitchen.

A sudden ghastly howling echoed from the hallway on the other side of the kitchen door. The small group huddled closer to the guy with the pistol. There were bloody paw prints everywhere they looked. Ken rounded the kitchen to look in the living room and leveled his pistol at an injured wolfdog.

"Hold it!" Robbie said, then looked in the den and the bathroom. It was clear. "You guys move over there and cover me. This guy is going out through the kitchen." Everyone moved as directed. Robbie carefully moved into the living room, hugging the far wall, until he was behind the large wolfhound. The wolfhound made no noise but simply looked at the human intruder and raised its upper lip and lowered his jowls to reveal and silently flex a ferocious rack of sharp teeth. Once in place, Robbie pulled the nunchucks from his waistband and started spinning and snapping the sticks and moving toward the wolfdog. It hauled itself up and limped painfully out through the kitchen with its tail between its legs, leaving behind a red spot where it had been sitting on its haunches. "Clear!" Robbie shouted. The howling continued to ricochet off the walls of the long hallway to the lighthouse off the kitchen.

All eyes however, looked in the opposite direction — up the steep, dark stairwell. Ken flashed his light upward. "That's a box spring." He looked at Robbie and motioned him over. "Excuse us, ladies, this looks like the aftermath of one of our frat parties." Both boys climbed the stairs and lifted the entire covering with their backs and tipped it over on to the side.

Kristy ran up. "Digger! Digger?"

They all congregated in the bedroom on the right and looked at the shut door on the left. "Here, let's get these out of the way," offered Ken. They passed the mattresses and box springs into the one open bedroom.

Kristy jumped for the knob of the closed room. It turned but the door wouldn't open. They all clearly heard a distinct groan. "Digger!" screamed Kristy. "It's Digger!" She started crying.

* * *

Robbie nodded toward Gretchen, who understood and pulled Kristy to the side. "Kristy, let the boys get the door open. Stay calm, honey. Breathe with me." Kristy did as she was told. The boys got on their knees and Robbie said loudly, "Digger, we're opening the door. Please roll out of the way on three! One, two, three!" Both boys pushed firmly at the base of the door. It held at first then suddenly gave way as Digger rolled away from the door.

Kristy ran in and fell to her knees next to him. "Digger, we're here. It's Kristy. You're gonna be okay."

Gretchen kicked some bedding over the bloodstain on the floor where

Digger had lain before Kristy could see it, and then placed her medical bag on the bedding and unzipped it. She started with a stethoscope and nodded to the boys to get Kristy out. Gretchen barked, "Quiet, I can't hear!"

Robbie lifted Kristy from Digger's side. "First Mate, step over here. Let Gretchen do her work."

Kristy looked into Robbie's eyes and whispered, "Will he be okay?"

Robbie half-carried her to the other bedroom. "Yes, he is gonna be fine."

She searched his eyes. "Do you pray?"

He whispered back, "Not since sixth grade."

Kristy crumpled to her knees and started whispering. "God forgive me for not believing, but don't do anything for me. Do it for Digger, please, Lord. He *is* a believer. He loves you. Save him, Lord, for his dedication to you, please. I deserve nothing. Do it for him, Lord. I love him. Ah-men." Rob echoed her *amen* and whispers of *amen* came from the room where Gretchen was working.

Gretchen strapped an oxygen mask on Digger and opened the valve on the mini-tank. "Robbie, or someone, have Kristy or anyone call in a medivac immediately! This guy needs serious help, ASAP!" Gretchen pulled out a small saline bag with tubes. "Ken, hold this up please." Gretchen washed a spot on Digger's inner arm and jabbed the port into a vein and hooked in the saline drip. She spoke calmly to her patient. "There you go, Digger. Your body is thirsty, and we are giving it a drink. Keep breathing that oxygen. Deeply now. That's it."

In the other room, Kristy was crying too hard to be of any use, so Robbie was on the radio. "Captain, we have one badly injured male named Digger."

Kristy whispered between sobs, "Davenport... David Adam Davenport, Junior."

Robbie continued. "Captain, correction, David Adam Davenport, Junior. Gretchen said medivac is essential. Over?"

"Roger on the medivac. Where's the first mate? Over?"

"First Mate is assisting, over. Please advise on an ETA on the medivac. Landing party standing by."

"Roger on ETA. *Performer* standing by."

Digger started groaning. Gretchen told him to save his energy, and that Kristy and the Coast Guard were working to help him. "Ken, tie that drip to the doorknob and let's align his body and check for fractures, okay?" Ken got on his knees and began rubbing down Digger's legs as he pulled him gently into a straight line. Gretchen tore open her patient's shirt. Her eyes widened at the sight of Digger's toned physique. "Uh, Digger, you look pretty good here. Let's check this arm." Gretchen unwrapped the bedding strips and saw the tourniquet he had made with the belt. "Not bad... it actually held. Hand me the peroxide bottle, please. I'm gonna need more sheets, too." She laid Digger's wrist out on the bedding and dabbed the wounds with peroxide. She noted aloud that the bite wounds had coagulated and had begun to scab over. She began to gently loosen the tourniquet. "Moment of truth here, fellas. We need blood in this arm if we're gonna save it."

Ken whispered, "What about infection?" Gretchen pawed through the medical bag and held up a hypodermic needle. "Right you are, Dr. Kildare. A mega-dose of antibiotics to the area ought to help." She cleaned the area and administered the shot. Digger winced, but let Gretchen bandage the wounds with clean gauze and white tape.

"Kristy, can you help me?" Gretchen called. Kristy stumbled to her feet and came into the room. "Can you talk gently to Digger and rub this forearm and these fingers here? We want the blood to return. Please stay away from the bandage and please let me know if you see any spotting."

Kristy wiped the tears from her eyes. "I would love to do that," she sniffed. Gretchen stood up and left the room. Ken followed.

The three crew members went down the stairs and out onto the lawn. Robbie brought the radio. Ken assumed point position with the pistol ready. Gretchen spoke first. "Who knew the mission was so personal to Kristy? Like, wow!"

Ken spoke over his shoulder as he kept his eyes straight forward on the lookout. "Is he gonna be alright?"

Gretchen nodded. "If we get him more help. Immediately. Can I see the radio, Robbie?" He tossed her the handheld. "*Performer, Performer,* this is landing party. Come in please. Over?"

"Go ahead, Gretchen. What's the status?"

"Davenport is stabilized with the best we can do. He is unconscious, dehydrated with dangerously low blood pressure. We need a medivac pronto. Over?"

"Roger. I can't get an ETA, just that it is coming from Portland and that was half an hour ago." There was a commotion in the background. "Correction, Gretchen. The crow's nest reports a white chopper has been spotted in the northeast sky. You got room for a landing? Over."

Gretchen looked at Ken, who nodded yes. "That's affirmative on the landing room. We will prepare for our visitors. Over."

"Okay. *Performer* out."

Robbie asked, "Ken, what do you say we unleash the hounds in that long room?"

"No, Robbie! Are you kidding?" Gretchen interjected as she jotted notes on a piece of paper. "Please wait until we launch the patient and we are in the boat. If you want to run back and open the door or something, knock yourself out, you bleeding heart!"

Robbie relented, "Okay, okay, let me check it out. I won't unleash the hounds yet. I promise."

All heads looked toward the east to see a white and orange helicopter coming toward them. Gretchen turned to enter the house. "Let's get him ready for evacuation. They better have a basket." The dogs started howling as the noise increased.

Rob muttered, "Must be a nocturnal-type species."

Gretchen entered the room where Kristy was gently working on Digger's motionless arm and fingers and speaking quietly to him. She looked up at Gretchen, stricken. "Will this work? He's not waking up. Gretchie, please, is Digger going to be okay?"

Gretchen smiled at both patients. "Yes Kristy, I believe he will. Help has arrived."

"Do you think I can go with Digger?" Kristy asked, pleading.

"Oh, I don't know about that, but you can ask. Let's get his stuff together."

Kristy looked around. "I think it's just that pistol and his backpack."

Ken came bounding up the stairs. "They've landed and are coming with a basket."

Gretchen handed Digger's handgun to Ken. "Can you make that thing safe for transport?" Ken snapped it open, emptied the chamber, and spun the round carriage of bullets and emptied them all into his hand. He dropped everything into Digger's backpack. "Nice piece."

They heard Robbie downstairs. "This way... up the stairs over here.

Do not open that door over there. We don't want the puppies to get out."

Ken said, "Let's move out of here and make room for them. Head to that room."

Three Coasties climbed the stairs in orange jumpsuits and heavy-duty helmets, gloves, and boots. The leader asked, "What we got, fellas?" He did a double take when he saw Digger in his blue uniform. "He's a police officer?"

Gretchen nodded and provided a quick summary of Digger's vitals and the interventions she performed. She handed the leader a sheet of paper covered with notes. She had signed it with her credentials and put her address as the *Performer*. "It's all on that paper."

The two other guardsmen placed the basket next to Digger. The basket was lined with a thin cushion and an unfolded blanket. One asked, "Captain, okay to lift?" Gretchen explained the skeletal exam she'd performed. The captain okayed the lift. The two guardsmen counted to three, then lifted Digger into the basket, bundled him in, and then applied the strapping.

The captain shook the paper Gretchen had prepared. "Thank you for this, ma'am. This is incredibly helpful."

She smiled and nodded appreciatively and then spoke quietly for Kristy, who was her own basket case. "Our first mate, Miss Riggins over there, is Officer Davenport's girlfriend. She's taking this pretty hard and was wondering…."

Before Gretchen could finish the question, the captain's head was shaking back and forth. He mouthed, *No passengers.* He looked beyond Gretchen. "First Mate Riggins?" He shuffled toward her, pulled off his helmet and gloves and set them down. He reached out for Kristy's hands and held them. "My name is Captain Thomas Bains, Portland Coast Guard Search and Rescue Team. I want you to know we are going to give Officer Davenport the very best treatment. Now, I need you to help these students get back on the *Performer* and get safely to port. I'm sorry I cannot let any friends in the chopper but hope you will be encouraged knowing we are doing our best for him. He is in good hands."

She nodded, blinking away the tears. The medics lifted the basket carrying Digger. As they moved toward the stairway, the captain said, "Hold up!" He turned to Kristy and asked kindly, "Miss, can you send him off with an encouraging word?"

Kristy stepped around the hulking officer and went to Digger's side. Only a small portion of his face was exposed by the blanket they had wrapped him in. She bent over to his ear. "Digger Davenport, we all prayed." She paused and changed her tone. "I want that Nose Warmer coffee with you at the Brigantine this summer. You promised." She peeled back the blanket from his face and kissed him on the lips. Digger licked his lips and gave a faint smile. The rescue team erupted with hoorays and applause. Robbie reached over and snapped Digger's backpack to the basket straps. The two Coasties carried Digger slowly down the stairs and out to the helicopter. Kristy and her crew waved as the chopper lifted off and careened to the northeast.

"Okay, gang, let's go home," said a decidedly calmer Kristy. As they gathered their gear and headed back to the launch, Robbie peeled off toward the lighthouse. He picked up a spool of rope that he had found earlier and attached to the door at the base of the tower. He started walking toward the team by the boat and played out the rope as he clambered across the rocks.

Kristy cocked her head. "Robbie, what in the world are you doing?"

He smiled. "I am releasing the hounds... when y'all are safely in the boat." He dropped the rope and helped them slide the boat to the water's edge.

Kristy looked around. A smile came over her face and she barked a command. "Sir Robert, release the hounds!" Robbie scrambled across the seaweed and rocks and pulled at the rope. He kept hauling and shortly the solar panel that Digger had used to block the door came skidding around the lighthouse. Robbie dropped the rope and started picking his way back toward the launch floating at the foot of the rails. He paused, bent down and picked up something in the seaweed.

The girls were screaming in the boat. "Here they come!" Robbie calmly looked back at the four wolfhounds at the base of the lighthouse, staring their way.

Robbie held the item in his hand and walked nonchalantly toward the crew. "Anyone looking for a set of boat keys?"

Kristy focused. "Those are Digger's! Hide 'em in the *Seahorse* and let's go, Marlin Perkins! *Wild Kingdom* is over. We're changing the channel. Get in!" Behind Kristy, Ken and Gretchen high-fived each other in reference to Kristy's newfound spunk. They mouthed the words, *She's baaack!*

The wolfhounds quietly, and in single file, came out and watched the landing party row away. Proto stepped to the forefront, stretched his neck toward the sky, and let out a long and lonely, solemn-sounding cry. Robbie responded quietly in the boat. "You're welcome."

CHAPTER 42

THROWING OFF THE SCENT

On Tuesday morning following the Fourth of July weekend, a package arrived at the receptionist's station at the Tuck School of Business at Dartmouth College. The same girl who had met Rick Eaton's alter-ego weeks earlier opened the package to find the stolen Hartson archives material lovingly cushioned in bubble wrap. She checked the items against the catalog of missing documents. Everything had been returned, down to the last page. She checked twice. The return address was Portsmouth Public Library. There was an unsigned typed note in the bottom of the box. *Sorry about the mistake. I thought these items circulated.* The receptionist called the chancellor's office. The chancellor called the college's general counsel.

The same morning, a brown UPS truck drove down Hartson's Beach Road to Jonathan Hartson's home at Crescent Point. Out on the point, one can watch any vehicle approach from across the beach for a full five minutes as it makes its way to the peninsula, raising a dust cloud in its wake. Thus, in keen anticipation, Jonathan Hartson walked down the porch steps to receive the delivery. The driver announced three packages for the Hartson family. Jonathan smiled. "Well, you are at the right place." He signed for them and offered a tip. The UPS man declined, citing corporate policy.

Jonathan brought the packages in and set them on the dining room table. He thought to share the excitement with family members but quickly remembered he was alone. The financial ruin hanging over his head ruined much more than just the balance sheets. He opened the heaviest package first. It was the gold Hartson crest, shined to perfection. There was no note. Next, he opened the large box. It was the telegraph machine, gleaming in mint condition. There was a thin paper tape with dots and dashes curling out from the shiny contraption. Jonathan scratched his head as he looked at the tape. Next, he opened the smallest box. It was the ship's log from the *Vigilant*. The return address for all boxes was the same: 33 Arch Street, Boston, Massachusetts. Jonathan's stomach tightened. How many times had he dreaded seeing the address of the regional office of the Securities and Exchange Commission? He called his lawyer.

* * *

Also that morning, which was almost two weeks since he had found the gold on Dog Island, Rick Eaton was busy in his attic hideaway. He turned off the recently acquired copy machine as the attic was starting to heat up. He had amassed several packets of documents and photographs of Hartson family members and properties. He called Sanford Beach, his father's attorney, who had challenged the Hartson bequest in court twenty years ago. A chipper-sounding secretary answered the phone. "Sandy Beach Attorneys. How may I help you?"

Rick was thrown off by the firm's name. *You gotta be kidding*, he thought. "Uh, is Mr. Sanford Beach there, please?"

"Who may I say is calling?"

Rick thought quickly and said, "A paying client on the Hartson probate fraud."

"Just a minute please." A jazzy tune came over the phone. Rick started grooving to the hold music. He was getting his suave, command performance mojo going.

"Sandy Beach here. How may I help you?"

"Hi, Mr. Beach. This is Bill Eaton's son, Rick. How are you sir?"

"Well, I am fine Rick. I remember our conversation after your dad passed. He was a great man and I miss him. How can I help you?"

"Thanks for those kind words, Mr. Beach. My dad thought highly of you as a person and as a technician of the law, and that's why I am calling."

"Say, Rick," the attorney interrupted. "Please call me Sandy, okay? But I must cut to the chase, young man. My receptionist mentioned something about Hartson probate fraud. As I explained to you years ago, we settled that case and you're living in the result of that settlement, unless you have moved. That property by the way, is getting valuable these days."

Rick let him take a breath and asked calmly, "May I be heard, counselor?"

It touched a chord in the attorney as it was the exact phrase he would use with a judge who was mowing him over. "Of course, Rick, go on."

Rick began slowly as he looked at his papers. "As to the settlement agreement, there must be a complete meeting of the minds. No party must be laboring under a mistake or a hidden set of facts. See the court decision, *Harvest Grain versus Lewiston Railway.*"

Sandy said quietly, "I know the *Harvest Grain* case. Go on."

Rick continued, "I believe I can demonstrate that the Hartson family knew or should have known they were sitting on textile assets worth millions at the time of the settlement, and if they had been disclosed, one, no settlement would have occurred, and two, the Eaton's twenty percent interest in the mill would have been paid to us…" Rick paused for dramatic effect and finished confidently, "… in gold."

Sandy coughed on the other end of the line. "I'm sorry, Rick, did you say *gold*? The mill was flat broke. It was in bankruptcy."

"Sandy, several days ago, I finally obtained proof after years of research that the Hartsons have hidden a cache of ingots of gold that are still available for attachment or whatever legal process you recommend. I'd like to show you my proof and see what you say. I would pay for your time to review and research our options. I think a preliminary injunction preventing the gold's removal is crucial, however." Rick let his words sink in.

After a brief silence, Sandy asked in a low voice, "How much gold?"

Rick knew he had him. "I believe the document identifies over seven hundred bricks or about fourteen tons. Are you available this afternoon? I can bring the retainer and we can discuss."

"Absolutely, Rick. Is one p.m. good for you?"

"That's perfect, Sandy. Are you still down on Talbot Beach on the main stretch of the beach road?"

"You got it," Sandy replied. "The white house with the turret. You can't miss it."

"I know the place. I'll bring my suit!" Rick doubted the man caught his double entendre because the line went dead too quickly.

In his office, the attorney hung up the phone and licked his lips. He reached for his morning bracer and happy pill with a noticeable tremor in his hand.

CHAPTER 43

The Impatient Patient

That same morning, Digger sat upright in the hospital bed, thumbing one-handed through *The Dog Island Diary*. He had pulled the leather-bound book from the backpack that had accompanied him to the hospital from Dog Island. The chief and Patty knocked on the door. Digger raised both arms, one in bandages. "I give up!"

The chief snorted and shook his head. "That's your problem, Davenport. You nevah give up." The chief took the journal from Digger's hands and showed the title to Patty. "See what I mean?"

Patty brushed the chief to the side and gave Digger a hug and bouquet of flowers. "When they gonna let you outta here?"

"When my blood levels are correct. Whatever that means. It's been over a week! Apparently, I had sepsis and now I have jaundice from the mega doses of penicillin. The cute little puppy gave me a world-class infection. And I did have to get a rabies shot, just in case. But I am feeling a lot stronger. Maybe tomorrow."

The chief sighed. "Well, that's good. Guess who handled Talbot Square over the Fourth?" Patty snickered and motioned her eyes toward the chief.

Digger exclaimed, "Don't tell me you worked the square?"

The chief nodded and looked around for a *No Smoking* sign. "Can you smoke in heyah?"

Digger pointed to the oxygen tanks on one wall. "Not a good idea, but hey, let's take a walk to the balcony. You can light up out there. I need the fresh air." Digger grinned. Patty rolled her eyes and helped Digger out of

---

the bed. He put a robe over his shoulders and grabbed his portable IV stand.

The three of them headed down the hall to an outside deck overlooking Portland's Casco Bay. "This is my favorite place," sighed Digger. "Although I no longer fantasize about living on those islands out there."

They all laughed, but then the chief got serious. "Dog Island was a minefield, Diggah. I'm sorry I sent you into it. I had no idea." The chief put his hand on Digger's shoulder. "I thought it was a picnic in the pahk. Fun in the sun… on the clock! I am so sorry."

Patty picked up where the chief left off. "I'm sorry too, Digger. When that dingbat Darla called in the request, I should have gotten so much more information. I talked to her over the Fourth and she casually mentioned how the guys on the *Jug Tug* were concerned about being waved off by a white guy wearing a red-stained shirt with a shoulder holster."

Digger's eyes got as wide as saucers, but he held his tongue. "Hey guys, It's okay. I get some R and R with a water view." He pointed out to Peak's and Chebeague islands and continued. "I forgive you. Don't think about it again. I can't wait to get back to the beat, honestly. It may be awhile before I ride the bike, but I think the doctor will clear me for light duty."

The chief raised his eyebrows. "Light duty, Unit 19? You got two weeks paid medical leave. Enjoy it. That's an order! Besides, the Dog Island matter is simply a missing person report. The bones found with the clothing weren't human. The bones are cow bones and the blood on the clothes was canine. Mr. Lincoln, the keeper, went AWOL, that's all. We contacted his ex-wife in DC. She says he'll be back when he's done betting on the trotters at Scarborough Downs. We have an APB out for him. Case closed for now."

Digger's brow furrowed. "Closed?" He thought quickly and changed his expression to a smile. "Great news, Chief."

His boss took a last haul on the unfiltered cigarette and flicked it off the balcony. Then he exhaled to the sky. "The lighthouse works and that's what counts. Lincoln will show up soon enough. Not our problem. Right, Diggah?"

Patty stood slightly behind the chief, signaling Digger to nod his head in agreement. "Right, Chief. Yes, that's good news. Probably best to keep any mention of the bones and blood analysis very confidential, just in case." That last phrase caused the chief to wrinkle his forehead. He reached for his second cigarette. He was obviously frustrated with trying to keep up with a college kid's insights into investigations within the chief's jurisdiction.

Digger looked through the glass back down the hall and was thankfully able to find an excuse to derail the conversation. "Looks like I have some guests…let me tell 'em I'll be right with them. We can take our time out here. I'll be right back."

"No, Diggah, we gotta go," said the chief. "We just wanted to apologize and show our respect. You get some rest, okay?"

"You sure? We don't have to rush," Digger offered cordially.

The chief shook Digger's hand. "We're off like a prom gown and remembah, you're not on sick leave. You're on our workah's comp program. You take as much time as you need. You'll be paid for every day missed and all the medical bills. No questions. Before we run, is there anything you need me to know?"

The chief kept a firm grip on Digger's hand. Digger thought about a few items. "No, Chief. I think my statement pretty much explained what happened. Thanks for coming and bringing this pretty woman. She's better than a bouquet of flowers." He bent over and hugged Patty.

"Flattery works for me!" Patty hugged Digger. "Get well. We need you."

Digger left them on the balcony and went to greet Kristy in the hallway. She was joined by Gretchen, Robbie and Ken. The sailors followed Digger into his hospital room, where he crawled back into bed. Kristy bent over and kissed Digger on the forehead. "As you know, this is the landing party that rescued you. I wanted you to get to know them, Digger. Plus they deserve some land time and the captain let me borrow the car so I could bring us all here."

Suddenly Kristy got emotional. "Gretchen saved your life." The other boys nodded in agreement. "And these boys…" Her tears were flowing. "These boys nunchucked and muscled their way past your barricade to your second-story hideout. They took on the hideous wolves."

Robbie, seeking to help Kristy, tried diluting the subject. "Actually, the creatures are more like an Irish wolfhound. The snout is hairy and they're much taller than a wolf."

"My arm is starting to throb just thinking about those beasts," Digger replied.

"Robbie is our resident zoologist," said Ken. "He set the dogs free from the hallway that led to the tower. When they got out, I swear they came to say thank you as we rowed away. It was freaky."

Robbie added, "They're a smart and unique breed, that's for sure."

"Oh yeah, and Robbie has good eyes," said Ken. "He found your boat keys in the seaweed!"

"Oh wow, thanks, man! That's still a mystery." Digger saw Kristy's face change at the mention of an ongoing mystery. He quickly changed the subject. "Gretchen, give me a hug, please." He brought her in for a long hug. She explained some of the emergency medical procedures she performed and Digger thanked her profusely.

He also shook the boys' hands and got to know a bit more about their respective interests in firearms and martial arts. "Geez, what a dream team, Kristy! You all could have your own TV series!"

Soon, Gretchen indicated that it was time to leave. "We're gonna get some ice cream downstairs. Take your time, Kristy." The three sailors made their exit and allowed Kristy and Digger to be alone.

"I saw the chief was here. Are you gonna take the rest of the summer off, Digger?" she asked pointedly.

"I've got two more weeks of paid leave," he replied. "But no, I'm not quitting. No way. I love this job!"

Kristy sighed. "You don't need the job, Digger. And who knows what was going on out there? You may be a target still. I am a basket case thinking about the harm that could happen to you. I was a blithering idiot when we came to the island. I lost it... I actually snapped and became very unprofessional, knowing it was you somewhere on that island, and then with all that blood everywhere..."

Kristy paused but she wasn't done. "I think I love you too much. I have been shaken to my core over this." Digger held his arms out for a hug. Kristy leaned in and wept. Digger couldn't speak. Her feelings were too deep for him to touch with words. He shoved over on the bed and invited her to lie down next to him. Digger reached over to pull the privacy curtain closed and the two held each other in a long, silent embrace.

CHAPTER 44

THE SHIFTY SANDY BEACH

Rick drove to the attorney's office, which was in a large white Victorian overlooking Talbot Beach. Sanford Beach's office was in his home, which featured a turret on one side and a widow's walk on the roof. A small white sign with black antique lettering announced *Sandy Beach, Esq.* and provided a phone number below. Rick brought a suitcase into the reception area. The receptionist stood and offered a seat and a cup of coffee. Rick accepted both. Before long, Sanford Beach descended the turret's circular oak stairs into the reception area. "Mr. Eaton, good to see you again. It's like looking at your dad. The resemblance is uncanny."

"Thank you, Mr. Beach. I take that as a compliment."

"You should, Rick. I loved your father. Such a hard worker. Say, Rick, please call me Sandy."

"Okay, Sandy, thank you. Do you have a large table? I have a lot to show you."

"Of course. Let's meet in the conference room over here." Sandy led the way into a large room overlooking the ocean and Beach Avenue. He lifted window blinds from the bottom of the window to halfway up the window. The blinds hid all the passing cars, surfers and people pushing strollers, leaving just a view of pure ocean. Off to the right, Dog Island was visible.

Rick began unpacking the suitcase. He looked up at Sandy. "Does the attorney-client privilege apply yet or do I need to pay the retainer officially?" He reached into his pocket and pulled out a banded packet of hundreds and put it on the table.

Sandy's eyes widened. "It attached over the phone this morning. Let's do it this way, you tell me your story. Make your case. If it's something I think I can help with, I will describe what I recommend and then I'll quote a fee for doing it, okay?"

Rick put the money back in his pocket. "Perfect. Let me just collect my thoughts and papers here."

The secretary brought in coffee. "Would you like an easel, Mr. Eaton?" Rick looked up and noticed her for the first time. "Yes, please, that would be great, Miss…?"

"I'm Jeanette." They shook hands. After a few minutes Rick was ready.

"Sandy, I'd like to start where you last left off in this case. Here is the settlement agreement where Dad accepted the property and trailer in full satisfaction of his, or actually what would have been his father's, claim to a bequest of twenty percent of Hartson Textile in Biddeford. Let's call it Exhibit One. Exhibit Two is the order of the court stating that the bequest of ownership in the mill had… what you lawyers call… *adeemed* because the mill was in bankruptcy."

Sandy nodded. "I remember the ademption problem like it was yesterday."

Rick continued, "This is the bankruptcy petition of Hartson Textile Ltd. I got it from the federal court in Portland. It cost a small fortune to copy it. Let's call it Exhibit Three." He let it thud onto the conference table. Sandy reached for it immediately and started thumbing through it. Then the attorney reached for the other exhibits and compared the wording in the documents. When Sandy looked up, Rick continued, "I think these documents show what the Hartsons *said* was the status quo of Hartson Textile. It did not, for example, address real estate on the beach and in Vermont, correct?"

Sandy nodded in agreement. "Correct. Your family's rights were only in Hartson Textile Limited."

Rick nodded agreeably. "And these documents paint a dismal picture of the mill, which made the settlement for a single-wide trailer in the woods look good, right?"

The attorney nodded. "It was the best I could get for your family."

Rick, invigorated by the attorney's acquiesce so far, continued. "I believe that in 1960 when Ted Hartson Junior's last will and testament was going through the probate court and my grandfather, Thomas Eaton, was about to be rewarded, that Hartson Textile was worth between $100 and $200 million dollars." Rick didn't skip a beat. "Here's Exhibit Four. It's a copy of an inventory of the company's vault on Bay Street in Savannah, Georgia, dated 1859. The abbreviations are a bit tricky but *VLT* is vault. You will see references to French, Spanish, and British currency and 'ings' or ingots worth $6.8 mille mille which is a thousand thousands or a million. In short, the vault for their textile operation contained $6.8 million worth of gold… in 1859. I'll let you review the document."

Sandy looked up. "Where's the original?"

Rick pointed over his right shoulder. "New Hampshire. At Dartmouth's Tuck School of Business."

Sandy got up from the table and shut the doors leading into the reception area and the door into the kitchen. "This wasn't stolen from their archives was it?"

Rick's face wrinkled. "That is what I hate about the news. They never tell you the good news. Dartmouth recovered every document, returned from the Portsmouth Library with a note apologizing for circulating the documents. Originals, if necessary, will have to be subpoenaed from the Tuck School."

Sandy looked Rick in the eyes. "Please don't tell me you are behind the Hartson heists at Dartmouth and the vandalism down on the beach."

Rick, feeling a bit perturbed at the attorney's pointed question, deflected. "As I said, the news never reports the good developments. I understand that as we speak, everything has been returned to the Hartsons." Beach's eyes scanned Rick's face for any twitch, smirk, or blink. Rick was cool as a cucumber, smug in fact.

Sandy made his mental notations and continued. "So, the textile company had money in 1859. So what?"

"So, in 1859 the Hartsons hid the yellow bricks of gold in their schooner and offloaded them on Dog Island. They've been hidden there ever since, until I discovered the mother lode this past week." Rick knew he was misrepresenting the date of his discovery, but figured Beach didn't need to know the whole truth. He reached down and lifted a gold ingot imprinted with the Hartson crest out of his suitcase, then handed the heavy ingot ceremoniously to the attorney. "If I am correct, there are seven hundred more of these bricks stacked under that window in the lighthouse tower on Dog Island." He slid over a picture of the windowsill in the tower showing the gold bars beneath the sill. "Exhibits Five and Six."

Sandy was slack-jawed and mesmerized by the bright golden light shining in his eyes.

Rick paused to allow the primal greed to attach thoroughly. "I analyzed shipping logs, telegraph transmissions, and personal letters to pinpoint where the gold was hidden. Then, by myself, I toured the lighthouse. It was completely abandoned, by the way," Rick lied easily. "Just a mess… taken over by wild mangy dogs. Anyway, using the blueprints for the tower, which was built in 1861, I found that the tower of the light is hollow and filled with these ingots of gold. Using your law firm, I'd like to lay claim to them. I believe there are a number of legal reasons for my claim. The easiest one is the inheritance argument of a minimum of twenty percent of the value in 1960. Add to that punitive damages for withholding the information. My other theory is known as finders keepers, losers weepers and I have here the case of *Beauchamp versus The City of Portland*. It is an actual legal doctrine."

Sandy looked pale. "What else do you have?"

Rick spread out on the table more contents from his suitcase. "Here are some photos of where the ingots have been stacked and photos of the abandoned state of the lighthouse today. I'd like to get an injunction over the lighthouse barring people from taking the gold out from under me. I'd like to do this today if possible"

Beach stammered, "Who else knows about this?"

Rick replied, "I don't know who knows about this. Possibly just you and me. But one of my theories is fraud and that would mean that the Hartsons alive today have full knowledge of this stash."

"Not necessarily," Sandy countered. "The subsequent generation may not know about this hidden gold. Why would they be selling everything if they knew they had all this?"

Rick ignored the question and cut to the chase. "So, Mr. Beach, do I have a case?"

Sandy stood and began to pace slowly, his head down. He reached for the bankruptcy petition and the inventory on company letterhead.

"Son, you have a heck of a theory but unfortunately, I do not think you have a case. First, it appears that the southern company is a different company than the one of which your family was given a twenty percent interest. Second, if what you say is true, then you are simply discovering

Hartson property *for* the Hartsons. Are you entitled to a fee by law for this discovery? No, the property you discovered sits on their land. By law, it's not lost."

Rick's thoughts swirled as Beach's negative opinions unfolded. In exasperation, Rick stammered and pleaded, "Mr. Beach... sir... the issue as to whether the gold was an asset of the northern company or the southern company... I... I know it appears to be two different businesses but look at the bankruptcy petition. The schedules of assets turned over to the trustee in the bankruptcy include the cotton gins! That sounds like the southern operation was a wholly owned subsidiary of the northern operation! That argument alone could earn us the twenty percent of millions... if we were to prevail on that theory."

"It's a theory, but to be frank, Rick, I just don't like the foul play that surrounds the case. In the law we call it *unclean hands.* Your position has been jeopardized by improper conduct."

Rick did his best to keep his cool as he argued his rudimentary understanding of the law. "Aren't *unclean hands* an equitable argument and our claims are based in black-letter probate law?"

Sandy showed a slight exasperation with a non-attorney playing legal eagle. "A court always sits in equity. They may give you an attaboy for the discovery, but when the truth comes out about the lengths you went to in order to get this information and the vandalism at the family home, I'm afraid I won't be able to keep you out of jail, to be honest."

Rick became incensed. "I didn't say I *did* that vandalism!"

Sandy stopped him. "Rick, don't try to kid a kidder. I see what happened here and I will get thrown out of court on my backside. I'm sorry, I can't help you."

Stunned, Rick returned his papers to his suitcase in silence. He put the gold bar in a velvet sack and added it to the suitcase.

Sandy offered lamely, "There might be another attorney who would consider this. Would you like me to inquire?"

Rick let the suitcase drop to the floor with a thud. He stuck his hand out to shake the attorney's. "Mr. Beach, I would appreciate it if you would forget I was ever here. Do I have your word?"

Sandy Beach shook Rick's hand vigorously. "You have my word." The two men parted, not as friends.

* * *

Sandy let Rick out and then ascended the circular stairs to his round-walled office in the glass-windowed turret overlooking the beach. He peeked through the blinds as Rick got into his late-model Ford. Sandy wrote the plate number down. When the car had disappeared, Sandy pressed the intercom button on the phone. "Jeanette, hold all calls please. I'd like not to be disturbed."

"Yes, Mr. Beach."

Sandy went to the other side of the round office and opened the blinds fully. He used binoculars to check out Dog Island. From his angle it looked like an uninhabited island of pine trees and rocks. He could see just a bit of the top of the tower and light. He muttered, "Beautiful!" He walked to an intricately carved armoire and opened both doors to reveal a wet bar and a large television. Above the TV on its own shelf was a Sony Betamax video recorder and player. A red light was beaming from the machine. He hit a button and the recording indicator light went off. He reached for a crystal tumbler and poured two fingers of scotch and sipped it neat.

He walked back to his desk and spun his Rolodex of contacts. He stopped at *James Pearson, Real Estate Broker*. Beach punched in some numbers on the phone. "Sandy Beach for Mr. Pearson, please." He was connected immediately. "Jimmy, you scallywag, what are you up to?" After exchanging pleasantries, Sandy got to the point. "So, Jimmy, are the Hartsons selling Dog Island too? Everything else seems to have a for sale sign on it?"

"Yeah, Sandy, it's for sale if you got two million dollars," replied the broker.

"Has there been any interest?" inquired Beach.

"I'm not the listing broker but I can find out. I hear it comes with a Coast Guard lease that requires the owner to power the lighthouse and allow them possession of the light occasionally for safety checks and repairs. Why? Are you interested?"

"I have a client who's interested. They want their identity to remain confidential. What does it take to get a showing?"

The broker replied, "It takes a letter from a bank indicating that the prospective buyer is good for two million dollars. Then I can show it or, better yet, you, being an attorney, can show it. I am not a water person. If you get me the bank letter, you can go out there and kick the tires. Are you any good with a boat? I hear it's tricky to land on the rails they set up on the island. But I guess you could anchor away from the rocks and row a skiff in."

Sandy pressed for more information. "I'm pretty good with a boat. I heard the island is abandoned."

"I am not sure about that." Pearson said thoughtfully. "A black fellow was living out there, last I heard. He's a friend of the Hartsons. And of course, the dogs are out there, you know. They're still there from when we were kids and they're still howling. But they don't bother you during the day."

"What's it take to put it under contract if we want to move quickly?" asked Beach.

"Sandy, this would be a commercial deal. I'd say a good faith deposit of ten grand on the contract with twenty percent down at closing and the rest could be bank-financed. That should do it, if your offer is in the right ballpark," replied the broker.

"Okay, thanks, Jimmy. I'll let my client know and I'll get back to you."

Sandy hung up and reclined in his high-backed leather executive chair and hit the power buttons on the remote controls at his desk. The TV sparked to life. He mashed the rewind button on the Betamax control, then hit "play" and watched.

On tape, Rick was looking in the direction of the hidden camera. *"So, in 1859 the Hartsons hid the yellow bricks of gold in their schooner and offloaded them on Dog Island. They've been hidden there ever since until I discovered the mother lode this past week."* Rick reached down and lifted a gold bar. He handed it to Beach. *"If I am correct, there are seven hundred more of these bricks stacked under that window in the lighthouse tower on Dog Island. I analyzed shipping logs, telegraph transmissions, and personal letters to pinpoint where the gold was hidden. Then by myself, I toured the lighthouse. It was completely abandoned by the way. Just a mess… taken over by wild mangy dogs. Anyway, using the blueprints for the tower, which was built in 1861, I found that the tower of the light is hollow and filled with these ingots of gold. Using your law firm, I'd like to lay claim to them. I believe there are a number of legal reasons for my claim…"* Sandy hit the pause button.

The lawyer spun his Rolodex again and punched in a Boston number. The phone was answered by someone with a thick Russian accent. "Popov's Fish Store."

Sandy Beach gave his best attempt at a Russian greeting. "Zdrahst-vooy-tyeh, Attorney Beach calling for Alex, please." There was a hearty laugh and a simple *okay*. Beach was put on hold.

" 'ello, dis is Alex. Who dis?" replied Popov.

"Alexander the great! This is your Maine attorney. And I mean Maine as in the state of Maine because I know you have attorneys everywhere, but I am your Maine attorney, get it.?"

"Da. I get it." Then the Russian added sarcastically, "Funny, comrade. Vut you vant? I pay you for dat last violation. I pay my fine to DEP too. Big fine. Vy you call?"

"You were lucky on that DEP violation. I saved your kapchunka, buddy!"

"Okay, okay, Sandy Beach. Vut you vant? You charge by da vord… keep simple for me."

"Alex, I have a business proposition. Do you have a boat?"

The Russian replied, "You funny man today. I have fleet of boats. I fish. You remember?"

Beach rolled his eyes. "That's right, Alex. Well, how would you like to become very, very rich?"

"I listening to my Maine lawyer now. Talk to me, tovarish."

Beach replied, "Here is the thing. I need you at my office tomorrow at 8 in the morning. I will show you something and then we will take my boat for a quick ride. I promise you, you will like this deal. We will make some serious kapchunka, comrade."

"Okay, you speak my language. I come to your office at beach at 8 tomorrow, yes?" confirmed the Russian.

"Yes, please, comrade. I will have the black tea ready."

"Dat is good. I see you in morning. Goodbye, Beach."

Beach signed off in Italian. "Ciao, baby."

CHAPTER 45

PROFESSOR KINGSLEY SPEAKS

After he left Sandy Beach's office, Rick drove home pounding on the steering wheel, yelling choice words about the attorney. He stomped into the trailer where Brenda was, as usual, glued to the TV. *Wheel of Fortune* droned away on the new Zenith console TV that Rick had recently bought. Ignoring her, he headed for the bottle of Old Grand-Dad in the upper cabinet of the small kitchen. Brenda punched the buttons on the control and the volume went up then down as she tried to figure out the newfangled thing. "What's the matter, Ricky? That was quick. Let me guess, the attorney was in court?" Rick ignored her until he had poured a second gulp in the small tumbler.

"No wonder my dad lost!" Ricky finally spat out. "That yellow-bellied sapsucker... good for nothing turncoat... wimp! He is a wuss!" Rick moaned, taking another gulp.

Brenda pushed the side lever forward on her new crushed velvet Barcalounger and lumbered to her feet. She came to Rick's side as he faced the cabinet and kept pouring single shots as he spewed angry words about Sanford Beach. Brenda put her hand on his shoulder. "Come sit here at the table and tell me what happened." She grabbed the whiskey bottle and his hand and pulled him over to the faded yellow Formica kitchen table. He followed and sat down. Brenda poured a few more ounces in his glass and said kindly, "What happened, honey?"

Rick's head was down as he sputtered, "He listened to everything I said, thought about it, asked me a couple of questions, and said he was declining to get involved."

Brenda zeroed in. "What did he ask?"

Rick stammered. "He a... he a... he asked if I... if I was behind the Dartmouth heist and the... the... the Crescent Point burglary. I admitted nothing! You know I returned everything to those snobs. Even a thirty-thousand-dollar slab of gold! I never should have done it. We need that money. I thought Beach was gonna take the case and we were gonna do it on the up-and-up. I didn't want that stuff derailing the legal case. Now, I want it back... All of it!"

"Okay, honey, okay, maybe you're right. But just hold on. Breathe. C'mon, let's go outside and let Samson out and you have a cigarette. Come on, Ricky." Brenda was speaking Rick's language. He slopped some more whiskey into his glass and followed Brenda to the garage. Brenda called Samson. The dog just looked away from her as if he was deaf. Rick slapped his thigh and the dog leaped immediately from his pen and ran into the backyard. Rick lit a menthol as he and Brenda walked to the deck overlooking the large, heavily overgrown backyard.

Rick was calming down. "That attorney got all of my information on the gold and now he ain't gonna help me. I don't get it. It's simple. There's a pot of gold out there on the island. I have a solid legal argument that I'm entitled to some of it. I discovered it, after all. We got ripped off in court years ago and today was supposed to fix that. Why wouldn't he take the case? Attorneys only need the slightest reasons to sue. And there being so much money involved, it makes settling easy! What's his problem!"

Brenda let him vent for a while. "What about getting a different lawyer? You don't need that chum bucket!"

"No! One blood-sucking coward is enough. Besides, the information is too sensitive to share. I cannot risk shopping this case around to lily-livered lawyers afraid to take on the Hartson dynasty."

Brenda labored to lower her pregnant self into the Adirondack chair as Rick continued to pace on the deck, chain-smoking. Samson brought a ball and dropped it at Rick's feet and cocked his head to the side. Rick absentmindedly kicked the ball out into the yard. Samson's eyes lit up as if to say *game on* as he tore after it. Rick paced more and then looked at Brenda with a gleam in his eye. "I could do this myself! I'll sue them myself! I know..."

Brenda interrupted, "Now the Old Grand-Dad is speaking. I was wondering when 'he' would come out." Brenda used her fingers to indicate two quote marks around the word *he.*

Rick ignored the dig. He slurred on, "I know what needs to be done. It is called a motion to knock out an old judgment."

Brenda rolled her eyes. "I doubt it is called that, counselor."

"It's something like that. You can blow up a previous order if there's been fraud. I would first ask the court to make the case top secret. They seal it from the public. Then I'd ask for an injunction to protect the gold and fight over my motion to revisit the old probate case. That will bring the Hartsons running to the settlement table. I just need to get them in that position. If my calculations are correct, there's plenty of dough to talk turkey with these thieves. It's time for payback… *lex talionis!*" he shouted, punching his fist in the air. Samson jumped and barked incessantly in reply. Brenda shouted at the dog to shut up, with no effect. Rick snapped his fingers and the dog sat and looked at the ball at Rick's feet.

Brenda thought for a moment. "If your argument is so good, and it does sound good, Ricky, why don't you just make your case to the Hartsons directly? Just go to Royal Orchard with your legal papers and proof and say, 'We can do this the easy way or the hard way.' Tell 'em you have a team of attorneys that will argue that it's all yours and that you'll drag the Hartson name through the mud. Shame on them for ripping off a common working-class family. Tell 'em it will drag on for years, but if they listen to you and your demands, everyone can do well. There's enough to go around, if it is as you say."

Rick threw back the rest of the whiskey and walked in the trailer for more as he contemplated Brenda's words. He yelled from the kitchen. "They'd probably try to arrest me for the Crescent Point job!"

Brenda looked toward the neighbor's house next door. "Ricky! Keep your voice down. Your Old Grand-Dad is talking too loud."

Rick returned, looking more subdued but with a full glass in his hand. Brenda picked up where she left off. "They can't arrest you. They're not cops. Besides, it would expose their own underhanded dealings… if, again, the facts are as you told me. It's simple. The things you were gonna say to a judge, well, you just say it to the Hartsons themselves. Write up a script just like you're going to court and stick to it. You're smart, Ricky. You've always been smart!"

Rick was thinking. He didn't want to mention Samson's pursuit of the lighthouse keeper on the island and the man's "natural death" by the wolves.

He kicked the ball again for Samson, who had been waiting expectantly next to the motionless ball. Rick looked up. "Everything's been returned, Brenda, and there is no proof I did those jobs..." His voice trailed off as he thought about Brenda's idea.

She added, "Well, you be sure you don't say anything that ties you to those capers and push the angle that the Hartson reputation has more to lose and they should drop their cockamamie accusations of burglary, especially when everything has been returned. As Professor Kingsley says on that *Paper Chase* TV show," Brenda used her best deep patrician voice, "No harm, no foul."

Rick laughed, bent over and kissed Brenda. "That's why I like you. You're funny. And you're smart." Brenda knew the alcohol was taking effect. Rick, feeling much better, mimicked the popular TV character Professor Kingsley by putting his nose in the air and bellowing, "No hahm... No foul!" Then he did his best imitation of the same actor's advertisement for an investment house. "They make money the old-fashioned way... They earn it!"

"That's right, Ricky! You go earn it, too. The old-fashioned way. You do a backroom deal with the Richie Riches of this country over snifters of one-hundred-year-old brandy. You tell them that you are not running to a courtroom, you're not doing what every low-class American does when injured. You're respecting their intelligence on this matter and doing a deal the old-fashioned way. You're earning it, man to man. I think it will work. If not, then run to court on your own, but let's hope it works 'cause you in the courtroom would get eaten up by their team of attorneys."

Rick was getting inspired. Whether it came from Brenda's idea or his Old Grand-Dad, it was hard to tell. He looked at Brenda sweetly. "Will you help me prepare?"

Brenda rolled out of the chair and hugged him. "Of course, Ricky. I'd be honored." Deep down Brenda knew she was being an enabler, but the truth was, he was nicer drunk. "We start tomorrow and we practice until you are ready, Ricky."

He held the embrace and started massaging her back. "We have to do it soon cuz I don't want someone else to scoop our gold!" Rick was slurring his words.

"Thursday is our visit to the baby doctor. You'll be ready to visit the Hartsons by Friday," Brenda calculated.

CHAPTER 46

DOG ISLAND DIARY

Later that same evening at the hospital in Portland, after the chief and Kristy had concluded their visits, Digger reached for *The Dog Island Diary* on the nightstand and began to read.

May 14, 1863

This is my first attempt at keeping a diary. Please bear with me, dear Diary, as I pen some preliminary thoughts about this endeavor. At Mount Holyoke, I learned what a diary was by studying Samuel Pepys's written diary ca. 1700. He shared personal feelings and historical observations. His work gave us an intimate insight into life in London during the Great Plague and the Great Fire of London. By Providence, I pray such calamities will not be shared here but rather I hope to share the salient events and my feelings as they unfold during our escape to Dog Island. It is hoped that the pages of this diary will be filled with joyous moments and be a testament to the love God has patterned for us. We leave behind the madness of a warring world. As I ink this, a civil war is raging among our fellow citizens in the southern states. Russia is crushing people in eastern Europe; Mexico is in flames.

If it were possible, my soul mate, Tombo and I would declare this island as a neutral country. Instead, we shall live here as if it were and share our life together, hopefully free from apprehension and violence. Our own relationship is under attack on the mainland. We both risk imprisonment because of our love. Tombo is Negro and I am white. Separately, we are decent, honest, God-fearing folk. Together in love, we are illegal, felons under the laws of the state of Maine. Dog Island is our refuge.

My father, Henry H. Hartson, wants to rename the island Liberty Island, as he is a staunch defender of that American ideal. He wants to exterminate the wild dogs that have lived harmoniously with the Indians during their encampments. I explain to my father that liberty, obtained at such violence to beautiful creatures, is not an ideal. Thus far we have prevailed.

Tombo is showing me how to appreciate the wild dogs and he has begun interacting with our fellow island dwellers. They appear in the evening and look larger than a coyote or a wolf with more colorfully variegated coats than the coyote or wolf. It is hard to call them wolves or coyotes as they have longer necks, thus making them taller, and they have fur around the snout more akin to the Irish Wolfhound. I have dubbed them the Wabanaki Wolfhounds and hope to make friends with them.

You will have to forgive me if I use the medium of this diary to express my feelings. I am an island dweller now. It can be a lonely life and I like the idea of conversing with someone, if only in the pages of this diary. In particular, I speak a testament to future Hartsons. This is your heritage. Your inheritance. Last year we built the Dog Island light. We were fulfilling the request of the Department of Revenue in aiding seafaring vessels. But it too served our purposes. It will be a lasting inheritance for Hartsons for generations to come. We commenced construction in the spring and lit the light on Christmas Eve 1861. The building materials used are most unique: yellow brick from Savannah, Georgia. This is the true inheritance, combining the rich resources of our fruits in the South with the Yankee ingenuity of protecting property and future commerce in the North.

Digger stopped reading and wondered why there were penciled stars in the margin of the diary at this sentence. He noticed a faint underlining in pencil of the repeated words *inheritance*. He continued reading.

The Department of Revenue has partnered with us on the creation of the lighthouse. They pay us a small rent to run the lighthouse. Their stated interest is for the safety of sailors. Their underlying raison d'etre, however, seems to be revenue from customs, taxes, and catching the excise evaders. In fact, this spring Congress and President Lincoln enacted the Revenue Act. It is a new tax called income tax. This will help pay for the war in the South. It requires a reporting of all assets and an annual determination of their increase in value and a tax on that value. For the Hartson textile mill and railroad operations, this is a significant development. Father, a big supporter of Lincoln and an avowed abolitionist, nonetheless, likes my idea, in jest, of declaring Dog Island independent and seceding from all such authority, especially after he has had a clarifying glass of port. Thus, the irony of Dog Island: It is a place to be free from authority while, at the same time, the authority pays us rent.

Finally, by way of introduction to our island life, my brothers, with the help of Tombo, and George Eaton, the foreman at Royal Orchard, have made every effort to convert the lifesaving station on the island to a habitable home for us for year-round. The boys erected a flagpole tall enough to be seen from Royal Orchard. Likewise, similar poles have been erected at Royal Orchard and Jonathan's new home under construction at Crescent Point on the beach. All three sites have signal lights for nighttime communication and signal cannons to get one another's attention. The piece de resistance, however, is Tombo's boat, the Jalibaas, which is a sturdy craft and can ferry us back and forth from the island. It is a steam-powered launch that provides heat and speed when needed. It does have a mast, but he rarely uses it. So rhetorically, dear Diary, I ask you, what could go wrong out here? I started this account with a reference to my alma mater, Mount Holyoke Female Seminary. I conclude likewise with her motto: "Go where no one else will go, do what no one else will do." Thus, begins our story. Sarah Hartson, May 14, 1863

Digger thumbed through the pages. Most of the book appeared to be in Sarah's handwriting. "This thing doesn't make total sense. Is she married?" he asked himself as he turned the pages. Toward the back of the leather-bound book, it seemed that the author and the penmanship changed a few times. Digger had to squint to decipher the cursive writing.

His eyes seized upon a sketch on one the pages. It was captioned "Window on Hartson Heritage and Inheritance." It was an incredibly realistic illustration of a simple four-paned window looking out on crashing surf. It evoked a feeling of beholding a tumultuous surrounding from a peaceful and protected place. The window was framed deeply in brick. Digger thought, *I'll bet that's the window halfway up the lighthouse.* Digger noticed another lightly penciled star in the margin next to the drawing's title. Digger repeated the words out loud. "Hartson heritage… Hartson inheritance." He studied the pencil drawing more closely. On the sill of the window was a symbol. Digger pulled the other light cord next to his hospital bed and bright light filled the room. As his eyes adjusted, he examined the drawing again and recognized the symbol as the Hartson crest. It was identical to the crest he had seen at Crescent Point. Digger turned the page of the diary and continued reading, utterly captivated.

August 6, 1863 Feast of the Transfiguration

Our Anglican calendar says today is the feast in remembrance of Jesus returning to heaven and so we are celebrating with a party at Royal Orchard. I am being honored for completing the murals at Royal Orchard. Thus, they have a feast planned in part for us. This is the difficult part of civilized life in Maine, it is not entirely so. Tombo and I remain aloof from one another in public. Twenty years ago, Massachusetts repealed their anti-miscegenation law. Twenty miles away, in New Hampshire, no such law ever existed. Now, however, forty-three years after Maine came into the union as a slave-free state, it still remains unlawful for us to marry. Tombo and I, both created in God's image must deny our affection for one another in public. Mr. Darwin's theories have not helped. The full title of his book says it all: On the Origin of Species by Means of Natural Selection, or the Preservation of Favoured Races in the Struggle for Life. Open discussion now abounds as to the necessity of cleansing "inferior" inherited traits and these ungodly ideas are now taking root. It is abominable. Tombo says it is the spirit of the anti-Christ and has been around for a long time. Indeed, Plato's work, The Republic, speaks of the superior society being achieved through mating of the upper class. Sparta was in favor of killing inferior infants! Could a society that makes our mixed-race marriage a crime devolve to the killing of children as acceptable? I pray not.

I am happy to be back from the reception for the unveiling of the murals. How very convenient we had to catch the Salmon Creek's tide.

It waits for no one, even Maine's governor, who was in attendance. I did not like explaining to him why Vigilant's cargo and the Dog Island Light were depicted in the mural using gold leaf. Only Jonathan, Ted and Tombo could understand the mysteries in the mind of this artist. It's the Hartson heritage, the Hartson inheritance.

Digger noted the underlined words yet again. His thoughts began racing. He pictured the murals in his mind. Turning off the bright light, he lay back and closed his eyes to concentrate. Some key words that he had read started illuminating *in medias res* in his mind's eye like the marquee in Times Square: *Yellow brick... inheritance... mysteries... testament to the future... coat of arms on compass... coat of arms on windowsill...window to inheritance... golden lighthouse... golden ship in Savannah... the lighthouse constructed... resources of the South protecting property in the North... Testament, inheritance.* Digger bolted upright and blurted, "This book is a last will and testament. Dog Island Light...or at least the window in the Dog Island lighthouse... There is something there."

Digger turned on the bright light again and began to read the diary cover to cover. He took notes and placed bookmarks as he examined the century-old text. When he was finished, he pushed the call button for the nurse and bolted across the room to pack his personal items into the overnight bag that his parents had brought on an earlier visit. A nurse entered the room. "Mr. Davenport, may I help you with something?"

Digger was dressed except for the shirt sleeve on his left arm. "Yes, please. Can you remove this tube-thing? I need to be discharged, please."

"I am sorry, Mr. Davenport, we cannot discharge you without a doctor's order and that will not happen at this hour. Our lab is closed and we need to be sure your white and red blood cell counts are healthy. But I'll note your desire for the doctor on tomorrow's day shift."

Digger sighed and thanked her. He looked at the clock on the wall and reached for the phone to call his father, Dr. Davenport.

CHAPTER 47

THE RUSSIANS ARE COMING!

"Comrade, here's your tea." The attorney handed the tall, dark, curly-haired Russian a mug.

"Thank you, Beach. Is a good day to discuss making money."

Sandy raised his coffee mug to toast the Russian. "To our success!"

Alex Popov raised his own mug. "To our success!" They both took a sip.

"So, Alex, did you bring the bank letter and the check for the good faith down payment for the contract that we discussed yesterday?"

The Russian patted his shirt pocket. "Yes, Beach. I have de letter and check, but first convince me I vant to buy dis island."

"You are not gonna buy the island, Alex. You are just putting it under contract so we... you... can do your inspections, like water tests, structural inspections, and the like. You will have thirty days to come and go on the island as you please. There's a lot to look into, no?" Beach said with a wink. "During that time, you will surgically remove the gold. Then when you're done and the site appears undisturbed, I will send a letter declining to make the purchase because of water quality or some other excuse. Your two million dollars will never leave the bank, and you'll get your deposit of ten thousand dollars back...every penny."

"Okay, okay, show me vy I vant to do dis. You lawyers talk fast. I vant proof dat gold is dere." Sandy smiled as he dramatically hit the button on the remote control. Alex spun around to watch the TV where Rick Eaton was speaking.

So, in 1859 the Hartsons hid the yellow bricks of gold in their schooner and offloaded them on Dog Island. They've been hidden there ever since until I discovered the mother lode this past week." The Russian watched intently as the kid speaking reached down and lifted a gold bar. He handed it to Beach. "If I am correct, there are seven hundred more of these bricks stacked under that window in the lighthouse tower on Dog Island."

The kid slid a picture toward the attorney. *"Exhibits Five and Six."* The tape continued to play.

I analyzed shipping logs, telegraph transmissions, and personal letters to pinpoint where the gold was hidden. Then by myself, I toured the lighthouse. It was completely abandoned by the way. Just a mess... taken over by wild mangy dogs. Anyway, using the blueprints for the tower, which was built in 1861, I found that the tower of the light is hollow and filled with these ingots of gold. Using your law firm, I'd like to lay claim to them. I believe there are a number of legal reasons for my claim..."

Sandy hit the pause button and looked at the Russian.

Alex asked, "Why you not take case, Beach?"

"Because that kid is a two-bit criminal," he answered.

Alex continued to pepper the attorney with questions. "Vut dogs? The kid say dogs. Vy you not tell me wild dogs dere? I hate dogs."

"Alex, uh hello... the place is called Dog Island. Big Alexander the Great is afraid of puppy dogs?" chided the attorney.

Alex ignored the question and asked, "How you get on the island?" Sandy rolled out on his desk a chart of the island and surrounding waters and Alex stooped over the desk to examine it.

Sandy swiveled in his chair and pointed out the window. "There's the island right out there." Then he returned to the chart and began to point out the landmarks. "Here's Portsmouth, Isles of Shoals..."

Alex interrupted, as was his pushy style, "Dis I know. Where's Gold Island on map?"

"Right here. It's *Dog* Island," replied Sandy.

Alex picked up the chart and peered at the little numbers around the island. "Horosho! It's deep dere. Dat is good. Vat's dis?" Alex pointed to a set of parallel lines extending from a small structure on the island.

"That's a boat ramp." Sandy replied.

"Vat, no dock? How I get on my island?" inquired the Russian.

"Uh, well, we go now and find out. My boat is ready. If you are ready, I will take you out now." replied Sandy with the smile of a slick salesman. He followed Alex's gaze out the windows at the beach and the sea.

"Yes, it is good day, let's go, Beach." Alex replied gruffly. Sandy patted his own breast pocket. Alex took the hint and handed over two items. Sandy examined the bank check and then the letter from the bank indicating Olga Karpinsky of Sobaka Corporation was approved for payment of two million dollars.

"Why is the letter from a different bank than the check?" asked Sandy.

Alex smiled, but without humor. "You not vant to know… and no ask who is Olga."

"Okay I don't want to know. Good. But if the broker calls this bank, this account and these names will check out, correct?"

Alex tilted his head to the side. "I sound like dumb Russian, I know. Dat is to fool you. Dis will all check out. Dis ain't my first road to hoe."

Sandy squinted his eyes. "You mean *rodeo*."

"Da. Dat's vut I say." replied Alex.

Sandy dropped the idea of giving the Russian a lesson in American idioms. "Let's go check out the island and, if you like, we can go to the broker's office and put in this offer." Sandy handed him a contract for the purchase of real estate. Sandy turned to a page and pointed. "This is the right of inspection clause. You can do bore samples, percolation tests, structurals, environmental tests… even air tests, anything! This means that when you bring equipment on and have helpers on the island going everywhere, that it will look normal. Got it? When you take your equipment back, it will just be a little heavier."

Alex nodded. "How vee split da gold, comrade?"

"Well, Alex, my friend, I say we are fifty-fifty partners. Like détente. You Brezhnev, me Kissinger. Even-steven."

Alex swore in Russian. "Fifty-fifty? Nyet. You get one-three. All lawyers get one-three. I take all da risk. My money, my name, my boat, my inspection, my carry gold to boat. I get seventy. You get thirty to sit at fancy desk and vatch with magnify glasses." The Russian pointed out toward the island.

Sandy smiled, undaunted. "Make it forty percent and we have a deal." Sandy extended his hand to shake. Alex spit on his own right hand and held it out to shake.

"Alex, that is disgusting." Nonetheless, Sandy spit into his palm and shook. They looked each other in the eye and held the tight grip for longer than usual.

Alex warned as they shook, "My team…Vee play, vee win."

"Good. I'm glad I'm on your team, comrade," replied Sandy.

The men set off for Dog Island. As they approached the island in Sandy's Boston Whaler, the *Sand Shark*, Alex examined the island through the binoculars. "I not see dogs. Dis beautiful land. Vut if I want dis property for real? I can buy, yes?"

Sandy was watching the waves and wind as he got closer to the landing rails. "Yes, you can buy, but I get more legal fees!" They both laughed. "Do you want me to land the boat or just drive around the island?" Sandy asked.

"I see enough. No one dere. Vindows broken. Door is vide open. Vere dis gold?"

Sandy turned the boat around to approach the south side of the island. "According to what the picture showed and what the kid said, it's right below the one window there in the tower."

"Dis might take time to get. Maybe best to pull tower down," replied Alex as he continued to scan with the binoculars.

"Pull down the tower?" Sandy erupted. "Are you nuts? This is a stealth operation, Alex! You want the $10,000 back… you do not want people asking you questions about what happened out here. No. No. No."

"Okay, Beach, I understand. How I get hundreds of bricks out of dat tower fast?" The men discussed various plans as Sandy did lazy figure eights in front of the tower and boathouse. Sandy suggested they set up a tented spot under the window, run loads to the boathouse, and then use a small skiff to run loads to Popov's anchored trawler.

Alex nodded in agreement and looked at his watch. "Okay, I like dis deal. We come tomorrow, Friday, and do our… vut you say? *Due diligence?* It vill take time to get my trawler here."

"Hold on, Alex, we need to get it under contract," said Sandy. "The sellers have to sign the contract. They may take a few days."

Alex barked, "Today you make offer good for twenty-four hours only. It is full price. They sign. We come tomorrow. It is simple, Beach. We go now."

Sandy decided he would rather not argue the point. He would make the offer valid for twenty-four hours just like the shrewd Russian insisted. "As you wish, Alex." He steered the *Sand Shark* back toward the Talbot River.

The men enjoyed a quick lunch at the Talbot Wharf Restaurant, which sat above where Sandy docked his boat. After lunch they parted with specific instructions. Sandy headed to the real estate broker's office with a "time is of the essence" contract signed by Olga Karpinsky on behalf of Sobaka Corporation, and a ten-thousand-dollar bank check.

CHAPTER 48

THE CONFIDENTIAL
INFORMANT

On Friday morning, as Digger was discharged from the hospital and being driven home, he had a few words with his father. "Pops, I thought you had visiting privileges at Maine Med. Why couldn't you get me out of there? I was hoping you could pull rank."

"Son, what's the rush? You're very lucky to be alive. The infection was severe, it compromised your lymph system, kidneys, and liver. And, for your information, I did pull rank. I told them to keep you until the lab results were to my liking, and that took two more days."

Digger exploded, "*You* kept me in? Wow... I just hope it isn't too late! I'm trying to help the Hartsons on a very serious matter, Dad. I lost *two more days* sitting in there watching reruns on TV!" They drove in silence after Digger's outburst. As soon as the car pulled up in front of Seaside, Digger exited and slammed the car door shut, then ran in the house to get some items.

As Digger started to head back outside, his father stopped him in the front hall. "Hold it, Digger. You're still on sick leave. You need to rest your body, son."

Digger sighed and dodged his father. "I'll be back soon." He let the screen door snap behind him to put an exclamation point on his feelings, and headed straight for Royal Orchard with the *Dog Island Diary* on the seat beside him.

He pulled into the long tree-lined driveway of the stately mansion.

He didn't recognize the two cars in the driveway, but he saw Holly's car over by the barn. He put the diary in his backpack and headed for the door. This time he used the brass knocker with the Hartson family crest on it. The *bang-bang-bang* was close to a "police knock." Holly's mother answered the door with a bewildered look on her face and squinted at the unexpected guest.

"Hi, Mrs. Hartson. It's Digger Davenport. I am sorry to bother you. I hope Mr. Hartson is feeling better."

A broad smile came to Faith Hartson's aging face. "Digger, why of course. What a pleasant surprise. Come in."

"I don't suppose Holly is around, is she?" asked Digger.

"Well, she is in a meeting…" Just then Holly came around the corner.

"Digger! I heard you got injured out on Dog Island. Are you all right?" Holly rushed to hug him. Mrs. Hartson stepped back. Obviously, there was more to this story than she knew.

"Holly, Mrs. Hartson, I really am sorry to intrude but I think I have some very important information that the family, the entire family, needs to hear."

Holly and her mother looked at each other with genetically matching furrowed brows.

Mrs. Hartson asked, "Good news or bad news, Digger?"

"Hartson news is always bad news, Mom."

Digger smiled to encourage them. "This actually could be great news, ma'am, if steps are immediately taken to protect what I believe is a Hartson asset." The women again showed similar hopeful expressions as if they were twins.

Holly said, "Well, your timing is impeccable. Daddy and Uncle Jon are having a family meeting. Stay right here? I want to be sure they can take a moment to have you explain it to us all at one time." Holly spun and ran down the long foyer and disappeared to the right. Mrs. Hartson offered a refreshment. Digger declined.

Holly re-appeared at the end of the foyer and gestured to him. "Digger Davenport, come on down!"

Mrs. Hartson followed Digger to the study where the gentlemen were meeting. Theodore Hartson the fourth sat slumped down in the red velvet throne chair that had belong to his ancestor Henry. Jonathan Hartson, also the fourth, stood up from his burgundy captain's chair and crossed to greet

Digger. Ted barked from the throne, "Davenport! Come in here. Tell us some good news. Forgive me for not getting up."

Jon shook hands with Digger. "Thank you for investigating the robbery down at Crescent Point. You found more in fifteen minutes than those Keystone Cops found in a week."

Digger replied, "It was a privilege to be invited in to help." He then crossed to shake Ted's hand. "Mr. Hartson, I hope you're feeling better."

As Ted lifted his feeble arm to shake Digger's hand, tubing attached to his arm followed. "Call me Ted, please, Digger. We're glad you came. I don't know why... but I'm all ears. Have a seat."

Digger took the chair Holly had been sitting in. She grabbed another matching captain's chair. Mrs. Hartson floated to a Chippendale at the other end of the study. Somehow in-laws instinctively know their place among the landed gentry into which they have married, and behave accordingly.

* * *

Digger cleared his throat, "I don't know where to begin but I'll just jump in. Mr. Har... Ted, like you, I had my IV tube removed earlier today from the injury I suffered at Dog Island when I conducted a safety check on the lighthouse keeper. Do you know about that whole thing?" Ted nodded.

Jon said, "We've been told that Tom Lincoln, the keeper, was fatally attacked by the wild dogs out there and that you, too, were attacked and had to be airlifted to the hospital. We're very sorry about that. Our family has been debating eradicating those beasts ever since I can remember."

"Well, I'm not sure Mr. Lincoln *is* dead, but let's just let that hold for a minute." The Hartsons looked at each other in wonderment but remained silent. Digger plowed ahead. "When I landed on the island for the safety check, I could just feel that something was wrong. Mr. Lincoln, or Link, was nowhere to be seen. Then I noticed blood on the couch and went to the radio in the house. It was disabled. Then I ran out to my boat and my boat and radio had been sabotaged, as well. Without boring you with all the details, I determined that someone else was on the island and they were up to no good."

Holly piped in, "Digger, you're not boring us!"

Then Ted, Holly's father, barked, "Holly, let him tell it his way. Please, go ahead, son."

Digger obliged. "After trying unsuccessfully to fix my boat or at least repair a radio, I determined I would be spending the night in the keeper's house. I secured the windows and doors, and looked for anything that seemed significant. There, in the office, amongst books about wolves and whatnot, I found this." He bent over his backpack and pulled out the diary.

As he brought the book toward the patriarch's throne, he quickly showed the cover to the others in the room. The journal still had Digger's bookmarks sticking out of it. "It's entitled *The Dog Island Diary*. I assume you all have seen this before, correct?" He gave it to Ted, who looked at the family crest on the front cover and began to turn the pages.

Holly answered Digger's question. "I've never heard of the book." Digger noticed Jon and Ted glancing at each other in a knowing manner. Digger sensed something was amiss. In the deafening silence, Ted offered the book to Jon for his inspection. Jon declined. Holly approached her father. "Can I see it, please?" Her father put up his palm, signaling Holly to stop, and pointed at her chair. She sat. The awkward silence continued.

Finally, Ted spoke. "May I have a moment with my brother?"

Mrs. Hartson stood up quickly and said cheerfully, "Digger, Holly, come try my authentic southern sweet tea on the Salmon Creek porch."

As Holly left, she said over her shoulder, "I thought this was a *family* meeting!" As Digger followed closely behind her, he heard his name whispered.

"Davenport!" Ted motioned him back. "I ask that the contents of this book not be discussed with the ladies, please."

Digger replied eagerly, "Of course, Mr. Hartson. I believe it may contain good news." Ted gave Digger the palm gesture too. Digger bowed, signaling his understanding of the elder's wishes for confidentiality. He pivoted and caught up with Holly on the porch overlooking the boat dock on the tidal river behind the house.

CHAPTER 49

Reaping a Bumper Crop of Whirlwind

Jonathan shut the door to the study with a click and returned to his chair in front of his elder brother. Ted lifted the book. "Have you read it?"

Jonathan conceded that he had. "Maybe thirty years ago when I was out there. Liberty or, as we knew her, Libby, was picking up writing in it where her grandmother Sarah left off."

Ted stared at the ceiling for a moment before speaking. "You know Jon-Jon, I'm dying in not-so-slow motion. It's good and it's bad. It's good because it allows me to come to terms with my mortality and my Maker. Faith, my dear wife, has been a rock in this reckoning... I guess living up to her name. The bad part of a slow death is that the pain is excruciating unless I vegetate myself with opiates. I really wish it were over quickly. But here's what I am learning as I prepare for judgment. There are some immutable laws in God's universe. Do you mind if I get spiritual with you, brother?" Tears welled in Jon's eyes. He nodded silently.

"One law is that we reap what we sow. The other is that God offers forgiveness to everyone no matter who they are and no matter what they have sowed, if you will. Obtaining that forgiveness, you know all about, if you listened in church all these years."

Jonathan whispered, "Believing in Christ's passion on the cross for my wrongs."

The older brother agreed, "Correct. Good. We're brothers eternally. Amen?" Jonathan whispered the word in agreement. Ted continued, "But

I want to talk about reaping and sowing as it pertains to us collectively in the Hartson family and as it pertains to our dirty little secret on Dog Island. First, you have to agree, we are reaping a whirlwind of misery right now. Every square inch of Hartson land is up for sale. I am on death's door fifteen to twenty years before my time. Frankly, I can't afford the dialysis… forget a transplant. You? You're looking at an SEC indictment. Your house was robbed. There's now a death, I guess, out on the island. Our archives were stolen from our alma mater. Our Biddeford operation's gone belly-up."

Jonathan added, "Yeah, we're reaping a bumper crop of whirlwind. My divorce, my son's addictions… tell me when to stop." Jonathan thought to update his brother on the Dartmouth matter and the return of the items stolen from his house but held his tongue to allow his brother to make his point.

Ted continued, "Do you not find it incredibly coincidental that the day after we sign the contract to sell the island, that this kid comes into our house with the revelation of our darkest secret out there? Is that not staggering?" Jonathan shook his head in disbelief. Ted had more to say. "Besides the contract on the island, which as we both know won't save us from our debts, the Hartsons have been reaping a whirlwind of bad news, brother."

"Faith and I have asked ourselves, where did we sow the wind or, sow foolishly… like bad seeds?" Ted mused. "Where did we deviate from godly conduct? Where did the Hartsons violate the golden rule? One area I keep coming back to is Dog Island. We have essentially banished our own flesh and blood because of their skin color, or worse, because of what others might think of us if they know our family is half Negro, or black, as we now say."

"We never had the family here for Thanksgivings or Christmases," said Ted with regret. "I don't even know their full names! It has been an unspoken rule. They stay there, we stay here. Oh, we have paid the taxes on the island and given them the navigational lease payments, but it's been more as if we are *keeping them!*" Jonathan nodded in agreement.

Ted continued, "As I head toward my Maker, I want to make amends for any part I have had in sowing bad seed, for any pain I have caused others. This is an area where I desperately need to make amends and had no idea it would be thrust upon us today. Jon, I was excited by this contract.

Until that kid came in here, I was fully prepared to transfer that island out from under the Lincolns with little or no notice. That's how wicked I can be, and here I'm on death's doorstep, trying to please my Maker. It is sick…I *am* sick!"

"Brother, don't be too hard on yourself," said Jonathan. "We have a deceiver who inserts himself in every way possible to frustrate God's plan. We are not alone in stumbling in this manner. Do you know the story of Malaga Island in Casco Bay, fifty miles down east from here?" Ted shook his head. "Well, on Malaga Island, whites and blacks intermarried against Maine's laws and lived out there to avoid criminal prosecution. They were squatters. The anti-miscegenation law was repealed in the 1880s but the families were not welcomed on the mainland and continued to squat on the island. The owner of Malaga got pressure to do something about *those people*, so he put the island up for sale. A Christian missionary society came forward to buy it for the mixed-race squatters. But our then-governor, who had been fighting against the missionary society over Prohibition, out-bid them for the island. In 1912, the state took title to the island and conducted a mass eviction. The governor incarcerated many into the Maine School for the Feeble-Minded. The state leaders destroyed all the homes."

Ted moaned and shook his head. "God help us."

"I'm not done," said Jon. "The governor then had them dig up the graves of the mixed-race inhabitants and shipped the jumbled remains to the so-called 'feeble-minded' school in Pownal, Maine, where they lie at rest today. So, brother, this sowing of bad seed is understandable when you are surrounded by like-minded people. I really think the eugenics movement and the way evolution was taught early on, really scrambled our brains. You're the exception, Ted. It takes courage to confront your motives like you have. I am proud of you, brother. Please, lead us back from the brink."

Ted shook his head in shame. "I'm no leader. I'm a deceiver. I need to bring my wife and children up to speed on our secret, and pronto."

Jonathan gently asked, "Faith doesn't know?"

"Not an inkling." The brothers were silent for a moment. "Would you ask Faith to come in here, please? On my road to making amends, I have learned to strike while the thought comes to me because our inner-being is wily and will resist coming clean." Jon stood and went to get his sister-in-law.

Faith walked in and shut the door. She had a worried look on her face. "What's wrong, Ted?" She sat in Jon's chair.

"Honey, you know how you have been helping me to prepare for heaven? How we have increased our charity and written letters to past business associates and all that?"

"Of course, dear. And we are clear that these activities do not earn us entry into heaven but are rather the kind of person God calls to be on this earth, right? Are we on the same page?" Faith asked.

"Exactly. If it weren't for you, I'm not sure I would've picked up the distinction from sitting in the pew. Anyway, I need to talk to you about an item of serious amending... where some very bad seed has been sown in the Hartson lineage for say, a hundred and twenty years, and I've never discussed it with you. I'm ashamed and I am sorry."

As Ted's words of confession of the true family lineage left his lips, Faith recoiled in horror. "We have *family* out there? Do you mind if I get Holly, please? The deceit stops now!"

"Of course, dear. She was next," Ted replied. Faith rushed out of the room and returned with Holly. Ted repeated the need for amends and apologized for being deceitful about the issue.

Upon hearing the full story, Holly stood up. "You mean that creepy black guy out there is my cousin? Oh, great, Dad. That's just plain weird. You're right! No wonder this crap keeps happening to us. So, I tell my friends the Hartsons are half-black, right?" In her indignant rant, Holly paused and asked in a whisper, "Does Digger know?"

Her father raised the diary. "It's all in here. I'm not sure what his bookmarks are for, but he most certainly knows." Holly bolted from the room and her parents heard her footsteps pounding up the grand stairway.

Faith looked quizzically at her husband. "Are those two dating?"

"I sure as heck hope so!" retorted Ted. Then he put his head down, shielding his eyes to think for a moment. Faith knew him well enough to be silent. Ted then looked up at his wife. "Can you ask Jonathan to come in? I'd like to close this topic off with a prayer of repentance. Please, can you lead it?" Faith nodded. It had become a familiar practice lately with her husband. Ted added, "If you can get Holly to come back, that would be great too. Where's the Davenport kid?"

Faith nodded her head toward Salmon Creek. "He's down at the dock pumping out our boat." Faith said with wink as she went to get the other family members.

CHAPTER 50

THE GOLD DIGGER

Jonathan whistled from the porch. Digger got the signal and waved. He came up from the dock, wiping his hands. Jonathan waited for him. "Sorry to hold you up. Faith promises us lunch when you're done with us."

Digger grabbed Jonathan gently by the arm. "Man, I had no idea I was setting off a bomb here. I thought with the crest on the book and all, that it was common knowledge."

"That book has never been on the mainland, Digger. But listen, what just happened in our family in the last hour is the best thing to happen to us in over a century. It wouldn't have happened without you speaking up. Come on in, son. We're looking forward to what you have to show us."

As Digger, again, took a seat in front of the patriarch's desk, he apologized to the group for his intrusion. Holly sat next to her mother, both on matching Chippendale chairs, at the other end of the study in the shadows. Ted led the meeting. "So yes, Digger, to answer your question of about an hour ago, we know all about Sarah Hartson Lincoln's diary..." Digger heard a distinct sigh of protestation from Holly behind him. He didn't turn. Ted continued, undeterred. "Why do you ask? And what are these bookmarks?"

Digger dove in. "Again, I don't know where to begin. I'm pretty sure I will be walking on some hallowed ground as, frankly, I don't know if you know what I'm about to share with you. So, I want to apologize in advance if you would rather I...."

"Get on with it, man!" Ted had been sitting too long.

Faith scolded him "Ted, please!"

Digger, a bit perturbed himself, blurted out, "Sir, I believe you have a ton of gold buried in the lighthouse. Did you know that? Sorry if I just blew another family secret. Oh, and most important, I believe someone else knows this and is trying to get it and will kill to get it. There, I'm done." Digger stood up as if he were about to leave. "Perhaps you've tired of me and I should leave now?"

The gaping mouths in the room signaled that they had no idea what he was talking about. Ted spoke first. "I'm sorry for my outburst. Please sit down. What are you saying?"

Digger sat slowly. "It's not really what *I* am saying. It is what *your* ancestors are saying. Sir, are you able to come out to the hallway? I'd like to start on the trail of evidence supporting my theory by looking at your murals." Ted gave a quick signal to his wife. Faith hustled to her husband's side and helped him up. She rolled out the wheeled IV pole from behind the red velvet curtain that decorated the Palladian window behind Ted's throne chair. Ted held onto the thin pole and his wife's arm and ambled toward the door and hallway. The rest eagerly followed.

Once everyone was assembled under the grand stairway, Digger pulled out a sheet of paper with notes. "First, can you all identify the brightest colors used on any of these murals?" Holly already knew the answer, but everyone waited for Ted to move around and look.

Ted pointed. "The schooner's hold and the lighthouse."

Digger nodded toward Jonathan, who had the diary in his hands. "Jon, can you open to the entry for August 6, 1863? As a bit of background, Sarah painted these murals even though she lived on Dog Island with Tombo. When she was done, the family had an unveiling and a reception here. She explains in the diary how her husband had to basically act like a servant at the reception to avoid detection of the fact that he was in a relationship with her, let alone in an illegal marriage."

Ted raised his finger as if to ask Digger to pause. "No wonder the Hartsons started sowing bad seed. The state law made the family hide Sarah and Tombo's illicit relationship. No excuses, just an interesting observation. Carry on, Davenport! I'm loving this. I am getting goosebumps and I haven't had those in seven years!" The rest of the family was relieved to laugh and see their sickly patriarch lighten up.

Digger looked back at his notes. "The part that is of interest is the second paragraph, beginning with the words *I am happy to be back.* Can you read that, Jon?"

Jon cleared his throat and read. "*I am happy to be back from the reception for the unveiling of the murals. How very convenient we had to catch the Salmon Creek's tide. It waits for no one, even Maine's governor, who was in attendance. I did not like explaining to him why Vigilant's cargo and the Dog Island Light were depicted using gold leaf. Only Jonathan, Ted and Tombo could understand the mysteries in the mind of this artist. It's the Hartson heritage, the Hartson inheritance.*" Jon finished reading and looked up.

Digger asked, "Jon, is there anything on that page to indicate the significance of the passage?"

"Uh, yes. The words *Hartson inheritance* are starred and underlined lightly in what looks like pencil." Jon passed the book around, pointing to the relevant text.

Digger said, "Okay, remember the concepts of gold and inheritance? Let's go back to the study. I have more."

Faith spoke up, "We will be right there." She nodded toward a door marked *Powder Room.*

As Jon and Holly walked with Digger back to the study, Digger commented, "I am sorry the *Vigilant's* logbook was stolen from Crescent Point. I think it has clues that have fallen into the wrong hands."

Holly whispered loudly, "Ricky Eaton!"

Jon put up his hand. "I guess it's time for true confessions. I was going to bring this up at today's meeting. I don't think it is Eaton. Everything was returned by UPS a few days ago. In fact, I have the logbook for *Vigilant* right here." Jon crossed the room to his chair and pulled the logbook from a satchel.

Digger shouted, "Freeze!" Jon stopped in his tracks. Digger reached into his backpack for a pair of latex gloves. "Sorry for yelling. Use these." Digger handed the gloves to Jon and asked, "Does Chief Nickerson know the ship's log was returned?"

Jon fumbled with the gloves and stammered, "Uh, no. I need to explain something about where the UPS boxes came from." Jon handed the logbook to Digger, who had also slipped on gloves.

Digger perused the pages. "What other items were returned?"

"Most significantly, the gold family crest and the telegraph machine," replied Jon.

Digger looked up. "The gold crest? That has to be very valuable and easy to melt down. This is an amazing development." Digger returned to the log. He put a marker on one of the pages.

"Another thing, Digger, I got a call from the Tuck School of Business at Dartmouth. All of our archive materials were returned from the Portsmouth Public Library with a note apologizing that they didn't know the items did not circulate."

Digger squinted his eyes at Jonathan as he explained these truly baffling developments. Ted entered, dragging his IV with Faith by his side.

Ted asked, "What did I miss? It looks important. The gloves are out."

Jon kept talking. "Two more things, Digger. The return address on my UPS boxes was the Securities and Exchange Commission in Boston, with whom I have a terrible fight pending. It struck fear in me. I called my lawyer but not the police department. I really didn't want anyone contacting the SEC about this, for obvious reasons. The last thing to note is that this piece of ticker tape was in the telegraph machine." Jon pulled a thin paper ribbon out of his satchel and handed it to Digger, who looked carefully at the dots and dashes on the ticker tape and grabbed a pen and his notebook from the backpack.

Again, Ted tried to speak. Jon put his hand up to silence his older brother. The room was quiet as Digger studied the strip of paper. He looked up. "*Lex talionis…* it says *lex talionis.*"

Jon burst out, "Unbelievable! It took me hours to figure that out. And I had to have a code book. Can you really translate Morse code in your head?"

Digger shrugged his shoulders as if to say *no big deal.* "Does anyone know what it means? *Lex talionis?*" Digger waited a few seconds for someone to answer.

Holly piped up cheerfully, "Lex means law. I know that part."

Digger complimented Holly and then answered his own question. "Literally, it translates as *the law of retaliation.* The closest idiom we use is, *eye for an eye, tooth for a tooth.*"

Ted looked confused. "Where are we, folks? Seems like we are on to other matters."

Jon responded, "My fault, Ted. There's been a couple of developments that I had not been able to explain to you yet. The archives were returned to the Tuck School and the items stolen from my house were sent to me by UPS on Tuesday. I had brought over the logbook and an odd Morse code message that was in the telegraph machine. The message simply states 'lex talionis.' Digger had us don the gloves and he was reviewing the logbook from *Vigilant*."

Digger looked at Ted. "If you would like, sir, I am ready to resume the journey on the trail of evidence establishing that your family has gold hidden on Dog Island."

Ted replied, "Please do. I am baffled by Jon's latest revelation that our property has been returned but carry on, Mr. Davenport."

"Agreed, Ted, most baffling," Digger replied. "The trail has gotten hotter with the addition of evidence from the ship's log, which I have been quickly reviewing here. I am going to say that it is entirely possible that you have…" Digger looked at the log. "And I am quoting, "…*seven hundred-eight* [gold] *bricks weighing fourteen tons on Dog Island.*"

Jonathan jumped up and peered over Digger's shoulder. "What? Where? Where do you get that from?" Holly and her mom swept over to peer at the logbook in Digger's lap.

Digger replied, "Well, every logbook has to identify its cargo. Here in the entry for January 20, 1861, it identifies the yellow brick. That's Hartson-speak for gold brick. In fact, look at how heavy these yellow bricks are." Digger closed his eyes for a moment then looked up. "Each yellow brick weighs about forty pounds! That's the weight of gold. A regular brick only weighs about five pounds, right?"

The Hartsons agreed as they returned to their chairs smiling.

Ted had been stuck at his desk but was actively punching buttons on a calculator. Without looking up, he asked, "Are there still sixteen ounces in a pound?"

The Hartsons answered in unison, "Yes."

Digger responded, "No, not in weighing precious metals. There's only twelve ounces in a pound."

Jon agreed. "He's right, Ted."

"Blast! I have to start over," Ted said joyfully. "Are there still two thousand pounds in a ton?"

The group looked at Digger, who nodded. They said, "Yes!"

Ted continued, "And we have fourteen tons, correct?"

"Yes!" the group responded with smiles.

"Jon-Jon, what is gold trading at?" asked Ted.

"Six hundred dollars per ounce, roughly," Jon responded, looking at the ceiling to help with his recollection of the market.

Ted banged at the calculator keys. "Anyone want to venture a guess?"

Faith cried out, "Ted! Spit it out, man!"

He chuckled. "It's nearly two hundred and four million dollars' worth of gold!"

Digger put the logbook in a plastic bag and handed it back to Jonathan before he resumed discussing the evidence. "Okay, before you get stars in your eyes, I could be wrong. Look at the start of Sarah's diary. She speaks of protecting the rich resources of the Hartsons from the South and protecting them in the North. She calls these resources the true inheritance of the family. She refers to the diary as a testament, as in last will and testament. She calls the yellow brick unique and again the true inheritance. Each of these references is either starred or underlined in pencil. Finally, turn to the sketch of the window. It's called 'The Window on the Hartson Inheritance.' Look on the windowsill. It's the Hartson crest."

Ted looked at Jon. "You remember that crest don't you... halfway up the stairs?" Jonathan had taken the book out of the plastic bag and was turning the pages slowly, but he was also keeping his mind in the room.

Jon replied, "I sure do. I wanted to pry it out but was afraid of the Lincolns beating me up. It was tense out there. Not to get off subject, but they didn't want us out there any more than we wanted to be there. I really don't think we should be too harsh on ourselves."

Digger let the comment hang and continued. He looked at Jonathan. "Your namesake, Jonathan the first, had the same symbol inlaid in the floor of your library at Crescent Point. The compass places the gold family crest on the same bearing as Dog Island. I believe it was a purposeful clue. In conclusion, when you take Sarah Hartson's painted murals in that hallway..." Digger pointed out toward the door, "...giving hints of the gold moving from Savannah to the lighthouse, and her several distinct hints about inheritance in the diary, and the weight per brick indicated in the *Vigilant* ship's log... and I bet there is much more in that book..."

Jonathan interrupted as he held the logbook and prepared to read. "How about this for another hint? It's from February 1861:

By 3 p.m. the boathouse was cleared. Bay door and back door secured with iron hasps and locks. Hinges re-bolted from inside. The rails were re-greased with sperm oil and bear grease. Jonathan and Ted returned to Vigilant to get the first load of [two words crossed out] *materials to shore.*

By sunset first load was secured in boathouse. Then a howl was heard from the east end of the island.

Jon looked up. "I think they crossed out the words referring to the gold and changed it to *materials*. You have to see this scratch-out on this page. And who cares to load bricks inside a building? They're weatherproof! And who takes great pains to fortify a simple boathouse on an island in the middle of the winter? But the most compelling thing is why would these refined folk do the labor themselves, in the middle of winter? They are trying to keep it secret. Digger, I believe you are definitely on to something."

Digger wanted to wrap it up. "These clues, combined with the odd thefts of Hartson records and the invasion of the island itself, lead me to conclude Dog Island Light, itself, is a vault for gold. In particular, gold bricks. Not yellow bricks made from southern limestone as family folklore explained. Finally, I believe the window in the tower of the lighthouse is where it is located."

Ted rubbed his forehead. "Jon, why wouldn't we know about this?"

Jon shrugged. "I don't know, Ted. The last time we looked at the trust and the wills there was no hint at any of it. I mean, it's over a hundred years ago."

Ted searched his mind. "Do you think our fathers knew and kept it under wraps in the Biddeford bankruptcy? Wouldn't they whisper something on their deathbeds? This is cataclysmic!"

"May I offer a possible answer?" Digger ventured quietly.

"Please, Digger, help us out," Holly begged. "Why is this news to the leaders of the family who apparently know all the other deep secrets?" She glared at her father and uncle.

Digger responded evenly, "It is all in the diary. Part of the reason has to do with the Civil War and the need to remove Hartson assets under secrecy. Part of it has to do with the new tax policies in 1882, again, all addressed in that diary. Part of it has to do with the untimely deaths of your namesakes during Maine's influenza outbreak, also in 1882. But most importantly, and I just realized this, part of it has to do with what was revealed here today: the cutting off of Dog Island and the Lincoln line from the Hartson family. When the progenitors died from influenza without wills or trusts naming the assets, then a break in relations and information exchange between those on Dog Island and those on the mainland occurred. Sarah was the keeper of the info. She could have written a will and named it or started throwing the bricks around and using them. But no, she wrote about them in code."

Holly spoke up. "That sounds like a true Hartson, all right."

Digger added, "And perhaps someone in the Lincoln line knows or knew or was close to discovery. That is what those stars and underlines mean to me. Or, maybe Sarah did that herself to help us."

Faith, noticing her husband sagging tiredly in his chair, stood as if to put a period on the meeting. "Lunch is served in the big dining room. Let's reconvene there in a few minutes. We can continue discussions."

Ted agreed. "Hear, hear! Capital idea, lovey! We are adjourned. When we resume, we will discuss who else may be on to this discovery and the impact of our contract to sell Dog Island." Digger's eyebrows raised reflexively but he was able to hold his tongue regarding the mention of the sales contract.

CHAPTER 51

Pep and Prep

Just up the road, Rick was putting his notes and exhibits together in preparation for confronting the Hartsons. Brenda had just returned from scoping out Royal Orchard.

"There is a pow-wow down there for sure, Ricky. I think the timing is perfect. Midday, it's just after their lunch hour. Remember, you can always say you're visiting for the purpose of setting a meeting in the future, but they may just hear you out."

Rick had put on his Sunday best again. No matter that Rick did not view Sunday as any different from a Saturday. "How do I handle the brick again?" he asked nervously.

"You say that you visited the island; it was abandoned, the doors were open and you took a tour looking for anyone and checked your theory out and found it in the tower. That's all. Also don't forget your fallback position is, if they aren't going to work with you, you will slap 'em with an injunction and litigate forever," Brenda said, getting a bit angry.

"Remember, too, you are putting them on notice about the gold, that you took pictures and that if they do anything with it, they will be temper'n with evidence." Brenda was now parroting back the legal theories he had shared with her from his research.

"I got it, Brenda. Thanks. It's *tampering.*"

"Right, Ricky. You're the Mayor of Gutsville! Show 'em that valedictorian brain you got!"

He smiled and looked at his watch. It was a little before one. "I gotta go."

"Ricky, we should pray."

"Oh, Brenda, you know how I feel about that.".

"I know. I know. But it can't hurt, right?"

"I don't know about that..." Rick looked dubious.

"Come here, this is how they do it on the *700 Club* on TV." Rick rolled his eyes as he stepped towards Brenda. She placed her hands on Rick's shoulders.

"Dear God, bless Richard Eaton. The Good Book talks about stolen inheritance. It must be important to you, God. Help Richard get his portion. Help him get his words out. Oh yeah, God forgive us our trespasses. Amen." Brenda looked up. "Are you crying, baby?"

Rick turned away. "I don't hear my name Richard much. It reminded me of my mom." He wiped away a tear, and headed for the car with his briefcase in hand.

* * *

At Royal Orchard, the discussion in the grand dining room had turned to the oddity of the Hartson memorabilia being returned. Holly was explaining her work at the probate court on behalf of the family attorney a few weeks ago. "As you know, Digger suggested trying to find out who had an axe to grind against us and that sent me to the probate court, right, Uncle Jon?"

He nodded, his eyebrows raised. "I figured any angle is worth pursuing."

Ted spoke. "I never heard if there was anything worthwhile from that effort, Holly. What did you find?"

She replied, "The facts are that the Eatons sued us in probate court over a codicil to a will where Theodore Junior promised a percentage of the ownership in the mill to an Eaton in 1920 or so. But because Junior lived so long, until somewhere around 1960, the mill had gone belly-up by then. So, when Junior finally died, the bequest to the Eatons of twenty percent of the shares of stock in the mill was worthless."

"I settled that case amicably with Billy Eaton," said Ted. "They got acreage and a new single- wide over by the blueberry bogs." Ted pointed inland toward the direction of the bogs and added, "It was a generous settlement given that they would have gotten nothing."

Jonathan added, "I believe his son, Richard, is capable of vandalizing and robbing, but I do not see him returning anything, especially putting the SEC's address on the return labels. How would he know anything about that?"

Holly blurted out, "Uncle Jon, it was in all the papers, remember?" Then she put her hand over her mouth when she saw her poor uncle's expression.

In the moment of awkward silence following Holly's exclamation, Digger wondered how he had gotten himself in the middle of all this and sought to move the conversation forward. "Regardless, someone is all over this secret, I fear. I am very concerned about this contract that you signed yesterday to sell Dog Island…"

Ted interrupted. "It's not a problem. I just talked with Attorney Stockton before lunch. She assures me that she can get us out of it during the due diligence period. Further, even if we want it to go through, we are entitled to remove our property from the island. That actually may be the best. We remove the property and let the transaction go through. We can make good with the Lincoln family and be done with those infernal, vicious beasts out there. Let the new buyer deal with them. And good riddance!"

The door knocker sounded an ominous two hard bangs. Ted looked at Faith. "I hate that knocker. Can't we get Westminster chimes or something?"

Faith stood, smiling. "Westminster chimes would be lovely, Ted. I'll be right back."

Jon continued the discussion without addressing the SEC issue. "There is no question we need to get out there to verify these findings. Also, I'd like to know more about Link. Digger, are you saying he is alive?"

Just then, Mrs. Hartson returned, white as a ghost. She gave Ted a look of alarm. "Richard Eaton? He's at the door and he wants to speak with you and Jonathan. He said it is a very important legal matter."

"Where is he now?" asked Ted.

Faith replied, "I asked him to wait in the little house living room while I checked with you."

"Perfect. Good job." Ted turned to his brother. "Jon, you okay meeting with this kid?"

Jon looked at Digger. "Let's say this guy is the one harassing and stealing from us. I mean, even with the stuff returned, there was some costly vandalism."

"The guy who tore up your house is not well," said Ted. "If there's a chance this is the guy, I'm not sure I feel safe in a room with him."

"Ted, could we have Digger sit in with you three?" Faith asked.

Jon nodded. "I'd feel much better."

Ted looked at Digger. "You up for playing the bailiff of Royal Orchard?"

Digger had been thinking. "I don't mind at all, but may I ask if you have any recording equipment?"

Ted looked at Faith. "That cassette player we use in the apartment in Boston for our books on tape, it has a record button and I think I have blank tapes in the study. Holly, run and fetch the portable cassette player on my bedside table, would you?"

"Sure, Dad." As Holly stood, she looked at Digger and whispered, with a look of vindication regarding her research, "The plot thickens!" She bolted without looking back and headed toward the kitchen and the back stairway.

Ted spoke. "Faith, tell him we're finishing lunch and we would be happy to meet with him in just a few minutes. Offer some of that killer tea you made. No pun intended."

Faith hissed, "That's not funny, Ted!" She stalked out the room.

Ted looked at Digger. "What else, Officer?"

"Can you and Jon sit behind the desk together? I'll sit to the side where Jon was sitting." Digger added in a whisper. "I will be armed. And I have half a mind to frisk the guy first."

Ted looked at Jon and wrinkled his face." I don't think we should frisk the boy whose family served our family for over a hundred years." Jon nodded in agreement. Ted turned to Digger. "But I'm glad you're armed, son. Don't tell Faith, though. She'd have a conniption! Anything else?"

Digger thought briefly. "Well, sir, if Rick wants to hand you something or you're gonna hand him anything, use me as a go between like a true bailiff in a courtroom. That's it."

Holly came back with the Sony portable cassette player and handed it to Digger. He said, "Let Holly and me set up now in the study, if you don't mind."

Ted dismissed them and added, "The blank tapes are in the top right drawer of my desk. Now by golly, I am going to enjoy this pear and ginger dessert with my brother. We will be right in, then Faith can fetch our guest."

Holly whispered to Digger as they walked toward the study, "Do you think Dad will let me sit in?"

Digger whispered back, "I don't know, Holly. This guy could be a real hothead. I'm not sure it's safe, but that's not my call. That's up to your dad." Digger quickly surveyed the room. "Put Eaton's chair right there. I'll sit over there and Jon will sit with your dad here." Digger inserted a fresh ninety-minute cassette in the machine and pressed "record." He placed the recorder in a large spider plant on a side table. "Say something, Holly, at a regular volume."

Holly responded with a controlled voice, "Testing 1-2-3. Hartson meeting with Rick Eaton Friday, July 11, 1980, testing 1-2-3."

"Good." Digger replayed it. It was clear and crisp. Next, he brought his backpack over to his chair where Jon had been sitting, and when Holly wasn't looking, Digger slipped his pistol into his waistband on his back and pulled out his shirttail to cover the weapon. He quickly strapped a small dagger in a sheath around his ankle. He looked up. Holly looked horrified but said nothing.

After a moment she asked very seriously, "Anything else, Officer?"

"We're ready. Can you let your dad know we're all set?" Digger replied with a reassuring smile.

"Yes sir," she replied dutifully and departed. Digger doubted he would see her for a while.

Once the men were seated, minus Holly, Faith was given the instruction to escort Mr. Eaton to the study. Rick entered carrying a briefcase and was dressed smartly in a white shirt, club tie, khakis and a blue blazer. His shoes were a dead giveaway of hard times, fake black leather sneakers dotted with small splotches of paint. Rick focused on both Hartsons and confidently reached over the desk to shake their hands. They exchanged pleasant greetings. Ted motioned toward Digger. "Do you know one another? Rick, this is David Davenport." Rick snapped his head to the right. He hadn't seen a third person in the room, let alone a cop and his smile weakened. "David, meet Rick Eaton. His family has been a tremendous blessing to our family for nearly a hundred years."

Rick corrected Ted as he shook Digger's hand. "One hundred and twenty-six years to be exact, Mr. Hartson. How do you do, Officer Davenport?"

Digger thought, *this guy is smooth*. Out loud, he said, "You can call me

Digger. I am just a friend of the family over for lunch. Off duty."

"Sure," Rick replied without smiling. "I'm sorry to interrupt a social gathering but I'm here to discuss a confidential business matter."

Ted responded before Digger could. "Davenport is a trusted advisor. He stays. Have a seat, Rick. I go by Ted and this is Jon. Tell us what brings you here today?"

"Thanks, Ted and thank you, Jon and Digger, for allowing me to interrupt your day without an appointment. I'll try to make this as brief as possible and to do so I need my notes." He flipped the buttons open on the briefcase while it rested on his knees. He did not lift the lid open but rather slipped a yellow pad out between the narrow opening. Even so, Digger spied something shiny in the case. Digger could tell the case was heavy just by the way Rick handled it. He noticed Rick was left-handed, corroborating his deductions in the Crescent Point investigation.

Rick looked at his notes and began. "The Eatons have served the Hartsons for over a hundred and twenty five years and during this time, the families became as close as two can get in an employer-employee relationship. There came a time when a gift promised to my grandfather became the subject of litigation in probate court. You, Ted, probably know more than I do, but this is the issue that I have come to discuss." Rick looked up at Ted and continued, "I'd like to make three points as to why the settlement reached in that litigation was unfair and, in light of recent information, opens the Hartson family to extensive litigation and embarrassment in the community."

"I could simply have had my attorneys commence litigation based on the facts I am about to lay before you, but I don't think people who have over a hundred years of helping one another jump to attorneys without talking first," Rick said. "In recognition of that extensive history of goodwill, I am humbling myself to come before you and make my case face-to-face. If, after today's discussion, accommodation cannot be reached, then at least you will have advance notice of what my attorneys will be suing for. May I continue with my points?"

Ted responded, "We're all ears. Continue."

"Point one. Pursuant to the codicil to Ted Junior's will, the Eatons were entitled to a twenty percent ownership share of Hartson Textiles, Ltd., or what we call the Biddeford mill. For reasons I will demonstrate in a moment and contrary to what your family said in court, the Company was *not* bankrupt. Far from it. Whether by active deceit or inconceivable lack of knowledge, the mill was worth and is still worth multiple millions of dollars. In legal terms…" Rick looked at his notes. "… the bequest did not *adeem* and should be paid at this time amicably. If not, payment will be forced legally through a motion to reopen the bankruptcy case and a motion to set aside the probate order based on fraud or mistake."

All the other men in the room collectively blanched at Rick's sophisticated command of legal language but were careful not to show it.

Rick continued, "Point two. The settlement given to my father, God rest his soul, was not only an insulting pittance, but now, in view of new information that I have discovered, it can be set aside by law…" Rick looked down. "There was no meeting of the minds and it can be rescinded. It was a sham. The Hartsons knew or should have known the company was not insolvent at the time of the settlement."

"That's how the attorneys say it." Rick went on. "But this is the way I want to say it. Even if Hartson Textiles was belly-up and wasn't worth a plug nickel, you all managed to enjoy your wealth out here in your oceanfront estates, attended your Ivy League colleges, and when it came time to recognize faithful stewards, you, Ted, reneged on the spirit of what your grandfather, Ted Junior, had wanted done for the Eatons. My dad was in no condition to fight you. You used the bankruptcy code to your advantage and callously ignored your obligation to the little people who had invested their whole lives for the Hartson family. The settlement you foisted upon my dad should be set aside on so many levels." By now, Rick was shaking with emotion.

Nonetheless, Rick pressed on, "Point three and I am done. I believe the Hartsons have had a hidden asset that I am entitled to lay claim to. Pursuant to the court case *Beauchamp versus City of Portland*, Maine has a finders keepers rule. Through my research, I have what I believe is overwhelming evidence, an earth-shattering revelation, and it entitles me to keep it all. I believe…"

Ted interrupted and asserted boldly a fact he was unsure of, except for Digger's convincing presentation. "Excuse me, Rick. Please don't tell me you think the gold on Dog Island is a surprise to us. Just drop point three. It's ludicrous."

Rick jumped out of his chair. "You guys knew about it? That's proof of the fraud right there!" He turned and looked at Digger. "I can't believe this. I was giving them the benefit of the doubt." He looked back at Ted and Jon. "You ripped off my dad!"

Ted was gesturing wildly for Rick to sit down. "Young man, please, please hear us out. I'm not saying we knew about the gold when we settled the case in 1960, okay? We did not have any idea about the gold in 1960. Like any family, we have our dysfunctions. Further, to argue that it was a part of the mill is nonsense." Jonathan nodded his head in agreement.

Ted continued, "I don't know if you know, but there has been a communication barrier in this family for generations; so, I'm not saying we can't look at the things you're raising and do something. So calm down. Are you ready to hear me out?"

Rick looked skeptical, the wind being so suddenly taken from his sails regarding the revelation about the gold. He took a breath and said, "Explain your side, sir. I have been holding resentment for years, you understand. I think that court battle back then advanced my dad's health problems. Maybe even contributed to his death, so you can understand why I'm a bit hot over this."

Ted paused before replying. "First, Rick, the mill was bankrupt and the gold is not part of that operation. The settlement with your dad was reached in a spirit of generosity as best we could do at the time with no legal requirement to do so. The mill was worthless. Your father, in fact, seemed very pleased. You're entitled to your feelings, but I was there."

Ted paused again to collect his thoughts and resumed. "But I want to move our discussion to a different level. I want to apologize for the way I looked at life back then. I look at life differently now. Just today before you came, we had been talking about reaping, sowing and making amends to those we have harmed. So, if you're looking for some... some *lex talionis*," Ted paused to let the word sink in, "then you are stepping off on the wrong foot. If however, you're here in a spirit of cooperation allowing for reasonable amends, then your timing is divine." Rick blanched when he heard his signature Latin phrase. His body language spoke a clear admission of guilt.

Ted wisely did not press on how he knew the origin of the phrase but simply continued. He had used the reference like a partial unsheathing and shining of a sword's bright reflection into the eyes of an opponent, signaling strength and readiness for battle.

Ted followed up cryptically, as he did not want to reveal that they had just found out about the gold from Digger, and yet he did not want to lie. He chose his words carefully. "A little background, Rick. Because of our own dysfunctions, the gold has not helped us at this time. Every square inch of Hartson land is on the market and has been for over a year. In fact, just yesterday we accepted a contract on Dog Island. It is in the due diligence period and will close in thirty days. But we would be willing..."

Rick's eyes widened at word of the contract and he interrupted. "Under contract? Oh, really? Who is buying, if I may inquire?"

Ted looked at Jon, who indicated he didn't mind telling. "It's some Russian-sounding company from Boston. We don't know the company." Ted reached for the packet of papers on the desk. "Sobaka Corporation, Olga Karpinsky. Ever hear of them?"

Rick stood up. "Do you mind if I stand? I don't like this. I know some Russians in Boston." Rick began to pace, looking down at the floor. The others looked at each other and raised their eyebrows. Rick asked, "When did this go under contract?"

Now Ted was concerned. Who *was* this kid? He knew Russians in Boston? He continued now with extreme caution. "Jon and I signed yesterday. We had twenty-four hours or the offer expired. Our broker deposited a ten-thousand-dollar good-faith check."

"Who is their broker, please?" Rick asked urgently.

Ted looked down at the papers. "It's Pearson, a local guy."

Rick pressed, "Is there an attorney for the Russki?"

Ted looked down again. "Yeah, a local guy too...Sanford Beach? Do you know him?"

CHAPTER 52

SANDBAGGED BY THE BEACH

Rick spun around, eyes blazing. "May I see that contract, please!"

Ted reluctantly handed the whole stack of papers to Rick and pointed to the signature. "Right there. Sanford Beach. Why?"

Rick looked at his watch. "What time did they get a signed contract from you guys yesterday?"

"Noon," Ted replied.

Jon stepped in. "What's going on, Eaton?"

Rick began cursing as he gathered up his notes. He looked at the brothers with his head tilted to the side. "Your... *our* gold is being stolen as we speak. If it's not gone already. I confided in that slimeball Beach about the gold! Everything... location... details galore! He kicked me out of his office and went behind my back to take it for himself. We've been set up! These Russians will move fast. I guarantee this company is fake. The bank letter is fake and Olga whatever her name is, *does not* exist!"

Digger jumped to his feet. "We need to take a telescope up to the widow's walk right now!"

Ted yelled, "Holly! Get in here!"

Holly came bursting through the door. "Yes, Dad?"

"Get these boys up on the widow's walk and fetch the telescope. Immediately." The three men followed Holly to the elevator. On the fourth floor, Digger knew what to do. He slid the roof cap back. Holly handed the telescope up while Digger set up the tripod.

Jon was looking through his own binoculars. "Yup, it looks like a trawler on the west side of the island." He handed the glasses to Rick, who knelt down and placed the glasses on the railing to steady them because his hands were shaking so badly.

He swore repeatedly. "I am gonna kill that son of a... Beach!"

Digger was focusing the telescope. "No, you're not, Rick. If you're right, the police are going to deal with him." Digger squinted into the telescope. "I see six men on the island, one skiff, and a trawler at anchor across from the boat rails."

Rick was pacing. "Digger, can you call in an airstrike or something?"

Digger looked at Rick. "I issue parking tickets, dude!"

Rick snapped back, "Did you tell that to my friend Chuck Branson when he was parked on Ocean Avenue two summers ago? I think you brought some serious heat then!"

Digger ignored the dig about the arrest he orchestrated in 1978 but simply responded, "If we know for a fact that crime is afoot, you bet, we'll call the police, the Coast Guard and the FBI in a case this big." Digger turned toward Jonathan. "Jon, can you tell what they're doing?"

Jon was bent over the telescope. "I can't tell. I think someone is rowing back to the trawler."

Digger looked down at the dock. Holly whistled and waved them to come down. "We're going for a boat ride, boys!" she shouted up.

Digger grabbed the binoculars and turned to look down at Holly and another woman beside her. "Crap, it's Annabelle, the horse wrangler, wearing double Magnum holsters." Rick asked to see. Digger handed the glasses to him.

Rick whistled. "And she's carrying a Winchester repeater and an ammo box. Game on, boys. Let's go!"

Jon looked through the telescope. "I can't see that they are doing anything illegal, but that skiff is certainly going back and forth."

Digger and Rick looked at each other as if to say, is he serious? The men rushed to the first floor by elevator. As they descended, Digger suggested they downplay any discussion of the preparations to engage the trawler. "We are just overseeing the due diligence process on behalf of the owners. Right?"

Jon opened the door. "I am going to stay here with Ted. I am under a microscope right now." Rick remained silent.

Digger whispered to Jon. "Do you know how to read nautical signal flags?"

Jon replied, "There's a flag chart around here somewhere."

Digger added, "Good. Just in case. Also, see if you have flags here. That pole out front can be seen from the island and there are flags out there which may come in handy. How 'bout a signal cannon, you got one?"

"Boy, do we! It's our July Fourth entertainment," Jon replied with wide eyes.

"Get it ready. Any diversion may be handy. Start firing the thing if you see us waving a jacket or something, okay?" Digger instructed.

"Got it. I'll take the cannon up to the widow's walk and I'll be watching with the telescope," Jon replied.

Digger added, "Bring the biggest flashlight too. Hopefully, we will be back well before dark." Jon nodded.

In the study, Faith was pacing and clutching her pearls. Ted was at the Palladian window with binoculars. He spun around in slow motion as Digger entered the room. "Are you going out there?"

Digger responded, "Yes. I will bring my police radio. At the first sign that something is amiss, I'll call the chief and the Coast Guard. Right now, we're just 'observing the due diligence process on behalf of the owners,'" Digger recited robotically.

Faith looked worried. "Please be safe and don't let Annie Oakley out there do anything rash."

Ted teetered over to Digger and looked him in the eye. "Keep an eye on my daughter, please. She's a great boat driver but remember, she's no Navy Seal candidate. She's precious, please!"

"Understood, sir." Digger assured him.

Rick spoke loudly to get everyone's attention. "Well, I think we can discuss my issue later. Job one is to make sure these guys aren't making off with the goods." Rick hesitated, then spoke to Ted and Jon. "Based on what I said here today, do you two think we have a fair basis to revisit the settlement of 1960? My fiancée and I are expecting a child this fall and I'd like to know that we're on the same page in terms of renegotiating something fair."

Ted looked at Jonathan. It didn't take but a nod to confirm their thoughts. Ted responded. "Congratulations on the baby. We need more Eatons. And yes, we look forward to setting things right, my boy. There may be some apologies on *both sides* that need to be made, but I do believe we'll reach an honorable and just resolution, if the assets are as you believe."

Even though time was of the essence, Rick paused to bend over his briefcase and flipped the lid wide open. The ingot of gold brightened the immediate area. The Hartson crest was unmistakable. Rick lifted the heavy brick out and brought it to Ted. "As you already know, here is what we are securing for your family and mine." All heads bent over to look at the stunning artifact. Their expressions clearly revealed no one had ever seen such a thing. As Ted held it, trembling, he was speechless. He passed it carefully to Jonathan.

Jonathan, not wanting to reveal that they had no idea about the gold until meeting with Digger earlier, did his best to feign familiarity. "Yup, that's from the Savannah operation, all right." He handed it to Faith.

Rick looked at his watch. "We gotta catch the tide to get out and back to the dock. I'll leave the ingot with you for good-faith safekeeping." An air horn sounded in the distance.

Ted extended his hand to Rick. "Holly is calling you. We will work things out. This will be safe here. You be safe out there and we'll talk when you get back." The brothers took turns shaking Rick's hand. Digger and Rick turned to exit but Faith called them back. She reached for their hands and pulled them in close to where Ted and Jonathan were standing. Without warning she bowed her head. "Heavenly Father, protect this mission to secure the inheritance for these families. Dispatch angels to guard and protect. In Jesus' powerful name, we pray. Amen." Faith looked up and urged, "Now, go!"

Before heading to the dock, the young men headed for their cars to get the items needed for the trip to Dog Island. Digger yelled as he ran, "I got to get my radio."

"Yeah," Rick replied as he wiped something from his eye. "I gotta get my backpack and ditch this briefcase."

CHAPTER 53

The Approach to Dog Island

As Digger approached the dock, he spied two kayaks sitting on the lawn. "Rick! Grab one." The boys bounded down the dock ramp, each with a kayak balanced on a shoulder and paddle in the other hand. Digger barked, "Annabelle, can you make some room for these, please?" Thankfully, Annabelle was wearing a jacket covering the arsenal strapped to her torso, because Ted and Faith Hartson were on the porch watching and waving them off. Digger grabbed life vests from under the gunnels. "Put these on, please." He handed a ski belt to Annabelle. "We can't cover those hand cannons with a vest. This belt will keep you afloat if Holly spins the wheel too hard," he said, winking at Holly.

Holly responded with, "Here we go. Hold on!" She pinned the throttle. The twenty-two-foot Aquasport roared to life with all two hundred twenty-five horses starting to charge in the Johnson outboard engine.

Digger made his way back to Rick, who was holding on to the rail of the captain's bench for dear life. "Do you have any problem with me leading the operation?"

"You're the cop in the boat. Lead on, copsicle. If I think you're blowing it, I will speak up. You got any problem with that?" asked Rick.

Digger clasped Rick's hand. "Two heads are better than one, for sure." He moved over to Annabelle and Holly and asked the same question. They agreed.

"Okay, guys! We are just gonna verify that they are conducting a legitimate inspection out there having to do with the sale of the island. As soon as we see anything otherwise, anything fishy, I'll call in the heavy artillery of the cops and Coast Guard, okay?" Everyone nodded. Digger continued, "We are not to fire upon anyone or anything like that. It could get us in a world of problems legally."

Anabelle yelled over the roar of the engine. "We can defend ourselves, right?"

"Absolutely!" he replied, though Annabelle was beginning to worry him.

Digger motioned Holly to back down on the speed. "Okay now, before we get too close, here's the plan. Rick and I are gonna disappear… get down low, right now. You girls are gonna blaze past the trawler to the west of it. Just like you are on a joyride or something. Rick and I will lie low on the deck and keep our binoculars on their operation. You girls will play like sassy wenches, whooping and hollering as you speed on by. If Rick or I signal something is wrong, Holly, you will do a lazy arc to the left to the south side of the island. Keep your speed up but not too fast. I'll alert the Coast Guard on the radio. You will keep turning to the left until we're out of sight of the tower, then make a hard left to the island. Rick and I will launch the kayaks and get ourselves onto the island.

"Once you drop us off, continue to do a wide circle around the island to the north side. As soon as you can be seen from the lighthouse on that side of the island, bring her to a stop and do some dancing. Raise cups toasting each other, look around like you have lost something. If they're up to no good, they'll be watching you closely, trust me. I need you to buy time for us to get into position. Then after a few moments, say, ten minutes in that position, grab that ensign on the pole at the stern and start waving it like it's part of your party dance. You will be signaling Jon on the widow's walk at Royal Orchard. He'll start blowing the signal cannon. Just hold your position. Can you handle this, ladies?" They both nodded excitedly.

Digger asked, "Anabelle, do you have a scope for that Winchester?"

"You betcha, honey!" she replied.

"Good. If you see a firefight erupt, use your best judgment but defend at all costs. And stay low, right, Holly?" She nodded.

Rick spoke up. "On the east end of the island, toward the Talbot River end, there is a cobblestone beach if you need to beach it. Also, generally if they can't see you, they can't shoot you. So, you can play the angles for safety's sake. Is that right, Digger?"

"Good word, Rick," Digger agreed.

Holly repeated the plan, making light of their expertise at being sassy wenches. The boys put cushions on the floor and got into position. Holly brought the boat up to three-quarter speed. Anabelle started her role early, raising a cup and drinking dramatically as the boat bounced along. She punched her fists in the air and danced about. Digger and Rick were getting pounded on the deck as the boat plowed through the seas.

Rick yelled up to Digger as his body was getting air and bouncing back on the deck, "You sure this is the right way to do this? Ouch!"

Digger gave a signal to back it down a bit. Holly acknowledged, "Once we head east, it'll be more manageable, you bilge rats."

Rick yelled from his crouched position, "Digger, keep your eye on the right side of the tower at the base. They would come out of the door on that side carrying stuff!"

Digger replied, "Wilco!... Holly, arc closer to the trawler, please."

Holly repeated Digger's radio lingo, meaning *will comply*. "Wilco."

Digger started fiddling with his radio to see if he could pick up transmissions from the trawler. Suddenly Russian dialogue came in on channel four. Digger turned it up. From the floor of the boat, he shouted, "Anyone speak Russian?"

Rick yelled back, "Nyet!" Rick looked again through the glasses. "Captain! Look at the guy by the boathouse. Is that a rifle or a shovel?"

Digger put down the radio and peered through the binoculars. "Checking... I think it's a survey tripod. Hey, wait a minute... where's my boat? My boat is supposed to be on that ramp! Dang it!"

Holly was dancing away as she drove and asked Digger, "Do you want me to wait or keep going?"

"Keep going, Holly! You're doing great. I'm just bummed my boat is MIA!" Digger responded. The Aquasport was almost even with the trawler but to the west by a hundred yards.

Rick peeked over the side again and yelled, "Look at the thing tied at the stern of the trawler! It looks like a yellow missile, what is it?"

Digger looked through his glasses. "Shoot! That's a Donzi! An offshore powerboat. They can make a clean getaway if needed." The girls continued their whooping. Both Digger and Rick yelled at the exact same time, "We're being watched!"

Digger added, "Keep it up. They like sassy wenches, apparently."

"Look in the tower, there's another one with glasses on us," said Rick. "Lie low! I think he has a high-powered rifle. You see that thing leaning on the window? I think it's a rifle with a scope. You see it?"

"Affirmative! Holly, start swinging to the east toward the Talbot River!" barked Digger. As the boat started moving left, the one window of the tower came into view.

Rick called out, "Digger! They're dropping shiny things from the window! That's it! A robbery is in progress!" Rick began cursing up a storm.

Digger interrupted him. "Rick, can you make out the name of the trawler or the Donzi and their hull numbers?" Rick grabbed his backpack and pulled out a pen and started looking and writing. Digger tuned in channel four again. The Russians were still talking up a storm, but he had no idea what they were saying. He clicked over to the police channel.

"Dispatch... Dispatch... Come in please? Unit 19 here. Come in, please. [*static*]. Port Talbot Police, come in please. [*static*]. Shoot! I can't reach the police department on the secure band! This handheld doesn't have the range." He tried a Hail Mary message. "Patty, this is Unit 19 on Dog Island. We need armed backup immediately. Russians are invading Dog Island and there is an armed robbery in progress. I repeat, armed Russians robbing property on Dog Island. Help! All marine units needed. I cannot confirm your receipt of this message. I'm out of range. If this is received, Patty, please transmit in three-second bursts for three times and repeat. I'm radioing the Coast Guard, too. Thanks, Patty. 19 out."

Digger yelled to his mates on the boat, "I'll try the Coast Guard. Keep your eye on the guy in the tower. They may be monitoring the channels and will be able to hear this transmission. I don't want to tip them off." Digger clicked to channel 16. "Coast Guard... Coast Guard... This is D-O-G Isle Navigational Aid off Salmon Creek. Need law enforcement assistance. Emergency. Repeat D-O-G Isle Navigational Aid. Need law enforcement backup. A Section 6-5-1 is in progress. 6-5-1 in progress. D-O-G Isle. Using code, Coast Guard, the 651 is armed and has ears on. Over?"

Digger's radio crackled to life. "D-O-G, D-O-G this is Coast Guard. Code message received message. Dispatching assistance. Out."

Digger replied, "Roger. Tag numbers are..." Digger turned to Rick, "Tag numbers!" Annabelle, still dancing, passed Digger a slip of paper. Digger continued on the radio, "Tag Romeo Indigo Alpha sixty-six, thirty-seven, seven. And the second vessel's tag is the same as the first tag, but the last digit is an eight. Caution urged. Out."

"Wilco. Portland CG out." replied the Coast Guard dispatcher.

"Hey, Digger they're watching us big-time! They are moving faster. I am seeing bricks fly out that window."

Digger ordered, "Holly, let's get around this island and don't look back at them!"

"You asked for it. Hang on!" Holly pinned the throttle. Annabelle started swinging her jacket and really whooping it up.

Digger was watching the angle on the tower. "Okay, hard to port. Take us in, please!" Holly cut a tight arc in toward the island. Digger stood up. Rick stood too, stretching his back.

Rick pointed to the right. "If we go just a few more feet to the east, we don't even need the kayaks. Holly can nose us to shore and we jump. Maybe beach one kayak there. But kayaking through this seaweed and surf will be a nightmare."

Digger agreed. "Holly, drop us near that beach over there, please."

Radio static punctuated the moment. Digger's eyes grew wide. "Shhh, listen!" Digger put the radio to his ear and counted, "Two, three." The static stopped. Digger counted again. "One, two, three." The static started and again Digger counted to three when the static stopped. The signaling repeated a few more times as Holly motored up to the beach. Digger looked up. "Good news, guys. Patty got my message. The cavalry is on the way, both cops and Coast Guard."

Digger gave the final instructions, "So, Holly, nose us into that beach. We will jump off. Anabelle? Send one kayak into the shore. It will be an emergency exit vehicle. Likewise, you guys will have an emergency launch still with you. Finally, if you see a green flag raised on the lawn flagpole, it means all clear. You can come to the boat ramp. Okay?" The women nodded in agreement.

Rick added, "Digger, I would suggest one more rule. If nightfall comes, do not come onto the island, period. The wolves or whatever they are become unhinged after sunset."

"What do we do?" asked Holly.

Digger thought and replied, "We will signal you with a flashlight on the north side where you're holding. One long flash means go home. Two flashes will mean it's safe to come."

The boys moved to the bow. Holly was coming in hot. She bellowed "Jump on three. One… two… three!" Just as their feet left the boat edge, Holly roared into reverse and pivoted away to the north toward Hartson's Beach.

As they walked up the stone-covered beach, Rick handed Digger three flares. "These may come in handy in case the wolves come and we can't shoot due to a need for stealth." After a moment, he asked, "So what's the plan, Stan?"

Digger was checking his ammo as he walked. "Well, let's think it through. We know enough right now. They're prepared for a firefight. We also know that help is on the way. One option is to hold positions, to monitor their movements until firepower gets here and their getaway boats are seized."

Rick nodded. "True, but it is possible they're almost done and if the gold is in that ocean racer, he could skedaddle and we lose it all. Under that theory, we're gonna have to disrupt as soon as possible to limit the amount of gold moved and force them into defensive activity. Even if the speed boat runs, it doesn't run with as much."

"You're right." Digger said. "What's disruption look like? Given their numbers and having the building advantage. Just fire some shots? What about just one of us walking up there like a birdwatcher and playing stupid, while the other covers from the tree line?"

Rick hesitated. "Uh, you wanna be the birdwatcher? I am afraid they'd pick you off as you approached and ask questions later. How about this? I know from the north along the shore, you can get to within 20 feet of the boathouse undetected by anyone in the tower. We make our way to the boathouse and take the boathouse as our fort, if you will, and defend from there. It will at least disrupt the offloading and give us a defendable position until help comes."

Digger was beginning to realize that Rick was a little too familiar with this island. Nonetheless he responded, "I like it. Lead on. Get us there. Disrupt and hold until help arrives. Look out for sentries on our way. Let's go!"

Rick began running and dodging like he was on patrol in the jungles of Vietnam. Once his approach on the south side, or ocean side, was coming into view of the tower, he took a hard right into the woods. They crossed the area where the bloody bones and clothing had been. Rick kept running due north toward the coastline facing Hartson's Beach. Once there, he led in a crouched position under the bush line with the water to their right. They could see Holly's boat pulling into position.

Digger whispered, "Hurry, the cannon is about to go off." They ran up to beside the boathouse and could hear men barking orders in a foreign language. Rick signaled for Digger to cover him as Rick would flank the boathouse to the left where the door faced the open lawn. Once there, Digger would go to the right and confront the thieves on the boat ramp, and theoretically overtake them with Rick coming from behind. Before Rick left, Digger pointed to the guy in the tower to make sure Rick had eyes on him if the tower sentry should try to fire at Digger when he stepped out at the boat ramp to disrupt.

Rick was off. He hugged the side of the boathouse facing the lawn and the flagpole, then slipped in through the open door. Digger scurried up to the corner of the boathouse nearest the ramp and saw a rowboat sitting low in the water, partially filled with gold bars. When the man approached the rowboat lugging a bulging canvas bag, there was a cannon shot in the distance. When the man looked in the direction of the sound, Digger stepped out from the corner of the boathouse and crouched in a firing position.

"Drop it, comrade!" Digger whisper-shouted. The man froze, then opened his mouth to yell. At that moment, Rick sprang from the double doors of the boathouse and clocked him from behind with a rubber mallet. The thief crumpled into a heap. Rick quickly dragged him back into the boathouse and shut the double doors. Digger dropped back into position, out of sight.

Digger heard rustling in the boathouse and then a whisper from Rick. "Secured! Here comes another. The lookout on the tower is looking toward the cannon sounds and watching the girls. No rifle in sight. You hear me?"

Digger whispered back, "I hear you. Let's repeat the procedure but watch the trawler. We're both in full view when we step out."

Digger could hear the next thug huffing and puffing toward the boat. As he was about to dump his canvas sack, Digger came out in a low crouch.

"Drop it, comrade!" Digger hissed. The man looked toward Digger, dropped the bag, and was putting his hands up when Rick snuck up from behind again and struck the side of the Russian's head with the mallet.

He too fell immediately. Rick dragged him back into the boathouse and slid the double doors shut silently. Inside the boathouse there was more scuffling and a muffled cry for help cut short by another blow.

Digger watched the movement on the trawler. He spoke to Rick through the wall of the boathouse. "Something's happening on the trawler," he warned. "I think they're lifting anchor."

Then Rick exclaimed from inside the boathouse, "The man left the tower! Here come three men... No, four men coming... it's the guy from the tower. They're running! They're onto us."

Digger replied, "Same routine but we disarm only."

Rick responded, "Okay, I will come around the outside of the boathouse after they gather on the ramp."

Digger waited for the group to assemble by the rowboat. They were waving and yelling urgently at the trawler. When two of them bent down to push the rowboat, Digger stepped out and spit out his words in a harsh whisper, "Drop the guns! Hands up!" Two men dropped their guns and put their hands up immediately. The other two pulled out pistols.

Rick jumped from behind them and yelled, "Nyet! Drop 'em, Russkies!" Rick kicked the discarded handguns toward the water and yanked the rifles off the shoulders off the two closest Russians. Digger remained crouched in firing position.

A shot rang out and one of the Russians closest to Rick keeled over. Rick hit the dirt and the Russians rushed Digger. He fired at the closest one charging him and the bullet hit the attacker in the gut, but he kept coming and jumped on Digger. While Digger wrestled with the large, well-muscled man, Rick took cover. He watched the two other Russians run past Digger toward the north shore. Sudden machine-gun fire hailed all around them. Digger positioned the weakened Russian as a human shield from the flying bullets of what sounded like an Uzi. The body of the Russian on Digger was instantly riddled with bullets.

Rick yelled, "I got no cover!" Then a distant shot rang out from behind Digger. He turned to look. It was Annabelle. She had expertly picked off the machine gunner on the trawler.

Digger yelled, "Fall back, Rick! Get behind the boathouse!" Instead, Rick scrambled over the rocks toward the trawler and crouched behind a large boulder.

"Or that..." Digger said half to himself and then yelled, "I'm headed to the tower with a rifle. Here's one coming!" Digger threw the weapon to Rick.

Rick pointed toward the north. "Don't forget you have unarmed Russians behind us, but I doubt they'll come back." Another shot came from Holly and Annabelle's direction.

Digger replied, "You got that right! Go, Anabelle!" As Digger surveyed the lawn and considered making a run for the keeper's house, he heard a helicopter in the distance. He used the distraction to make the run to the house. Once there, he did a sweep of the rooms downstairs then dashed down the long hall to the tower of the lighthouse. There were gold bricks mixed with regular bricks everywhere. He clambered over the mess and climbed the stairs. He heard the machine-gun start up again. Rick was clearly being targeted and it sounded like rock was splintering everywhere. His shield was getting reduced quickly by the bullet fire. Periodic shots from Annabelle caused the machine-gun to pause, giving Rick the opportunity to seek a different rock as shelter.

As Digger reached the top of the tower, he heard the unmistakable sound of the Donzi starting up. Two men were on the boat that was pulling away. Digger could see gold in the boat and took aim with the rifle. *Click.* It misfired. He pulled his pistol out and leveled it at the driver and fired. He missed but shattered the windshield. The driver looked up and pointed his way. The other man in the Donzi pulled a rocket launcher from the low-profile cabin of the speedboat. He lifted it and aimed at Digger.

Digger ran around the rim of the light toward where the roof of the hallway connected with the tower. He paused briefly enough to hear the hiss of the incoming missile, then jumped fifteen feet down to the roof over the hallway below. The explosion of the tower blew Digger off the roof and he fell another story to the ground. Digger was showered in glass and sizzling shards of brick. He had just enough strength to cover his head with his arms and breathe. He had narrowly escaped the epicenter of a fatal impact and was only semi-conscious in a pile of rubble.

The helicopter had gotten near enough to witness the rocket launch and explosion and immediately veered to the south out to sea. The trawler was weighing anchor and moving off. From his post, Rick aimed for the engine compartment and any movement he could see, but the trawler kept pulling away. Rick watched as the Donzi got smaller and smaller in the distance. Every now and then a shot would ring out from Holly's boat and make a noise pinging off the trawler as it finally hauled in its anchor. Rick decided to make a run to see if Digger was alive. He ran a zig-zag pattern up to the house and drew no fire. The trawler was chugging away as fast as it could in the same direction as the Donzi.

Rick heard groaning over by the smoldering, topless tower. Rick pulled bricks and lumber off the spot from where the sounds emanated. He knelt beside Digger and urgently whispered, "Digger! Digger! You okay?" Digger moaned.

Rick insisted, "Don't move. I'll be right back." Rick was going to get water but then remembered the two Russians in the boathouse and ran down to check on them. He raised his pistol as he entered the boathouse, his adrenalin peaking. They were gone. Their ropes had been untied. He went out to the deck where the skiff was filled with gold. It was shot up pretty badly. He disabled the boat completely with the mallet. He looked for the guns he had kicked toward the water. They were missing. He thought to himself, *Great! We need to establish the high ground and wait for darkness.*

He returned to Digger. In the distance, Rick heard a police siren and saw a tubby center-console boat with a flashing blue light pursuing the trawler. Suddenly, three F-15 Tomcat fighter jets buzzed low overhead and headed in a triangle formation in the direction of the Donzi's escape route.

"Digger! The calvary is here! Are you alive? Please be alive!" Digger barely lifted his head and moved his arm forward and gave a weak thumbs-up. Then his head fell back. Rick was encouraged. "Thank you, God. Good job, copsicle! Now we need to get you inside before *the dogs* come!"

Digger lifted his head quickly. His eyes were like saucers. Being reminded of the dogs was like a shot of adrenalin. Digger moaned, "Help me up! Get me inside. I hate those dogs!"

Rick knew the mention of the dogs would be like a shot of go-juice. He put Digger's arm around his neck and lifted him to his feet. As they walked from the rubble, they heard rocket fire in the west. Rick rotated with Digger in time to see a missile trail climbing from the ocean toward the sky where the jets were mere specks. The missile trail from the Donzi was cut short. The missile was detonated before it got near the level of the jets. The jets had utilized a flare and chaff countermeasure, causing the rocket to explode before getting near the jets. Then three missile trails emanated from the jets toward the Donzi and an explosion created a huge fireball and a mini mushroom cloud off in the distance.

Rick helped Digger as they limped toward the house, and asked jovially, "Are you any good at scuba diving?"

Digger snorted with a short laugh. "Hopefully the Donzi didn't have much on it."

Rick situated Digger in the living room and got him water. After a few minutes, Digger groaned, "I feel like I've been hit by a ton of bricks!"

Before Rick could laugh, a piercing howl came from the woods.

CHAPTER 54

HOWL HOLE

Rick looked at his watch. "You going to be okay here for a minute? I want to look around."

Digger nodded. "You got a weapon in case any visitors come? Furry or otherwise?"

Rick handed him a pistol. "It's one of theirs."

Digger moaned. "Oh, great, that wasn't much help in the tower." Digger checked the action. It had a seven-round cylinder fully loaded. "Da! Dat's good!" Digger laid his head back down on the couch.

Rick started to leave the room for the tower. "I'll be right back. Hopefully that helicopter will come back or that police tub."

Digger raised his head. "Chief Nickerson?"

Rick sighed, "Oh God, I hope not! That guy is a jerk!"

Digger rested his head again and called out as Rick headed toward the hallway. "Not if he gets us off the island before dark!"

Just then the door to the kitchen opened. It was Holly and Annabelle. "That's our job!" announced Holly.

Rick spun around in a shooting position and asked, "Where'd you come from?" Holly pointed toward the rails at the boathouse. "We took the train. Riding those rails is tricky, especially when two tons of gold brick are in your way."

She rushed to Digger's side and knelt. "You okay?" She started brushing embedded brick particles from his face and hair.

Digger looked her in the eyes. "Boy, you're a sight for sore eyes. But we didn't raise the green flag. You'll be court-martialed in the morning."

Holly stood. "Yeah, you're okay." She went to the kitchen for a cloth and water.

Rick observed Annabelle standing like a sentry at the door. "There are some Russkies out there somewhere."

She replied with her southern drawl, "I know I got one for sure and hindered another."

As Rick headed down the long hallway to the tower, he said, "Keep an eye peeled. I'm gonna survey the damage at the tower."

Annabelle called over her shoulder as she kept watch on the lawn "Looks like World War Two out there!"

Holly ministered to Digger on the couch. Annabelle surveyed the house briefly and went upstairs. "I may get a better lookout up here!"

Out of the blue, the barking of a dog rang out. Annabelle yelled down the stairwell. "Holly, take a gander over by the woods!" Annabelle went back to the upstairs window and trained the scope of her rifle on the single white wolfhound barking on the ridge just out of the tree line.

Holly went to the living room window. "It's a white dog or wolf or something. It's beautiful… it's the size of a small horse!"

Digger whispered, "It's Proto, I think he's a friend to the Lincolns, believe it or not."

Anabelle yelled down, "Don't shoot. He's friendly-like!"

Digger moaned. "I wouldn't say that."

Holly went to the kitchen door and yelled, "Proto!" The wolfhound, who had been doing circles and barking like any pet dog, immediately sat on its haunches facing Holly. She called again. "Proto, come here pup!" The dog came forward a few feet and started barking again, then turned and went toward the woods a few feet, turned toward Holly and barked some more. Holly called out from the front lawn. "This dog is behaving more like Lassie than a wolf. He is telling us something."

Annabelle was in the window of the house above where Holly stood. "He wants us to follow him."

Digger heard that and rolled off the couch and staggered to the kitchen door. His head was pounding and ears were ringing. He immediately sat down on the stoop. "That's Link's dog."

Holly ran back to Digger. "You should rest."

Annabelle squeezed past Digger at the kitchen door. "They call me the horse-whisperer, but dogs 'n me are tight too. This fella has sumptin on his mind." She began walking toward Proto. The dog showed excitement and went deeper into the tree line and turned around and barked more. Annabelle and Holly advanced toward the dog.

Annabelle called back, "It's clear as day. He's askin' for help. I'm goin' to help!"

Holly added, "I am going too!"

Digger yelled. "Holly! Get back here! Not all Russians are accounted for." He almost passed out from the exertion. He lay back on the kitchen floor and turned his head toward the hallway and gave it his all. "Rick! Rick!"

After a moment Rick came running down the hall and saw Digger lying on the kitchen floor. "Digger, what's going on?"

Digger lifted his arm and pointed toward the woods. "The girls… following Proto." Rick jumped over Digger and started running toward the woods. He could see Holly disappearing through the trees.

Rick called, "Holly! Stop!" He looked back toward Digger. "Stay inside, Digger! I'm going after them!" Rick looked at his watch and then at the western sky. He took off in a run. Digger didn't move.

* * *

Annabelle and Holly were in a full trot as Proto kept beckoning them deeper into the woods.

Holly called ahead to Annabelle. "Do dogs set traps?"

Annabelle yelled back. "No!" The dog had stopped at the mouth of a cave and sat ten feet from its opening. Annabelle peered in and turned back to Holly, who was catching up. "They don't set traps… they save people." Holly looked in at what seemed to be a lifeless body.

Holly exclaimed, "It's one of the Russians!"

Annabelle, crawling in toward the body, said, "Only if he's a black Russian." Holly crawled in too. The smell of infection and rotting fish was overwhelming. A nearly naked black man was sprawled on the floor of the cave. There were large shells and fish carcasses littered all about the body. There were signs of fresh camping provisions as well.

Holly, the premed student, started to assert herself over the traumatic scene. "I think they call this cave Howl Hole." She moved closer. "Excuse me, this is my forte. Let me see if he's alive. It's Mr. Lincoln, I believe."

"The lighthouse keeper?" Annabelle asked, incredulous.

Holly grabbed the man's scabbed arm and felt for a pulse. "He's alive!"

Rick, finally catching up, bent over at the opening to the cave. "Who is it?"

Annabelle crawled out. "It's the lighthouse keeper. A black guy." Rick's eyes registered fear. Annabelle added, "Holly, we gotta get him outta here. We need a stretcher or somethin'."

Rick crawled in. "He's alive? I thought the keeper was killed by the dogs." A moan came from the near-lifeless man.

"That says it all, right there. He's alive. This is Link, the keeper." Holly paused and looked at Rick. "He is my cousin. Let's get him out of here."

Rick said, "Hold on, let me scan for broken bones." He looked at Holly. "I was pre-med too." Rick started behind the neck and gently manipulated the vertebrae and moved to the shoulders. Link's eyes opened like bright lanterns and looked into Rick's eyes. Link's eyes widened in fear and he started to squirm and moan.

Rick said, "Link, don't move! We're here to help." Link moaned. Rick asked, "Got any water?"

Rick and Holly looked around. Rick noticed remnants of his own camping provisions, which he had left near the beach when he and Samson had made their hasty exit.

Holly yelled. "Annabelle, got any water?"

Annabelle, who was in sentry mode, replied, "Fresh out."

Holly looked around the cave. "Check this out." She lifted a large shell carefully. A pool of water shimmered in the shell.

Rick propped Link up. "Link, drink this." Holly leaned in and brought the shell to his lips. The water dribbled all around his cracked lips. Reflexively at first, Link's lips pursed, and then he started to accept the water, his throat moving as the water began to revive him.

Holly looked around and grabbed another large clamshell with water in it. "Here's another." She repeated the nursing. Link began to cough and sputter.

Rick lifted him higher. "Good, take his legs. Let's go. Annabelle, grab a leg!" They dragged him out as gently as they could manage. Rick bent over and with the girls' help, placed Link on his shoulders for a fireman's carry.

The girls steadied Rick as he stood up. Rick groaned. "This guy is big!"

Holly quipped, "We Hartsons are part Mandinka."

As they turned to head back to the lighthouse, Annabelle whispered, "Don't freak or anything, but look over there… to the right." Forty feet from their position on a raised area of land stood approximately twenty wild dogs who had assembled in complete silence.

Rick swore. "Let's get out of here. They look hungry." Rick started staggering back toward what was left of the lighthouse. Annabelle turned back to look at Proto, who had remained on his haunches ten feet from the cave the whole time.

Annabelle knelt. "Good Proto! Good puppy! Link is gonna be fine. You saved his life. Good Proto!" The stately wolfhound stared unflinchingly at Annabelle.

CHAPTER 55

NAVY-SEALED LIPS

As the rescue committee surfaced from the woods near the keeper's house, a squad of military men in camo surrounded them, rifles pointed. Holly and Annabelle put their arms up.

Holly's voice hit a high pitch. "We're friends! We're Hartsons!"

A soldier rushed towards Annabelle. "Keep your arms up!" The man roughly disarmed her.

"Don't lose those, G.I. Joe. I want them back," Annabelle responded. Another soldier disarmed Rick as he carried Link. An officer stepped forward and gave his squad hand signals to assist Rick and yelled toward the house, "Medic!" Another man in camo with a bright red cross on his shoulder came running out of the kitchen with a knapsack and yelled toward the boathouse, "Stretcher!" The soldiers helped lift Link off Rick's back and the medic took some vitals and began to set up an IV and plasma rack.

The officer approached the youths. "Well, kids, have you had enough fun for the day?"

Rick remained serious and pointed toward the north shore. "I think four Russians escaped that direction about an hour ago."

Annabelle spoke up with a wry smile. "Make that three. There should be a bright red trail to follow to find one of them."

Rick added, "And they're armed and could be watching us right now."

The first lieutenant yelled to the men as he pointed toward the woods, "Establish a perimeter to the east. Three hostiles, armed and dangerous!"

Annabelle ran up to the officer. "Tell 'em not to shoot the wild dogs, please! They're under federal protection!"

The officer looked to his left. "Murphy, gimme that commo." The officer put the bullhorn to his lips. "Listen up, team! Do not engage the wild dogs. I repeat, do not shoot the dogs on this island. They are protected by federal law." The officer looked at Annabelle. "How's that, young lady?"

Annabelle blushed. "That's great, thank you."

Rick stepped forward. "Sir, in an hour or so, the dogs will engage your men. That's feeding time. Can I suggest you let the dogs bring the Russians to, er, justice? Cheaper, safer and the puppies are quite reliable."

The lieutenant said, "Thanks for the heads up. We will take it under advisement."

"Sir?" the medic appealed to the officer.

"What is it, Bones?"

"This man needs a lift," the medic replied.

"Tell Murphy to call a helo," commanded the officer.

Holly and Annabelle headed into the house. Rick walked with the lieutenant a bit. The officer led Rick by the arm toward the boathouse. "Let's get off the firing range. What in Sam Hill happened here, son?" Rick explained the situation. They were standing next to the remains of the skiff partially filled with gold. Behind the skiff was Holly's boat, and behind Holly's boat were two large black inflatable Zodiacs bobbing in the shallows.

Rick asked, "Geez, the parking lot is full. Where'd you guys come from?"

The officer nodded toward the west. "Originally Portsmouth Naval Shipyard but we launched from the *Millinocket* over there." He pointed to the south at an Expeditionary Fast Transport vessel, an odd-shaped hovercraft. "We get excited when we hear Russians are in the neighborhood."

Rick couldn't help but ask as he nodded to the glowing skiff. "Everybody trustworthy on your team? I mean the spoils of war and all..."

The lieutenant paused, then laughed at the spoils of war comment. "I don't think we earned any spoils today. You did the heavy lifting. But yes, the Navy SEALs are professionals. No worries. Besides, these are too big to pocket."

Rick headed into the boathouse and returned with a tarp and covered the skiff. Then he pointed over to the smoldering remains of the lighthouse. "Well, over there, if we could keep that area restricted, the Hartsons would appreciate it. It's hunks and chunks of gold everywhere."

The officer squinted. "*Hartson's Beach* Hartsons? What the heck is all this all about?"

Rick reached under the tarp into the skiff and pulled out a gold brick. "Yes. The Hartson's Beach Hartsons. This is the family crest. Three bucks or *harts* as deer were called in old English." Rick pointed to the emblem and then pointed to the tower. "Their vault for storing the gold got blown up today. Can we keep that area restricted?"

The lieutenant said, "Sure, but let's take a look at it before I restrict it."

Rick agreed and stuck out his hand to shake. "I am sorry, I didn't get your name." The officer pointed to his breast pocket. *Johnson* was emblazoned above the pocket.

He shook Rick's hand. "Scott Johnson, and you?"

"Richard Eaton, nice to meet you."

As they headed to the strike area, a grey helicopter was coming in from the direction of the strange naval vessel at anchor. Johnson turned toward the lawn and yelled, "Murphy! Guide the bird in!" Then the officer followed Rick around the curve of the tower to where the missile did the most damage. The officer looked at the partially destroyed tower and gasped. He was speechless as he gawked at a fifteen-by-ten-foot wall of gold bricks largely intact, now visible due to the explosion.

Rick was the first to speak. "I think the rocket blasted off the surface material but the gold was much heavier and remained intact behind the outer layer of brick." Rick walked around with his head looking down.

First Lieutenant Johnson was still looking at the wall and whistled. "I have never seen anything like it. It's like King Tut's tomb or something, hidden in an old lighthouse in Maine. Brilliant! Literally!" Johnson looked toward the water and the chopper in the distance. "I didn't notice it when we came in at top speed but, yeah, I would get a tarp on this thing quickly. I could see a news crew here in no time and this just glows!"

Rick replied, "That's a good word, Scott, thanks. You see these shiny melted blobs? That's golden shrapnel. I'd just like to keep this area secure. You know what I mean?"

The lieutenant was climbing up the smoldering pile of gleaming rubble. "Roger that on securing this site. I'm just looking for evidence of the type of rocket they used. It's deep with gold bricks and melted shrapnel back here too." He picked up a metal fragment and brought it down to show to Rick. "Russian-made Willow class rocket. Still hot." He smelled it then handed it to Rick to examine. "They're crap missiles. Do you mind if I take it with me?"

Rick handed it back and replied, "Not at all, thanks for asking."

The officer added, "Oh, and I am sure you will have more investigators combing through this pile. The US government doesn't scramble Tomcats and the Navy SEALs without seeing why!"

Rick's wheels were turning. "Do you talk to the investigators?"

"Of course. That's why I am in this pile of gold," Johnson replied.

Rick smiled. "Okay, remember two words as to the person behind this Russian mess. It's a Maine attorney, probably a spy, his name is two words, Sandy Beach." The officer flipped open a pocket in his cargo pants and pulled out a pad and pen and started writing. Rick added Beach's address and phone number. "It's actually Sanford Beach. He was tipped off on the location of the gold and called the Russian agents. Here's my name and number if the investigators need further information."

The officer was scribbling when his name was yelled out from around the tower. "Lieutenant Johnson?" A team member was pointing to the incoming whirlybird. Johnson ran around toward the front of the lighthouse. He yelled back at Rick as he ran, "Tarp it, Rick! I'll make sure it's off limits while we are here."

The SEAL team member approached Lieutenant Johnson. "Sir, we have one wounded enemy combatant over here." There were two stretchers side by side. "Not sure he will make it." The officer looked at the dark-haired man lying next to Link.

"Did he say anything?" asked the officer.

The sailor notified the officer that the prisoner's speech was *Fouled-Up Beyond Understanding*. "It was FUBU, sir."

Johnson ran over to the landing zone and helped guide the helicopter down. He then ran up to the house and walked into the living room to see Holly kneeling by Digger, who was now sitting upright and alert. She appeared more interested in him than all the gold in the world. Annabelle was watching activities out the window.

The officer turned toward Digger. "How 'bout you, son? You need a hop to the Naval Hospital in Portsmouth?"

Digger thrust his hand out. "Can you haul me up, sir? Let me see how this goes." The officer leaned back as they shook hands. Digger stretched his arms to the ceiling, did a torso twist, raised each knee to his waist and walked to the bathroom for a moment and returned. "Plumbing's good. I only have a ringing in my ears. I'm okay, thanks. I'll pack out with them."

The officer looked at the stitched-up bite wounds on his left arm. "What's that?"

Digger replied, "These? Oh they're from my first tour of Dog Island. The furry enemy combatants out there got their licks in." Digger nodded toward the woods.

Annabelle spoke up. "They are not enemy combatants. They're motivated by basic instinct."

Digger showed Johnson the broken glass windows with blood around the edges of the glass. "They broke the glass with their teeth and lifted the window with their snouts in the jagged opening. That is an instinct more basic to a burglar from the Bronx." Everyone laughed, except Annabelle.

Johnson looked out the window. "Speaking of enemies, look at what we have here…" Everyone ran to the window to see two men with their hands in the air marching toward the lawn.

"Fantastic! That accounts for everyone now. I believe," said Digger.

Rick came rushing into the house. He passed Johnson as the officer beat feet toward the approaching prisoners. Rick looked around to see who was present. Seeing that it was safe to discuss the gold, he said, "Holly, I got some tarps from the boathouse. We've got to cover the tower ASAP. We can expect news stations out here any minute, according to Johnson. If they broadcast footage of the gleaming gold brick tower, there'll be the Dog Island Gold Rush of 1980. So we've got to hustle. Once it's tarped, you guys can go. I'm gonna keep a vigil on this island until this stuff is in a vault on the mainland." He turned to look in the fridge. "I'll survive."

Digger nodded toward the stairway. "Use the box springs to cover the stairwell. It was effective." Rick nodded. He knew enough not to pat his revolver in front of Annabelle.

As they all headed toward the kitchen door to the long hallway to the tower, Digger pulled on Rick's shirt. Rick called toward Holly and Annabelle, "Start spreading that big ol' sail and those tarps, we'll be right there!"

Digger leaned over and whispered as he pointed to the kitchen counter, "If I can find my pistol and backpack out there, I'll leave the gun in this drawer with about a hundred rounds. Those beasts can be demonic!"

"Thanks, Digger, you're not bad for being a cop." Rick reached to shake Digger's hand.

Digger quipped, "The lawyers in Police Court say, the only difference between a cop and a robber is their uniform."

Rick laughed and slapped Digger on the back. "I gotta remember that one. Oops, I'm sorry, did that hurt?" Digger gave a wincing smile.

CHAPTER 56

THE AFTERGLOW

Digger looked out the open door and saw the flagpole. "Oh, shoot. I gotta signal Royal Orchard. I'll meet you at the tower in a minute. The officer is right about the press. Tracy Thomas from First Responder News will be here any moment." Digger started to walk toward the boathouse at a measured pace.

Rick yelled, "Tracy can interview me anytime!"

Digger teased, "Racy Tracy. Y'all could keep a vigil together!"

Rick quipped, "Wolves are one thing, but I don't know about a cougar too!" They laughed as they parted.

Rick watched as the Navy SEALs loaded the prisoners, the injured and the casualties. Link was still on a stretcher waiting to be loaded onto the helo. Dread overcame Rick as he remembered his fight with Link and siccing Samson on him that night. His mind began to race. *This guy could have me put in jail for a long time.* He heard Brenda's voice in his mind. *"Apologize, Ricky! That's all!"* He ran toward the chopper. Two team members were lifting Link's stretcher. Rick yelled. "Hold up!" They set the patient down for a moment and looked at Rick running toward them waving his hands.

Link, who had been slowly reviving with saline and plasma drips, turned his head to see what the commotion was about. His eyes widened as he recognized the man running toward him. Rick looked at the soldiers standing by. "I just need a second, do you mind please?" They retreated a few feet and signaled to the chopper pilot to hold up.

"Mr. Lincoln, I want to apologize for what happened that night.

If I had been straight with you, this would never have happened. I am really sorry, and I hope you fully recover. I would like to make it right with you in whatever way I can."

The anger visibly subsided in Link's eyes but he was still distrustful. "If you're not John Schreiber of the Massachusetts Life-Saving Station Historical Society, who the heck are you and why?"

Rick answered, "Remember the Eatons? I am Bill Eaton's son."

Link nodded. "Bill was good people. What happened to you?" Link was not letting Rick off the hook easily.

Rick sighed, "He did his best with me, but I was cut loose a little early in life and I'm still learning things my dad tried to teach me." The sailors gave a wrap-up signal.

Link lifted his arm weakly to shake Rick's hand and said, "I was cut loose early, too. My dad died too soon. I forgive you, man, but I'll take you up on making good from that night. Say, did your dog survive? Proto's team can be efficient."

The sailors stepped in and lifted Link and started moving toward the chopper. Rick walked alongside. "Yeah, Samson's fine."

Link replied, "I like the name Samson. Did you teach him to climb trees? That was a freak-out!" Rick withheld his laughter and pride.

As Link was being loaded, Rick yelled, "I'll be watching over your home until you're better. Any tricks to calling off the dogs?"

Link tried to sit up and answered excitedly, "Yes, the whistle in the drawer in the desk in the study. Three short bursts means retreat! Also feed 'em at the flagpole with a side of beef once a week from Revell's meat store!"

Rick couldn't help it. "I thought those were your bones!"

As the door was being shut Rick heard Link yell. "That was the point!" Rick gave a thumbs-up through the window and to the pilot. He then ducked down and ran from the now-roaring chopper toward the tower. He noticed the pretty array of flags on the flagpole snapping wildly as the chopper lifted off. Rick looked at the activity at the boathouse. Lieutenant Johnson and his team were loaded in the inflatables and pulling out. Johnson saluted Rick, and he returned the gesture.

Rick rounded the tower to see the girls draping it in a colorful spinnaker sail and Digger securing the fabric with rope against the tower before the breeze lifted it away. Rick helped by spreading tarps over the debris on the ground. Everyone watched as the military chopper headed west by southwest toward the *Millinocket*. As soon as the rotor sound seemed to dissipate, a similar sound started to increase. They looked toward the skies and saw a colorful small helicopter coming in from the east.

Rick yelled to Digger, "Here comes Tracy!"

Holly looked at her watch. "Boys, we gotta run if we're gonna get up the creek. I got no time for dirty laundry!" Holly nodded towards the helicopter and added, "Are we good here, Rick?"

Rick yelled back "It's a wrap...literally!"

* * *

As the news chopper circled overhead filming the scene, Digger peeled off toward the house with his dusty backpack in hand. Inside the kitchen he started loading his ammo in the kitchen drawer.

Rick came in. "Keep your ammo. I got the dogs under control. Apparently, they obey a whistle, according to Link."

Digger kept filling the drawer. "Just bring it back when you're done out here. Between us chickens, I'm not one hundred percent sure that only three Russians got away. There's the four that got past us at the boathouse and ran to the north. They're accounted for. A Russkie could have peeked around the tower when we were disarming the group down at the boathouse and decided to run away the other way, to the south and east. And remember, there's that kayak over there on the east end."

Rick pointed at Digger. "Good point. I'm gonna grab that before sundown."

Digger looked out the window to the west. "You better hurry."

Rick handed a scrap of paper to Digger. "Can you call Brenda and tell her all is well and I am babysitting some dogs and bricks out here? I'll be home when all is secure. Oh, and Link said he gets a side of beef at Revell's for his dog team each week. If you're returning anytime soon."

Digger thought. "I'll see. I don't know where my boat is. Someone sabotaged it here and now it's gone." Rick was pondering a response when a police siren clicked on and off briefly. Digger looked toward the water. "It's the Chief. I gotta run. Good luck out here."

Rick looked toward the boathouse. "The last I saw him he was chasing the Russian trawler in slow motion."

Digger yelled as he ran, "That's Chief Nickerson, slow, methodical, by the book, and effective!"

Finally, the obnoxious news helicopter had veered off toward Hartson's Beach, making communication easier on the ground again. Digger jumped in Holly's waiting boat. She motored at Digger's request over to the chief. Digger introduced the parties and made it known they were trying to catch the tide at Salmon Creek.

The chief, wearing a wide smile, pointed to a pile of gold bricks in his boat. "The Coast Guahd helped me intercept the trawlah. They briefed me on your afternoon, and loaded me up with this gold. I recognize the Hahtson crest. Diggah, let's take a minute and load this on youah boat. I was informed the Navy is taking jurisdiction, Thank God. This stuff can be turned over to the Hahtsons. Besides, my good friend, Ted, will be happy-ah knowin' that I'm not sittin' on his gold. I've taken enough from him on the golf course." The chief turned to Holly. "Tell Ted I hope he's feelin' bettah and I wanna see him on the fairway soon. I may see some of this gold again… if he still slices the golf ball like I remembah!"

Holly smiled. "Of course. I'll tell him exactly what you said. It will lift his spirits for sure. Thank you, Chief."

* * *

Holly plowed home with the heavy ballast weighing the boat down. They paddled into the dock at Royal Orchard. They came up the hill from the dock just in time to see the First Responder News van driving down the driveway. They used the remaining minutes of light to bring the bars of gold into the wine cellar.

On Dog Island, Rick retrieved the kayak and put it in the boathouse. As he returned to the house in the dark, he heard howling in the woods and then the unmistakable sound of a man yelling for help in a foreign language. Rick listened. "I guess Digger was right. They are efficient."

* * *

At Royal Orchard, Mrs. Hartson yelled from the study, "Holly! Digger! It's coming up on the news next. It's the lead story!" Only Digger and Holly entered the study. Annabelle said she would watch the news at the manager's house and left the big house without fanfare. Jonathan Hartson handed a snifter of rum to Holly and one to Digger. Jonathan raised his glass and toasted to the success of the mission. Everyone sipped. Faith Hartson crossed herself and turned up the news. "Here it is."

Tonight's lead story comes from Dog Island off Port Talbot on our southern seacoast.

An aerial view of the island shared half the screen with the talking head.

Today at approximately three p.m., a naval and air force operation thwarted a Russian racketeering and fraud operation being perpetrated on one of southern Maine's most prominent families. According to a statement just received from the Naval Public Affairs Office and interviews with family members, the Hartsons of Hartson's Beach fame were allegedly the subject of a racketeering and fraud operation. The plot included a false real estate transaction and theft of artifacts from the historic island. The lighthouse, which was fired upon with a handheld rocket launcher, was partially destroyed.

A view of the lighthouse covered in tarps filled the screen.

The Coast Guard said the island is necessary for navigation of international trade, and according to a spokesperson for the Navy, a temporary light structure will be placed on the island.

The Portland headquarters of the US Coast Guard requested the Navy and Air Force to assist when the rocket was fired at the Coast Guard's rescue helicopter. A separate missile destroyed the historic lighthouse. A Navy SEAL team was deployed to the island and three jets from Pease Air Force Base were scrambled. Both military services encountered enemy fire. Details on casualties and prisoners are being withheld pending further investigation. The FBI was dispatched to the law office of Sanford Beach in Port Talbot.

The TV showed Sandy Beach getting into an unmarked vehicle accompanied by FBI agent Johnny Barnes.

The attorney was taken in for questioning in connection with the Russian transaction. Mr. Hartson was reached just prior to broadcast. Our own award-winning Tracy Thomas has more from Hartson's Beach. The camera cut to a pretty girl talking into a microphone with ocean surf crashing in the background.

Thank you, Charlie. This afternoon an insidious re-make of the movie The Russians are Coming! The Russians are Coming! unfolded on the beautiful shores of Dog Island. Our sources tell us that Port Talbot's famed Bicycle Police Officer, David Digger Davenport, ferreted out a Russian plot to deprive the prominent Hartson family of their most precious asset at Dog Island.

The camera cut to a view of Royal Orchard and then a close-up of Ted Hartson on the porch.

The patriarch of the family, Theodore Hartson, was contacted a few moments ago and had this to say:

"So much of our commerce is built upon trust. We had no idea that we were being subject to a Russian hit job. We have received word that our family is safe on Dog Island and we are grateful for the service members who put their lives on the line for the protection of the international navigational aid known as the Dog Island Light. Special thanks to Digger Davenport and longtime family friend Richard Eaton for their quick action on the behalf of the Hartson family."

The camera cut back to Tracy.

Charlie? Mr. Hartson was quick to say the Dog Island light will be rebuilt and dedicated to the side of the Hartson family that has cared for the light since the 1860s. Mr. Hartson indicated ...

(Tracy glanced down at her notebook)

that back in the 1860s his great-great-great-aunt, Sarah Hartson, married Tombo Lincoln, a freed slave from Georgia. This resulted in several generations of Lincolns living on the island and protecting sailors for over a hundred years. Hartson said a celebration of their heritage and the contributions of the Lincolns will be held on the island at the dedication of the new lighthouse, hopefully in the early fall. The public will be invited. Charlie, we will keep Channel 8 viewers informed on the developments in this blockbuster story from Port Talbot, yet again.

CHAPTER 57

Sowing New Seed

Theodore Hartson's friendship with US Senator David Whitten, who summered on Whitten Point at the far end of Cape Talbot, was key to the rebuilding the Dog Island Lighthouse on an expedited schedule. The Army Corps of Engineers, with directives from the Office of the President in a campaign season, resulted in the tower being completed by the end of September. The best part of the operation was the construction of a "temporary" deep water dock that allowed large vessels to tie up and unload. The Corps' concept of "temporary" seemed to mean temporary for this century.

The attempted heist by the Russians led by Alexander Popov was determined to be the Russian mafia operating out of Brighton Beach in New York. The organized group, known as the Bratva, had been using the fish store in Boston for an expansion of their territory. The failed attempt led to six deaths, including that of Alexander Popov himself, and five indictments, including attorney Sanford Beach.

Beach was charged with a host of crimes, the worst of which was six counts of felony-murder even though he had remained at his office watching the debacle through binoculars. Beach compounded the difficulty of fighting the murder rap by representing himself in court, giving life to the adage that a lawyer who represents himself has a fool for a client. Maine's felony-murder rule required a participant in a crime to be charged with murder even when the victim was an accomplice, killed by the police, or in this case, killed by the military and law-abiding citizens acting in self-defense like Digger and his crew. The felony-murder rule required that it must be foreseeable to Mr. Beach that the criminal enterprise could lead to the use of deadly force. A reliable witness placed Beach at the wharf on Seaport Boulevard in East Boston when Popov and company loaded up the weapons and headed to Dog Island. Proceedings had not gone well for Sanford Beach. While he was trying in vain to arrange bail, the Maine Board of Bar Overseers issued an emergency order suspending his license. Rick Eaton did not have to say a word. It was safer for Rick to keep his mouth shut.

* * *

Within days of the skirmish on Dog Island, Rick, Digger, Annabelle, Holly and Jonathan moved the gold ingots and a surprising amount of old foreign coinage to Royal Orchard. From there, Rick's portion was calculated. The total haul included the bars found in the wreckage and cremains of Alexander Popov and his Donzi resting 65 feet underwater on a ledge at the bottom of Bigelow Bight off the coast of southern Maine. The total mother lode returned from Dog Island Light and Bigelow Bight was worth $204 million dollars at the then-current exchange rate.

* * *

The Hartsons' attorney, Sharon "Mama Bear" Stockton, assisted in the settlement agreement and distribution with Rick Eaton. She followed Ted Hartson's guidance and wishes to make amends with those who had been harmed by the Biddeford Mill bankruptcy. She calculated set-asides for retirement accounts and death benefits for the former factory employees and their heirs. Then Stockton, using Rick's copy of the bankruptcy petition and schedules, identified the former creditors and negotiated set-asides for debt payoffs for pennies on the dollar under the guidance of the trustee of the bankruptcy court.

Stockton even established a set-aside for income taxes. She advised that, given that the money was made in the 1800s and given the proof of tariffs being lawfully paid on time by the Hartson family back then, no argument for tax fraud could be made. With these set-asides deducted from the mother lode, Stockton fairly estimated the value of the Hartson textile company and the cotton business, which Ted insisted on treating as one business known as the Biddeford Mill, to be at least $170 million dollars, and this was the figure upon which the Eaton bequest should be calculated. Stockton tried to convince the Hartsons that none of the gold was the property of the defunct mill and should not be subject to bankruptcy or Eaton repayment. She tried to explain the difference between Hartson Textiles, Ltd. and Hartson Cotton, Ltd. (the Savannah operation).

Ted cut her arguments short. "We Hartsons are honorable and when we see a wrong, we correct it. We are coming out of the shadow of Dog Island Light. No more technicalities, Mama Bear. Do the math! We are sowing new seed!'"

Rick's share was negotiated downward to account for the damage he wrought at Crescent Point, and the harm done to Digger Davenport, Tom Lincoln, and their property. A deduction was made for the gold family crest and the trailer property that he already possessed. Rick held his tongue. He read through an inventory of precious items destroyed at Crescent Point but he made no admissions of guilt. He coolly waited for the attorney to get to the bottom line. The Hartson attorney negotiated that Rick receive $20 million dollars, which was twenty percent of the supposed value of the mill, minus a one-third imaginary (in his view) attorney fee. Hartson's she-bear argued that Rick would have not seen the one-third (approximately ten million) anyway. Rick argued that while he would not have received that percentage, it would not have been the Hartsons' to keep, either.

Ted Hartson spoke up. "We will give that one-third fee to those who laid their lives on the line for all of us. Davenport gets sixty percent of it. Annabelle gets thirty percent. Digger gets more because he was out there twice at great personal risk, not to mention that he had to be airlifted and hospitalized after his first trip."

* * *

Digger, back on the beat as Port Talbot's bike cop, had no idea what was in store for him in the settlement. He finished out his summer without further incident. Mama Bear Stockton talked to him about the evidence of Rick's culpability for the Crescent Point job and the sabotage at Dog Island.

Chief Nickerson was blissfully unaware of the Hartson matter. He had only commented on seeing the for-sale signs come down. At the end of the summer, the chief offered Digger a full-time job after Digger completed his upcoming senior year in college.

"Sir, I must respectfully decline, since I'm hoping to go to law school because I want to become a prosecutor," Digger replied.

The chief thought for a moment and said excitedly, "Well, law school doesn't start until the fall. That means you can do another summer as the bike cop!"

Digger smiled and replied coyly, "Maybe…"

* * *

On Labor Day, at a meeting at Royal Orchard, Rick signed papers settling the feud for twenty million dollars. Rick made sure the settlement included iron-clad releases from both of the Hartsons and Tom Lincoln for any and all liabilities, criminal or civil, with a mutual covenant not to participate in any proceedings brought by third parties unless under compulsion of law, just in case a governmental entity decided to pursue any charges. Mama Bear Stockton included a nondisclosure agreement, much to the relief of all concerned.

When Rick returned home from the Labor Day settlement meeting, he found the very pregnant Brenda pacing in the rocking trailer. He explained the settlement terms.

Brenda's eyes bulged upon hearing the final amount. "Twenty million dollars? Are you kidding me, Ricky?" She started screaming uncontrollably and jumping around the trailer like a winning contestant on *The Price is Right*. She stopped her antics abruptly and looked down. "Uh, Ricky? Ricky? I think you better get my suitcase. I think my water just broke! The baby is coming!" She looked up at Rick and exclaimed, "It's gonna be our million-dollar baby!"

CHAPTER 58

THE ISLAND DOG SHOW

Four weeks later, the new Dog Island lighthouse dedication ceremony was held on a fine Indian summer day. Students who had sailed on the *Performer* returned from school for the weekend to man the schooner for the occasion. Due to the renovations, the ship was able to motor to the dock and tie up with its nautical flags flapping in the breeze. The event brought out a who's who of Port Talbot citizens. A temporary stage was placed in front of the lighthouse, which was covered in a colorful spinnaker. Boats, including a large Coast Guard cutter, were moored on the western edge of the island so their passengers could view the festivities from the water. Loudspeakers insured the speeches could be heard. On the island, Link offered tours of the immediate grounds. He had made sure to place signs warning against entering the Wabanaki Wolfhound habitat.

Jonathan Hartson was the master of ceremonies. He welcomed the guests and gave a shout-out to the boaters watching from their moorings. Air horns and boat horns rang out in response. He then called Father Brad Jones of St. Peter's to give a convocation of dedication. "Dad Brad" waited for the calm to come over the crowd. A light breeze registered through the speakers. "Let us pray. Father, we come to dedicate this instrument of safety on the seas. Your word says that we have been created to reflect your glory. That our talents, our endeavors, indeed, our very reason for existing, are to bring you glory and honor. Forgive us for thinking it's all about us. It's about You," he said as he pointed one finger heavenward.

"This is your lighthouse, God. The Hartsons and Lincolns have authorized me to affirm that symbolic and spiritual transference to you publicly. We pray the words of your Son over this beacon of safety: 'I am the light of the world. Whoever follows me will never walk in darkness but will have the light of life.' We therefore dedicate the new Dog Island Lighthouse to the glory of God in the name of the Father, Son and Holy Spirit, Amen." A lone trumpeter belted out the Navy Hymn. The Navy SEALs on the dais stood at attention. Those who knew the words mumbled along.

At the conclusion of the hymn, three F-15 Tomcat fighter jets buzzed over the island in a triangular formation, split apart and then climbed heavenward and out of sight. The boaters sounded their horns and the crowd applauded.

Jonathan took the microphone, waited for quiet and began by introducing the parties responsible for defending Dog Island. Each participant stepped forward to applause as their name was called: Digger, Kristy and her rescue crew, Annabelle, Holly, Rick, Chief Nickerson, Captain Ronnie of the *Jug Tug*, the Navy SEALs, two chopper pilots, and three Air Force pilots. They returned to their positions on the platform and Jonathan added, "Another defender of the island that I would like to introduce to you has spent his entire life here."

"His ancestors spent their lives here. His ancestors are *my* ancestors. We are one blood!" Jonathan told the story of Tombo, whose freedom was purchased by a Hartson and how he fell in love with and subsequently married Sarah Hartson. There were murmurs in the crowd. Jonathan concluded, "So please give a special thank-you to my cousin Thomas 'Link' Lincoln, who has a special presentation to make."

Link, also a newly made multimillionaire, stepped forward to the microphone wearing his signature red and black plaid flannel shirt. Applause and horns rang out. When silence came over the crowd, Link lifted a silver whistle to his lips and blew a signal. Immediately a cacophony of howling erupted from the woods to the left of the crowd. Horror rippled over the faces of the crowd, which started shifting *en masse* to the right toward the dock. Link spoke up with a big smile. "Hey folks, it's okay, they won't hurt anyone. I promise you. They are just saying hello."

"Now I am going to introduce you to one another," he continued. "Just remain still and behold the beauty of the dogs of Dog Island." He blew another signal and approximately twenty wolfhounds slowly came out from the shadows of the woods. The crowd gasped and looked terrified. Link gave another shrill blast. As one, the wolfhounds sat on their haunches. The crowd applauded and boat horns rang out. Link blew again. All the hounds began to howl again. Link signaled again. They stopped. He blew the whistle again, and the cacophony of howls erupted. He blew to silence them.

"It's a little like choir practice, isn't it?" Link joked. The crowd showed their agreement with applause. "Now I would like to introduce you to their leader. Without his leadership, and about a ton of beef from Revell's meat shop, none of this obedience could be achieved. Please welcome Proto, the alpha male." Link blew the high-pitched whistle and a white wolfhound stepped out in front and sat. The crowd was in awe. Link blew another signal and Proto, alone, cried a distinctive low howl. "Now meet his wife, Lupa, the queen of the pack." Link gave another signal and a speckled wolfhound came forward and sat next to Proto.

"These are the dogs of Dog Island. They are not to be trifled with. They and their habitat are now protected by the Endangered Species Act, but mainly protected by me and their own survival skills. Please, I am warning you, friends, do not think you can come to the island for a picnic lunch and pet the cute doggies. You'll end up being lunch. Seriously! Visitors are welcome here by appointment set up in advance through the harbormaster, Mr. Hatch, or my cousins, the Hartsons at Royal Orchard. In closing, please give a warm welcome to my son Tombo and daughter Sarah, up from DC, and their lovely mother, Denise Lincoln!" After the applause died down, Link finished. "Thank you for coming out today and seeing a bit of our world." Link blew the whistle and all the dogs ran back into the woods. The crowd erupted with applause.

CHAPTER 59

THE CHRISTENING

Jonathan stepped forward with his older brother. "Theodore Hartson is the patriarch of our family and without his leadership, none of us would be here. Ted, please take us to the next level."

Ted adjusted the microphone down to accommodate his diminishing frame. First, Ted credited his wife, Faith, with being the true strength and wisdom in the family and indicated that she would be introduced momentarily. He then introduced his daughters Agnes and Holly. They stepped forward waving and intermittently wiping tears from their eyes. Ted directed everyone's attention up toward the lighthouse. Rick and Digger stepped from the platform and grabbed ropes at the side of the tower.

Ted raised his voice. "Ladies and gentlemen, in recognition of the many years in which the Lincoln side of the Hartson family faithfully tended this very special lighthouse, we present the newly named *Lincoln Tower!*" Digger and Rick ran with the ropes and the silky spinnaker sail slipped off, dramatically revealing the new gleaming white tower. Horns and applause heralded the moving event. The tower was encircled with two decorative wide bands, one yellow, and one black.

When the applause died down, Ted explained, his voice choked with emotion, "The lower yellow band is actually yellow brick from Georgia. It is a brick made from lime indigenous to the South and the Hartsons will always hold the yellow color as a reminder to the family and to the community of our roots and our blessings. The black band, as many know, graced the chimneys of the homes in the North in the mid-1800s as a signal for blacks seeking refuge and safety. These two colors together signal how deeply the Hartsons value our heritage founded in both worlds."

"Now, I would like to introduce my wife, Faith Hartson. Please direct your attention to the top of the tower. Honey, are you there?" Faith stepped out a small glass door and walked around the railing toward the crowd. She was wearing a red windbreaker with a matching red headband and carrying something in her hands.

She lifted a microphone with one hand. "Yes, dear, I'm here. It is a beautiful view from here. You all really must tour the tower and the long hall leading to it. We have established a small museum in the hallway highlighting the Hartson-Lincoln history of the island, the dogs, and, of course, sailors in distress. The pictures of Link working with the wolfhounds are astounding. So please, come visit. Now, it is my honor and pleasure to christen the new tower." With her other arm, she raised over her head a magnum of champagne tied to a thin red rope which was also attached to the railing. "I hereby christen this beacon of hope to be known henceforth as the Lincoln Light in honor of the Lincoln family. God bless all who turn to this light for direction!"

Faith threw the bottle out over the railing. Its tether caused it to swing back and smash against the brick of the lighthouse, making a distinctive *ker-pocksh* sound as if it were a large heavy light bulb. More honking and applause followed. Then the Coast Guard cutter sounded its sirens and spouts of water shot sixty feet into the air from multiple fire hoses.

After the sirens, horns and applause died down, Jonathan thanked the community for coming and invited the guests to partake of the hot dogs and potato salad set up outside the boathouse. As Jonathan and the others left the platform, a disc jockey took over. He started with a song from the movie soundtrack of *A Clockwork Orange* entitled "I Want to Marry a Lighthouse Keeper" by Shorty Long. The lyrics and festive tone were perfect for the mixed-age crowd.

CHAPTER 60

FRESH STARTS

As the crowd dispersed to the various sights and activities on the island, Holly and Agnes Hartson headed for the hot dogs and became engaged in stimulating conversation with Ken and Robbie from Kristy's rescue team on the *Performer*. The boys were explaining how they found Digger upstairs in the keeper's house. Holly was visibly enamored with the charismatic Robbie and his reenactment of scaring the wolfhound with his nunchucks. Ken rolled his eyes and turned his focus to Agnes.

Not far away, Digger elbowed Kristy and nodded toward Holly and Robbie. "They are made for each other."

Kristy, whose arm was interlocked with Digger's, pulled him closer and whispered, "She is perfect *for him*." They heard Holly ask Robbie if he had ever been up on a real widow's walk. Kristy whispered, "I told you that you have to watch out for Holly Hartson!" Digger held his tongue and nodded agreeably with a smile as he recalled his own evening up on the widow's walk.

Digger and Kristy turned to see Rick and Brenda come up beside them. Digger introduced Kristy. Rick introduced Brenda as his wife. Their new baby, Henry Eaton, was strapped in a carrier on Brenda's chest. Rick's story of the marriage ceremony in the hospital between contractions, with Pastor Joe officiating, went untold. Kristy complimented them on the cuteness of the baby and his name. Brenda, who had peeled back the folds of the carrier to reveal the baby's face, also revealed a huge diamond ring and wedding band.

Brenda bubbled excitedly, "We liked the name and wanted to honor the Henry Hartson who built the whole empire. We're already calling him our little Hanky Panky." The girls giggled. Brenda leaned over and whispered to Kristy, "Truer words could not be spoken!" They giggled more and started a huddled conversation of their own.

Digger raised his soda can to Rick. "Cheers, Rick. Here's to a fresh start!"

Rick replied, "Cheers, Digger! It is unbelievable. Wealth, marriage, and fatherhood all at lightning speed. We are reeling."

"Why don't you check out a house on our side of the river in Cape Talbot?" asked Digger.

Rick coughed. "You're funny, Davenport. Brenda and I wouldn't feel right with the hoity-toity crowd over there. No offense to present company. We're Maine-ahs. No, we're gonna sit tight. Brenda's nesting instinct this summer resulted in a sweet spot for Hank right at home. We're gonna enjoy it and get the gold invested through a money manager and just breathe easy for a while. I may start working for the Hartsons again. Annabelle needs help with the farm, and I like that work."

Digger replied, "Sounds like a smart plan. The stories of the lottery winners crashing and burning are common."

Rick stiffened at a perceived insult and then smiled. Using his best British accent, he quipped, "At the Eaton residence, we make money the old-fashioned way. We eaaarn it!" The men laughed at Rick's imitation of the Professor Kingsley character.

Digger raised his soda can in another toast. "*Lex talionis!*"

Rick was raising his own soda but stopped halfway and changed the toast. "Here's to forgiveness!" They clinked cans and drank. Rick added, "*Lex talionis* is crap. It eats you up on the inside."

"That's a good word, Rick. Say, I meant to tell you someone found my boat up Salmon Creek, sitting peacefully on the marsh grass."

Rick, again not admitting anything, inquired, "Can you forgive the person who disabled your boat?"

Digger thrust his hand out. "He's forgiven." They shook hands. Digger looked over at Kristy and Brenda. Kristy was gaga over little Hanky Panky.

Rick elbowed Digger. "Uh oh… the clock is ticking for you, buddy."

In the distance, away from the crowd, Jonathan and Ted Hartson were looking across the water toward Royal Orchard and Hartson's Beach. Jon, the younger brother, looked at Ted. "Well, brother, you gave away the farm, so to speak, and it has never felt so good."

Ted replied, "Well, hopefully our kids and the Lincolns can invest it wisely and keep the good name for years to come. Thankfully, now they'll always have the real estate, if needed. Didn't you hate those tourists gawking around the houses like every day was an open house?"

They shared each other's reasons for being grateful. Jonathan had settled with the SEC and was focused on his son's rehab. Ted had been approved for a kidney transplant. The gift to the hospital did not hurt the approval process.

Looking at the sea and possibly far beyond, Ted shared a deep thought with his brother. "It's an amazing new harvest when new seed is sown."

* * *

As previously promised to her viewers, Tracy Thomas of First Responder News was on the scene, interviewing and providing a live feed to the Channel 8 news team. "Charlie, in a dramatic turn of events, the Hartson-Lincoln clan have restored the tower and restored a sense of safety not only to the sailors but a new start for the entire community. Standing next to me is a young man, well known to you all, who has yet again assisted the Port Talbot community to rout out crime. I am of course speaking with David 'Digger' Davenport of the Port Talbot Police Department. Digger, what are your thoughts today after having fought off a Russian mafia attack on this island?"

"Tracy, Port Talbot is very lucky to have the leadership of Police Chief Nickerson. He single-handedly chased down the Russian trawler right over there." Digger pointed beyond the lighthouse. "I am just a bike cop and love working for him and the people of and visitors to Port Talbot."

"Digger, I know that next summer is far away, but let me ask you, will you be coming back for your fourth season as Port Talbot's Bike Cop?"

"I don't know, Tracy; I am applying to law school and can't say what next summer will look like for me. Besides, given the mayhem that has occurred each summer that I have been on the job, it may be safer for me to be a beach bum."

Tracy replied, "Digger, you have been a tremendous asset to this community, and we wish you success wherever your endeavors take you." Tracy shook Digger's hand.

"Thank you, Tracy, and thank you to First Responder News for always being there," Digger replied.

Tracy looked at the camera. "That is the report from Dog Island, Port Talbot, Maine. Back to you, Charlie."

Digger scanned the crowd and saw his mother and father talking with a small family at the flag pole. Kristy was in the middle of a conversation with the *Performer* team and the Hartson girls. Digger headed toward his parents. As he approached them, he recognized his birth mother, Cissy, with her husband and two children. He paused to watch her son and daughter kidding around with each other. One moment they appeared to be fighting, then the next, tickling each other. It dawned on him: *This is what siblings do.* As he reflected on what he missed as an only child, Cissy hailed him over with a dazzling smile. With some trepidation, Digger approached his new extended family.

"I hope you don't mind we came up for the festivities. This event is news throughout New England," said Cissy with a broad smile.

"No, of course not, Cissy," Digger responded gamely. "It's great to see you and your brood."

Cissy leaned in and whispered to him, "These guys wanted to meet their hero big brother of sorts. They know our secret and are very understanding."

Digger whispered back, "More a brother than a hero, that's for sure."

Cissy introduced her husband, Dr. Roderick Traub, her twelve-year-old boy, RJ, and her sixteen-year-old daughter, Clara. After the exchange of pleasantries, Meredith and David excused themselves to go speak with Ted and Faith.

Digger turned to the young boy. "You like football?"

RJ responded, "Football's okay. I like soccer!"

Clara spoke up. "He does everything with his feet. It's obnoxious."

RJ pulled a Hacky Sack from his pocket and started tapping it into the air off his foot. Digger put his own foot out. "Pass it here!" he urged, and dribbled it in the air too. As he passed it back to RJ, he asked, "Who taught you how to do this ?"

RJ kicked it over to Clara. "She did." Clara popped the little sack over her head and caught it behind her back on the side of her shoe, then passed it back over her head to Digger. Cissy and her husband backed away to give them room. They played the game for twenty minutes, after which the three of them explored the *Performer* together. Then Digger, oblivious to the social setting, taught them how to skip stones at the water's edge.

While they were away from the crowd, Clara asked, "I guess you're kinda like our big brother of sorts, huh?"

With an expert side-winder throw, Digger sent a small rock bouncing out across the water and then looked at Clara. "I guess that's true, and you'd be my little sister. Is that okay with you?"

Clara's dark blue eyes blinked. "It's okay with me, if it's okay with you."

Digger looked at RJ. "It's okay with me, if it's okay with my little brother."

RJ smiled and added exuberantly, "It's okay with me, if it's okay with you!"

This prompted Digger to repeat the phrase and point toward Clara, who repeated it. She pointing at RJ, who kept the word game going several more rounds until they ended in laughter.

Cissy called to them from the dock. Clara looked at her brother. "C'mon, RJ, we gotta go!"

With a gleam in his eye, Digger said, "Wait! We need to play the *fruit de mere* game! Let's find the coolest item on the beach to give each other as a gift until we meet again. Maybe a shell, or a rock, or sea glass. Go!"

As the three started scanning the beach, Cissy called out, "Kids, let's go!"

Digger responded like a whiny brat. "Hold on, *Mom*! We're busy!" Heads turned, but most assumed Digger was being just funny. Digger bent over a log of driftwood and used his pocket knife to pry something out, and then he picked up a blue mussel shell. "I'm done!"

Clara called out, "I'm done too!"

RJ came up from the water's edge. "I can't find anything!" He kept running around looking at the ground.

"Ladies first," said Digger. "Clara, what's your fruit of the sea that you would like to share with me?"

Clara blushed as she handed Digger a small heart-shaped rock. "This is not a heart of stone. This is a sign of love that is like a rock."

Digger teared up a little, grateful for the warm reception by his newfound siblings. "Oh, you're a poet and don't even know it!" He held the opened mussel shell out to Clara. "This shell is the color of your beautiful eyes. One half is for me to remember you by." Digger carefully separated the two halves. "The other half is for you. Remember that the matching part of the shell is with me, your big brother who will be thinking of you."

Clara had tears in her eyes and reached over to hug Digger. She whispered, "Thank you!"

RJ couldn't contain himself. "I got something!" He looked up at Digger and Clara with both hands in his pockets, then shrugged his shoulders and nonchalantly pulled his hands out of his pockets, causing the Hacky Sack to drop to the sand. "Oh wow, look what I found!" RJ picked it up. "It's a fruit of the sea now! And it is my gift to you, Digger!"

Digger loved the kid's inventiveness. Clara seemed to be ready to scold her brother for cheating, but Digger smiled at her and she held her tongue. Digger then crouched down to get on RJ's level. "What do I do for job in the summer?"

"You're the Bike Cop!"

Digger rumpled the boy's hair. "That's right! And when the bad guys try to get me but miss, it means I dodged a bullet." Digger reached into his pocket and pulled out the slug he had pried from the driftwood. "RJ, I hereby present you with a genuine Russian bullet meant for me but God protected me. I dodged that bullet and I want you to have it as a symbol of God's protection and a big brother who will be there for you."

RJ's eyes were wide with amazement. He hugged Digger, said a quick thanks and then ran off, yelling "Dad! Dad! Digger gave me a real Russian bullet!"

Digger rolled his eyes at Clara. "Can you teach him some discretion?" Digger walked with Clara back toward the dock where Kristy and the whole family waited. As he surveyed the faces of his loved ones and friends beaming at him, he had a shuddering flashback to dodging bullets at this very site. He paled for a moment and whispered to himself, "Thank you, God, for seeing us all through the shadows."

Kristy grabbed his hand. "Everything okay?"

He kissed her and whispered, "*Everything* is okay."

THE END

ACKNOWLEDGMENTS

I would like to thank the lighthouse keepers of Goat Island, Cape Porpoise, Maine. Karen and Scott Dombroski and their dogs allowed unfettered access to the lighthouse and provided their hospitality and expert counsel on island life.

Next, in connection with the lighthouse and the island on which it sits, I would like to thank the Kennebunkport Conservation Trust, and in particular, Tom Bradbury, for his leadership in keeping Goat Island the way it should be. Photograph credit for the landscape image on the front cover is given to L. E. Fletcher, Cape Porpoise, Maine, circa 1907 (in the public domain).

The artistic cartographer of the Dog Island Map is Faith Victoria Bruner, of Tallahassee, Florida. Thank you, lovey, for the faithful rendition. My editor, Kate Victory Hannisian of Blue Pencil Consulting in Danvers, Massachusetts, was so patient with my passive voice and point of view mishaps. I am grateful for her watchful eye and expertise in the craft of writing. Kudos to my graphic artist, Isabel Rubin, of Tallahassee, Florida, and now Boston, Massachusetts. She took a 1907 postcard and turned it into the front cover. Dropping dogs in, taking them out, adding trees, hues and badges effortlessly! Thank you to my book designer, Grace Peirce of Great Life Press in Rye, New Hampshire. Grace allows the author to write; she gets the work to market.

For pre-Civil War research, I thank Dr. Jayson Hayes, PhD, DD, owner of The Book Mine, Tallahassee, Florida. Special thanks to my Navy brother, Todd Bruner, Sr., for guidance on radio talk and transmission etiquette.

I would like to thank my beta readers Steve Post and John Drake, who social-distanced to get it done. John deserves credit for steering me correctly on sailing directions and terms. I have learned so much sailing on the SV *On Eagles Wings* with John.

Thank you to my best bud, Dutch Dwight, of Amesbury, Massachusetts, for overall counsel and keeping me in the center of the fairway as the project progressed.

Finally, a very special thank-you to Sally and Wilhelm Hojer for helping with plot development. I'll never forget the three-hour ride to Amelia Island with Sally that saved or enhanced many peoples' lives herein. If Ricky, Brenda, Link and Kristy could only speak, they would have nothing but gratitude for my daughter's input.

Note: No dog or any other animal was harmed in the writing of this book.

The Bike Cop Series

Book 1
The Bike Cop in *The Greater Weight of Evidence* [June 2018]

In the summer of '78, the chief of police for Port Talbot, the quaint tourist trap on the southern coast of Maine, has chosen David "Digger" Davenport to be the bicycle officer to help with traffic and parking. Digger is a college kid who is the son of summer folk who live out on Ocean Avenue.

For Digger, the summer starts as it should: Hot with tons of college kids working in the resort hotels who are looking for love in all the right places. Soon it becomes, as they say in Maine, "wicked cold" and deadly when a waitress, a Southern belle, is found lifeless on the beach and a black bellhop is immediately arrested for her murder.

Port Talbot is thrown into turmoil on multiple levels: North versus South, white versus black, summer folk versus townies, and the lobstah mobstahs versus the candidates for sheriff and district attorney. One kid on a bike with a badge pursues a different scent in the search for the true killer. Introducing Port Talbot's Bike Cop in *The Greater Weight of Evidence*.

Book 2
The Bike Cop in *Son Over The Yardarm* [June 2019]

Nineteen-year-old Digger Davenport is eager to return to Port Talbot, Maine, for his second summer as the town's Bike Cop. Instead of directing tourists and writing parking tickets, he is caught up in mysterious events that seem connected to the town's fabled Abenaki curse, which is hounding members of a blue-blood Ocean Avenue family to death. Digger's crime-fighting efforts are complicated by revelations of a Davenport family secret—and helped by sailing instructor Kristy Riggins, a new friend who's as beautiful as she is brave. Join Digger and Kristy as they take on the ungodly evil harassing idyllic Port Talbot in this standalone sequel to *The Greater Weight of Evidence*.

Book 3

The Bike Cop in *Shadows of Dog Island Light* (in your hands) [August 2020]

In the third book in The Bike Cop series, Digger Davenport returns from his junior year of college to resume his summer job with the Port Talbot Police Department. While his ongoing romance with Kristy Riggins faces new challenges on land and at sea, Digger investigates a brilliant criminal's scheme to get revenge on a prominent local family that's been hiding many secrets on a small island just off the coast of Port Talbot. Making emotional new discoveries about his own family secrets, Digger finds himself in a harrowing race against time and a mysterious menace at the Dog Island Lighthouse. This season, Digger's summer adventures have a real bite.

Join the Talbot Club for participation in events and book development, at www.thebikecop.com.